FURIOUS

SWARM
BOOK 3

JT SLOANE
MIKE KRAUS

FURIOUS
Swarm
Book 3

By
JT Sloane
Mike Kraus

© 2022 Muonic Press Inc
www.muonic.com

---

www.MikeKrausBooks.com
hello@mikeKrausBooks.com
www.facebook.com/MikeKrausBooks

No part of this book may be reproduced in any form, or by any electronic, mechanical or other means, without the permission in writing from the author.

CONTENTS

Special Thanks	vii
Untitled	ix
Book 1 Summary	xi
Book 2 Summary	xv
Chapter 1	1
Chapter 2	9
Chapter 3	20
Chapter 4	28
Chapter 5	36
Chapter 6	44
Chapter 7	55
Chapter 8	64
Chapter 9	72
Chapter 10	82
Chapter 11	93
Chapter 12	103
Chapter 13	113
Chapter 14	122
Chapter 15	134
Chapter 16	141
Chapter 17	150
Chapter 18	162
Chapter 19	171
Chapter 20	181
Chapter 21	189
Chapter 22	199
Chapter 23	207
Chapter 24	217
Chapter 25	228
Chapter 26	238
Chapter 27	246
Chapter 28	256
Chapter 29	265
Chapter 30	275

Chapter 31	284
Chapter 32	292
Chapter 33	303
Chapter 34	313
Chapter 35	322
Chapter 36	332
Chapter 37	341
Chapter 38	353
Chapter 39	362

WANT MORE AWESOME BOOKS?

Find more fantastic tales right here, at books.to/readmorepa.

***

If you're new to reading Mike Kraus, consider visiting his website and signing up for his free newsletter. You'll receive several free books and a sample of his audiobooks, too, just for signing up, you can unsubscribe at any time and you will receive absolutely *no* spam.

***

Thank you for checking out Swarm! This series was written as a collaboration between Mike Kraus and several individual authors listed below, the collection of which appears on the cover as J.T. Sloane, and is the result of many months of hard work. We hope you enjoy it!

Aidan Pilkington-Burrows
J. Mannix
E. L. McCabe
Michael Raymond
S. E. Gilchrist
B.K. Boes
Liam Pickford
Jack Caspian
Kate Pickford

***

Special Thanks

Special thanks to my awesome beta team, without whom this book wouldn't be nearly as great.
Thank you!

SPECIAL THANKS

Special thanks to my awesome beta team, without whom this book wouldn't be nearly as great.

Thank you!

READ THE NEXT BOOK IN THE SERIES

**Swarm Book 4
Available Here
books.to/ZhUkQ**

The locusts covered the face of the whole earth, so that the land was darkened; and they did eat every herb of the land, and all the fruit of the trees which the hail had left: and there remained not any green thing in the trees, or in the herbs of the field, through all the land. – Exodus 10:15

BOOK 1 SUMMARY

A swarm of mutant cicadas emerges in America's Corn Belt, killing everything it touches and leaving a trail of deadly venom in its wake. While out in California, wildfires rage. It's not just the fire that kills, it's the smoke.

In rural Iowa, Dr. Diana Stewart, Senior Crop Scientist for Matreus Inc., a firm with deep roots in agri-business, witnesses one of the first cicada-induced deaths which leaves an orphaned boy, Jesse, in her care.

When her bosses demand her silence, Diana fears they're hiding something—if not illegal, at least *very* suspect—so she sets off ahead of the cicadas to find answers. The brood multiplies, emerging faster and in greater numbers than anticipated, while her bosses hunt her down. Diana and Jesse escape several attacks, but finally make it to her colleague Sam Leary's lab at the University of California, Berkeley.

Sam and Diana dissect her cicada samples, noting how their morphology differs from the standard cicada carcasses but their research is interrupted by Diana's ex-husband-turned-cop, Garrick. On Matreus Inc.'s orders, Diana is kidnapped, leaving Jesse in mortal danger.

After witnessing a raging fire start in a Teff field and overtake the farmworkers, including her father, California journalist Anayeli Alfaro rescues Cricket (the dog), collects the rest of her family, and rushes them to safety at her apartment so she can file her story about the fires with her newspaper editor, Sid.

When she finds Sid dead in the newspaper offices, Anayeli abandons her story in favor of finding basic supplies, rushing to Sid's house where his much-loved dog, Roxy, greets her enthusiastically. Sid's upscale neighbor is less enamored of Anayeli, threatening to call the authorities, but the young reporter tussles with the woman and then makes a run for it, leaving the pushy women bleeding on the street.

The gas stations are swamped and Anayeli is forced into a gritty neighborhood store where she encounters her sullen neighbor who's already showing signs of sickness. When she makes it home, the neighbor's young daughter, Bailey Rae, begs Anayeli to come and help her father, but it's too late. He dies in a pool of his own blood after extracting a promise that Anayeli will protect his daughter.

When the rampaging fires threaten the city, Anayeli and her family—complete with the neighbor's girl and the two dogs Anayeli has inadvertently adopted—are forced to flee again, this time taking refuge on a raft, on the American River. When a bully challenges her for the use of the raft, pushing her asthmatic brother, Ernesto, into the churning waters, Anayeli takes aim and fires, killing the challenger and taking the raft for her own family. But the current is strong and her family is exhausted. They lose her youngest sister, sweet Luz, to the churning foam.

When the tattered band finally make landfall, the line to gain admission to the Evacuation Center stretches down the street. Anayeli begs the officials to admit her ailing brother and when they refuse, deliberately goads her mother into a fight in order to make Ernesto's asthma worse. The gambit works, but at a price. Anayeli and Ernesto are escorted into the camp, while her mother, the two girls, and both dogs are left outside the gates to fend for themselves.

Further south, at U.C. Berkeley, boy genius Sam Leary gets a call from his friend Dr. Diana Stewart about the killer cicadas that have exploded out of the ground, leveling crops and humans alike. Diana offers to bring him samples, hoping he can figure out what's going on with this new species.

As Sam waits for her to show up, his colleague and academic rival, Frank Dorset, goes on the rampage, insistent that he be allowed to take possession of Sam's flannel moth research which, Sam discovers, is tied up in government contracts. Stuck between self-preservation and keeping his promise to wait for his friend, Sam must devise a way to keep himself and his research away from Frank while remaining at his post.

Hostilities escalate and Frank brings fire and then water to Sam's lab in an effort to flush him out. Sam hunkers down with his most loyal and trusted friend, Henry (the dog), but also reaches out to his science-geek-internet buddies, leaning heavily on the brainiac known only by his handle, "Cockroach."

Cockroach urges Sam to leave Berkeley, but Sam has given Diana his word that he'll stay put until she arrives, so he toughs it out, Frank hounding him at every turn. When it looks like all is lost, Sam begs Cockroach to come to his aid.

Frank intercepts Cockroach, threatening to kill Sam's friend; it's only then that Sam discovers Cockroach is a girl.

Incensed by Frank's cruelty, Sam devises a plot to trap him beneath the ribs of the T-Rex that graces the departmental lobby but the trap malfunctions, crushing Frank beneath the T-Rex's humungous skull. Sam and Cockroach hide Frank's body just as Diana and orphaned Jesse show up with the cicadas.

Sam and Diana have barely begun their work when Diana's ex kidnaps her, trapping Sam and Jesse in Sam's lab, with the doors and windows sealed and a fire hose pumping water into the confined space.

Meanwhile, way over The Pond, Ron Frobisher, fixer to the rich, is summoned to the ancestral home of his patron, Ann Pilkington, and tasked with escorting unidentified, live cargo from England to the west coast of Africa. Ann gives Ron a small box, suggesting that the contents are deadly.

Ron runs the box through and MRI machine, only to discover

that he's in possession of some kind of beetle. He digs into his patron's web of companies in an attempt to uncover what, exactly, he's transporting, but the clues are scant and he's left wondering whether Ann's latest venture, *Bio Better,* has put him in charge of 'a new protein source' and/or 'a miracle cure for cancer.'

Ron supervises the loading of *Bio Better's* crates, only to discover three crates have gone missing. A sojourn to the seedy side of Southampton's underbelly leads to a brutal, bloody, coke-fueled confrontation, and—to Ron's horror—the release of an entire crate of mutant cicadas onto the streets of Great Britain.

BOOK 2 SUMMARY

When out of control wildfires with abnormally lethal smoke threaten Sydney (Australia), café owner Kim Walker embarks on a perilous journey to check on Emma, the child she gave up for adoption. But what is normally a three-hour drive turns into a fight for her life.

Kim's forced off the road and robbed, but quickly hitches a ride with Toby, the stoner. When they pass a couple whose car has broken down, Kim begs Toby to stop for the pregnant woman and her ailing husband. The trek to the hospital is beset by fires and panicking citizens, the hospital parking lot jammed with the sick and dying. Kim is forced to deliver the newborn right there on the roadside, just as Toby abandons them to their fate.

When Kim is sure that both baby and mother are healthy and the new dad is making a remarkable recovery, she steals a police car and resumes her pilgrimage to find her daughter.

Sydney is in chaos and neither Emma nor her adoptive parents are at home. A neighbor says he saw Emma leaving for school in the morning, but when Kim arrives at the school gates she finds them locked and bolted. The authorities declare a curfew, thrusting Kim into a race against time to find her daughter.

Boulder has been mostly shielded from the unfolding mayhem and Dr. Keiko Sato leads the scientific community's effort to isolate a cause for the cicadas' rapid breed cycles and to discover an antitoxin. Her world collapses when a rogue gang of white supremacists, the Boulder Boyz, assault her babysitter, Netsy, and burn down her house.

Keiko, Netsy, and Keiko's young daughter, Maiko, flee to Keiko's lab, but the good doctor and her friends are banished from the laboratory and forced to run for their lives. They take refuge in one of Keiko's favorite restaurants, but the white supremacists hunt her to ground, killing the proprietor and his family before Netsy takes a stand, shooting one of the Boyz.

Keiko calls in a favor, promising her Zoomshare driver, Raoul, that she will not only pay him to drive them out of Boulder, but also grant him safe haven once they reach their destination.

Choking on toxic smoke and directly in the path of the advancing cicada hordes, the survivors flee to the mountain village of Breckenridge and beg sanctuary from Keiko's ex-husband, Christopher. At first, Keiko's ex won't entertain the idea of her hunkering down at his place. She's burned all her bridges with her self-serving hubris and complete lack of respect for their marriage vows. But when the gangsters who forced Keiko out of her lab return, Christopher joins forces with Keiko and Netsy in a bid to keep their daughter Maiko safe.

The Boulder Boyz hound the family at every turn, killing Christopher before Raoul takes them down in a deluge of lighter fluid and flame, allowing Keiko, Netsy, and Maiko to escape.

Keiko reaches out to her former lab assistant, Gretchen, apologizes for her many missteps, and is welcomed back into the scientific fold.

Émile Harris—who's something of a stickler for rules and regs—manages the longshoremen at the shipping port of Redwood City, California. Émile is vigilant in his care of the workers and the company and doggedly determined to stay on task. When he loses more than half his crew to the swarm, the distraught manager must battle his past, killer insects, and his coworker, David Sackman, who wants to take over leadership of the survivors.

Word is the cicadas can't survive over water, so Émile leads his crew to the dock where they find an abandoned boat. The craft turns out to be little more than a floating coffin and two of his people die in the ensuing fire.

Frantic but unbowed, Émile steers the remaining longshoremen to the railroad, where they liberate an abandoned train and head for freedom. The trip is beset with trials, both internal and external. The cicadas are relentless, Émile is consumed with fears around food insecurity, and his feud with David deepens with every challenge.

But when his crew are set upon by looters, Émile steps up and gives his life to protect his men and women. Content to have been of real service to the people he loves best, Émile dies as the train pulls away to safety.

Anayeli Alfaro has secured treatment for her kid brother, Ernesto, but there's something going on in the medical facility, adjacent to the evacuation center, that has all her reporter antennae on high alert. The nurses take too many blood samples and give too little in the way of explanation, though Anayeli notices that everyone—medical personnel, patients, national guardsmen, and civilians—are fitted with color-coded wristbands. Exactly what the code means remains a mystery.

Anayeli tracks down her sister, Carlota, and neighbor, Bailey Rae—in the tent city outside the med unit—but Mama remains at large. Determined to find her mother *and* solve the mystery of what's behind the blood draws, Anayeli befriends National Guardswoman, Fatima Kassis, who gives Anayeli a black, all-access wristband, so she can roam the camp at will.

During one of her many sorties, Anayeli stumbles on a transport van packed with dead bodies, their wristbands a multitude of colors; a revelation that raises more questions than answers.

Jeremy Curtis is on a mission to bond with Brandon, the son who barely acknowledges his existence. The pair hike the famed Half Dome in Yosemite National Park, but the acrid smoke drives them—and all the other hikers marooned on the treacherous slope—up the Dome, to the promised air lift.

The hike up the sheer granite is treacherous on a good day, but with so many people jostling for a place someone slips, tumbling and sliding past Jeremy toward the cliff edge. He grabs for the woman a second too late and is left with a chunk of her scalp as she careens to her death.

A pecking order quickly emerges with a hiker named Nash bullying his way into a leadership position. When the chopper lands, Nash takes point steering 'his people' to a seat on the bird. But the pilot collapses and dies, leaving the crowd to determine who to evacuate.

An older man steps up, claiming that he knows how to fly even though his wife says he had one lesson and no more. When the mob rushes the copter, Jeremy holds Brandon back but leaps to save a little kid who's dangling from the chopper's skids. The whirlybird lifts off and plummets, plunging down the side of the Dome, killing everyone on board.

With no rescue in sight, the survivors hike back down into the forest fire, desperate for an escape. Nash's friend, Max, dies and his girlfriend, Tosh spirals into despair. When the group finds an abandoned Forest Rangers' cabin, Nash sets his goons on Jeremy, pummeling him to a pulp. When he wakes, everyone has left except Tosh who's drunk more than her bodyweight in beer.

Gutted that his son would abandon him, Jeremy commandeers a Ranger's vehicle and sets off to find him. Jeremy and Tosh pass one of Nash's thugs, but the man's dying of smoke inhalation and there's nothing they can do to save him. The dying man's location points them towards the hotel at the heart of the forest, where Nash is forcing his people to commit acts of great violence to prove their loyalty to him.

Jeremy sneaks up on Nash, but when he sees the bully has his son held hostage, he offers his life in exchange for Brandon's. Jeremy lays down his weapon, but a shot fells Nash.

Shocking everyone, Tosh has sobered up enough to follow Jeremy and kill her ex. Nash thinks he has the final laugh, reaching up and stabbing Brandon in the thigh before Tosh empties her gun into his sorry body.

Ron Frobisher might be a contract killer, but he's no mass

murderer. Determined not to allow Ann Pilkington's deadly cargo to reach Africa, he stocks up on bug killers, locks himself in the *Fairwinds'* hold with the *Bio Better* crates and studies how best to kill the mutant cicadas.

But when the *Fairwinds'* captain tells him that Ann has ordered them to dock in the Bay of Biscay, Ron comes clean, urging Captain Alva to join him in destroying their poisonous freight.

The crew lower the crates over the side of the ship, one at a time, determined to drown the entire swarm, but one of the charges that Alva had set—to blow the boat, once they'd exterminated the arthropods—explodes ahead of schedule, forcing them to abandon ship.

A dark cloud hovers over the burning vessel but the fact that it has form and function means it's not smoke. In spite of his best efforts, Ron has brought the ravenous insects to the Cradle of Humankind.

Dr. Sam Leary, and his faithful companion, Henry, escape Sam's waterlogged laboratory and haul Jesse, the kid Diana Stewart left in Sam's care, from California to Colorado in order to deliver Dr. Diana Stewart's cicadas to Dr. Keiko Sato, the only person Sam believes is smart enough to make sense of them, in Diana's absence.

Dr. Sato is cold and aloof, dismissive of Sam's many intellectual gifts, taking him and Jesse into more and more dangerous situations. Sam decides to remove Henry and Jesse from Sato's influence.

Most of Breckenridge is heading for the hills and Sam refuses several offers of transportation, but is cornered by Sandie, a junkie, and her bruiser of a boyfriend. The couple try to rob Sam, who doesn't have a nickel to his name, but are interrupted when a vehicle slams into their van.

Worried that Sandie is injured, or worse, Sam stashes Jesse behind a tree ordering him to take care of Henry, and climbs into the van. Sandie's badly injured, but that doesn't stop her from launching herself at him and latching onto his arm with her teeth. The two tussle, spilling out of the van and onto the street. Sam thinks it's over, but Sandie has one more trick up her sleeve. She pulls a gun and aims it at him, but Henry leaps into the fray, taking a bullet for his best friend.

Sam begs Henry not to leave him, but the sweet dog dies in his arms which leaves Sam no choice but to take out the trash who killed the only creature who's ever truly understood him.

Sandie dies at Sam's hand just as the fires roar into town. Broken hearted, Sam and Jesse accept a truck driver's offer of a ride out of hell.

CHAPTER ONE

KIM WALKER. SYDNEY, AUSTRALIA

Screaming, Kim slammed her fists against the steering wheel of her stolen police car. Then she stopped her thumping and squinted once more at Emma's school, one of the most prestigious schools for girls in Sydney and probably Australia. Clouds of smoke swirled around the locked gates and the empty, well-kept grounds. Of course the school was shut. The city was in lockdown after all. But that man in the apartment building had definitely said Emma'd left home this morning dressed in her school uniform. Kim threw herself back onto the leather seat, squeezing her eyes shut while her hands throbbed and just about every part of her body ached. Including her heart. She had to start thinking and not reacting. She had to stop making wrong choices. She had to find her daughter.

She snapped her eyes open and straightened, her gaze zeroing in on her phone. No signal. Her mouth flattened as she set the car into motion and drove slowly down the street. Right. Schools were shut. Emma's parents either not home or at work. Any young teenage girl in her situation wouldn't return home to spend the day alone. No, she'd be with friends. Or, Kim sucked in a breath, at the mall, with or without friends. Even in lockdown.

Swerving into a vacant car spot, she snatched her phone off the charger. Her fingers lightning fast she found her emails and scrolled through the saved messages from Emma. There weren't many. She had not only saved them to her cloud server, she'd printed them out and often re-read the brief snippets of her daughter's life that she'd chosen to share with her. They'd exchanged emails occasionally since then, but Kim only ever responded to Emma's messages, she never initiated contact herself. She'd thought at the time she doing the right thing for both Emma and herself. Waiting until she could show her daughter, she was someone Emma could be proud of—all those wasted opportunities when she could have attempted a connection. Maybe even forged something deeper, something more special than simply being a name on the end of an email.

Her lower lip wobbled as she continued to search through the messages. She was positive Emma had mentioned a favorite shopping mall. There! The World Square Shopping Centre—a large development that filled an entire city block and which was within walking distance from Emma's school.

Kim swung out onto the road and headed through Darlinghurst and into Sydney's central business district. The certainty that Emma was inside that shopping mall grew stronger with each beat of her heart and each spin of the car's wheels. The orange hued smoke hung low and ominous, making it impossible to see the skyline of skyscrapers and the distinctive steel arch of the Sydney Harbor Bridge. Pity. She loved that bridge, loved its graceful curve, loved its Aussie nickname, 'The Coathanger.' While for many the sight of the bridge filled them with pride, for Kim its solid strength symbolized continuity and hope that a better future could be achieved by anyone.

North of the Sydney Harbor Bridge, the streets had been virtually empty, but in the central business district the streets were packed with cars and people jammed the footpaths. People of all ages, sizes, and nationality—all of them hell bent on one thing: looting. She checked her door locks for the hundredth time as a man in a gas mask smashed the window of a Chinese herbalist and stormed inside. Some of the thieves carried loads of grocery supplies in bulging bags, others had stolen goods piled high in their arms. And yet others trudged along the concrete pavement, grim faced and silent, pushing shopping trollies filled to the brim, or dragging bulging suitcases. Many coughed. Some even hunched over while they struggled to breathe. The majority wore masks and those without, had scarfs or bandanas wrapped around their noses and mouths.

But no one stopped to help the fallen—curled up in fetal positions on the unforgiving concrete, blood coagulating on their clothes and faces, while others convulsed, blood gushing from their eyes, noses, mouths as they writhed in their final death throes.

And all the while the wind blew the smoke further and deeper into the city as if determined not to miss any crevice or alleyway, pooling between buildings so it formed a thick fog.

Kim rubbed her burning eyes, wanting to look away but unable to, in case she missed her daughter's face, and continued to cruise slowly down the road in her stolen police car.

Sirens blared, shop alarms shrieked—strident calls for help that remained unanswered in a city where tension sizzled like live electrical wires. Here and there, shop owners hauled out sheets of timber and boarded up their windows while other businesses lay in darkness behind locked doors. It was as if the city had split in two: on the one side were business owners and the other criminals. There was no other type of human left. Apart from Emma, of course. She wouldn't get caught up in that nonsense.

A group of four young teenagers ran out in front of her and she had to slam on the brakes to avoid hitting them. Two boys. Two girls. Ash settled on their hair and blew in their faces from the gusting wind as they turned to look at her. None of them was her daughter. Kim's racing heart slowed then jumped again when one of the boys banged on the hood with his clenched fist and waved a bottle of liquor at her. Laughing with more than a touch of hysteria the teenagers danced across the road. They might have acted like they didn't have a care in the world, but Kim had stared into their eyes and seen it all. Fear. Despair. Anger. Even resignation.

A deep sorrow twisted inside her heart, when one of the boys ran up to the closest shop window and tossed his bottle through the glass. He clambered through, followed by his friends. They'd seen her police uniform and hadn't been fazed. Control of the city was descending into a darkness so impenetrable all light might be vanquished forever.

Kim flexed her tense fingers where they gripped the wheel and shifted her cramping legs, edging her way ever forward through the snarl of traffic. Two BMW sedans and a Lexus SUV, along with several smaller, cheaper sedans, appeared to have been abandoned, while a pickup truck, a Mercedes coupe, and a Mini had crashed into each other, causing more congestion. A motorbike lay wedged under the pickup. Some drivers had simply stopped where they were, their passengers running into shops and returning with goods before starting up again. Road rules had been forgotten. And, of course, there were those who'd died at the wheel.

The smoke was thickening, and visibility had reduced to a few yards in front of the car as Kim drove closer to another intersection. The deadened traffic lights rocked from side to side in the wind that surged around the skyscrapers and along the streets. A massive pile-up of mangled cars and a furniture truck blocked the intersection.

Kim stopped and ran her fingers along the buttons and dials on the dashboard until she found the car's strobe lights. Hoping the flashing blue and red lights as well as her headlights would be sufficient warning for any oncoming vehicles, she mounted the curb, pedestrians scrambling out of the way as she leaned on her horn. At the corner, she squeezed the police car in between a parked car and motorcycle, scraping the metal all down one side as she pushed out onto the road again.

Ahead of her, a red blinking light cut through the haze and an ambulance with its siren shrieking careened down the street. Stomping on her brakes, she looked for somewhere to go but the road was a wall of metal. The ambulance swung wildly, broadsided a pickup, then rolled over and over until it shuddered to a halt two yards from the front of Kim's police sedan, steam hissing from the engine. The siren cut out.

Kim stared at the emergency vehicle's cracked windshield splattered with blood. A hub cap fell off one of the wheels and clattered to the road. The noise broke through her shock and turning off the engine, she left her car. Scrunching down she peered through the ambulance's side window. Seeing the driver upside down, his head at an unnatural angle blood everywhere, sent nausea roiling through her belly. Hand over her mouth and swallowing hard, she stumbled to the rear doors which had opened, spilling the occupants out onto the road. The patient was still strapped in the stretcher, eyes staring blankly into eternity. The paramedic who'd been treating him lay on his back, his skull crushed.

Kim stumbled back to her cop car, fumbled with the car keys, and eventually found the ignition. Her foot trembled so badly she had difficulty keeping it on the pedal but she inched down the sidewalk scanning the looters for signs of her daughter.

The glow to the west had deepened to a dark red. The wind howled outside the car sending litter and ash blasting in all directions. Another particularly vicious blast rocked the car. Kim clenched her hands over the steering wheel in a death grip. Tiny burning particles hammered onto the windshield and she unlocked one shaking hand to flick on the wipers. She leaned closer to the glass. Not leaves on fire, no, more like tiny sprays of seed pods. She'd seen something similar before, in Branxton moments before the fire hit the town, and couldn't shake the thought that it was a bad omen.

She pulled over, and after ensuring—again—that all the car doors were locked, had a long drink of water. She had to find out what was happening out in the wider world. The police radio crackled into life at the touch of a button.

"...latest update on the bushfire situation. The premier is becoming increasingly concerned that Sydney could be cut off by a ring of fire should the fires continue on their current trajectory. The Wollemi National Park fire has diverged into two immense fire fronts: one is coursing through Yengo National Park all the way down to Ku-rin-gai and..."

Yawning and rubbing her eyes, she splashed a little water on her face. She had to concentrate. She couldn't afford to zone out.

"...Blue Mountains fire and is predicted to impact the towns of Upper Colo, Mount Wilson, Blackheath within the next eight to twelve hours. The premier has declared a State of Emergency for the Greater Sydney region. All police members are to remain at their posts and contact their area command for further orders. Members of the public are already displaying signs of panic buying and looting. All perpetrators are to be charged on sight and imprisoned. The Sydney curfew comes into effect at seven p.m. and will be enforced by..."

Kim switched the radio off. The word *'enforced'* had her blood running cold. She had to find Emma and get her to safety before the streets became too dangerous. She pulled out onto the road and took the next turn to the right only to stop dead in the street. Every nerve in her body tensed. Ahead towered the World Square although every level above the second floor was shrouded in smoke.

But the smoke wasn't the worst of it. The street and footpaths were a heaving mass of shouting, furious people throwing bottles, cans, and rocks at a line of riot police, shields held in front, batons at the ready, attempting to push back the crowd. Mounted police pressed through the jostling herd of people with loudspeakers, ordering them to move on, the center had been closed. But no one listened.

Three men dragged a mounted policeman off his horse. The officer still clutched at the reins for an instant, struggling against his attackers, but the horse was panicked and scrambling, trying to bolt but hemmed in by the mob and pulled away. As the officer disappeared into the jeering throng, a shot rang out like a thunderclap and his horse reared, trampling those closest to him. Fresh screams and shouts erupted, the air pulsating with fury, and the crowd surged like a tidal wave toward the police line.

Through the roar of the riot came the faint 'whomp-whomp' of choppers overhead. Over to the left on the fringe of the protestors, a fire truck stood silent and forlorn, doors wide open, the driver slumped over the wheel and three other firefighters collapsed on the rear seat. One firefighter was huddled on the ground, almost buried beneath a thick layer of ash.

A silent wail built up inside as her traumatized mind jolted into survival mode. *Run. Get out of there.* The Liverpool Street entrance to the shopping center was a lost cause. Bunching her shoulders, she slipped the car into reverse and turned her head to check behind when something slammed onto the hood. Her foot went to the brake in reflex and she spun around, her poor heart doing overtime in her chest.

A balaclava clad man wielding a cricket bat pounded another dent into the car. "It's a cop! Get her!" His high-pitched screech cut into her head like a drill.

Kim pressed the window down a few inches, and somehow infused authority into her voice. "Stop or I'll arrest you."

Too late. Several people broke from the rioting pack and pelted toward her. Heart hammering and moaning in earnest now, Kim went to put her foot down on the gas when the trunk received a hail of thuds. More people had circled around her to attack from the rear. If she kept reversing, she'd run people over. She hesitated, froze. A moment that cost her precious time as another swarm of furious, frightened men joined in. They waded in with sticks, broom handles, even furniture legs and more bats, pounding and smashing her car, shattering the strobe lights on the roof bar and killing her headlights. With each crack and thud, she flinched and let out an involuntary squeal.

She gripped the steering wheel with one hand while the other fell to the dead policewoman's utility belt she wore and the holster with the gun. Her throat tightened, her body one rigid pulse of fear.

Her lungs burned for air. She'd forgotten to breathe! Her shocked fog lifted as the mob grabbed both sides of the police sedan and began to rock it. The car shifted onto its opposite wheels, tilting at a dangerous angle before plunging back down on all four wheels. Up it went again. In less than a minute, the sedan would be on its roof.

But she wasn't ready to use a weapon on these people. They were frightened, desperate. Emotions she understood all too well. She whipped her hand away from the holster—she'd seen too many dead already, she couldn't and wouldn't add to that number.

Instead, she gunned the engine. Several men sprang backward, swearing in surprise. She spotted the opening and went for it. Ramming the car into drive, she stomped her foot on the accelerator. The police car rocketed forward, going full pelt, straight ahead. The thin stream of people in front of her, flung themselves out of the way. She was going to get Emma. Nothing was going to stop her. She kept her foot flat to the floor right until the very second when the car plowed through the storefront window.

CHAPTER TWO

DR. DIANA STEWART. MATREUS HQ. CHICAGO, ILLINOIS

The flare of pain in Diana's shoulder was excruciating. It left her gasping, but it burned away some of the fog in her brain, if not the slackness in her body. She forced her eyes open. She was belted upright in the back seat of a car. She didn't recognize the driver. Then again, the back of one head looked a lot like another. There was a man to her right, in uniform, but she wasn't sure what organization he belonged to. Army? Security detail? The stitching over his top pocket looked like words, but it was difficult to focus enough to read it. The light hurt her eyes. She couldn't think straight. "What—?"

The man in the front seat twisted around to look at her. "You're back with us, then?"

"Garrick?" Her stomach clenched with fear.

"And you remember our friend Emmet, of course?" He gestured to the man beside her, who grinned like a shark.

"No." That made them both laugh. Diana lifted a hand to rub her eyes, but it was too heavy so she let it drop again. She was so confused. They were sitting in a passenger vehicle of some kind, maybe a taxi. She was in a wheelchair. "Where are we?" Perhaps she had been in an accident. That made her afraid too.

"We're in sunny Chicago, of course. We're taking you back to your desk."

But—she struggled to compose her thoughts—she should be going to a hospital if she'd been in an accident.

Garrick turned back to the driver. "Are there fires in the city?"

The man was just a pair of eyes in a mirror. "Riots broke out earlier today, sir. We'll have to avoid the main road, but we can take a back way."

The traffic had come to a stop in their little backstreet. Diana had lived in Chicago for twenty years, and had developed that "city sense" that pricks at the back of the mind when something's not quite right; the homeless man's mutter turning to a roar, the push that becomes a shove, the squeal of brakes and honking of horns. It was a million little things that blared, *trouble*. When that tension started to accumulate, it was time to leave. There were storm clouds threatening, and she had a horrible feeling that it had to do with her. She racked her brains. She didn't remember where she had been or why; or even with whom.

Smoke drifted between the buildings, picked out here and there by the sunshine. People streamed toward the stalled vehicle and surged past, out onto the main street. Then there was a shout, and a huge bang made her jump. People screamed and scattered; a young man stumbled and was pulled to his feet by his companions. They ran to a gate which blocked off an alleyway; it was locked but two boosted the third up and he held a hand back to help them up and over.

"Tear gas!" someone yelled. A man pulled out water and wet a scarf, and covered his face. He sprinted toward the woman curled on the sidewalk, just feet from the car, clutching at her eyes and coughing.

"Get out of here!" Garrick snapped.

The driver revved at the engine but didn't move forward. "We're shut in!"

Behind them, cars were bumper to bumper. Up ahead, a line of police marched around the corner in full riot gear, using their shields to shove people out of the way.

Garrick slammed his hand on the dash. "Do it. Move us."

A police officer casually leaned in through the car window, a couple of cars ahead, and sprayed pepper spray, leaving the driver and her passenger screaming.

"They don't pay me for this!" The driver bolted into the surging crowd, leaving the door open.

"Son of a bitch!" Garrick scooted across into the driver's seat and slammed the door. Reversing hard, he smashed the car behind him out of the way and drove across a row of bicycles to get onto the main road. The triumph was short lived. The road ended in a plaza, all exits jammed with vehicles. Garrick flipped a U-turn to avoid the police vehicles and veered into an ornamental garden. An SUV crunched their back bumper, pushing them into a VW full of wailing children. It was the world's worst game of sardines, albeit in cars.

A line of cops raked their way through the madness, making good use of their batons and pepper spray, but not their weapons. Diana could make no sense of what she was seeing. The city was in the grip of a bloody free-for-all with the lid jammed down tight, making everyone doubly nuts.

Emmet unfastened his seatbelt and twisted to look around. "We should go, boss. Just leave her and run."

Pepper spray filtered in through the vents, making Diana's eyes sting. She realized with a jolt of fear that she was defenseless if they left her. She could hardly keep her head upright.

Garrick unfastened his seatbelt. "You're a cop, Emmet; go show them your badge and ask for an escort. We're on their side; they're not gonna go after us, are they?"

"Huh. Yeah." Emmet spilled out of the truck and approached the troops, but as he reached out with his badge, there was another bang and a puff of smoke and he doubled over and fell to the ground.

"Great. Rubber bullets." So much for not using their weapons. Garrick picked up his phone. "Hey. We're on the way, but there's trouble. I don't know, can't you tell from the tracker? Yes. And hurry. We have maybe ninety seconds before you lose your friend here to the locals."

Diana felt sick. Her eyes were still streaming from the stink of pepper spray and she could barely see more than a few feet in front of her hand. She grappled with the doorhandle, but her grip was limp and lifeless.

The line of cops got as far as the front of the taxi. Someone smashed the window and opened the driver's door. A stronger drift of pepper spray wafted by, and all she could do was cough and cough, helpless to wipe the tears from her eyes. Garrick was speaking to the cop, and there was the static of a radio transmission, the cop yelling to be heard over the din, but she was coughing so hard that she couldn't get the details. Another exchange, and the door slammed and then there were bumps and smashes and jolts. Garrick must be ramming his way out of the line of cars. She tried to wipe her eyes, but it did little to help. A police siren wailed ahead and after a couple of nasty jolts – hopefully the bikes again rather than protesters—the movement continued rather more smoothly.

After what seemed like an eternity, she managed to catch her breath, and concentrated all her energy on breathing. Her lungs burned and so did her eyes, but once she'd gotten over the initial shock, her mind was much clearer. The taxi was moving, and there was a police car leading the way. Though there were shouts and screams, and the occasional bang, they were getting fainter. Diana couldn't tell whether her sight was darkening or the light was somehow starting to fade. She shivered at the idea of losing her vision, here at Garrick's mercy in the middle of a rioting city.

"Decided not to choke to death, have you?" Garrick's eyes were framed in the mirror, ice blue and striking as ever. "Good. I didn't fly halfway across the country for the good of my health."

"Not very good for my damn health," Emmet wheezed. She had not realized he'd returned but he sat in the front with Garrick, hunched over.

She recognized where they were now; not far from Matreus' HQ, which was lit up like a Christmas tree. The streets were awash with police, though they drew aside to let the cop in front through and the taxi after them. The other side of the police cordon was chaos.

The taxi drew to a halt, and people surged forward, banging on the windows, and screaming insults. Diana jerked away as the window was smashed. There was shouting all around and then, quite suddenly, their windows were blocked by black uniforms. The banging stopped, but the screams of rage didn't.

Metal screeched on metal, and the taxi darted forward and then halted. Another screech, and Garrick leaned back in his seat and whistled. "That was close. A pretty hot reception for a scientist!" He put his head out of the window. "Where do you want her, boys? Your man jumped ship once it looked like it was getting interesting."

The next few minutes were a confusing mash of people and movement. Garrick drew the car up to a brightly lit doorway where two security guards waited.

"Dr. Stewart, nice to see you again. You look like you've been through the wars." One had a vaguely familiar face, and he unhooked the wheelchair and extracted it from the taxi.

She tried to stand, but her knees wouldn't take the weight and she collapsed back into his grip. "Oh!"

"I've got you." He lowered her gently into the wheelchair. "You might be better staying put for the moment. You're not too steady."

A suited woman marched up to Garrick. "Good work, Sheriff. We were very worried about Dr. Stewart being trapped in the fires. Thank you for tracking her down." She turned, dismissing him. "Dr. Stewart, Mr. Victor has asked us to bring you up to the penthouse apartment. He'll be dropping by later when you're feeling less *jetlagged*." The security guard frowned, but blanked his face when the woman turned to him. "Bring her."

As the guard wheeled her into the building and the lift, a wave of relief washed over her. There was no immediate threat here; it was familiar territory. The citrus smell of the air freshener, the brightness of strip lights on pale wood and plastic, the pattern of the carpet; this was as much home as she'd ever known. But the familiarity was tinged with unease. As they wheeled her out and to the penthouse flat, she became more convinced of it. There was something very important she wasn't remembering. Something urgent. Something *bad*.

The suited woman put her keycard through the lock on the door. "We'll leave you here, Dr. Stewart. Mr. Victor will be along shortly." She left, beckoning Garrick to come with her.

The security guard wheeled her into the corporate apartment and helped her onto the sofa. "Anything you want, Doc, you know where to find me." Nodding at her in a friendly way which made her skin crawl, he left before she could gather her wits to reply.

The door had not even closed when there was a tap and Victor hurried in, followed by a nurse. "Di, they said you're in a wheelchair? Are you hurt?" She blinked at him, trying to make his face come into better focus.

"I believe your men sedated her, Mr. Matreus, and they don't seem to have been particularly careful with their dosage." The nurse behind him bustled forward, lay her hand on Diana's forehead and took her pulse. She shone a light in Diana's eyes, and then turned to Victor. "She needs to sleep. She'll find it difficult to make much sense of anything right now. Come by tomorrow and chat then."

Diana was fading fast. Victor said something, but the nurse was wheeling her into the bedroom. She made one last effort to get out of the wheelchair and fell onto the bed, which hurt like hell. Then she drifted off into an uneasy unconsciousness.

She woke up in darkness, apart from the lamp in one corner. She licked her lips, cleared her throat. "What the hell?" Her voice was a bit slurred but understandable at least. She threw the cover back and caught her breath; everything hurt. Everything. She didn't recognize the room she was in; it was all wrong. "Where the hell am I?"

She eased her legs out of bed, but it was too painful to sit up, so she shifted over onto her side and let herself slide to a kneeling position on the floor. Her head swam for a moment, but it subsided and from there she used the bed to clamber to her feet and stumble to the doorway. She turned the handle and staggered into a well-lit room. Sofas. Kitchen. TV. The lights of the Chicago skyline blinked at her through the windows. She was high up. Ah, yes. The penthouse flat. She'd been there before. But it didn't comfort her. Something bad had happened, she knew it. It had to do with Garrick. Who, it seemed, was sitting on the sofa watching TV. "Garrick, how did we get here? What happened?"

He grinned like the Cheshire cat, enjoying her discomfort, and got up, coming over to lead her to the sofa. "What happened, my girl? Well, apart from the cicadas and the fires?"

"Cicadas. I was bringing them to... Berkeley. Oh no." And with that it all came flooding back. Garrick had been in Berkeley. Sam. Jane and her kids. Jesse. "Oh, Jesse....!" She buckled at the knees and he pushed her so that she fell on the sofa rather than the floor.

"Now you've got it." He dragged her upright.

The pain made her cry out. She had to take a moment to get her voice under control again. "Garrick, tell me you didn't—"

"Of course I didn't. What do you take me for? I got Chad to go back in after we left." He waited two beats, and just as she relaxed, he added, "They were dead, the pair of them. The water had filled up fast. It was so cold, I guess they got too numb to hold onto anything. The dog too, in case you were wondering. But we couldn't have Chad leave his handcuffs on the door. That would just be dumb."

She gasped as if she was in freezing water herself. One of the worst things about Garrick was that he lied with such ease. The next worst thing about him was that he loved—as in took deep, dark pleasure in—causing other people pain, be it physical or psychological. There was pretty much no way to know if he was telling the truth or toying with her. She had to play it cool if she was going to keep him on her side. She forced a smile in spite of the dread chill in her chest. "You didn't kill them. I know you didn't..."

"You believe what you want, hon." He brushed his hand over her hair. "But even if they weren't dead when we left, how long do you think they'd last? The fires were getting very near. Wouldn't it be ironic if the water saved them from the flames, having killed them with cold already?"

It cost her everything she had, but she managed to suppress the shudder that threatened when he touched her. The door opened and to her immense relief, Victor came in. Garrick would behave with someone else in the room.

"Di! What the hell happened to you? You look terrible! And you'll be the Sheriff who brought her in, I guess? Thank you for seeing her safely here. If you go down to the seventeenth floor, anyone will show you where the cafeteria is."

Garrick straightened, his snake-smile just as convincing as ever. "Thank you, sir. Can you tell me where to find Mr. Matreus Junior please? I'm to report into him when he arrives."

"Bryce has been delayed, I'm afraid." Victor opened the door and stood back to let Garrick through. "Are you staying in the dorms on the second floor?"

"Family block, yes sir."

"Excellent. Bryce should be with us by tomorrow; I'll have someone call you when he arrives. In the meantime feel free to avail yourself of the staff facilities. On us."

"Thank you, sir."

Victor waited until Garrick had closed the door behind him, then moved to the cupboard. "The usual, Di?" He set out glasses and whiskey and brought one across to her. "You've slept for hours. The nurse said you might; you've been in the wars. What happened?"

She dropped her head in her hands, and misery gripped her.

When she'd given him the barest bones of her story—the first gruesome death, her suspicion that their fertilizer, FeedIt, was somehow implicated, how she'd been shut down and cut off from her own data by Matreus insiders, Dan tracking her, trying to kill her, ending up a victim of a cicada attack himself—Victor got up and poured them both a second shot of whiskey and left the bottle on the table. "Diana... I'm so sorry you had to go through all of this. If I'd known what Dan was up to..." He got up and strode to the window, looking out over the smoke-smeared sky for some time.

She swirled her glass around, watching the dancing light in the golden liquid. "We have bigger fish to fry. The cicadas are starting to lay eggs. They're far too early. They hatched out too early. I'm afraid their cycle is becoming faster. And they had no right to be in California. We have to warn people—"

Victor took another slug of whiskey. "The wildfires are raging out in Cali. Could be a good thing? Kill off the cicadas?"

He was so *casual,* blasé almost. Diana couldn't wrap her head around his nonchalance.

"Bryce and father have called a meeting of the key shareholders."

A glimmer of hope, then! He could get the word out! Warn people!

"Diana..." He sipped his whisky and the world tilted, ever so slightly, on its axis. "I know you want to get the word out, but we're all bound by our NDA's, me included. We need to talk about how to handle this."

"But people are dying! There isn't time for meetings—"

He held his glass up. "I've got people readying extra PPE, all sorts, but I need a few more hours to have it ready. We'll hit the ground running, I promise you."

She took another sip. The rich fumes of the whiskey stung her nose. "Victor, this shouldn't even be a question. I know what your father's like, but Bryce worries me. He puts profit before people and—"

He flicked a piece of lint from his shirt. "I didn't realize how much damage it would do to refuse him that sportscar. He was 18 and a big-mouth, and it humiliated him. And because it followed on from trying to make the company more sustainable. He got it into his head they're linked. As if I did it on purpose. And my father swooped in to save the day, like always. They're inseparable now. It's my own fault; I was never any good at being a father, so I guess he looked elsewhere."

Diana finished her whiskey, determined not to let her outrage show. The world was in free fall and Victor was assessing the past! His past! His role as a father! She hadn't taken him for a narcissist, but he was putting that assumption to the test. Still, better that he was talking to her, than not. She set the glass down next to his, but couldn't think of a single thing to say to him.

"You're a good friend, Diana." He stood, smoothing his hands over his hair. "There aren't many people I can talk to like this. I appreciate it, truly."

He left the apartment, and she slumped back on the sofa. The world was spinning out of control and her one-time mentor was worried about his legacy 'as a father.' Then again, she had to give him credit for at least *trying* to understand his son.

The tears threatened again. Her own father had left his house—moved away, not let her know where he was going—signaling that she wasn't even an afterthought. Her heart ached and her brain fritzed. "Parents," she mumbled. "A rum lot…"

Jane! Now, there was a parent who lived up to the name. Jane had promised to look out for Sam and Jesse. If Garrick was lying—and there was a chance, however slim that he was, Jane—might be able to put that lie to bed.

There in the corner: a landline. She tried to get up and stumbled. She moved across the sofa a little at a time, stopping to gasp when it hurt her shoulder and ribs too much, then pushed herself upright. Standing up made her feel dizzy and sick again. She tottered halfway across the room and fell heavily, but gritted her teeth against the pain and crawled over to the desk. When her head had stopped spinning she pulled herself up onto the chair.

"What's the number? Come on!" Jane's number escaped her, so she rang the operator and asked for Motel 8 in Auburn.

After an eternity, the phone began to ring and was picked up by a man. "What do you want?"

"I need to speak with room 17."

"If they're still there."

She had no idea what he meant by that, but she waited impatiently. Sam's lab would take a long time to fill with water. It couldn't be watertight. They must've gotten out. And if Jane could just find a way to get down there… she had no idea how, but Jane would find a way to get them safe…

"Hello?"

Diana stifled a sob. "Jane!"

"Di! Oh, thank the Lord! Is Jesse with you? Tell me he went with you, for goodness sake!"

Her gut plummeted. Jesse and Sam hadn't made it back to the motel. She closed her eyes and steadied her voice. Jane had enough on her shoulders, she didn't need to hear her blabbing. Where to begin? "He hid in my car and came all the way to Berkeley, but it went bad. Very bad. Jesse and Sam were shut in." Diana's voice wobbled.

"Where? Where are they?" Jane demanded. "The fires, Di, we're nearly surrounded. We have to get out—I don't know how, but we have to get out!"

"They're in Berkeley, in the University—"

Behind her the door opened but she ignored it.

"It's cut off." Jane's voice was frantic.

"What?" Cold clutched Diana's heart.

"The fire crossed Highway 80 at Sacramento. We can't get anywhere to the West."

Shouts echoed through the background of the call. "Woah, lady, what are you still doing here? We have to leave, now!"

"Di, I've got to—"

An iron grip clamped on Diana's shoulder; black spots danced in front of her eyes and the phone dropped from her fingers.

"Orders from Mr. Bryce, Di. No phone calls to the outside world!" Garrick tutted at her.

"No! Garrick, please!" She struggled to pick up the phone, but he was too strong. He threw her back in the chair, then took the phone and ground it under his heel.

CHAPTER THREE

CLAIRE MOONE. PRESTBURY, CHESHIRE, ENGLAND

Claire's heels clicked as she hurried down the empty boarding school corridor. Attendance had been thin the last few days, with parents already snatching their children and running from the oncoming disaster. From the hillside on which the Prestbury school stood, she had a clear view across the Cheshire Plain to the horizon blackened by the heavy toxic clouds that were ravaging North Wales. There were new reports that fires had destroyed vast areas of farming land and were beginning to threaten towns and cities. Panic had quickly spread through the countryside, even though the rural idyll of Cheshire had yet to see a single spark.

She flung open the classroom door, and the children stood, ringing out a hearty, "Good morning, Miss Parker."

The school was in the wealthy area of Prestbury – home to many footballers, musicians, and television personalities. There were expectations of how the education would operate, with an eye for formality and the use of polite language. There was an elitist undercurrent, hidden beneath the ideals of inclusivity and classlessness. "Be seated."

She reached into her bag, took out the folder marked 'Lesson Plan' and opened it at the page she'd bookmarked the night before.

"Today, we are going to..." A small, raised hand flailed and waved, demanding her attention with some enthusiasm. She lifted her gaze from the text. With a smile, she engaged. "Yes, Matthew? Do you have a question?"

"Miss, do we all have to wear masks again? Isla said we do."

To his left a girl pressed her hands on her desk. "I never, Miss. I never said that."

Within seconds, arguments and counter-arguments filled the air, as half the class engaged in animated discussion. The noise rose, point and counterpoint ping-ponging around the room. "Settle down, please. We can talk about what's happening by listening to each other rather than shouting."

It took a few moments for her controlling presence to calm them enough that the room was There was a sense of achievement in that ability to manage an unruly mob, without having to repeat her instructions or become more insistent. She'd had to practice speaking in such a way, toning down the assertive edge of her normal speaking voice. "For fourteen voices, you do make a considerable noise when you all speak together. Let's see if we can work this out, shall we?"

An insistent rapping of knuckles against the old glass panel of the classroom door made every head turn. The Headmistress pushed the door wide open and held it in place with her foot. "Kori. Briony. Come with me immediately, please. Your parents are here to collect you."

Several girls' faces crumpled and all the children looked about anxiously. It was near to impossible to maintain any sort of calm or routine with constant interruptions and the darkening sky looming outside.

Claire had no experience of children panicking en masse, but she could feel the tension in the room rising. She needed to do something to calm them, as their classmates gathered their things. "I know this is very strange for you all, but we do this at the end of term, don't we? We say goodbye to each other, knowing we'll see our friends when we come back to school."

The panic ebbed with the reassurance of her words. She understood the sense of loss they experienced. She'd been at so many boarding schools, had to move from country to country, and had to let go of so many childhood friends. "Kori, before you go with Mrs. Muir, give everyone a really big hug and tell them you'll see them next term. Briony, you do the same. Everyone else, wait by your own chair, please." She waited for everyone to say their own goodbyes, before kneeling and opening her arms. "Now me. Come on."

The girls threw themselves at her, grasping at her as though they were afraid to be anywhere else. She hugged them back, then stood and held their hands. "Let's get you to your parents. They'll be so pleased to see you."

As the older woman at the door took the children, she smiled at Claire. "Well done, Miss Parker. Very well done, indeed."

When the door closed, Claire turned to the remaining group. There were a few sniffles, but the sudden upset had passed.

Rebecca, who was positioned in the middle of the classroom, had been less animated than her classmates and yet every few breaths, she would sigh. Her hands were clasped together on top of her desk, her eyes brimming with tears.

It was hard to see a child in any anguish. "What's the matter, Rebecca?"

The tears ran down her cheek. "It won't be long before my dad comes for me, too. He always says we have somewhere safe to go, if there's a crisis or any trouble. He says that I have to leave my friends, my school, everything."

To her left sat Clara, blond curls bouncing as she insisted, "You can't leave. It's dangerous."

On her right, Pippa leaned across. "You can come stay at my house, until all the fires have been put out."

"Will we all have to leave our homes, Miss Parker? Like Rebecca?"

"If the smoke comes here and we breathe it, will we all die?"

"Are we going to die, Miss?"

"Can we stay here, with you?"

Claire had watched the news reports, keeping herself informed of the incidents—eruptions, really, there was no better word to describe what was happening—that were disrupting the country. There were reports of people getting sick and being taken to hospitals that had quickly become overwhelmed; many were already dead. And that didn't even account for what was going on in the rest of the world. Not just fires, but bugs, too.

She continued to cue her students to speak, but her thoughts raced beyond their questions and concerns.

"Miss, will we have to?"

They looked at her for reassurance. She'd gained their trust since the start of the year. She'd always been fair and honest but how honest could she be, given that she was already lying to them about who she was? With all their faces turned to her, she had to say something but whatever she said, she had to avoid patronizing them. "It's hard to know. Your parents will make those choices for you. You might have to leave your homes for a short while. I don't know where will be safe, but I'm sure there'll be places. Let's talk about safe places, shall we?" First, she chose one of the boys sitting on the edge of the group. "Stuart, where would you go?"

"High on the hills, Miss."

"Vanessa, what about you?"

"My dad has a yacht, Miss. It's called Escape Velocity. I think we'd use that."

"Rebecca, where will your dad take you?"

The mousey-haired girl didn't hesitate. Blinking her big brown eyes, she looked straight at Claire. "My grandfather is Scottish. He lives on a small island. It's called Iona. It's close to a bigger island. That one is called Mull. We haven't been for a year. Dad says it will be very safe up there."

"An island? Wow!" Claire covered her pleasure at learning of a truly viable escape plan by sounding enthusiastic. "That sounds like a great place to go to. How do you get there?"

"By boat, Miss. It's an island and they don't let people have cars on it."

In a bid to further cloak her minor interrogation, Claire opened up the conversation. "What other ways could we get to an island, everyone?"

A shrill trilling interrupted the discussion. In the months she'd been there, her mobile phone had never made a sound. Reaching into her coat pocket, she withdrew the slim shiny handset. The screen displayed a number without any contact details. Swiping the green button, she answered. "Hello."

The voice was familiar, but there was a protocol to follow. "Opcode?"

She was so close to discovering what she needed to know from Rebecca, only to have the moment disrupted by a check-in call from her superiors. "Seventeen seventy-six."

"Op scrubbed. Be at the intersection of Springfields and Scott Road in five minutes."

The line went dead. The fresh faces of her class peered up at her. She had to leave and there was no time to waste in saying goodbye. "I have to go to the office!" It was the simplest excuse she could make. "Take out your reading books and be good while I'm gone."

In the bustle of children digging for their textbooks, she popped her phone back in the pocket of her jacket, lifted it from the chair and grabbed her bag. She was being repurposed and no longer needed to smile and simper and play the concerned teacher. The muscles in her face relaxed, as she turned to the door.

"Miss." The youngest of her charges ran to her desk. "Don't forget your glasses."

As she turned to take them from him, she tightened and contorted her face into that of Miss Parker, once again. "Thank you, Dylan. I'll need those, won't I?"

Not a soul noticed her march down the hall. She pulled open the heavy oak door of the main entrance and walked out across the parking lot full of demanding parents and disorganized staff, then onto the sidewalk of a tree-lined avenue without a single word or glance from any adult.

Scott Road was lined with single-family homes, set back from the road with driveways and large gardens. The school was out of view and the junction with Springfields was ahead, a hundred yards around the long curve of the empty suburban road.

From the other direction, something bigger than a car turned and accelerated toward her. The engine revs changed as the driver shifted up through the gears, then the moment they began to brake, shifting down. Tires squealed. The front of the van drew level with her peripheral vision. There was a clunk and the characteristic sound of a transit van side door being slid open.

As the vehicle halted, she stopped walking. Turning to face the black metal panels of the front door, her eyes met those of the dark-haired front seat passenger. He said something that only the driver could hear above the engine, before mouthing the word "Sorry" to her.

Stepping from the curb, she walked toward the side of the van. A calloused male hand stretched out and offered her some assistance, but she ignored it. She made it a point to always be self-sufficient. As soon as she was in, the guy threw the sliding door shut. Even with the beard he sported, she recognized Mickey by the sheer size of his frame. He was a Colossus of a man. He braced himself against the forward bulkhead, then flicked a nod to her.

Claire raised her hands, grabbing the overhead straps. "Go!"

The van sped forward. She compensated for the turns, tugging at the straps as though she was using a parachute. Mickey gave no indication physics was something as insignificant as gravity affected him.

For ten minutes, neither of them said a word. Their eye contact was unwavering, even as Claire was tossed and bounced in every possible direction. She'd already taken in the details she needed. He was wearing his usual black jump suit with extra webbing. There was one large backpack fastened down and labelled, "C.A.M." – Claire Adele Moone. Once she unzipped the bag, Miss Parker would be no more. She was already becoming a faded memory, as were all but one of the children. She'd already filed Rebecca and the Scottish islands into the 'if all hell breaks loose' corner of her brain. Because whatever she'd told the children, safe places were going to be at a premium, if things were as bad as they seemed. She'd seen the news out of the States and Australia. There were ops and then there were options.

"Where were you three days ago?" She yelled. That's when the first parents started pulling their kids. Granted, most of the parents at Prestbury were the helicopter type, but still. "Seven months I was in there. Seven months, two weeks and three bloody days," she yelled.

He grinned. "How many hours?"

"Nine hours and forty-seven minutes." She was always aware of the details, and accurate in all she did.

"Uh huh." The grin widened. "But who's counting?"

Taking in a deep breath, she exhaled through her nostrils. "Yeah, Mickey. Who's counting?"

There was a constant drone from the tires as they ran over smooth motorway tarmac. The big man eased his shoulders, pulled a manila file from beside her bag, then produced a mobile phone from his trouser pocket. Claire took her hands from the strap and sat down on the floor of the van. Mickey handed her the file and the new mobile phone. There was a single sheet of paper inside the folder. The word 'Artemis' was unsurprising. At least her personal and professional goals were in line for the time being. She dialed the number she and her team knew by heart.

"Hello Moone. Had to scrap that mission. Higher priority and all that, from the Prime Minister." Cavendish knew who she was before she'd said a word.

Her heart sank. That confirmed her worst fears—the ones that had been nagging her since the first reports of fires and insects came out of the United States. The world was *definitely* going to hell in a handbasket if the PM had asked for her and wanted a mission dropped because of a change in *priorities*. Accepting the reassignment, she acknowledged with a simple "Yes, sir," ended the call and passed the phone back to Mickey.

The van slowed down with a swing to the left, before the driver shouted, "We're here." There was a sudden staggered series of bumps, as the wheels passed over an obstacle.

Once it stopped, she kicked off her shoes and began to unbutton her dress. Shedding her clothes, she dragged open the zipper of her kitbag. "Who let the nerd drive?"

"Don't look at me. I was in the back the whole time."

The van rocked as the driver and passenger exited the vehicle. The side door opened. Mickey closed his fist around the handle and slammed it shut again. "Not now, you idiot."

Claire stepped into her jump suit and zipped it up. She grabbed her Kevlar bodyshell, popped it over her head, then reached for her boots. As she tied the laces on the second, she checked inside the duffle. "Weapons?"

Mickey opened the door. "In the Range Rovers, ready to rock and roll."

She stepped out before him, surveyed the armor-clad group of four before her and raised her hand to bring them to attention. "The mission is to retrieve and transport Artemis." She raised her eyes skyward for a second. "So – let's go and get my Dad."

CHAPTER FOUR

TERRI CURTIS. OUTSIDE LONDON, ENGLAND

Terri Curtis had just given a cheery nod she didn't feel to the switchboard operator and taken five steps toward the kitchen to pour herself a coffee when a call came blaring across the loudspeaker. "Recovery vehicle and medics to RTA, M25 Hemel Hempstead turnoff, junction 21, M1. Articulated Truck overturned, shed load, probable casualties, police en route."

Terri forgot about the coffee and kicked into action, zipping up her utility vest as she speed-walked—she'd been trained never to run—across the ambulance station to the parking area where their ambulance waited. Her partner Bob was already in the driving seat, buckling up, the engine was running.

He grinned back at Terri as she opened the passenger door and patted her seat. "Come on in and tell me all about it, kiddo."

"Mind reader." Terri hopped up and strapped in. They'd worked together so long, they could practically anticipate each other's movements, long enough her daughters sometimes called Bob her wusband. "Let's go. I need to get into another headspace."

"Tough morning?" Bob kept his eyes on the road as he swung out of the garage.

Terri let out a sigh. "I'm so frustrated. At breakfast Dale had the nerve to suggest I give up work as 'we don't need the money.'"

"Ah, he wants a housewife, does he?" Bob gave her a wink.

"I nearly bit his head off. I gave the twins a small loan to get their new business off to a proper start, which I haven't told him about yet, not that he would mind, but... Ooh that man drives me crazy sometimes. And then, with the news out of the States, and not hearing from Brandon..."

"Gotcha." Bob pulled out onto the road and turned on the lights and siren. "Follow me—I know just the thing to take your mind off your troubles."

Her troubles. Terri's heart sped with the slight rise of adrenaline. Her husband's comment chafed, grinding against her years of experience and responsibility. For her skills to be dismissed with the wave of a hand and a flippant 'we don't need the money' grated. She gripped the safety handle over her head as Bob weaved through the heavy traffic, focusing on the job ahead, letting the sense of anticipation she always felt when she was heading out to a scene rise, the fear and excitement of *not knowing*—what to expect, how bad it might be, how she might help—blending, the closer she got to the accident.

Eight minutes later, they pulled past a queue of police vehicles along the hard shoulder of the motorway. A policeman, placing bollards to block the entrance to the slip road, waved them through to where an articulated truck had jackknifed. The cab had smashed into the side barrier, almost tearing through, and two other cars had been knocked into each other and forced onto the shoulder. The passengers were milling about by their vehicles, confused and dazed, their pale, anxious faces turned up to the cab of the truck in consternation.

Terri took a deep breath and steeled herself as she and Bob slid out of the ambulance. She had decided to guard against becoming indifferent when attending emergencies when she chose medic as her career path. Whoever was involved in this accident was a person, with parents and maybe a partner and children. If ever her own family were ever in trouble, she would want someone who cared to treat them. Not if ever, *whenever.* Terri's heart wrenched thinking of her eldest Brandon, who had been exposed to some awful fire ordeal while trekking with Jeremy—his dad, in name only—in the States. They'd gotten only the barest of details. But Brandon was fine—*would be* fine. That's what Jeremy had said.

But now she had a job to do, someone else's baby to help. So as Bob moved toward the traffic officer who had waved them in, Terri went for the cab of the truck, bringing herself back to this moment, this accident.

The velocity of the impact had caused the trailer to overturn, its cargo tearing through the tarp sides, making a tangle of straps and broken crates, and spilling millions of fine, brown, tiny seeds everywhere. Even though many of the crates had exploded into splinters as they hit the tarmac, she could still make out a familiar bright green logo emblazoned across some of them: Matreus, the company her sister-in-law worked for.

Her feet slid from under her and she went down so quickly that she barely had time to put her hands out to break her fall. She made an embarrassing half-grunt, half-huff as she landed flat on her back on the asphalt, a cloud of seeds spraying up around her torso and shoulders, flying into her face and hair. She sat up quickly, and coughed some seeds out of her mouth but the real irritation was the seeds that had found their way up her nose. She stood up, taking care not to slip again as she brushed herself off, blowing her nose and shaking the seeds from her hair. She didn't have time for this nonsense, she had to assess the crash victims—starting with the passengers of the cars that had been shunted into one another and to the opposite side of the road. They didn't seem to be seriously injured, but it was impossible to tell from a glance, and a few were now staring at her, with the glassy looks of shocked patients.

"Hey guys," Terri kept her voice bright. "I'm guessing this wasn't on your itinerary this morning. How are you doing, are you hurt?"

"No broken bones, thanks." The most alert of the women lifted her hands and wiggled her fingers as if to prove her point. "We can wait—but I'm not sure the same can be said of the guys in the truck." She motioned toward the cab and its passengers.

There were some things Terri would never get numb to, no matter how many crashes she'd worked. Death. Suffering. The horror of a passenger, ejected from a vehicle. In this case, the passenger had been thrown halfway across the hood of the cab, but at least it had been quick. From the look of his forehead, the poor man had been dead on impact. But she still had a job to do. She quickly reached up for his arm, searched for a pulse, found none.

The driver was obscured by his airbag, but there was a smear of blood on the white canvas and terrible, pitiful sounds coming from the cab—the kind that made her wish she didn't have to look. *Please let him live. Please let me help.* Because that's why she kept this job—not for the money, but because she could truly *help*.

Terri reached up and opened the driver's door and did a second take. The airbag had deployed as it ought, and unlike his mate's, the driver's seatbelt was secure, but the man was in obvious distress as he writhed in his seat. There was blood everywhere—not just on the airbag. It dripped out of his mouth, his nose, his ears and eyes, soaking his collar, his chest—so much blood! Terri could almost taste the iron in the air as she stood, frozen. It didn't make sense that the driver had been protected by the truck's safety features yet suffered such extensive injuries. Before she could even do anything, the poor man hacked up a storm of bloody bubbles.

"Help me, please, help me." His cry was plaintive, even childlike as his eyes focused and met Terri's, searching her for some hope in his helplessness. She took a mental inventory of the way his body shook, the beads of sweat that appeared on his forehead and face, and the fact of his right eye bulging strangely, the whites suffused with blood. His chest wracked with a violent convulsion.

"Sir, I'm here, can you hear my voice? Terri's training and years of experience kicked in. "First I need to take your pulse while you tell me your name, alright?"

The driver grimaced as though he had been asked to perform some impossible feat, his face a mask of pain and fear, and she didn't wait for his answer, *couldn't* wait. She laid a couple of fingers on the man's exposed wrist, felt his bounding pulse. Far too fast.

"It's Edmund," he finally managed. "They call me Ted."

"Great, well done Ted. I'm Terri and my partner Bob and I have come to help you." Terri took her multitool from the utility belt at her waist, wondering how much longer Bob would be. She was going to need his help. "Now, Ted, first order of business is to get you a little more space and then we'll see about getting you down from here. Sound good?"

The man gave what she thought was a nod, followed by something that was part groan, part sob, and part cough.

"Okay, here we go with step one." She used the point of her multitool to pierce the airbag and the cutting edge to slice through the safety belt in a fluid motion.

There were footsteps to her left—Bob's from the slight shuffle—and then his voice rang out. "What have we got, Terri?"

She ignored the question, her focus trained on Ted. She didn't like the gurgling hitch in his breath, or the way his eyes were bloodshot. "Ted, I'm just going to bring your legs around to face me so Bob and I can help you down from the cab, are you ready?"

But before she could maneuver to get her arm behind his legs the driver's face contorted with agony as some violent reaction tore through his body. He screamed as his bulging eye exploded in its socket. Terri's stomach turned and she retched, bile souring her mouth, she staggered back from the cab and clutched the side of the door to stop her from falling back with the shock. Sometimes there was a limit to training and experience, and she'd found it.

"What's going on, Terri?" Bob's voice came from right behind her, the edge in it telling her he was worried.

Terri stepped back, giving Bob a clear view of the cab and the driver. Bob was a professional, but she heard him suck in a breath as he got a glance of the scene, and Ted broke into another hacking cough.

"Let's get Ted more comfortable, shall we?" Terri's voice was just a touch too loud. She hoped Ted could hear her and know they were there to help. They needed to get him to the emergency room, and into the care of a surgeon, and they had to act soon. Whatever was wrong with him was getting worse.

"Bob, can you spot me?" She took her position back on the step, and got her arm behind her patient. "Same plan as before, right Ted? I'm going to swing your legs around and—" Ted's coughing jag had brought up another froth of blood. The sight of blood, of body fluids, or the other unpleasantnesses that came with her job had never bothered her before but a wave of nausea swept over her and the scene swam before her eyes. Now was not the time to be going soft. She took a deep breath and turned back to the driver.

As she started to swing Ted's legs around he shook again. "Easy Ted. Stay with me—" He kept writhing, gurgling blood through his strangled screams as cerebrospinal fluid tinged red flushed out of his nose. Terri couldn't keep hold of him. She had never felt so helpless, as a paroxysm of spasms shook him in his seat. Then, just as suddenly as it had begun, the convulsions stopped and Ted collapsed, his head dropping forward onto his bloody chest, suddenly, terribly still.

They got him down quickly, Terri and Bob together, even as a heavy silence settled over the pair of them like a sullen cloud. As soon as they'd laid him on the stretcher, Bob began CPR, while Terri reached for Ted's wrist again. "Ted?" She pressed her fingers against flesh that was already lifeless.

"I'm calling it." Bob sat back on his heels, slightly out of breath after they'd taken turns for the requisite twenty minutes.

Life was so short. So unpredictable. Her husband Dale's face flashed through her mind as Ted was declared dead. She winced inwardly, wishing she hadn't reacted so aggressively to his suggestion that she slow down and take some time for herself. She pushed the thought away, instead wondering what she had missed in her assessment of Ted. It always felt personal when she lost someone; always.

"What happened, Terri?" Bob's voice was gentle as he planted a warm hand on her shoulder. She almost lost it then, but Bob was staring at her, waiting, so Terri pulled herself together.

"They're both dead." She hated that word so much. Dead. "Driver's mate immediately, on impact with the windshield by the look of it and the driver, well...."

Bob frowned when she didn't go on. "Well, what?" There was a touch of impatience in his voice. He brushed past her and climbed on to the step on the driver's side of the cab. "Was it airbag failure? Impact with the steering column?"

"No, he had some kind of multiple seizure. But even before that, there was blood seeping from every orifice in his face, and then his eye exploded...."

Bob's face blanched as he finally managed to push away the airbags. "Good Lord!" he exclaimed. "It's like a butcher's shop in here." He stepped down and away from the cab, his face drawn as he came alongside Terri, silently guiding her back toward their ambulance. He took his work personally, too. It was one of the reasons he was such a great wusband.

As they passed the battered cars and their passengers, the same woman Terri'd spoken to before was on her knees, retching. The sight compounded Terri's own nausea even as her training pulled her toward the woman. "Bob, we ought to—" Terri swallowed hard against her rising gorge.

"Hey, what's this stuff?" Bob bent forward, scooping up a handful of seeds. He lifted them to his face and sniffed. "Huh. Grass seed or something."

But Terri couldn't answer. She swayed slightly and had to steady herself on the side of the truck, not wanting to mention Natalie's connection to the company. "Looks kind of like poppy seeds," she said, but the words didn't sound right when she said them.

"Terri, are you okay?" Bob cast the seeds to the side. "You look like hell!"

"I'll be alright. I just need a moment to gather myself." Terri dabbed at her itchy nose, narrowing her eyes at the blood staining the back of her hand. She wasn't prone to nosebleeds, and she fought against the bubble of panic that rose deep in her gut, as Ted's bloodied face flashed through her mind. *Get yourself together, girl.* But a hysterical giggle rose up in her belly. Here she was doing everything she could to present herself as a consummate professional and her body was betraying her. She bent over and vomited her breakfast onto the road.

"Bob, these other victims, we haven't properly assessed them—" But she couldn't even finish before she was coughing, a spatter of blood landed atop the mess on the asphalt. She felt shaky as she straightened. Dale's face drifted into her mind's eye, an oasis of reassurance in her present chaos. Her last words to him had been ones of anger—*Not last words.*

Bob was right there, hand to her head, then taking her pulse. "I'll call for another unit. Get in the van, you're going straight to hospital."

Terri crumpled onto a bed of smooth seeds. Something trickled down her cheek. Fear snaked through her gut as she swiped it away. There was blood across her hand, bright and fresh and most definitely hers.

CHAPTER FIVE

ANAYELI ALFARO. SACRAMENTO, CALIFORNIA

The bodies that had spilled from the back of the truck—like meat, rather than people—haunted Anayeli. Back in her own quarantine zone, inside her own tent, with Carlota and Bailey Rae safely asleep on their blankets, she couldn't stop seeing the dead. She hadn't slept all night because they came back to her, every time she closed her eyes. Piles and piles of bodies, inside the refrigerated truck and flopping, rolling, spilling out its open doors, all of them with geometric shapes cut out of their cheeks. She tried to sleep, but her brain played tricks on her, made her see those bodies with faces she recognized—the faces of her own dead, Papa, Sid, Luz mingled with Josh Bertoli, the China Box Lady, Bailey Rae's daddy, Jason—those known faces mixed in with so many more unknown ones. Every time she replayed what she had seen, the arms and legs canted at impossible angles, the heads lolling too far to one side or the other, the stiff dullness of the skin, she thought of Mama. Mama could have been among those bodies haphazardly stacked in any one of the trucks and

Anayeli would never know. Except she *did* know. Mama wasn't on those trucks. She was as certain of that one fact as she was of anything.

"How's Ernesto?" Carlota's gravelled voice, thick with sleep or smoke or emotion, made Anayeli flinch, worse than if she'd watched a horror-flick. She hadn't known Carlota was awake.

"Better. Off the ventilator. You should visit him, if they'll let you." If Carlota would go, Anayeli could focus on finding Mama. And once she found Mama, she would tell Master Sergeant Kassis everything she knew about Teff and Matreus and be done with the whole story.

"I already tried. When you were gone so long. They won't let me go anywhere." There was accusation in Carlota's voice. *Your fault. Everything bad that's happened is your fault.* "Did you find Mama, at least?"

"She's still here."

"You saw her?" The fierceness in Carlota's voice, the quickness with which she sat up, set Anayeli even more on edge. Her sister had a *tone* when she was hangry, and that timbre of voice meant she was one provocation away from being a dynamite stick with a short, lit fuse. Anayeli scooted farther away from where Bailey Rae still slept, her hair sweat-stuck to her face. Little kids always slept so hot.

"No. I haven't seen her yet." Anayeli wasn't going to lie, but she couldn't tell Carlota the whole truth either—not about the bodies. It was guaranteed Carlota would become a raging explosion if Anayeli told her she still had no idea *exactly* where Mama was, or that no one else seemed to know either. She did not have the energy to cope with a Carlota-bomb going off. So she told Carlota what she could. "I would know it if she were gone. I can feel her, you know?" And then she couldn't say anything else. Her throat closed around a hard painful lump, because of the ones she couldn't feel anymore. Papa. Luz.

But where Luz would have said "me too," with one hand on her heart and one on Anayeli's arm, Carlota planted one hand on her hip. "You can't just say stuff you can't possibly know, just to make me feel better. Because it doesn't work, okay? Nothing will make me feel better—"

A better sister—a sister like Luz—would have acknowledged the fear in Carlota's voice, the way it cracked with anger that barely concealed grief. "I'm not trying to make you feel better! I'm telling you the truth!" She had to work to keep her voice down. She wasn't about to admit it was only a half truth, and if Carlota pushed her any further, she would say something worse than regrettable, something about how a nearly-grown woman ought to know herself well enough to know when she was hungry and eat instead of walking around like a ticking bomb all the time. Instead, she shoved off her own blanket and went to the door.

She knew she shouldn't but couldn't stop herself. "I don't have the bandwidth for this." She yanked the zipper and forced her way out the partially opened flap. She needed space more than sleep.

She needed to think, but walked instead, because moving made her feel like she was taking action, even if she wasn't. She shoved her good hand in her pocket to keep from punching something—a tent wall? The chain-link fence? She needed at least one functioning hand. But her fingers touched something fleshy, and dry—the slab of ham Slumpy had given her. She'd forgotten all about it. Just the idea of meat made her shudder, her stomach roiling at the thought of all those bodies, but the dogs—if they were still there—they would make her feel better. They would be happy to see her. Feeding them would be some kind of accomplishment, anyway. And then she'd have actual good news to report to Bailey Rae and Carlota when she came back—the dogs are okay, she'd tell the girls. They were hungry but I fed them and petted them and they wagged their tails.

The guard at the orange section's gate had just let her out—accepting her "I'm headed to visit my brother in the hospital" reason so easily, she had to wonder if Carlota really had tried to go see Ernesto—when a beating throb battered her ears.

There was nothing visible in the sky at all—the smoke was too thick—but the sound got louder and louder, beating against her eardrums, making her want to cover her ears with her hands, except she couldn't risk blotting out any sounds. She had to be alert for anything, she had to take in everything. A blinking light seeped through the dense haze, dimly at first, then growing brighter. She shrank back at the wind and noise as a helicopter—some kind of military one—sank beneath the layer of smoke, headed directly for the empty expanse of parking lot she had to cross to reach the hospital. She would've run for the hospital entrance, the same one Kassis had escorted her through, except two officers followed by a phalanx of National Guardsmen came hurrying out as the helicopter circled above, before lowering to the parking lot, its blades sending grit into Anayeli's eyes. She shielded her face with the crook of her arm and waited, wishing there were something to hide behind.

By the time the helicopter had touched down, the two officers—fully protected with gas masks, proving the National Guard was taking the smoke seriously— had stepped forward to greet the passengers. From taut, wiry build and his confident bearing, one of them had to be Silver Fox—Colonel Wilson. The other was much shorter in stature, but moved through the space with a similarly powerful stride. If it hadn't been for the woman's earlier reluctance to go out into the smoke, Anayeli would have thought it was Master Sergeant Kassis. Behind the two officers, the other soldiers formed an armed corridor, leading to the hospital entrance. Whoever was on that helicopter was important, then.

Anayeli moved closer as the helicopter's blades slowed, the buffeting noise easing, and finally the passengers disembarked, ducking as they went beneath the span of the helicopter's still spinning rotors. There were six passengers, all decked in full-face respirators. The first was wearing a black suit and Anayeli couldn't shake the feeling that she'd seen her before—more than once—though it was hard to tell who anyone was under all that protective gear. She moved closer, trying to keep the helicopter between herself and the armed guards, staying as inconspicuous as possible as she angled for a better look at the others.

Three of them sported lab coats, and one had already taken out some device which she held out in front of her, as if she were taking samples or readings. Behind the lab coats were two men who sported logo'ed polo shirts—the kind uniformed employees wore. Their swiveling gaze reminded her of a pair of periscopes, their eyes sweeping over the hospital, the tents, the smoky sky. One of them turned toward her.

"*Ay, Dios!*" It was involuntary, spoken on an exhale, and covered by the noise of the helicopter—still powering down—and Silver Fox's greeting to the suited woman.

"Madam President! Come this way!"

She barely managed to stop herself from exclaiming again—that's why the suit had looked so familiar! The woman right in front of her was the freaking Vice President of the United States—she must have heard wrong when Silver Fox had addressed her. She wanted to shout after the VP, but she needed to keep quiet to avoid attracting attention. Everyone hurried toward the hospital, except the second officer, who broke away from the Guardsmen and headed for the helicopter pilot, who was the last to disembark from the aircraft.

Anayeli skirted behind the helicopter, praying not to be seen. As much as she would've loved to voice her concerns about the Teff fires directly to the VP, she needed to talk to the polo shirts more. Because that's what had made her gasp. The giant M logo on their shirts. It matched the one from the Matreus website, where she'd found Dan Jenson's and Taylor Muckenfuss' names. This was her big chance. She could ask them the questions Dan had dodged by hanging up and Taylor had refused to answer. She could ask about the Australian Taylor had mentioned. And if she could get close enough—because the VP and Silver Fox were already making their way through the armed phalanx of soldiers—she could ask, once and for all, if Silver Fox knew where Mama was. In front of the Vice President, he'd be forced to answer, because if anyone styled themselves as the voice of the common man, of the immigrant, it was the VP.

She darted past the lab coat trio, who were all huddled around the one with the monitor, which was making a weird ratcheting clicking noise. "That's not good," Monitor Man said.

"Shhhhh." One of his colleagues pushed the monitor down, as if to hide it from Anayeli. She'd talk to them next—that move alone had guaranteed it. But first—the polo shirts.

She went for the oldest one, assuming he had the higher position, her mouth going dry. She could not blow this. "Excuse me, sir?" She grabbed the man's sleeve, and he whirled, eyes bright with indignation and startlement. She used the element of surprise and didn't give him an opening. "Can you tell me what's in the smoke that's making everyone here so sick?"

With eyes that were cold and detached, he raked her from top to toes. The last time Anayeli had seen a mirror was back at her neighbor's, days ago. Before she'd had a messy braid, river-washed clothes, and grimed mask. Polo Shirt's expression said, *Look at yourself. You can't possibly be important.* "You don't seem sick."

"You're right. I'm not. But I've watched at least a dozen people die—blood pouring from their noses and lungs—and I'd like to know when Matreus is going to take responsibility for it." For a split second, she was sure she'd surprised him, that her arrow had found a chink in his armor. "No comment." But the guy was well-practiced, a professional. And this was definitely not his first public appearance at a crisis.

"Who are you?" The younger polo shirt had stopped walking, and stood blocking her path, while Professional Polo Shirt barged ahead, making a beeline for the VP. She didn't have much more time.

"Hey!" Professional Polo spoke loud enough that it was clear he was addressing anyone in the general vicinity. "What kind of lax security is this?"

Private-Citizen Anayeli wanted to run straight for the chain-link fence where she hoped Cricket and Roxy would be waiting. But Reporter-Anayeli dug in, because indignation and irritation she could pry at, maybe get Young Polo Shirt riled enough to answer before he thought better of it—or before she was ushered off. She tried another tack. "I was told an Australian from your company would be helping address—"

The guy snorted. "Natalie?" He gestured to the smoke-shrouded sky. "Like she can fix this!"

It was something. She could use it. She had a name. Natalie. "Can you tell me Natalie's last name, and when she'll be arriving?"

But Professional Polo Shirt had jogged ahead, and caught the Colonel's arm—and attention, bellowing about security lapses. Colonel Silver Fox whipped around, laser focused on her. His voice, when it came, carried. "Master Sergeant Kassis! I thought this woman was to be confined in her containment zone?" It was the tone bosses used when someone's head was about to roll, but instead of making Anayeli cautious, it made her reckless. It was Kassis who had accompanied Silver Fox out of the hospital to greet the helicopter's passengers. Anayeli hadn't recognized her, hadn't noticed the hijab Kassis wore, hidden beneath her gas mask, but the woman's identity was obvious on a second glance.

She could have lied or pretended to be someone else—just a regular concerned citizen. But Anayeli had an ally: Kassis was on her side. The VP was looking at her. And this was the freaking *United States*. Where Free Speech and Freedom of the Press were enshrined in the Constitution. Where she had protections.

So she spoke the truth. "You can't lock me up. I'm a reporter with the Sacramento Bee." And that was a mistake.

Silver Fox made a sharp, forward-chopping gesture with the flat of his hand and with a response so precise they might have been automatons, the two National Guard personnel nearest the helicopter—Kassis and the pilot— peeled off from the group. Meanwhile the phalanx of soldiers, all but two more who kept their weapons trained on Anayeli, closed around the visitors, hustling them into the hospital.

She'd squandered her best chance to get the information she needed, and in her attempt to learn more about the Teff fires, she'd completely lost any opportunity to press Silver Fox about Mama's whereabouts.

She was boxed in, with nowhere to run. The pilot and Kassis stormed toward her, their speed and the intensity of their movements furious. Doubt pricked at Anayeli. Maybe she had misjudged Kassis. Maybe the woman's earlier assistance had all been a ruse, or worse: a trap.

"You can't arrest me. I'm a citizen and a reporter!" Even if the newspaper she worked for no longer existed, she was forever a reporter.

"I told you not to draw attention to yourself." Kassis' voice was hard, tough, befitting of the Silver Fox's right hand.

"I can explain—"

But Kassis was looking over her shoulder, toward the hospital. Everyone had made it inside, except for Silver Fox, who stood, legs spread wide, watching. Whatever fight had gone out of her when she'd recognized Kassis came roaring back.

"I have to take you into custody." There was no apology in Kassis' voice, only a hard edge that meant Anayeli had taken her investigation too far, and the even harder grip of the helicopter pilot's broad hands on her arms.

CHAPTER SIX

DR. DIANA STEWART. MATREUS HQ. CHICAGO, ILLINOIS

Diana was lying on the bed fully-clothed when the phone on the bedside table rang. She fumbled to pick up. "Jane? Are you—?"

"Hello, Dr. Stewart?" It wasn't Jane. "My name is Patti Simmons. I'm the nurse. Mr. Matreus asked me to take you down to the medical suite for treatment."

Diana shut her eyes. *Of course. How could it be Jane?* She'd fled the fires. There'd be no phones where Jane was going.

"Dr. Stewart? Are you there?"

"What time is it?" Daylight, of a sort. The night had been lit orange by fires, and had faded slowly to half-light.

"It's nine a.m. Would you like me to come up now?"

No. "Could you give me half an hour please?"

"Yes ma'am. There are clothes in your size in the wardrobe, and we can get any other necessities you require. I'll be up at nine thirty." The line went dead.

Diana sat up with some difficulty and set the phone back on the hook. Then she paused, and picked it up again, but there was no dial tone.

It beeped then a voice cut in. "Switchboard, can I help?"

Hope flared just for a moment. "Can you get me an outside line please?"

"I'm sorry, lines are down, ma'am. We've been told the fires in the city have destroyed the telephone exchange." The woman was still speaking but Diana set the phone down. It didn't matter if it was the truth or a lie. She couldn't call outside the building.

She rubbed a hand over her face. She wanted to get back into bed and hide under the covers and never come out, pretend this was a world where everything was normal and Sam and Jesse had not drowned or burned alive. She was cold and empty inside, as if something had hollowed her out, and every part of her hurt. She didn't much care how bad her injuries were. She deserved them.

It took two or three goes to get out of bed, and she had to lean on the back of the chair to catch her breath. Outside, the sky was dirty with smoke. There was a row of flashing lights all around the base of the headquarters, and outside that, a crowd. Occasional plumes of smoke fanned up, making spaces in the crowd. An old man ran, slowed, clutching his chest and then dropped to the ground, choking. The fires still burned in places, leaving gaps in the familiar silhouettes of the city, with smoldering wreckage beneath. *Even the city is bleak and hopeless.* She turned away and went to shower and dress before the nurse arrived.

There was a battery of tests and scans and checks, but as the nurse was helping Diana back on with the smart jacket she'd found in the apartment, Victor knocked and stuck his head into the medical suite. "Morning, Di. They tell me you're a pretty mess, but nothing that won't mend. Have you eaten?"

"No."

The nurse intervened. "You should eat, Doctor. Take it easy today and I'll check in with you tomorrow and see how you're getting on." She was an older woman, whose smile lit up an otherwise formidable face.

Diana followed Victor into the corridor.

"Let's try here." He checked a nearby office was empty and gestured her to go in, then shut the door and leaned on it. "Di... I spoke with the Fire and Rescue people. The Berkeley Campus was burned to the ground. There were no survivors."

Exhaustion swept over her so that she staggered, and he had to catch her arm. She couldn't reply; her throat locked up with tears she refused to shed.

"I'm so sorry." He brought her close into a hug, loose enough that she could step away if she wanted to.

She leaned her head on his chest, while pain gripped her so that she couldn't breathe. *I can't bear it. Not again. I can't bear it!* Her heart thundered so that she thought it would explode, and her breath didn't bring her any oxygen. Her grip became tighter on his arm.

Victor stepped back, but didn't let go. "Another panic attack?"

She nodded. *Panic attack. Not suffocating.* But knowing it and believing it were two separate things.

He led her to a table. She leaned back on it, trying to stay calm. He sat next to her, keeping hold of her hand. "Focus. You need to ground yourself. Everything is too much, so we need you to bring your focus right in to just a few things. You remember how?" He kept his voice low and calm, just as he had used to when they worked together more. "Five things you can see, yes?"

A coffee stain on the floor. His signet ring. A graze on the back of her hand. His cufflinks with the Matreus insignia on them. That bloody awful tie he liked.

"Four things you can smell."

His aftershave, cedarwood and citrus. The sharp tang of the antiseptic spray the nurse used. The musty smell of old coffee, faint but there. The slightest tang of smoke, things burning.

"Three things you can hear."

The ding of the lift doors. The low murmur of conversation. And far off, muffled by glass, sirens.

"Two things you can taste."

The metallic taste of fear, overlaid by the harsh mint of toothpaste.

"One thing you can feel."

Victor. His hands holding hers, keeping her anchored. The closeness of him.

She seized on that thought to keep away the panic for a few seconds while her breathing normalized, holding on to him so as not to drown.

The touch helped. It was something real, something tangible. She sometimes regretted that when it had been a possibility, the two of them getting together, the timing had been wrong. He'd still been married and she'd kept a distance between them because of it, only to find when he divorced his wife that he'd been cheating with various other women anyway.

He'd become a trusted mentor in any case but sometimes, just sometimes, when she was lonely and lost and needed a safe shelter, she wondered how things would have been if they had gotten together, and what she had lost to those sacred principles of hers. Certainly she hadn't ended up any the happier for them. Or wiser, given her failure to save the boys.

She took a slow, breath, and another one, waiting as her heart rate slowed to something more bearable. "I haven't had one of those in years." Apart from that one the other day, a little voice noted, but she ignored it. "I... I just really, really wanted there to have been a miracle, that by some fluke of fate the boys hadn't been hurt." She couldn't bring herself to say their names. That would make it real.

Victor nodded. "Just tell me how to help, Di. Whatever you need."

She had to clear her throat before she could speak. "I need to keep going. If I stop and think about it—I just can't." She drew her hand away from his, not without reluctance. "Coffee, please. And then tell me what's been going on the past few days."

He stood "Are you sure?"

"I need to keep busy, Victor. Help me to keep busy." She looked away so that he wouldn't see the moisture on her cheek, dashed it away with the back of her hand.

"Coffee it is, then."

It was quiet in the cafeteria at that time of day, and Di was grateful for it. Victor bought them a coffee each and something for her to eat and loaded them onto a tray. "Let's see, when did we last speak? Three days ago, maybe? So much has happened here, and so fast, I can hardly keep track of it."

They went to the private booth by the window which had been their favorite, once upon a time. She lowered herself carefully into the seat as he set down her coffee and a sandwich on the table. "Thank you."

He took the seat opposite and added three sweeteners into his cup, balling the papers up into a tight bundle. "It's been an insane few days. Besides the wildfires in California, and the cicadas which seem to have come early and eaten half our test crops, there have been a couple of storms in the Atlantic which have caused huge delays to the supply chain and then if that wasn't enough, the cicadas hit us here in the city. The police couldn't cope, people were trapped in their houses for a day and a half, and then someone started setting fires and the fire service just couldn't keep up with it as half of their staff were injured. And things got complicated as we had to suddenly start moving staff around to make sure we have all the people we need on hand."

Diana leaned back in her seat. "This is no time to mess around with office moves, Victor. Things are moving faster than you know. The cicadas are starting to lay eggs. They're far too early. They hatched out too early. I said this before, but it bears repeating: their cycle is becoming faster. And they had no right to be in California. We have to warn people—"

"Damn..." Victor took out a notebook from his inside jacket pocket and made a note. It was one of his evasion tactics.

Unless her memory was playing tricks on her, she was *sure* she'd told him about the eggs and the reproductive cycle speeding up. Or had that been Garrick? The days blurred together, her confusion compounded by her exhaustion and pain. She frowned. "You had the stakeholders' meeting last night, right? So you're sending information out to the emergency services today?"

"It didn't go exactly to plan, I'm afraid. They voted no, and until they release me from my NDA there's not much I can do about that."

Diana set her cup down. "It makes no sense to delay when people are dying right, left, and center!"

He shoved the notebook back in his pocket. "I tried to persuade them, but my father says it has implications for something Bryce's team is working on and he can't risk putting it in jeopardy. And there isn't a damn thing I can do about it because the old man has given his shares to Bryce, and now my son owns 51% of the company and runs his own division."

Diana rubbed her eyes, once again masking her rage. "Bryce has the controlling interest?"

"For a few years now. And he does everything my father ever told him to. They're cut from the same cloth, those two."

"Lives will be lost, Victor!"

"I was overruled by my father and my own son! I'm just the CEO, who am I to have an opinion?" Victor leaned forward and dropped his voice "But I found a way around it. I couldn't tell the emergency services anything, but I had my people source all the PPE they could find, and ship it to them. So they're as protected as I could make them." He looked so pleased with himself that she wanted to grab his shoulders and shake him. He dismissed it with a gesture. "But Di, I've given your theory a lot of thought. Here's the thing, there is no FeedIt in this city. I don't think the emergence of the brood *can* be due to FeedIt. It makes no sense that a fertilizer could cause this kind of mayhem. There must be some other agent or reagent involved. To say nothing of the fact that we're not even supposed to get cicadas for more than a decade. We had Brood X a couple of years ago; it's way too early for them to be back again."

"Maybe." She picked up the sandwich and nibbled on it. It tasted like ashes, but she chewed it grimly anyhow. "So, what next?"

Victor went on. "When the cicadas made the news, a crowd turned up and smashed in the front windows of every building on the street, and the city has started having brown outs. So we brought in some extra security."

She cocked an eyebrow, trying to swallow the bread.

He checked his phone and then set it on the table to one side. "The guys we brought in at first weren't the best, but they were all we could get. A few of them panicked and beat up protesters, but in the heat of battle, what can you do?"

Diana wasn't convinced that battle was the right word, but with a mouthful of sandwich, she didn't have time to interrupt.

"We sorted it all out with the police, and our guys have been told to be more careful. It's caused some bad feeling amongst the rioters, of course; hence the ramping up of the security measures. But don't worry, we're completely safe here. We have our own water supply and generators, and we have an underground pipeline that will keep them running for as long as we need." He picked at a piece of cookie. "But in the meantime, we're having trouble in some of the other sites. They're being raided for PPE as far as we can tell, and we're moving our staff back here from fire-torn areas."

"You're working up to something. What haven't you told me?"

Victor fiddled with his cufflinks. "Bryce is coming here, with his family. It's the safest place to be, so far, and I just want to know they're all safe."

Great. Diana really didn't need any aggro from Victor's son. "I'll move out of the apartment this afternoon, if the dorms are still functional?"

"No need, we have the family suites on the other side of the floor. And I need you well and functioning. We need to work this thing out before any more lives are lost."

If only she had his casual cheer and unrelenting positivity. But she didn't. They'd already 'lost' more lives than she could count. That terrible truth seemed not to have made it into Victor's brain. Not really.

"We've pulled everyone out of the onsite labs that are in the way of the fire, along with the most valuable equipment." Victor stood and held a hand out to help her up. "In the first instance, you'll know better than any of the admins what instruments and chemicals to prioritize. And then once that calms down, we'll get reports from anyone who's seen the cicadas and we'll work out how best to sort out that problem."

He made it sound so clean and logical, as if the solution was just a couple of test beakers away. What they were facing was as deep as it was wide, with roots that stretched deep inside Matreus, Inc. Of that she was sure. She stood with difficulty, and walked back to the elevator with him.

He hit the button and the doors closed. "It's busy-work, Di. If you'd prefer to go and rest—?"

"Busy-work is what I need right now." She needed a shield between her and her grief and guilt. "It's how I manage. I have to keep going."

"Very well. But as soon as you need to stop, don't ask. Just stop." He stood aside to let her go out as the doors slid open.

She paused in the doorway. "Thanks, Victor. For everything." She meant it. The man hadn't done *all the things* she'd hoped for, but he'd at least flexed in the right direction. Having PPE wasn't *nothing*. Sad as it was to admit her mentor wasn't as powerful as she'd always imagined, knowing how the playing field was stacked had to be to her advantage. Bryce was the one to beat; she had to refocus her efforts there.

He twisted his signet ring on his finger. "We haven't had much time together this past few years and I've missed our chats."

"I thought you were avoiding me." She fell into step beside him as they took the corridor to the offices.

He flicked an imaginary piece of lint from his sleeve, a gesture she was coming to see meant he was about to confess to *something*. "I was. But not because of anything you did. My father and Bryce kept me busy with the new lab down in Texas, and then there was a big argument and I didn't want to bring you into it. Bryce was being particularly unreasonable about the FeedIt project. When we lost Ed I told them I wanted you to head the project. My father grumbled, but Bryce absolutely refused unless we brought in Dan as your line manager."

"Bryce refused? But I'm more than capable, and have been part of this project right from the start." Diana was stung. "Why would he? Oh. Don't tell me it's personal."

Victor paused by the door to the offices. "The thing is, Di, it's his mother's influence."

"His mother?"

"When our marriage went wrong, we tried not to let him see the worst of it. And it worked a little too well, it seems. He wasn't there much until he finished his degree. But when he did and we were in the last stages of divorce, it was quite a shock to him. He thought I was having an affair. With you."

"With me? All your other women, and he thought it was me?" Diana shook her head. "Your type tends more toward the bikini babe."

Victor shrugged. "He and his mother both knew that sort of thing was just a fling. But she was jealous of the way we could talk, and laugh, and understand each other. She cared about that more than any one night stand. So when we divorced she knew it had to be something more than a fling, and that's what she told Bryce. He assumed it was you because we spent so much time together back then."

"That makes so much more sense of things." Di frowned. "You told him it was no such thing, right?"

Victor looked away. "The thing is, I didn't want to admit that the affair I was having was with my wife's sister so..."

For a second she thought she'd misunderstood. Then hot anger rushed to her head. "You didn't? Victor, did you let your son believe I slept my way to the top? No wonder he thinks so little of me." She stopped in her tracks. "That sort of nonsense can poison a person's entire career. You better start thinking of a way to tell him in such uncertain terms that no one ever dare think it again, or..." She searched for the right words. "Or I'll leave. Don't think I won't resign over this, because I absolutely will!" She paced away from him. "Did that ever get out? You've put my professional integrity at risk and undermined everything I've ever achieved here because... why? Because you didn't want your divorce to be messier than it already was?"

"Look, it was hard enough to stop Elise from trying to take half of this company. I couldn't give her any more ammunition or she'd have had her pound of flesh and then another on top of that."

The door opened, and one of the lab techs halted. "Sorry, am I interrupting something?"

"Yes."

"No." Victor spoke at the same time as Diana. "What is it, Caulfield?"

"Call from the Austin site, sir. They've evacuated all non-essential personnel."

"We'll be right through." Victor waited for the man to close the door again. "Look, I'm sorry, Di. It was cowardly of me. But it was fifteen years ago, and no one remembers. If you dig it up we'll have to go through the whole thing all over again and it really will follow you around. I don't think anyone in this company doubts your integrity now, if they ever did before."

"Apart from Bryce." She rubbed her ribs. They hurt.

"Okay, apart from Bryce."

She could feel her breaths coming faster again. She would not be able to manage another panic attack and after this Victor would hardly be a calming influence. She stalked away from him, crushed her anger down ruthlessly into fierce embers and took a moment to get herself under control.

"Di— Look, it's really not that big a deal." Victor scuttled after her, wringing his treacherous hands and bleating at her like some lost lamb. As if that would work on her now. "I shouldn't have done it but—"

She rounded on him. "I should walk away, just go back to the apartment and not come out again until..." She swallowed a sob. *Until what?* "There is nothing left for me, Victor. My friends are gone, my parents walked away from me and even Jesse..." Her fingernails bit into the palms of her hand at the name. "I thought there was one thing I could be proud of, one small thing that was mine. I stayed in this stupid dead-end job because I thought I could make a difference. I trusted you to be the mentor you promised to be. And now you tell me that the entire company thought every achievement

I worked for was given to me because I was sleeping my way to each promotion?"

Victor didn't answer—didn't even try.

There was nothing left. Nothing. And it was overwhelming. She couldn't cope with anger and hurt and betrayal and grief and hopelessness all together. It would eat her alive. All she had was busywork. "We'll talk about this further, Victor. But right now I don't have the bandwidth for it." She pushed past him and into the office, heading for her desk. As soon as she had her own research safe and sound, she was leaving Matreus Inc., and never coming back.

CHAPTER SEVEN

CLAIRE MOONE. M6 MOTORWAY. SANDBACH, CHESHIRE, ENGLAND

The parking lot of the gas station was busy, the worst of the traffic clustered around the entrance to the stores. People were lined up outside the grocery store, no doubt stocking up on stupid things like toilet paper and brownie mix when they ought to be getting water and canned goods. But despite the lines, there was little sense of urgency or impending doom—more like general unease and the kind of well-masked pique that came from waiting in line for longer than one felt was necessary. It was a very *British* kind of panic; polite, but irritated.

Governmental reassurances could only hold the masses steady—or ignorant—for so long. Take your pick. Beyond the throngs having nervous conversations—that opened with lines like "did you hear—" and "can you believe—" and "do you think it will reach us here?"—Claire and her team moved from the black van to three black Range Rovers, customized for all terrain, with bull bars and snorkels. They were parked in the least accessible or obvious location, hidden by overgrown bushes and the electrical substation.

All five of her team were dressed in black, as was she, and equipped with lightweight body armor and combat boots. She and those in her immediate command were Team One, six of the twelve Paladins. She hadn't been briefed on what the other half were doing. "Where's Team Two?"

A Scottish voice answered her. The man's nickname was 'Grouse,' for his tendency toward the use of profanities, not for the Highland game bird. "They're grabbing Gandalf, boss."

She pointed at him and the man on his right. "Second bus. Mickey, with me. You're driving. Plank and Nerd, rear. Nerd, you're on nav and comms." She threw a glance back toward the grocery store. Maybe they should pick up some essentials—water, food—just in case. But there wasn't time to navigate the lines. And their attire would certainly raise alarms. The vehicles would have some basics—water, anyway.

As her team moved off, she held her position. "Why are we this far south, if you all knew the mission brief before I did?"

Nerd, the youngest of the group, turned. "There are reports of fires on the Welsh border, close to Chester. The smoke is poisonous, but it's travelling east quickly. The public are fleeing toward Manchester and Liverpool. It's going to slow us down. Main roads and motorways are already snarled up."

Definitely no time for gathering supplies. After, then. Her assessment was immediate, like a reflex. "Get us moving north on the motorway. Scout alternate routes. Off-road's fine. Unmapped, too. Just get us there."

She joined Mickey, settling into her seat in the black SUV. The engine roared into life as he hit the start button. Even from within the luxurious, insulated interior of their vehicle, they could hear the same beast-like growl from the other two Rovers.

"If they want Artemis and Gandalf, it must be a full gathering of the Lazarus team." She was only half guessing. There weren't many other plausible explanations.

Mickey moved off behind the lead car. "We're taking them to Patterdale, so it's serious."

"'Lazarus' is apocalypse-level, full-blown crisis management and recovery." She pulled her seatbelt across her body and clicked it into place. "They're definitely worried. They've not been this serious since..." The list of misses, hits, and near-misses—most of which the public never heard about—reeled through her mind. "...last time."

Keeping up with the accelerating car in front of him, he gunned the gas. "We've done drills before."

The vista of the Cheshire Plain opened to the west of them. The flatland brought the sky down to earth in a long, wide horizon. In the brightness of the day's sunlight a darkness threatened. A cloud of black smoke rose thousands of feet, spreading out for at least ten miles. "This feel like a drill to you?"

"Nope."

At first, their progress was steady. They were able to keep to the speed limit of seventy miles per hour for ten miles. At mile eleven, they had slowed to a crawl. Then traffic came to a standstill. Picking his way through the congestion, Grouse moved from the fast lane to the middle, then to the slow lane. Mickey and Plank followed as close as was possible in the snarl of cars, without bullying their way in front of other drivers. It was better to be polite and ask. Even an SUV couldn't mess around with a truck carrying a full load.

Once all three vehicles were in the slowest lane, the lead car moved onto the safety lane. With the convoy assembled, they sped up. Claire pressed an auxiliary button on a panel in the middle of the dashboard. Blue lights flickered in their front and rear. A second button made their headlights flash. The other vehicles did the same. At approaching one hundred miles per hour, all three Range Rovers ran the tight passage between the fencing barrier of the motorway and the hard shoulder. Claire tensed with every deviation, each bump in the road.

Ahead of them, Grouse's rear lights flared. Mickey stamped on the brake.

Clare snatched up the hand microphone for the two-way radio. "What's going on?"

"Exit ramp traffic is blocking our path to use the hard shoulder."

A third voice broke into the conversation. "We can take the fields on our left, push across the side road traffic and rejoin when we can."

"Good work, Nerd." She trusted them all to make smart choices, even simple ones. "Take point. Grouse, follow. We have the rear."

The lead car surged ahead, turned ninety degrees and powered up the embankment at the side of the road. Claire grabbed the handle above her door and the 'off-roading bar' secured to the dashboard. She'd made ready for a rough ride before. It wasn't her first rodeo.

Splinters and soil kicked up into their windshield as she and Mickey crested the ridge into the crop of wheat that had grown undisturbed for a season. Smashing a single track through it all, the three Range Rovers etched a direct line to the sideroad feeding the intersection. Horns blared when Plank drove through the wooden fence on the far side, straight over the sidewalk and pushed his way onto the highway. The cars on the far side had nowhere to go, stopped by the traffic ahead of them. Three massive black SUV with blue lights flashing and headlights blazing, had come out of nowhere to transect a gridlocked road, not something covered in the 'Highway Code' for British drivers.

The team stopped their vehicles in a staggered order, giving Claire the best tactical view of the situation. "Clear a path, Nerd."

Nerd opened his door, stepped out and pointed at the bewildered face of the driver in the Audi A6 in front of them, then at where he wanted that car to be. Claire noted the energy in his body language. He said nothing, made no apology, and gave no thanks. He looked at the car behind, a big Mercedes. The driver had his hands raised in surrender. So long as he stayed put, their way was clear, other than having to destroy another fence or two and cut a swathe through another field of ripened crops in order to reach their objective: the Barton Bridge.

The massive mile-long viaduct of Barton Bridge spanned the River Mersey and the Manchester Ship Canal at their closest point from the coast. Ocean-going cargo ships could make their way inland to the port of Manchester, at Salford Quays. To attempt another high speed drive along a tight 'emergency only' lane over a bridge, one hundred and twenty feet from the earth, with only a steel railing to keep them from falling, could've been considered suicidal, but Claire's team zoomed along. She wouldn't allow even a rational fear to slow their progress.

Once on the far side, as the road rested on hard ground, Nerd broke radio silence. "M6 is at a complete standstill from M62 northbound. We need to go off-road into Warrington, then thread toward St Helens. I have a route."

Claire accepted the change of plan. "Received. Take point."

For the drive across open parkland, the team used a staggered formation, rather than driving in a single column. It tore up more of the ground but gave them better visibility. Startled deer scattered in every direction, leaving a path for the speeding Range Rovers. The ground undulated, sometimes dropping away beneath their wheels. Grouse had the lead, as he twisted and turned past stands of trees or hurtled across open ground. He slowed, approaching a dense forested area. Mickey did the same, then fell in behind him. It was a tactical choice, easier to thread through constriction if they were back in line.

Claire grabbed the bar. The black SUV ahead lurched left. A solid brick wall lay ahead of them, but a footpath led beside it. She was still holding tight, when they came to a sudden halt in front of the curving ironwork of a pair of old ornate gates.

Trigger jumped out, ran to the back of the vehicle and swung the rear door open. He pulled out a sledgehammer then moved around to the front. He delivered a powerful blow to the mid-point of the structure, smashing the locks. He dragged one wide, then the other, and returned to his seat.

They made their way through the sprawling estate without any challenges, sheep notwithstanding. And then they were back on tarmac, heading north. Road markings were more regular as they approached the outskirts and housing districts of the town they had circumnavigated. Clear of the snarl of traffic on major routes, they sped up again.

A long, straight stretch of road took them into a blind curve and pulled up on blue flashing lights. Trigger yelled over the radio. "Roadblock." At the same time, Grouse hit the brakes so hard his wheels locked. The tires smoked, leaving lines of burned rubber.

Two police interceptors blocked the road. Sleek, fast, and light, Claire evaluated the political fallout of ramming them out of the way. But they'd trained for encounters with enemy obstructions—police were even easier to deal with. "I'll handle it."

Everyone but Claire moved to the rear of the vehicle, opening the door that would give them access to weapons. "Hold position."

Ten yards from the front of her convoy, four unarmed male police officers stood at the ready. "Gentlemen. Before you begin to ask awkward questions, allow me to present my card as identification. On it, you will discover a Whitehall telephone number. Call your control room, relay the information to them and the situation will be resolved."

The older looking copper stepped between the shiny white Skoda Octavias. Balding, fifty-something and taking charge, he looked her up and down, then peered behind her to the Range Rovers and the men taking cover behind them. "Who the hell are you? Why are you driving around like maniacs? We've had reports of you all the way from—"

"As I said." She handed him her business card. "You'll need this. We'll wait while you call it in."

"You look military. Where's your insignia, your MP identification?" He waived his finger at her. "You can't go pretending to be police, putting blue lights on your cars."

Claire's annoyance rose steadily as his questions became time-consuming. Ramming them would have been quicker in the short term. "Take the card. Make the call. Do *not* waste my time." Her assertive tone, and the clipped articulation of every syllable, was enough to get him to snatch it from her hand.

He turned his back and put his hand to the microphone of his walkie-talkie. "Control, this is Foxtrot-Five-Seven, over."

Claire didn't need to hear the rest of the one-sided conversation. Returning to the team, she knew things would be resolved within a minute or two. "Mount up!"

Grouse grinned as they passed each other. "Nice one, boss."

She returned the smile. "Be ready to roll as they move back."

Foxtrot-Five-Seven stood with his hands on his hips when the Range Rovers moved past. There had been no need for further conversation. The police cars were withdrawn, opening the road ahead. In common politeness, Claire gave him an acknowledging nod. "What a reasonable chap."

Mickey hit the button for the blue flashing lights. "Did he have an option?"

"No."

As they rejoined the busier main roads toward other sections of motorway, the volume of traffic doubled. Claire checked the dashboard clock. "Dammit. School home time, then rush hour." And that was assuming daily life was still running on regular schedules. She knew enough from her too-long classroom experience to know how quickly a group could go from reasonable routine to chaos.

Mickey made no suggestions, so she broadcast to the other cars. "We're going to hit more traffic. Give me some suggestions."

Nerd was immediate with a response. "Take the next left. Two hundred yards on the right, there's a motorcycle dealership."

"Solid solution." She'd have to split them up. Artemis would not be comfortable on the back of a bike. They'd need the cars, once they'd secured him.

The dealership had a wide forecourt with ten lowrider style bikes parked side by side. Mickey whistled. "Nice Harleys."

The men armed themselves with Glocks and MP-5s. The three drivers stayed alert and with the vehicles, undistracted by the mechanical marvels beside them. Trigger and Nerd followed Claire, their guns pointed at the ground.

The showroom had glass walls on three sides, floor to ceiling, with themed sections for American, British and Japanese road bikes —the inventory already picked clean. Claire headed straight for the 'Adventure' section of higher-seated all-terrain monsters. Her armed escort held back, covering a side window each.

A young man, late twenties, blond and athletic, rose from behind a wide desk. He wore jeans and a tight-fitting white T-shirt. The company's 'Bike-s-mart' logo highlighted his pectorals, while the snug sleeves emphasized his bulging biceps. "Well, hello, miss. I'm Charlie. What can I help you with, today?" His patronizing tone grated on her every nerve. Even dressed as a soldier, a woman didn't always command the respect she deserved.

"I want those three KTM Dukes, fuel for each, and three helmets."

Charlie chuckled, opting for being too friendly instead of the business-like manner she would have preferred. "Ah, going all Terminator on me, eh? You're not the first one coming in here the last few days, looking for more efficient transport."

Without a word from her, Trigger turned, making himself and his piece obvious to the salesman. There was no threat. It was a simple exposition.

As she took a step forward, the blond took a step back. "Here's a credit card, Charlie. Put everything we take on that. Do you have fuel?"

Blushing, he put a hand on his desk as if to stabilize himself. "Those three are sold. I thought you were going to steal them."

"Add twenty percent to the price. We'll take them now." Claire walked away. "What boxes do you have that will clip onto the rack of the Duke?"

His tone had changed from confident to compliant. "They're custom KTM ones. Over at the back of the display."

"If we don't damage them, we'll send them back to you. You can resell them, second hand."

"Blimey, you're serious." At his desk, the young salesman started to scribble notes on a pad. "What helmets do you want?"

Nerd stepped up to stand next to Trigger. Claire directed his attention back to the cars with a single glance. It was all she needed to do. No words necessary. "Want me to drive car two, boss?"

She grinned. "Good man. Sort two Glocks for me. Same for Mickey and Trigger."

He acknowledged, took the MP5 from his compadre, and went outside.

On his way in, Mickey's gaze rested on every gleaming bike he passed. "What's the score, boss?"

"Fit the three KTMs with those slimline back boxes. We're going to be a bit light on firepower."

As Mickey and Trigger moved past his desk, Charlie looked up at them. "They're not registered. You can't use them on the road."

Mickey's eyes were widening, taking in all the metallic beauty. "Oh, we can. We *really* can."

Their transaction and preparation were complete, the bikers made ready to pull away.

Claire summarized the plan. "The three of us are going to follow the Sankey Canal, then cross Lord Derby's land. It'll keep us away from the main roads. You guys can meet us at the old windmill at Ormskirk. It's not a race. Get there safe. We'll secure my dad."

She pushed the helmet over her hair, checked her radio headset was comfortable, then tightened her chin strap. There was nothing else to say. The car drivers huddled over the map.

One by one, the bikes revved then moved off. The first mile was on tarmac, which gave her a chance to feel out the way the KTM handled. Inside her helmet, her headset beeped. "What is it?"

Nerd's voice was flat. "We've got a problem. Chester is burning. The fires are out of control. There's a cloud of the toxic smoke blowing this way."

CHAPTER EIGHT

TERRI CURTIS. OUTSIDE LONDON, ENGLAND

Terri coughed for the hundredth time. As soon as it passed, she picked up the radio, set on finally reaching Control.

"Van 1652 to Control, en-route to Watford." Only static in response. "Van 1652 to Control." Still nothing. Her throat constricted —whether from her own cough or being unable to help the accident victims, she wasn't sure.

She tried Control one more time. Like she'd been doing ever since they got back on the road and were promptly stopped in traffic. No sense in lights and sirens, she'd told Bob. She might be sick, but she wasn't dying.

Her control buzzed to life. "Roger 1652, copy."

"Two fatalities at the scene, transport required. Instruct attending personnel to cover up in hazmat suits. There's something fishy going on. Medic sick, cause unknown, we're heading to Watford General Hospital. 1652 out."

Terri hooked the handset back on the clip and reached for her canteen of water. If she hadn't felt so strange, it would have been a relief to finally make contact with Control. She didn't know what was happening, but she didn't like it. Her head was spinning with a hundred different thoughts as she revisited the crash scene, going over each element meticulously. Her mouth was dry, and her head was on fire. She took a long draft of water and swallowed down another wave of fear. An hour ago, she'd been as fit as a fiddle. She'd attended an accident scene, witnessed the bloody demise of a crash victim, had minimal physical contact with him—all with gloves on—and now she was manifesting some of the same symptoms that he had. Was it airborne? That was preposterous, it had been mere minutes... Her heart rate increased. It was probably due to the stress of the day. But she'd just convinced herself of that when another wave of nausea hit. Maybe they were all symptoms of this mystery illness. "Bob, what was that back there?"

"I don't know, kiddo, but it wasn't normal, I can tell you that." Bob hit the lights and siren. Cars pulled out of their path and he accelerating hard, sending the ambulance racing along the motorway.

Terri got back on the radio. "1652 to control, inform police that those remaining at the Road Traffic Accident should keep their distance while recovery of the bodies and vehicle is undertaken and while the shed load is being cleared, out." It was probably too late—the police had long been on the scene. But still... if she could help one person...

"Control to 1652, copy."

Bob pulled into the ambulance bay at Accident and Emergency, Watford General Hospital. "Okay, kiddo, let's get you checked... Terri, your lips!"

Terri smiled wanly and nodded. She could feel that something had happened to her mouth. She pulled down the sun visor in the cab and stared into the vanity mirror. Her lips were blistered and swollen to double their normal size. She opened the door and staggered out of the cab.

"Help me." Her legs buckled as she put her weight on them.

Bob was already there, guiding her back on her feet and lifting her arm over his shoulders as he supported her waist and walked her into emergency and straight to the reception desk.

"Hey, Jean," Bob called through the screen, "Let's get Terri in for an immediate triage, she was upright and in good health maybe thirty minutes—no, an hour ago."

Jean recoiled, then quickly mastered herself, even as blood trickled from Terri's nose again. When Terri went to wipe it away, she felt the bump of blisters that were forming on her cheeks. She must look like something from a horror show. Bob took her through the double doors into the triage unit, helping Terri out of her utility vest before easing her onto a gurney.

"Thanks, Bob." It was hard to get the words out, hard to breathe. "Pass me my phone mate, I need to speak with Dale."

Bob reached into the side pocket of the utility vest, pulled her phone out and handed it to her.

She had a message from Dale. "Sorry for upsetting you baby, you're the best. And you're right. Do whatever's right for you. Dx."

A lump formed in her throat and her eyes welled up. She really had chosen the most loving man to be her husband. She thought the world of him. He was nothing like her ex, Jeremy, the biological father of her son, Brandon.

She flicked to Dale's number and hit call. The phone rang twice and then switched to a text message: "Sorry, I'm in a meeting, I can't talk right now."

Terri sighed and scrolled through her address book. There, Jojo! She hit call again. After a few rings Jojo picked up, her cheery voice like music to Terri's ears. "Hey Mum. It's not like you to call me when you're on shift. What's up?"

Terri cleared her throat and tried to speak in a calm, even tone. "Jojo, I've had an allergic reaction to something. I'm getting checked out, just a precaution. If you hear from your dad, let him know I'm at Watford General Hospital."

"Mum, we're coming to see you."

"No sweetie, I'm just going to be checked out by the triage nurse, don't come, you'd just be sitting in the waiting area for hours. I'm sure I'll be out of here today; I'll see you tonight. Say Hi to Kitty for me. I love you girls!"

"Bye Mum, we love you."

Despite feeling like there was a battle going on in her body, her heart warmed from her brief conversation with Jojo and the thought of her family.

Terri let her arm and phone drop to her side when the triage nurse came into the bay and pulled the curtain around her. "Okay Terri, I wasn't expecting to see you on the gurney today, you're normally bringing them in to me. Let's have a look at you."

"Hey, Giselle."

Giselle pulled the canvas cuff of the sphygmomanometer up to Terri's upper arm and wrapped it around, pressing the button on the monitor. As the cuff was inflating, the nurse took Terri's temperature with a thermometer gun. The base monitor beeped within a nanosecond of the thermometer. "BP 140/90, Pulse 86 bpm, Temperature 39 C. Mrs., you ain't going anywhere fast. Let's get some fluids into you girl and get the duty doctor in to see you."

Terri thought back to the scene she had attended with Bob. Confusion and fog crowded her mind as she traced her steps. She'd gotten out of the ambulance, walked to the cab... The fall, the seeds! She fell face down in a deep blanket of seeds and had inhaled them. That had to be it.

Giselle put a cannula into the back of Terri's hand and set up a saline drip, which she connected. Then she took some Petroleum Jelly and applied it gently to Terri's blistered lips.

Bob stuck his head through the curtain. "Hey, kiddo, I'm going to head back to the station. You take it easy you hear? We'll manage without you somehow." He winked at her and turned to go back to the ambulance.

Bob had taken a handful of seeds and put them up close to his face. Why wasn't he on a gurney? Nausea gripped her stomach as she struggled to make sense of how she had come to be a patient in her local hospital instead of delivering someone there for help. There'd been strange news reports of fires and toxic smoke somewhere way up in Wales—and of course in the States where Brandon was hiking with Jeremy—but America and Australia were always on fire. None of that could be connected to her. It wasn't even smoky in London.

Giselle adjusted the drip, explaining she was about to administer 650mg of liquid Acetaminophen in the top of the canula. "Right, I'm going to find that doctor, back in a jiffy."

Terri barely had any strength—not for talking, not for even the slightest nod. Her head was throbbing, and she was shivering although she simultaneously felt like she was burning up. She wanted to go back to the moment she'd sat down for breakfast, to start afresh and not bicker with Dale. She drifted into a fitful sleep.

Terri woke to see a doctor standing over her, looking at her chart. She couldn't see Dale. They had to have called him and told him what had happened, surely. She cursed herself again for getting snarky with him over breakfast.

"Well young lady, what have you been up to that brings you in here in this state on a Wednesday morning?"

"It's still morning?" It couldn't be possible. But it didn't matter. She had to give the doctor anything which might give him a clue as to the cause of her sudden sickness. "RTA, two dead, seed in the cargo, shed all over the slip road, must have been tons of it. I slipped and fell face first into it, got it in my mouth and nose. The driver of the truck at the RTA was having major convulsions, bleeding from his facial orifices, the only things out of the ordinary that I can think of."

"Well, I'm Dr. Dasgupta and I'm going to keep my eye on you. Nurse, get her up to Heronsgate Ward, they've got a free bed, I just discharged that chap who had the triple heart bypass. And you young lady," he turned back to Terri, "I've got some ward rounds to finish. I'll come and check on you once I'm done. Try not to develop anything too exotic."

With that the doctor left the triage bay and Terri drifted off again. Just the effort of talking was exhausting.

When she came to again, she was on a ward. The curtain around her bed covered one side of her bed, offering her a little privacy. The other side was open, revealing a woman in the bed opposite and a bank of windows opening out onto the beautiful, cloudless sky. Terri sat up, an action that sent her into a fit of rasping coughs. As the coughing subsided she put her hand to her cheeks. There were welts scattered like giant freckles across her face, all over her forehead. It made no sense. Her symptoms added up to nothing she'd ever heard of.

The ward nurse approached Terri's bed and asked her how she was feeling.

"Like death warmed up." As she was talking, sweat trickled down her forehead. She used her forearm to wipe it but was horrified to see her arm covered in blood.

The nurse smiled kindly at her and wiped the blood away with a damp washcloth. "Don't worry love, it's hematohidrosis, it happens when people get extremely stressed. There's something stressing you big time." She turned and went back to her station.

Terri reached to her locker and picked up her phone. She hit Dale's number. It rang for an eternity, then he answered.

"Dale Curtis"

"Dale, I'm at Watford General Hospital, come now. I'm really sick and I'm scared." Terri heard the panic in her voice and thought how she might be sounding to Dale. The last thing she wanted was to come across as a hysterical wife, but she wanted him to understand the urgency of the situation without portraying herself as pathetic.

"I'm leaving now baby; I'll be with you as soon as I can."

Terri leaned over to put the phone back on her locker and was overtaken with a coughing fit. The phone clattered to the floor.

The ward nurse came to Terri's bed, retrieved her phone, and lifted her up into a sitting position. Then she plumped and propped the pillows up behind her. "Can you sit back against the pillow, love? I want to see if we can reduce this coughing."

Terry eased herself into a sitting position, a herculean task when it should have taken no energy at all. Baffling. She all but fell back onto the pillows, her breathing labored and way too fast after such a simple task.

"I'll go and get you some water, love. You still look parched. I'll be right back."

The nurse hurried away, and Terri reached for her phone again, her body aching as she did. She opened the camera app and switched it as if to take a photo of her face. She made a noise that was almost inhuman, half gasp, half shriek. She didn't recognize the woman looking back at her in the camera. The whites of her eyes were blood red, her lips blistered, swollen and cracked, there were weals on her upper face, some of which were weeping blood and puss, her eyelids cracked and red raw.

Dr. Dasgupta drew back the curtain. Behind him was the nurse, who had a jug of water and a small plastic tumbler. "Right my dear, my best guess is that you've had an extreme allergic reaction."

"No kidding, doctor." It was the seeds. She was 99% certain of it. *I had a reaction, but Bob didn't.* The driver had a fatal reaction but maybe his mate had symptoms too, before he headbutted the windshield. They were sitting on top of a few tons of the seeds, so it seemed possible there was a toxic effect, like a hay fever sufferer manifesting allergic symptoms when they were exposed to pollen.

The doctor was still talking. He was calm but forceful, but there was something in his tone she didn't like. Worry? Lack of certainty? If she hadn't been so addled, she would have been able to read him. "I would have said anaphylactic shock, but your blood pressure is high so that's unlikely. Your combination of symptoms defies description. So, we're going to take a belt and braces approach. Firstly, we're going to dose you with some hydralazine to bring your blood pressure down. We're also going to give you a dose of tranquilizer to bring your stress level down. We're going to give your body a couple of hours to relax and then we'll reappraise the situation."

It was too hard, too painful, to speak, so Terri nodded her assent, grateful that someone was doing something that might make a difference. The water in the cup the nurse held for her was a great relief on her tongue and throat, quenching a fire.

She was startled awake again when Dale took her hand in his. She opened her eyes.

"Terri. Sweetheart." Dale gazed at his wife.

Her heart swelled with love for her husband. No one else had ever looked at her the way he did—with pure adoration and gentle compassion, even when her face was ravaged. "Dale, there's something wrong sweetie. That truck we attended, the RTA, there was a shed load, seeds, millions of grass seeds. They got in my mouth, my nose. The state the driver was in, it wasn't due to the crash." Terri's voice went shrill, cut off as she burst into another furious bout of coughing, spitting blood over the sheet covering her.

Dropping her hand, Dale bolted to the door. "Nurse! Please!" Before he'd even finished calling for the nurse, she came rushing in.

Terri's lungs protested and the coughs tore at her already tender throat, but she had something important to tell him and he needed to listen at least this once. "Seeds, Dale, the seeds!"

"I'm sorry sir." The nurse guided Dale toward the curtain flap. "We're going to have to take her down to ICU. Leave your number at the desk, we'll let you know if there are any developments.

Terri fumbled to reach her husband's hand but her arm was too heavy to lift. Her entire body was too heavy. It was as if a giant weight crushed her to the bed, squishing her organs to pulp.

She couldn't even muster the strength to protest when an orderly hurried across the floor and with a few simple actions had transformed the bed to a gurney.

Terri was torn. She desperately wanted to feel better and just yield to the care of the professionals in the hospital, but she was scared. More than anything she wanted to hug Dale and tell him she was sorry for snapping at him over breakfast. There was so much more she needed to say. But a coldness slithered through her veins and a blackness inside her mind crept ever closer.

She needed to apologize. She needed to tell him...

"Dale," she started mouthing the apology when the last of her available strength diminished like a guttering candle and she passed out.

CHAPTER NINE

SAM LEARY. I-70 WEST OF BRECKENRIDGE, COLORADO

Before the sky rained mutant fricking toxic bugs and the earth burned with poison plumes of choking smoke, Interstate 70 had been a boring stretch of asphalt. No more. The traffic on the three westbound lanes trickled past burned land and disabled cars. Doors, tires, electronics, and even seats had been removed from the wrecks, leaving skeletal frames littered across the expanse of wasteland.

It hadn't gotten any better overnight.

The dim pre-dawn light filtered over a freeway jammed with cars, only a few of which were moving. They wove through the stalled out vehicles clogging the lanes, pushing past when they could, using the shoulders when they couldn't. Some of the cars that had run out of gas had been pushed off to the side of the road, their humans using them for shelter. Maybe? That's what Sam hoped anyway. The other alternative was much worse.

Sam sat in the passenger seat of the semi, his arm around a sleeping Jesse. They were squished together as the trucker eased the behemoth into the left lane. It was slow going, maneuvering such a big vehicle through the tight lanes.

He'd kept the grief at bay as long as he could, but the instant Jesse was asleep, the scenery blurred from the tears that ran down his cheeks and the memories that swept through his mind relentlessly. Henry bleeding to death from Stacey's ill-aimed shot. Stacey screaming as he lit the match. The van exploding. The fire bearing down on them. And it all circled back, again and again, to his best friend dying in his arms. His heart beat faster and he lashed out, kicking the gym bag. The trucker started, swerving before correcting his course as a car horn from behind them blared

"Sorry, involuntary twitch." Sam shuffled his feet, and the duffle bag of supplies he'd gathered rolled to its side. The contents he'd dumped proved that Stacey was nothing more than a hustler, selling things that weren't hers to people who couldn't care less about anyone but themselves. Henry was his proof. Sam's insides were a tidal wave, pounding his senses into fine gritted sand, and his heart dropped into his stomach. If he hadn't left Dr. Sato and the crew, he wouldn't have run into Stacey, and his dog would still be alive.

The trucker, who'd introduced himself as Bill, pinched a clump of red gummy bears with three fingers and stuffed them into his mouth. "At this rate it'll take three days to get to Utah." The statement sounded more like grumbling than an announcement. He slammed on the brakes, grinding the semi to a dead stop.

Sam and Jesse pitched toward the dash, the seat belt locking with a painful jerk. Sharing a seat wasn't the safest thing to do, but there were only two captain's chairs in the cab. A motorcycle ripped up the center lane, letting out a high-pitched whine as it wove between moving cars and threaded through the jumble of abandoned vehicles. As they watched, the motorcyclist slammed on the brakes. Smoke rose from the back tire as the entire back end of the bike fishtailed stopping just before rear-ending a slow-moving sedan.

Bill shook his head and stuffed more bears into his mouth.

"Young 'uns are going to get themselves killed if they don't watch it." He eased the semi forward into a steady crawl again and the biker shifted his motorcycle onto the shoulder, doing a wheelie as he took off. It only took moments for the biker to disappear into the darkness beyond where the morning's dim sunlight filtered through the smoke.

Jesse's head dipped forward, a slight snore escaping as he slumped against Sam. He shifted to the right, and the boy slipped further onto him. Taking care of a child wasn't something he wanted or enjoyed doing, and he'd already given up more than he was prepared for and then some. The trip to get the kid back to Diana had cost him his furry pal and put him in danger at least twice, and they were only at the beginning of the journey. The quicker he got rid of the tagalong, the better. He pushed on the superhero's shoulder to right him, but the boy shifted back.

"Put him on the bed, he won't roll around too much." Bill hiked a thumb at the back of the cab. "Shoulda told you sooner, but you both dropped off so fast."

The captain's chairs were backed by two square columns with an opening between them that led to a full-size bed. Sam unbuckled the seat belt and half shoved, half rolled the boy onto the mattress. The kid was worn out and he barely stirred before falling right back to sleep as soon as he lay down. As Sam turned to rejoin Bill in the cockpit, something behind the driver caught his attention.

The column that separated the cab from the bedroom had three cubbyholes. One cubby cradled a microwave while the other two held blankets and books. Curiosity overrode his grief. "You can cook while on the road?"

Bill chuckled. "First time riding in a semi with a sleeper, eh? Yup. I can live out of this beast for about a week before needing to stop for supplies. Although things smell a little ripe at that point." They slowed as Bill navigated another snag blocking the lane. Bill hooked a thumb at a small door above the microwave. "That's my mini fridge and the bottom is where I keep cups and plates." He shifted his arm to point behind Sam. "Got a TV, spots for clothes, and under the bed there's a storage compartment where I can hide my private stash should I take on a passenger or two. I'd blow the horn if the kid wasn't sleeping. They tend to get a kick out of that."

Sam stared at the truck driver. "Why trust me with that information?"

"It's all right, son. I've been on the road long enough to know a killer clown when I see one. Experience has taught me that anyone trying to protect a kid the way you're doing can't be all bad." He tossed a bandanna that had been knotted around the rear-view mirror to Sam. "Better wrap that around whatever part of you is bleeding. We can take a look later."

Sam tied the cloth around his calf, the muscle burning. Bill must've seen his bloodied and torn pant leg when he'd helped Jesse into the back.

The road cleared up the farther they got from Breckenridge, but they were still barely moving. He could've walked faster than they were driving, but Jesse couldn't, and anything was better than being out in the smoke. It felt safe in the semi until Bill pulled the lever for the blinkers and got in the right lane, headed for the exit. Sam squinted at the green signs as they came into focus. "Why are you getting off the Interstate? Wouldn't 70 cut straight across to Utah?"

The driver dug an atlas out from the front and handed it over to Sam. "It would, but there's too much traffic and it's going too slow. We'll take 91. It'll take us south. Once we hit Montrose, I can use the CB radio and see if anyone out there knows if 70 is clear enough further on."

Sam pulled at the medical mask he'd been wearing since he'd snagged it from Stacey's things. The new route worried him. Maybe he should ask to be let out. But he didn't want to take the risk of inhaling more poisonous particulates from the smoke. And if the new route still got them closer to where they wanted to go, perhaps it was best to stay put.

Bill turned the wheel, directing the truck onto 91 and stepped on the gas. The diesel engine grumbled and roared as it chugged up to cruising speeds. "Relax. You don't need that mask in here. The air's recirculated in the cabin and filtered from outside. No smoke inside."

Sam left the mask on. It was only a matter of time before the truck's air filter was saturated.

They passed an abandoned truck that had tipped into the ditch. It hadn't been pillaged, and the body looked to be in good condition. For a heartbeat, Sam imagined stopping and trying to get it running, but there was no guarantee that it had enough fuel to get Sam and Jesse back to California. Instead, he watched as it grew smaller in the mirror until it disappeared behind the smokescreen. Few vehicles traveled their way, and those that did raced around only to vanish into the haze that even headlights couldn't cut.

Sam went back to his brooding as the conversation dwindled, every cat's eye marker working its way into his subconscious. Their flash was a distinctive reminder of the dog he'd loved and lost. There was no way to replace Henry, and even if he could, it would never be the same. He bit his lip to stop the tears. He didn't want Bill to see a grown man cry. Besides, while he wasn't a prisoner, he had little choice but to travel with the stranger. That still didn't mean he trusted the man. And there was Jesse to consider. He needed his family, and the only way he was going to see them was with Sam and Diana's help. He rubbed the dried dark red spot on his pants and sniffed. Diana had better be there when they arrived, or he'd dump the kid with the first friendly face he saw.

Sam jolted awake and blinked to remove the sleep from his eyes. His brain wanted to explode as another horn blast made his head throb.

Jesse bounced on the bed in excitement, his mask lying beside him. "Do it again, do it again." Bill grinned and pressed a button. The horn bellowed. It was rude to play with things that made loud noises when someone was asleep. But, the kid was happy and it'd make the trip seem faster if everyone was getting along.

The entire windshield was awash with the sun's glare and traffic was impossible to see, but Bill looked over at him anyway. "Mornin' sunshine."

"It's not morning. And how can you be so chipper?" Sam stretched his back and arms, wincing at his injuries.

Bill bit off a chunk of granola bar. "It's just a phrase Sam, relax.

We made a pit stop an hour ago and I made sure your wound was dressed proper too." He handed Sam a wrapped bar and went back to navigating the road.

Sam pulled his mask off, unwrapped the bar, and tested the corner, nibbling until crumbs fell onto his shirt. They should have woken him up if they'd made a stop. And how had he slept through his wound being tended to?

Jesse hopped off the bed as if he'd been given two energy drinks and pointed at buttons along the dash. "Look. That thing tells us which direction we're going. Mr. Bill says we need it just in case the GPS isn't working."

Sam glanced at the compass on the dash showing a large white W as a sign flashed past by informing drivers they were on Highway 50 about to reach Montrose. Little Spiderman leaned against the driver's seat and watched the gauge needles.

Bill pulled the radio handset from the console and keyed it up. "Breaker one nine." He turned a knob on the unit up a notch and flipped channels. "Breaker one nine. This is Cinnamon Bear. Anyone got their ears on?" He waited a minute until the line went clear and a tinny voice came through the speaker. "I read you Cinnamon Bear. This is Skateboard Lizzy."

He chuckled and shook his head. "Hey, Lizzy. Looking for a ten-thirteen for Seventieth Street westbound." There was more silence and the radio keyed up before going to static. "Lizzy, did you copy?"

The speaker hissed and popped as Lizzy's voice came through. "You're breaking up, switch to channel one."

Bill reached for the radio knobs, flipping the first one all the way to the left. The readout showed a red number one in its rectangular box. "This is Cinnamon Bear. Lizzy, come back."

Lizzy's voice came over the speaker crystal clear. "Copy Cinnamon Bear. Ten-nine"

Bill keyed the radio and put it within an inch of his mouth. "Is 70 clear?"

Lizzy cleared her throat on the air. "Steer clear of 70. East- and west-bound lanes are packed with gear jammers past the split at U.S.-Six. Had to take a jaunt through the woods due to a couple of meat wagons. A crotch rocket hit some gators and became road pizza on the back of a roller skate. Whole damn place is a mess. Best to use the boulevards unless you have all the time in the world."

Bill slowed down as they hit the city limit sign and stopped at the intersection. There was no one around. He put the truck in park and shut off the engine. "Copy Skateboard. May God have mercy on their souls. Need some location information from 50th Street to Salt Lake."

"Negatory. A mamma bear has been using a plain white wrapper and several four wheelers on 80th Street near Clive to brake check semis and others that might carry precious cargo. Best to flip-flop or become a bobtail so you can outrun the bears."

Bill slammed his fist on the dash. It was the first time he'd lashed out and Sam wasn't sure if he was showing a darker side to his jovial demeanor or if something had warranted the outburst. The conversation was in a language he didn't understand. He pulled Jesse closer to him, ready to jump out of the cab at the first sign of true aggression.

The trucker squeezed the microphone until the veins stood out in his hands. His arms shook and his face reddened as he whispered into the unit. "Skateboard. Home twenty is west and I can't drop payload because of a rumor. Did you have eyeballs on the situation?"

"Negatory Cinnamon Bear. Heard it over the waves as a distress call. They said the lollipops past yardstick 50 had all been destroyed and that they'd been doing double nickels when several skins blew out and had to slow down. Bears caught up to them shortly after on the hammer lane and surrounded them. If you're going that way, make sure it's before noon. Good luck. Skateboard out."

Bill placed the microphone back on the radio's clip and pushed the GPS map around until Interstate Seventy ran across the center of the screen. He ran his finger down the red line and used his thumb to measure out the distance to Salt Lake City. Then he measured out the distance, heading south. "I don't like it, but we have another eight hours to go if Lizzy was correct." He started the truck and turned south. "At least we have enough diesel. Sorry about that little outburst. This world's gone to hell and taking the good uns with it."

Sam knew about the good ones going bad. Even rational people were turning on each other for scraps. He pushed Jesse back toward the bed, and the boy complied and jumped onto the mattress without a word. "So... Could you explain the conversation you just had?"

A smile returned to Bill's face as he set the cruise control. "What you heard was trucker language. Interstate 70 is still packed and will be so for the near future. Some knucklehead on a motorcycle ran over some tire tread and bounced off the back end of a car—maybe that guy we saw? The ambulances that were headed to help were creating a blockage. She told me to use alternate roads to get to my location. She also warned me that there's been a female cop and some cars raiding semis and that we should turn around or detach the trailer so we wouldn't become a target."

Sam leaned over to see the readings on the dials. They had over three quarters of a tank to get wherever they were going—Sam hadn't even bothered to ask and Bill hadn't said. Plenty of fuel for there and more. It took time, but every move Bill made, every button he pushed, Sam mentally recorded for later, just in case. *Just in case.* But the big rig seemed simple enough to operate; most of it was automated. The red circle of sun rose higher in the smoky sky. If they continued on the path the trucker was talking about, it would be hours before they reached his destination.

Hours of blacktop later, Bill pulled the semi onto a dirt road. "Welcome to Rush Valley, the smallest town I know." The lights from the semi cut through the smoke enough to light up a house as he turned, its sides burned to a crisp charcoal black. They bounced down the uneven path with the weight of the trailer until reaching a fork in the road. He took a right and chugged up the hill. The fields around the area were blackened and the two trees that were still standing had been hollowed out. At the top of the hill the headlights swung to illuminate the side of a house, its bright yellow paint an homage to survival.

Sam's jaw dropped, and he leaned forward. "How's this place still standing?"

The truck trundled in a large arc, circling the house, bouncing back and forth as Bill turned so that it faced the main road. He pushed the gear selector into reverse and the annoying beeping of the warning backup sounded. They reversed until reaching the garage. "My brother's smart. When the fires first started, he plowed all the plants under. Over fifty acres and the fire had nothing to burn. I'm sure the smoke was intolerable, but they called me to give me a heads up. Now it's time to unload." He put a mask on and hopped out of the cab, motioning for Sam to follow.

Three men from the house joined them, and Bill opened the back of the truck. They unloaded box after box from the trailer until everything was out. Once the garage door closed, Bill wrapped an arm around Sam's shoulder and steered him toward the truck. "Let's get the little guy inside for the night and find you a bunk."

Sam withdrew, sidling sideways until out of reach, afraid Bill would hear the thundering of his heart. "I'd rather not move him while he's sleeping. And I don't want to leave him alone either."

Bill shrugged. "Suit yourself. I'll leave you the keys should you need air conditioning in the night." Tossing the keys to Sam, he ambled toward the house and Sam crawled into the cab.

Smoke obscured the sky, and Sam leaned against the steering wheel. It was quiet in the dead of night. Two reflective orbs bounced across the tilled ground and Sam straightened. Henry! It couldn't be. He shook his head and blinked. The eyes bounced closer and the outline of a rabbit shone against a stump. Sam leaned back in the captain's chair and crossed his arms. It was stupid to think that his beloved boy could come back to life. He glanced in the rear-view mirror at Jesse's sleeping form. Logically speaking, part of the blame rested with the kid. If it hadn't been for Jesse, they wouldn't have been on the stupid trip. He had to get rid of the kid and, if the map was right, it was only another ten hours to California. There was nothing else for it. Clenching his jaw, he buckled himself in and turned the key in the ignition. "Sorry Bill, but I need the truck."

The engine chugged to life, he put it in drive, and pressed on the gas pedal. The cab jerked and the trailer rocked back and forth, a horrendous bang echoing. Even though the engine was running he wasn't moving. He'd forgotten something.

He fumbled over the dials and buttons as the back door to the house flew open.

Bill stood framed in the doorway, his checkered plaid impossible to miss.

Fingers trembling, Sam pushed every knob and lever again. Nothing happened, but the same three men from earlier all rushed out of the house and past Bill on the stoop, headed straight for the semi. One of them raised a gun.

CHAPTER TEN

DR. DIANA STEWART. MATREUS HQ, CHICAGO, ILLINOIS

Diana glared at the Matreus logo painted large on the opposite wall as she marched to her desk. Victor's team could sort out the evacuations. Let him do his own busywork! She wanted nothing to do with him, and less to do with his damn company.

She sat down and went through her belongings. Certificates, newspaper clippings, twenty years' mementos of her achievements, it all went into the trash. Her notes as well, why not? She wasn't staying with the firm and she didn't feel inclined to leave them for the company to use when they finally decided to put the blame for the cicadas' mutation onto her. She piled the files on the floor next to the trash can, checked in her desk drawer and slammed it shut.

When she wasn't so burned out she'd be furious and mortified and all the rest but right at that moment she just wanted to run away, to somewhere isolated and curl into a ball and hide. Everything she'd been so proud of, everything she had thought she had earned, all of that had been a lie. And she'd patted herself on the back for winning respect in a company that was not inclined to respect women. *So much for that.*

There'd been a few instances in the early days where people had made odd remarks. At the time she'd been irritated that they thought she was a teacher's pet, because she worked closely with Victor and her star had seemed to be rising, her career promising. Probably just as well she hadn't known they thought she was paying for her progress with sex.

She picked up the stress-ball from her desk, a pink foam pig the size of her hand, and squeezed it viciously a few times, and then paused. She'd meant to jettison it in the trash with everything else but Ed Greenbaum, her previous boss, had given it to her before he died. He was one of the few who had respected her for who she actually was. But Aaron and Dan had killed him, or someone from the company had. She weighed the pig in her hand and considered its cheerful expression.

"What a mess, Ed. I wish you were here to help me clear it up." She set it down on the desk, turned the computer on and waited for it to boot up. "Maybe Garrick was right after all. He always said I shouldn't base things solely on my own judgment. Can't tell a lie from the truth."

She'd always assumed that his statement was just another way to undermine her, but it seemed that he was right. That was a hard admission to make, but she'd been wrong about so many things, after all, and failed so many people. She logged in, half-amazed and half-furious that the computer system was still working, and began to go through her files.

It was self-indulgent to throw a tantrum in the middle of all the mayhem. Some of the people out in the city had no electricity, no water, no food—let alone working phones and computers. Matreus' wealth and power meant she had access to comforts so many others no longer had. People were dying, and even if her professional reputation was in rags, she still had a brain and it was still functioning after a fashion. There was no excuse for sitting around feeling sorry for herself.

A rap at the entrance of her cubicle. "Doctor Stewart?" Andrew was the guy she had been mentoring before it all kicked off. "Wow, your head! That looks painful! Did you get stuck in the riots?"

"Not entirely." She straightened a pencil so it was at right angles to the keyboard.

"Glad to hear that. It's madness out there! Kicked off in like ten seconds flat, and now here we all are, hiding in the Tower!"

"Hiding? From the riots?"

"Yep." Andrew came into the cubicle and leaned on the file cabinet across from her. "And they only got worse when we started having brownouts. You can't be sure your lights or your freezer or anything will work right now, and people are kicking off. The governor's talking about deploying the National Guard, but you know young Mr. Matreus. He's brought in his own security force already. I mean, rumor has it that half of them *are* National Guard, but whoever they are, they're keeping us safe here."

Diana paused, thinking back to the foggy details of the day she got back to Chicago. "They were guarding the gates when I arrived."

"Young Mr. Matreus, Mr. Bryce is very hot on security," Andrew added. "He's very hot on everything, though. I watched his video on the intranet. He's looking for good people to help him take this company forward into the future, he said. I'm kinda hoping to get transferred over to his department, but Texas is a long way from my mom. Still, if the right job comes up, I want to be where it's at, and Lord knows that's not here, even though it's the head office." He must have seen her expression sour, though she tried to keep a poker face; he dropped his chatty manner and stood up. "Anyhow. The sooner it all gets sorted out and we can go back to our own beds, the happier I'll be. Is there anything you need? I was supposed to be in a meeting but they canceled."

"No thanks." Her gaze fell on the files of notes on the floor. "Actually, yes. It's a boring job but when you have a moment, would you be able to scan these in for me? There doesn't seem much point in leaving them to attract dust when we could save them in pdf. Save them to the Documents folder, one file per category and call it 'Notes' and the category name, okay?" That way if anyone was paying attention to the files, it would not look like something she had added. And if she left—no, *when*, when she left—she could take the files with her.

"No problem, Doc." Andrew did not look pleased, but he scooped the files up and bustled off.

Diana turned back to her computer. Her files were still gone. And Dan's laptop must have gone up in flames with the van when the wildfires hit the campus. She swiveled her chair around to face the cubicle doorway, and beyond it, Dan's office. In theory, if the data was still retrievable, that's where it would be. She just had to work out how to get at it.

She fished in the trash, took out a thumb drive, and plugged it into her computer. There was nothing of use saved there, so she deleted everything. *Right. Now I have a terabyte of space. Let's see what we can fit onto that.*

She started off by sorting through the files she had access to from her own computer, deleting anything irrelevant and saving anything that might be important. If Dan was Bryce's man, she should be okay until Bryce got there; assuming that no one else was reporting on what she was doing. But if they realized what she was up to, she'd be in trouble; even if they didn't intend to find flaws in her data, removing it from the system was strictly against company policy.

"That didn't seem like such a big deal—standard operating procedure for an international agricultural firm—but that was before they tried to kidnap me," she murmured to the stress pig.

Some files were not clearly named, so she ended up reading through them, and with the cicadas in mind, apparently trivial comments started to make more sense. She opened a document and pasted them all in. They'd need rearranging and sorting through, but there were so many little loose threads, one of them must be the right one.

"Done, Doc!" Diana jumped as Andrew placed the files next to her. "Wow, you were really zoned out there! Have you even had lunch?"

"Lunch? It's only..." She straightened. Her shoulders were stiff with stooping over the keyboard. "What time is it?"

"Four-thirty." He laughed. "You've been sitting there all day."

"The perils of hyperfocus!" And now that he mentioned it, she was cold, tired, achy, and really thirsty. She pushed her chair out from the desk. "Thanks for doing all that, Andrew. Much appreciated."

"You're welcome, Doc. Want me to shred them?"

"If you have the time, please."

"Sure." He picked up all the files, and hesitated. "You're more likely to talk to Mr. Matreus than I am. If you end up chatting, could you put in a good word for me? About Texas."

For a moment she went hot and cold all over. "Mr. Matreus?" Was Victor's scandal still talked about enough for an intern to have heard of it?

"Young Mr. Matreus. He's due here in the next day or so, they said."

"Oh, Bryce, you mean." She relaxed. "A word from me would not help you there, I'm afraid. You'd be better off getting one of the others to talk to him."

Andrew shifted the folders, which were starting to slip. "Okay, I'll do that."

She watched him go, then scooted the chair back into place. Navigating into the shared drive, she saved the pdf files to her thumb drive then deleted all the originals. "At least I have my notes," she told the stress pig. "But now what I need is coffee."

She locked her computer, slipped the thumb drive in her pocket and stood. The clock was ticking; if she wanted to get the files from Dan's computer before Bryce arrived, she'd need her wits about her. But she couldn't risk doing it until her colleagues had left. She headed off to the cafeteria for something to eat while she waited.

The cafeteria was on the seventeenth floor, a lot nearer ground level than the penthouse where her apartment was. Once again she took her tray to the window, and sat with her back to the room, facing out over Chicago. It was not the Chicago she knew. This new, unfamiliar Chicago was wreathed in smoke, great swaths of the city lying burned and damaged. Leaning nearer to the window, she could just see the edge of the wide plaza around the bottom of the tower. It had been blockaded around the perimeter with Jersey barriers and heavy duty ten foot fencing. Armed men teeming on the inside, and rioters on the outside.

"Dr Stewart, I'm glad to see you're eating. May I join you?" It was Patti Simmons, the nurse.

"Please." Diana waved her cup at the scene below. "What's going on? Looks like they've made this place into some kind of fortress. A bit excessive for riots."

Patti slid into the opposite seat. "For riots, yes. But they've had problems with fires, and they're keeping the plaza clear to give us a bit of room in case one of the buildings around us goes up."

"Are you expecting it to?"

The nurse laughed. "No dear, I don't think we are, but there's Mr. Matreus Senior here, and young Mr. Matreus, Mr. Bryce is heading this way with his family. I think Mr. Victor wants to be double-sure his father and his son's family are safe, and he's made a space for anyone in the city or in the labs who wants to come."

Diana looked out over the disruption below. "It's one way to keep work from being delayed. Put people in here and what else have they to do?"

Patti laughed. "You're a cynical one, aren't you? Not that you're wrong, but even so..."

"It's been a hard few days." That was all it had been! One week ago she'd been feeding the stray cats in the alley behind her apartment and packing an overnight bag for her trip.

Patti nodded. "We're insulated from it up here, but every morning people come in smelling of smoke and pepper spray, and we've had to patch up quite a few people in the infirmary who were caught up in the fray. The brownouts are causing real problems in the hospitals and everywhere else. The governor's set a curfew for 8 p.m. while they deal with the riots, and they've called in local police forces where they can but..." She shrugged. "It isn't pretty out there right now, and I wouldn't go out there if I didn't have to."

Diana set her cup down. "It's like watching it on a movie screen. It doesn't look real."

"Oh, it's real sure enough." A new voice: Garrick, coming out of the line for the register with a can of Coke. Diana's shoulders tensed, but he was in public, of course. He nodded at the nurse. "Hi. I'm Garrick, Diana's husband. Mind if I join you?"

Diana growled, "Ex-husband," but the comment was lost in the scrape of the chair as Patti stood up.

"Lord, no!" The nurse laughed. "If my husband was still alive, I'd be stealing what moments I could with him as well. I've got to get back in any case. Dr. Stewart, I've sent your next batch of meds up to the apartment, and I've added in some arnica for that shoulder of yours. It'll be painful for a while, but the bruising should ease in a few days if you put the cream on as prescribed. I'll check on you before the weekend, but you know where to find me if you need anything."

"Thanks, Patti." Diana was still waiting for Garrick to show what he was up to.

"You look after that lady of yours, sir! Don't make me come after you!"

"Oh, you can be sure I will, ma'am." Garrick winked at the nurse and stood back to let her past. Then he sat and reached across to take the other half of Diana's sandwich. "What is this crap you're eating, Di?" He swallowed a bite and chucked it back onto her plate, washing it down with a mouthful of soda.

She pushed the plate away. "What do you want, Garrick?"

"What do I want? Isn't that a nice question to put to the love of your life?"

She should have responded to that but she was tired and stiff. If twenty years of being single had taught her anything it was that love and hitting people were two different things.

Garrick leaned forward. "Why the long face? Has something happened?"

"Other than you killing the boys?"

"You know as well as I do that I did no such thing, Di."

"You might as well have pulled the trigger. You shut them in and they drowned." Her eyes teared up. Dammit.

Garrick leaned back in his chair. "What? They didn't drown and you know it." He rubbed his chin. "Are you okay, Di? You don't seem quite right..."

"The boys, Garrick!"

"Di.... I don't know what you're talking about. Of course the boys didn't drown. And it kinda hurts to hear you call me a murderer." He picked at the edge of the napkin, tearing little strips into it. "I can't believe you'd even think that. Okay, I've thrown the occasional punch —sometimes at you, I grant, and I'm not proud of that. But to believe I'd kill children... That cuts to the bone."

Her throat thickened with tears, though of fury or hope she did not know. It was always this way, Garrick said something outrageous, then backed off and played coy. Twenty years, she'd been free of him. *Twenty bloody years!* And still he could wind her up and set her into a panic as if no time had passed and she'd learned nothing about staying calm and steering around his relentless bullshit. *He's a liar, Di. Remember that. Keep saying it. Ignore everything that comes out of his mouth.*

"I had Chad put his handcuffs on the door, so the kids wouldn't try anything while we got you into the car. But he went back and took them off, I told you that. If you weren't listening and you misunderstood, I don't think you can really blame me for that." He took another swig of Coke. "Chad told them to stay put for twenty minutes, or he'd shoot the dog. But he left them perfectly healthy. We've been through this!"

She wracked her brains. He'd *told* her the boys were dead. She was sure of it. The trip to Chicago was pretty much a blank and her brain had been fuddled when she'd arrived. The sedatives?

"You were off your head with the sedative." Yep, there it was, Garrick saying what she was thinking. Uncanny how he could read her. "I'm sorry we had to sedate you, but I'd been told you were in danger from some guy who was following you—David, Derek, Dan, some name like that?—and I thought it was best to get you away quickly. You had a bad reaction to the sedative; bad dreams, by the sound of it—but I didn't realize it was that bad." He took her hand. "You're okay now, right? Not still dizzy or forgetful or tired?"

"All of those things," she admitted. If Jesse was alive, the only way to get back to him was to weedle the information out of her exhusband; that meant playing along. He was a liar, but the problem with liars was they always tripped themselves. Too many details meant he was bound to contradict himself eventually. She summoned a smile from who knew where and let out an exaggerated sigh.

"Go rest, and get your head a bit clearer. Come on, let's get you back to your room." He held out a hand.

She pushed herself up from the chair. "You know what, you're right. Rest is what the doctor ordered."

He smirked. "Go sleep and I'll check in on you tomorrow."

"No need. I'll leave a message in the dorm if I need you."

He took her hand and stroked his thumb lightly across her wrist, as he had done when they first started dating. "Oh, you do. Need me, I mean. You maybe just don't know it yet."

Diana slid her hand away and forced a smile. She didn't need him, but he didn't need to know that. The world might be on fire, the people rioting, the cicadas eating their way through the Midwest, but nothing could tempt her back to Garrick—not loneliness, not self-doubt, nothing. This final lie, with its unending cruelty—the lives of children, for crying out loud—was a bridge too far. He might think he was charming her, or bamboozling her, or playing her for a fool, or whatever it was he did to her, but the tables had turned and, at last, she was the one in the driver's seat. She turned her back on him, and went back to the apartment, taking the precaution of locking the door and wedging a chair under the handle before she retired into the bedroom to sleep, sweet and long and dreamless.

A muffled announcement from the speakers in the lobby outside the flat woke her. "Please note, the gates will be shut for the night at seven o'clock. Please note, the gates will be shut at seven o'clock. Anyone wishing to leave the building tonight, you have thirty minutes. Please make your way to the security gate."

Diana waited twenty minutes and then wandered back down to her office. In the kitchenette at the end of the floor she poured herself some coffee. She leaned against the counter by the door where she could see the rest of the floor and watched the people finishing for the night. They filed past, checking their phones and settling bags over shoulders. The chatter had a worried edge to it, people murmuring in hushed tones instead of the usual raucous spate of farewells. The main crowd passed and the last few stragglers hurried through.

"Night, Doc! Nice to see you back!" Andrew was assiduous in making sure he was among the last to leave.

"Night." Diana did not allow her face to reflect her thoughts; the intern's work was mediocre but he was extremely good at office politics. The boy would go far.

She waited while the elevator lobby emptied; then, when everything had been quiet for some time, checked to make sure the thumb drive was still in her pocket. It was. She did a round of the floor with her cup in one hand, and a sheaf of papers in the other, walking with purpose as if she were on an errand. There were only a couple of people at the far end, and they were packing up too, bantering as they did so.

When they had gone, she slipped across the corridor and into Dan's office. She retrieved Dan's password from the slip on the underside of his drawer, where he kept useful information, and logged in.

"Right, you dog! Let's see what you have here, eh?" She tried to copy the entire shared drive but it was way too big. Her only chance was to go through the files one at a time and hope against hope that her own files were there too, moved rather than deleted; but she didn't have much time.

She froze at the sound of footsteps, and then the door opened. "You! What are you doing in here?"

Diana did not have to look up to recognize that voice. *Bryce. Now I'm in trouble.* "Bryce. It's been a while." Diana tried to keep her tone casual.

"That's Mr. Matreus to you." He strode into the office. "What are you doing here?"

"I've had some injuries recently and this chair is better for my back than mine." It was a weak excuse but at least she looked the part.

"You can leave now. And use your own desk tomorrow." He waited, damn him.

She logged off, leaving the thumb drive in place. He couldn't see it from the doorway.

"How've you been?" She didn't care that much, but it would keep him distracted. "Your family's all fine?"

"Are you joking?" He stepped forward, then stopped himself. "You must know that my mother just died."

"Oh! Oh Bryce, I'm so sorry. Mr. Matreus. I had no idea." She stood and pushed the chair back.

"You mean my father didn't tell you?" Bryce pushed the door open. "That seems unlikely."

"I wish he had." She edged past him.

He slammed the door behind them. "So you could gloat, I suppose?"

"No, because I never wanted to cause you pain, and grief is cruel."

"You never wanted to..." He was virtually spluttering, red-faced. "Get out. Leave. You've done nothing but cause pain, for years. And if you never wanted to, you're even less competent than I thought, and that's not an easy feat. My father can't protect you forever, and when he isn't here anymore, the first thing I'll do, the very first thing will be to fire you."

Diana had very little fight left in her. "Yes, Mr. Matreus." She turned and walked away.

"He won't be able protect you for much longer. I'll see to it!"

She shivered as she left the office floor and all her files behind.

CHAPTER ELEVEN

CLAIRE MOONE. ST HELENS, MERSEYSIDE, ENGLAND

Claire and her team still pushed north toward her Father, outrunning the pillars of toxic smoke that darkened the evening sky, fifteen miles away.

She'd gotten updates from Command, as they trekked along the Sankey Canal towpath, above the sheer walls of the dry lock. Chester was in ruins. It lay on the Welsh border, where the fires raged out of control and the crops and forests that surrounded it were either aflame or burned to ash. They were still no nearer understanding what was causing the massive inferno or the extreme reactions to the smoke, though the reports echoed those coming out of the States. The twin cities of Liverpool and Birkenhead were separated by the width of the River Mersey. Liverpool was taking refugees, in ferries across the water and through the two tunnels that lay beneath. An almost abandoned Birkenhead braced against the oncoming firestorm. It was a matter of when, not if, the buildings would burn. Claire planned to avoid both cities.

The dusty terrain was open to the elements, even in the suburban sprawl of a large town. The chalk-white heathland was dotted with clumps of scrub grass, toxic and scarred. The expanse lay at the end of the canal that once served long forgotten chemical plants. It was the furthest north the waterway went and forced Claire to take a route through a semi-derelict housing estate. At the best of times, it was a no-go area for police and a roll of the dice for ambulance and fire crews.

Some residents had chosen to leave but were stalled at the first main junction. Claire weaved between the vehicles and out into chaotic congestion. Threading her way past fenders, through narrow gaps between car doors and down the dashed white line in the middle, she jinked and twisted her way along, always pushing her motorcycle as fast as she could without losing control. She had to get to her father, he was essential to the Lazarus Think Tank which was, in turn, more important to emergency management than ever before.

A footpath followed the curve of the access road. With a blip of the throttle, she popped the front wheel off the ground, bouncing the rear of the bike onto and over a high curbstone. Ahead, a large dog pulled its owner toward her, growling and barking, reacting to the sudden appearance of three motorbikes. Claire braced for impact, anticipating the crunching and whining that would follow. Jaws snapped at her thigh, but the owner of the dog yanked it back.

The path split where people left the prepared route to take a short cut up a slope. She didn't want to follow the car-packed motorway, even on an open sidewalk. It wasn't the most direct route from their position. Traversing the embankment using the trodden down vegetation as a guide, Claire took them up to the single lane Blue Bridge.

Another well-trodden line of dirt split a square field of tall and ripening Brussels sprouts into two green triangles, providing a short cut onto a back road. It was empty, but for the three of them. On a tight corner, Claire took a hidden lane that ran parallel to the Rainford Bypass. It was suitable for farm vehicles with its potholed surface of loose chippings and gravel the size of a child's fist.

She stood high on the foot pegs, bent her knees to absorb the impact, bumped and bounced over the jaggedness. Something tall, white, and wide spanned the entire path. At two hundred yards distant, it was enough for her to wind the throttle back and let the engine slow the bike down.

"Who the hell puts a gate across a road?" There was a sign across the middle of it. Angry, she read it out loud. "Sandwash Golf Course. Private Property. No road vehicles." She kicked the side-stand of the bike down with a twitch of her foot, leaned over and dismounted. The single bolt that held the gate closed was easily released. "That's lucky. We're not on *road* bikes."

Mickey and Trigger drove through then dismounted.

Claire closed the gate and joined her crew. Trigger handed her a bottle of water, somehow intuiting that she was parched. She was relieved they had some survival supplies after all—she hadn't seen Trig pack them. But then a brief flash of worry surged through her that her burning throat was the result of the smoke. She pushed the anxiety away. *Focus.* "We've got another few miles to go. We'll head to the club house and out through the parking lot. There's an industrial complex to go through. That will get us onto an old military road. After that, it should be clear enough to use the roads of the village, all the way to the windmill."

Trigger swigged his own water. "Your dad lives in a windmill?"

"Yeah. He's quite the eccentric."

"Is it a working mill?"

"No. It's just the old building. No sails, as there's no millstone or mechanism.

Mickey dropped his empty bottle back into the hard box containing his pistols. "You weren't with us on the last scoop up, Trig. I think you've always been on the other team."

Claire tossed her bottle to him. "Break's over. Let's get back to it."

Their engines fired up. The aggressive tread of their tires gouged into the well-tended rough that delineated each hole. They churned their way across two of the emerald green fairways, spattering mud and grass. She could just imagine the consternation and disbelief of the golfclub-shaking members when they discovered the destruction —assuming they ever did. The course was deserted, likely owing to the encroaching smoke, and if the fires spread, the verdant beauty would be nothing but charred hillocks and bunkers.

There was a raised paved area connecting the first tee with the club house and the golf pro's shop. A couple of older ladies steered their motorized golf cart across it, hurrying back to the clubhouse from the looks of it, worried expressions on their faces. They halted at the approach of the three big bikes, which was good. At the speed she was doing, the small but sudden rise from the grass to the flagstones was enough for Claire to become airborne. Her tires squeaked.

A middle-aged man ran from the shop, waiving his hands wildly, yelling "Stop" and "You're trespassing," as the bikes hurtled toward them, as if any of that mattered when toxic fires were burning not twenty miles away. *Nero fiddles while Rome burns.*

Shifting her weight, leaning hard on one side, then the other, Claire managed to avoid the suicidal idiot.

Compensating again, she steered around a Porsche Cayenne, a couple of big Audis, and an Aston Martin Vantage in the parking lot, all of them vying for the exit as if in a great hurry. With no warning, a Lotus Exige turned into her path. The startled driver blared his horn in the split second it took Claire to see him and avoid riding straight onto the hood and over the top. Driving during a national emergency turned out to be something of a sport.

The three wove their way onto the drive leading out to the main road. A police car swerved into their path. Claire banked her bike to the right, changed up a gear and sped away.

Trigger came over the radio. "Was that cop there for us?"

"Maybe. We're not staying on the road, anyway." Claire slowed, seeing the entrance to the disused railway line that would take them through Rainford. The tracks ran through an old army base, abandoned since the general demobilization in the 1950's. It was the last mile of their journey, before reaching Artemis.

The afternoon had been dry and warm, making the ground dusty. Ahead, where the thin strip of public parkland intersected and crossed over a road, there was another dust cloud, much larger than the one the bikes were kicking up. Claire slowed.

"Car to our rear." Mickey's voice cut through the sounds of their rough riding. "That cop. Lights on."

Trigger confirmed. "Definitely after us."

Blue lights flashed to her left. Another car, hidden behind bushes. It pulled out behind her, blocking the guys from following. Dust swirled around the car, blocking her view to the rear. "Loop around. Stay hidden. Cover me from the sides. On foot, if you have to, but not armed. We don't want anyone to get cocky."

Up ahead was a police blockage, three cars, six cops, all business. Claire didn't like their chances. She dropped down through the gears, slowing and closing the distance to the blockade, then stopped and killed the engine. Pulling off her helmet, she studied their flat, confident expressions. They thought they had her, though to what end wasn't clear. Was someone trying to scupper the mission before it had begun? Maybe. Artemis was a prize worth capturing and she wanted possession of the target before anyone beat her to it.

"Officers, we're in a rush." It was always the same, but that didn't make her job any less difficult. "I would like to present a card to you. On it, there is a Whitehall number for you to call. It will help clear things up, so we can be on our way."

Three stepped forward. The one in the middle looked her up and down. *Yeah, sorry buddy, no badges or numbers to help you work out who I am or what I do.* The latest design in armor and materials. "Whitehall, eh? Who do you work for?"

His colleague scanned the road. "You've been abandoned. The other two left you to be arrested on your own. You lot have been riding on the road, on unregistered, untaxed vehicles."

Okay. Weird. The world was going to hell, but someone somewhere had managed to dispatch six police officers to stop her and her men from reaching their target.

He slid something from its clip and flicked it out. She recognized the sound and shape of the telescopic steel baton, *a viper*. Hell no, no way she was going to allow him to beat her. Sweeping it over his head, he aimed for her hand and missed.

Her palm met his wrist. She backed away, tugging him toward her, off his feet. With a crunching blow, her elbow hit the side of his head, crushing the cartilage of his ear against his skull. He yelled in pain, dropping the viper. She bent at the waist and grasped it, avoiding a strike from the policeman on the right.

Smashing the steel bar into the back of the second copper's leg, just behind his knee, she brought him to the ground too. Catlike, she leapt forward, bringing her knee to the chest of the last of the three. Wrapping her hand around the back of his neck, she used her momentum to land standing, towering over him as he fell backward. With any luck, her display would convince the remaining three officers she wasn't worth the trouble. She needed to get on with her mission.

It was only then that a female officer she hadn't seen moved on her position, gun drawn.

Well, damn. Claire had left her bike untended and the officer—sergeant, WPC, whatever—had helped herself to the contents of the bag.

Claire dropped the baton. She was no match for an armed officer. "I'm unarmed. I surrender." Raising both her hands, she offered her wrists. "Call the number on the card."

"You can call your lawyer at the station." The female officer placed the plastic handle of the cuffs between Claire's hands and clicked the catches closed. The woman looked at the other two officers still back by their vehicles and shook her head. "Go and help them, then. They'll need medical attention. There's going to be a ton of paperwork."

"It's not my lawyer, call Whitehall—"

The WPC yanked the cuffs. The steel bit, hard. The policewoman was doing her best to show she was 'in control' and 'as good as the boys.' Claire knew the type. No way would she lower herself to 'make a phone call.' The only option was to allow the charade to play out for the time being.

"We'd best get to it quickly, in that case." Smiling at the WPC,

Claire continued to speak as she was shown to the car. "Excuse me for a moment." She stood still. "It's alright chaps."

Not ten feet away, her companions stepped out of the tree line. "Meet you at the station, boss?"

"Help this bunch, then gather the team." The woman opened the car door for her. Claire bent down and shuffled in.

The drive was silent, and smooth—nothing compared to the pounding she'd endured riding cross-country. The officer drove, unaccompanied. She glanced at Claire many times in the rearview mirror, her tension obvious from the way her jaw ticked tighter each time their eyes met.

Turning into the compound that was no more than a parking lot, Claire read the sign that identified the building – Merseyside Police. Rainford Station.

Without any exchange of words, the officer led Claire inside, leaving her standing on a white line a yard back from the custody desk. A barrel-chested sergeant sat behind it. He raised a pen to make notes in the Arrest Book. "Tell me about the incident, PC Clement."

The officer came to attention. "Sir. Three motorcyclists were reported travelling off- and on the road, using unregistered vehicles. When stopped, the young lady surrendered for questioning, after a brief misunderstanding."

"A misunderstanding? Merrick already radio'ed in that she assaulted three officers, Clement. How's that a misunderstanding? The world's on fire and these lunatics are causing motorcycle mayhem while we're trying to organize an evacuation." His face flushed, then returned to its previous pink-ish tone. He peered down his nose at Claire. "Well now. Does the young lady have a name?"

"One of your officers has my card. I suggest you call the number on it. Immediately." Claire gave a wan smile that did not reflect her extreme irritation at the delay. She was so close to her mission's first objective, and there wasn't time for bureaucracy.

He continued to look at Claire, but spoke to the arresting officer. "Read her rights, Clement?"

The young policewoman tensed again. "No, sir. She's not under arre—"

His glance flicked to the girl. "Don't tell me you've not even arrested her. Why is she cuffed, if she's not been arrested? You know better than this, Patricia."

"She's dangerous, sir. She downed several officers before I was able to subdue her. I had to bring her back so we can phone this number." She raised a soiled business card to show the sergeant. "It's a Whitehall-"

The other police cars pulled up outside. Their occupants struggled to get out. "Put her in the cell. Just put her in the nearest one and get your backside back here." He threw his pen down on the table, stood up and put his hand over his eyes. "What a mess. What a bloody mess."

Within the flat grey walls of the cell, PC Clement fumbled with the key. Claire angled her forearms to give access to the lock. When the key was turned and the cuffs fell into her hand, the girl said a quiet "Thank you."

Claire spoke her first words since leaving the car. "Can you do me a favor?"

The PC shot a look over her shoulder. "Depends what it is."

"When my colleagues come, tell the one called Mickey to phone Cavendish." Claire sat on the inch-thick mattress that lay on the concrete slab.

"Er... Okay." Clement backed away, watching as Claire raised her feet and lay down. "If he comes, I'll tell him."

The door was silent, until it sealed and latched. The light went out. Closing her eyes, Claire resigned herself to the wait and let the memory of the combat wash through her mind. She'd been smooth, efficient, and used the minimum force necessary to defend herself. It would be in her report. She wondered what it looked like from the other side of things.

She didn't check her watch. She didn't need to. The roads might be congested, fire ravaging the countryside, and the power lines down, but Mickey would get a message to Cavendish. Her release was already in motion.

It was hours she didn't have before there were heavy footsteps outside, coming along the corridor. The light went on. Keys turned in the lock, there was a loud click, and the door was pulled open.

It was the sergeant, blustering and full of importance. "I want your name, rank and serial number. What outfit are you from? What's your regiment?" When he got no response, he shouted louder. "I want your name, rank and serial number. Now!"

Claire put her boots on the floor, sat up and put her hands on the mattress, either side of her. "We are not at war. I am not your prisoner. You are not my enemy. Be *really* thankful those three things are true."

"Are you threatening me, little miss?" He stomped forward a pace, every bit the caricature of a provincial bully who'd been given a badge and just a little bit too much authority. "Are you refusing to cooperate with an officer of the law?"

More footsteps came from the hallway. A smart uniform stepped into the cell. The sergeant turned, stood to attention and saluted. "Sir?"

"Blanchett, Chief Superintendent Blanchett." Looking at the bewildered sergeant, his brow furrowed, yet he spoke to Claire. "I understand you were hindered by my officers."

Claire stood to attention, offered her hand and shook his when he took it. "Thank you. Simple misunderstanding. Glad it's cleared up."

With an embarrassed smile, he showed her the door. Escorting her along the corridor, he became conversational. "We're on high alert, trying to keep people safe. You and your chaps were in a restricted zone, you see. The army base. Not quite as abandoned as they say, if you take my meaning. We had no choice. Had to stop you, see?"

"No harm done, Chief Superintendent. You were only doing your job. Ops in former MoD locations are always difficult to keep under wraps."

They parted with another handshake and three more apologies. The man really didn't want his name in her report.

Outside, Claire saw the reassuring shape of Mickey as he slept at the wheel of their Range Rover. The night sky was an unusual color, even for Liverpool-Manchester. It was too red. In the hours she'd been incarcerated, the western horizon had been overcome by fire. The mission to get Artemis, her father, was only more urgent and more at-risk than before.

CHAPTER TWELVE

DALE CURTIS. LONDON, ENGLAND

Dale needed to brace himself. He poured another mug of coffee ignoring the girls' whispers behind him—the odd twin language only the two of them understood. It seemed like lately they'd been even more secretive than usual, and constantly on their laptops. But that was teenagers for you. He allowed himself one sip, then sat down at the kitchen table with Kitty and Jojo.

"Girls, Mum's not well, I'm heading back to the hospital now, I'll let you know how things develop."

Jojo stood and took a step toward him, as if she might stop him from going. "You won't, we're coming with you!"

"Yeah, there's no way we're staying here while you go check on Mum. We're coming." Kitty always let JoJo take the first risk, but both girls stood tall, their chests out and chins up. Dale couldn't recall ever hearing either girl speak with such a firm voice.

They weren't leaving room for negotiation, and he didn't have it in him to argue. Terri would want to see the girls. Maybe they would bolster her spirit. "Okay, we all go, but be prepared that we might have a wait before we can see her. She was being taken to the ICU when I left, and I haven't been able to get a sense of how she's doing on the phone."

They were silent in the car as they drove to the hospital, the trees, traffic, intersections slipping by, so that Dale kept finding himself surprised at how far they'd travelled. He couldn't stop turning the events around Terri's illness over in his mind. She'd always been fit and taken good care of herself. She wasn't one for headaches or allergies, he couldn't remember the last time she'd had a cold. The thought of her sudden manifestation of symptoms chilled his heart. She'd always been a good-looking woman. He'd fallen hard for her smile, the first time his brother Jeremy had brought her to Thanksgiving dinner. His throat tightened at the thought she might never smile like that again. "Girls, the doctors don't know if this is an allergic reaction or illness, but it's messed with your Mum's face. Just prepare yourselves, you may be shocked."

Jojo's voice dripped with contempt. "Dad! Mum's been there at every step of our lives. Patching us up when we've grazed our knees, holding us in the night when we've had a nightmare, listening to our every grumble when life's handed us lemons. She's our Mum. We're coming because we love her."

Rebuked, Dale pulled into the parking lot and led the girls in through the main entrance, stepping up to reception. "We're here to see Terri Curtis, she was taken to ICU earlier today—"

But the receptionist waved him away. "Make room! We need a clear route to the ICU!"

The double doors to the entrance swept open from the ambulance bay and a gurney pushed by two paramedics, wrestling a saline drip so it didn't teeter and fall, thundered through the portal; followed by two more. Dale shrank back as the first crash victim passed, the blanket covering him soaked in blood from some injury obscured from sight. The second and third victims didn't appear so bloody until the third gurney went by, the patient still wearing his helmet. The visor streaked with blood.

That didn't look good, surely helmets were supposed to protect the head. He went back to the receptionist, but she was busy with another call—urgent from the tone of her voice. Worry clutched at Dale, his stomach souring, making him wish he hadn't had that second cup of coffee. He didn't have time to wait around for permission to see his own wife.

He placed a hand on each of the twins' backs and nudged them forward. They followed the gurneys into the Intensive Care Unit. The convoy of trolleys turned the place to a bustling hive of activity. It was abuzz, nurses busying themselves with heart monitors, drips and shifting the patients from the gurneys to beds. The commotion was too thick to move through, and as much as he wanted to rush to Terri's bedside, he wasn't going to get in the way of another patient's critical care.

Dale's head swam as he caught snatches of conversation as the scene unfolded before him.

"Help me with this one," the nearest nurse called to her colleague, as she prepared to move the guy still wearing his helmet. She pulled the blanket back as her colleague placed the PAT slide on the edge of the gurney and under the motorcyclist's side.

Dale's stomach lurched as the man's leg was revealed. The guy had obviously come off his bike and travelled on his side, the road wearing away his jeans through the length of his thigh, along with his skin and flesh, exposing a bloody femur, bits of roadway or debris or what looked like seeds embedded in what was left of his skin. Blood soaked the gurney, and his arms hung to each side, his chest barely moving. Folding his arms across his chest they slid him from gurney to bed

"Unhook his helmet strap, I want to see what we're dealing with here."

All that blood on the visor. The kind of sight that couldn't be unseen. He put a hand on each of the girls' shoulders, steering them away. They'd seen too much already, from the looks on their faces. "Girls—go out into the hall. I don't want you to—"

But JoJo and Kitty linked arms. JoJo's face was pale, but her voice was anything but weak. "We're not leaving 'til we see Mum."

The nurse supported the motorcyclist's neck as her colleague eased the helmet from his head. The man was unconscious, his eyes closed, but as the helmet was lifted clear his forehead erupted in a fresh stream of blood, a gash showing from his brow to his crown. His face was swollen—like Terri's. But it couldn't be for the same reason. This man had been in a terrible crash.

The woman on the gurney next to him was sobbing, choking her tears back, her hand reaching out to the rider's still form. "We were coming off the motorway on the slip road, there was a spill. Phil hit the rear of the truck head on. Jon was riding behind, he managed to pull off to one side and we hit the side barrier. Is he going to be okay?"

A doctor moved across the bay to the bedside, turning to the nurse on reception, his voice sharp. "Get the operating theater notified we're coming in, and to be prepped. Page Dr. Gibson"—the receptionist opened her mouth as if to protest, but the doctor seemed to read her mind. "Yeah, I know he's not on-call tonight but we're going to need the best neurosurgeon we have! And find out which orthopedic surgeon is on duty and call him to the theater immediately."

The nurse pulled the vanity curtain around the bed and Dale shook his head to free himself of the sight. He hurried to the nurse's station, suddenly afraid they'd wasted too much time, taken too long to get to Terri. The twins shadowed him, so close he could feel the warmth of them at his back. "Terri Curtis please, we're here to see her."

The nurse at the station checked the chart behind her with the various bays and beds written up on it. Dale read ahead of where the nurse's finger trailed. There it was! Terri's name scribbled over bed three in the bay marked Mountbatten. He whirled around, the girls somehow melting out of his way as he strode toward the patient bays.

"Sir! Excuse me! Sir, you can't—you'll have to go in by yourself. This is a critical time for your wife." Ordinarily he would never ignore a nurse's instructions, especially when her tone was so firm, but this was not the time to be ordinary.

Kitty and Jojo rounded on the nurse, but Dale stepped in front of them and took each of them by the hand. "Girls, we're in this together. Come with me and wait outside the bay. We can rotate—I'll make sure you get in to see your Mum."

But as they turned toward the patient bays, the ICU's double doors burst open again. This time two orderlies wheeled another patient in on a gurney, this one covered with bloody chunks. A nurse scurried after them with a doctor rattling out a stream of orders.

"Insert a peripheral central catheter, rectal thermometer, heart monitor, and get her onto a bed. Nurse! Where's the PAT slide? We're going to move her once, as soon as possible. And get her in the recovery position. If she vomits again, I don't want her choking to death."

Just as quickly as the area in front of the doors to the ICU had become a bustle of activity, the first bay became frenetic. Nurses swarmed around the gurney, one working to insert the IV, another moving blankets, a third positioning the patient. More nurses transferred the patient to a bed with military precision while the apparatus the doctor had rattled off was being set up and attached to her.

Leading the twins gently but firmly by the hands, Dale reeled from the vision of the injured and sick patients. His mind swam with a dizzy sense of otherworldliness with people critically injured on show. He felt a hysterical giggle rise from his belly, as he recalled the biker's wrecked leg. *That's one sight we won't forget.*

"Come on girls, it's just down here."

Beyond the activity of the first bay, the ward seemed almost quiet. At the third bay on the left, he stopped. The entrance was covered by a curtain screen, and Dale's heart thudded heavily, fear making his mouth cottony. *Please be okay*, he prayed, then turned and kissed Kitty and Jojo on the forehead before moving one of the curtains aside.

He slipped into the bay, surprised to discover that bed three was surrounded by another privacy screen. It couldn't be a good sign. He steeled his nerves, then side-stepped around the screen and drew up to the bedside. Her back was turned to him, one hand lying pale against the white sheets. "Terri?" He kept his voice to a whisper, in case she was sleeping, but he couldn't stop from taking her hand—to comfort her, to ground himself. But she turned to him—not asleep at all.

Her face was a battleground. His heart faltered. Angry purple and red welts scarred her cheeks, seeping yellow pus while tiny droplets of blood trickled from the corners of her eyes. There were wires attached to a monitor joined to her by sticky pads. Leaning over to kiss his wife, Dale hesitated, afraid to hurt her more. Instead, he took up a cloth from the tray at her bedside and gently dabbed blood from her lips which were swollen and bruised, one of her teeth chipped.

"Sweetheart, your mouth..." he started.

"I had a seizure." Her voice was a rasping whisper. "They were trying to intubate me at the time, but when I seized they thought better of it apparently, savaged my throat and nearly ripped my teeth out." Terri sank further into her pillow, her voice becoming fainter.

The curtains around Terri's bed snapped—the girls! But it was only a nurse, checking the chart hooked onto the end of Terri's bed with brisk efficiency. "You'll need to keep it short, sir. She had a grand mal seizure and it's cost her dearly. She needs to rest." The nurse left the enclosure.

Dale turned back to his wife to reassure her, but she was trying to speak. He leaned in to her.

"Dale, go and bring Brandon home. He's not safe over there, I can't bear it, promise me you'll bring him home."

"Look Terri, you're going..." He couldn't go anywhere now, not with Terri so sick. Certainly not to the States. Even if he could leave, there were so many things to consider. According to the frantic call they'd gotten from his mother two days earlier, Jeremy was in trouble, as usual. Wildfires were spreading across the country and leave it to his little brother Jeremy to be out in the thick of it somewhere with Brandon. Jeremy had always hoped that he and the lad would bond from the weeks he spent with him each summer, but Terri had voiced what they both knew to be true: Jeremy had never been one for taking responsibility. God only knew what was going on over there.

"Dale! Your brother can't be trusted to tie his shoelaces, never mind look after our son while the world is going to hell. Promise me!" There was steel in her voice now.

Dale squeezed Terri's hand. "I promise, darling, I'll bring him back."

Terri smiled wanly, but doubled up in pain, rasping for air as her body went into a violent spasm.

"Nurse! Doctor! Someone! My wife, Bay Three!" No one came and Dale tried to steady Terri, holding her shoulders, and was shocked with the force with which she shook under his hands. Her eyelids opened for a second, her eyes thrown back in her head. The bed trembled with the violence of Terri's seizure. His blood ran cold at the sight.

"Sweetheart, I'm here. TERRI!"

"Daddy! What's going on! Can we—" It was Kitty, her voice pitched high with worry.

"Go find a nurse, girls! Your mum needs help!" The last thing he wanted was to scare the girls, or for this to be their last memory of their mother. Better to send them away, make them feel useful. He couldn't go anywhere, couldn't leave Terri. Not like this.

"Terri? Babe?" A small trickle of blood streamed from the side of her mouth, staining her pillow. The heart monitor on her left showed a continuous flat line, an alarm sounding briefly in the nurse's station, as the pain in his own heart blossomed. This couldn't be happening. "Nurse! Please!"

Footsteps pounded from down the hall and nurses rushed in, one placing a defibrillator on the table next to Terri's bed, another barging past him, deftly pushing him out of the way. Dale took two steps back as the first nurse placed paddles on his wife's chest and side. "Charge two-hundred, clear."

Terri's body jolted as the current hit her heart. The heart monitor remained a flat green line.

"Charge three-hundred, clear."

A second jolt, still a steady green line on the heart monitor.

The nurse pulled the paddles and placed them on top of the defibrillator and started chest compressions. The blood drained from Dale's face and nausea gripped his stomach. The dizziness swept over him again as he steadied himself against the bed opposite Terri's. This couldn't be happening. This was madness. Just this morning they had eaten breakfast together.

The nurse placed an oral dam over Terri's mouth and gave her two rescue breaths before starting another round of compressions.

The doctor came to the bed and spoke in a muted voice with the nurse who was counting out the compressions. He looked at his watch and said, "I'm calling it. Time of death 19:24."

"No! You can't!" The words shot from Dale's mouth.

The doctor turned to Dale. "Sir, was this your wife?"

From somewhere far away, a twinned sobbing wail rose. The girls?

"Yes, she's my wife, what do you mean *was*? *She is* my wife."

Dale pushed the doctor to one side and stepped to the bed. They must be wrong; this couldn't be happening.

"She's fine. Please! Just keep—"

The doctor patted Dale's arm, cold, remote. "Sir, I'm sorry to tell you your wife was declining when she arrived today. I saw Dr. Dasgupta's notes. He seemed to think she was in anaphylactic shock. Not so. We need to get to the bottom of this, but we've had people presenting at ER for the last three days with similar symptoms. Respiratory problems, convulsions, bleeding from orifices and organ failure to name a few. Has your wife visited Wales recently?"

"What? No! She's been here. Completely normal until today. I can't understand—this can't be happening!"

"I'm truly sorry, sir. We did everything we could to help her rally today, but there was no coming back from this one. I am sorry for your loss. Do you want somewhere to sit while you gather yourself?"

Dumfounded, Dale looked at the young Doctor in front of him. "Dead?"

He nodded.

Dale stumbled to the bedside and took Terri's hand again.

"Terri, my love, my heart." His words choked in his throat.

Dale stumbled backward and turned away from the bed and out of the bay back toward the entrance. The twins. He couldn't bear telling them, but they were waiting. His heart was numb. All around him nurses and doctors went about their business like what had happened was normal, but he was suffocating. And the twins were looking expectantly at him, their identical brows creased with worry, and he had no idea what to say, how to explain. As he tried to make sense of this alien world Jojo strode past him.

"My turn."

"Jojo no. Mum, your mum's...." Dale started walking after Jojo, reaching for her but she lengthened and quickened her stride.

"No way, Dad, you said we would rotate, it's my turn!" She tore back the curtain and marched up to the bed before Dale could reach her. "Mum." Jojo's shoulders dropped as she saw her mother's still body, the bedsheet covering her face.

The nurse gave her a sad smile and turned to Dale. "Sir, we've got your details, the certificate of death will be available after the postmortem."

Dale caught Jojo as her legs gave out under her.

Jojo faced her Dad, her eyes hard. "Why? You said we would rotate! Why did you leave us out there? Why did you let her die?"

The words pierced Dale's heart. It was the question he was asking himself. Why hadn't he been able to save his wife?

The two of them walked back and joined Kitty. Jojo took her by the hand and led her to the bay.

"No, girls—" He didn't want their last memory of their mother to be of her swollen and bloodied face.

But Jojo looked over her shoulder and kept walking. "We're going to say goodbye!"

He couldn't get his mind clear about what was happening in front of him. *Promise me.* Those had been her last words. And he had. He'd squeezed her hand and said he would bring Brandon home.

If anything happened to Brandon, if he lost his son too—he'd never even thought of him as his nephew; Brandon was his *son* and he loved him—he'd never forgive himself. He had to get to the States. It was urgent. He needed to focus. He wasn't going to fail at this. When the girls returned, interrupting his thoughts, their identical faces streaked with mascara and tears, he made the announcement. "We're going to the States. Tomorrow."

"What? No!" Jojo's voice was thick with grief, her expression one of horror.

"Mum's just died!" Kitty's voice carried a sense of disbelief. "We can't just up and go to the States. What about funeral arrangements?"

With every word Kitty was more resolute, even defiant. Jojo too.

Dale couldn't allow this to draw out into a prolonged debate. "This isn't a democracy girls. We're going to honor your Mother's dying wish, get over there, find Brandon, and bring him home."

CHAPTER THIRTEEN

KIM WALKER. SYDNEY, AUSTRALIA

Kim cringed as she picked her way over piles of rancid garbage and scattered food scraps. Her footsteps echoed far too loudly over the tiled floor of the food court located on the ground level inside the World Square shopping complex. The last thing she needed was unwelcome attention either from the mob rioting outside the center's newly installed wide glass doors or the looters currently scurrying through the building like rats raiding a larder. The smart thing to do would be to ditch her noisy heels for something more functional, say sneakers or even a sturdy pair of hiking boots. But she didn't want to waste one more second, not with a curfew looming and a mob battling the police containment line.

The problem was, without wheels she had no idea how she was going to get her daughter safely home through toxic, smoke-filled streets to her adoptive parents' apartment. The police car she'd stolen was wedged fast inside a shop window with a bunch of fear-fueled men busy tearing the shop apart. There'd been a few heart-stopping seconds when she'd thought she wouldn't evade them, but it appeared their interest in her had been diverted by the store's camping gear.

Using the dead policewoman's flashlight, she swept the beam over the glass shop fronts, checking the interiors for signs of life; someone hiding inside, someone simply foraging for whatever they could find to survive, someone deciding *'what the hell'* and stealing an expensive piece of jewelry or the latest iPhone.

So far, she'd found evidence of all four—but no sign of Emma. There were too many places to hide, too many shops to search. All she had was her gut instinct to go on—start with Emma's favorite shops, then fan out from there.

The closed shops were dark inside, however a few lights here and there illuminated the corridors and walkways. Either only some of the power circuits were functioning or the authorities had deliberately cut the power to certain sections of the complex—possibly as another signal to the general public that the center was shut, or hoping it would be a deterrent.

Chest as tight as a drum, Kim pushed herself to keep moving while she fought the urge to rip off her long-sleeve police shirt to cool down her clammy skin. With the air conditioning system shut down, the air inside the center was hot and stuffy but so far, she hadn't detected the stink of smoke. She patted her shirt pocket to check her mask was still safe and snug, then adjusted the revolver where she'd shoved it under her bra between her breasts. She'd also removed the holster from the utility belt, popping it into her reusable shopping bag. Walking about armed with a weapon she had no idea how to use wasn't a wise move—not when civilization was on the brink of destruction—but walking around with no means of defense seemed equally stupid. And besides she didn't want to leave a weapon lying around so someone else could use it—either against her or heaven forbid, her daughter. At least this way, the gun remained hidden beneath her buttoned-up shirt and if she had to, she still had access to it.

Voices whispered in shadowed corners as she passed dark shop fronts, while shouting and yelling issued from the supermarket. It was unbelievable how fast everyday people had turned criminal.

The smashing of shelves had her whirling around to check the source of the sounds, the accompanying shouts sending her pulse kicking up a gear. Flicking off the flashlight, she merged behind a concrete pillar as a bunch of people careened out of the supermarket, each pushing a laden trolley. A store employee carried a case of water in her arms. The employee's eyes bulged and her lips flattened when a middle-aged man dressed in an Armani suit tackled her to the ground. They wrestled for possession of the bottles, kicking and cursing. More people charged out of the store—some held bags of canned food in their arms and ran off in different directions wailing and crying, others were empty handed, their red faces engorged with rage as they raced after the trolley pushers. One female desperado reached the slowest trolley pusher, an elderly man with sparse gray hair sticking up like a cockatoo's comb. She grabbed his shoulder and whirled him around, sending the trolley clattering onto its side and skidding over the floor, vegetable produce, water bottles, meat trays scattering everywhere. The old man shrieked as he reached for a tray of steaks and had his arm trodden on for good measure. Five or six people fell onto the goods like a starving horde, swiping them up, pushing and shoving and then a fist fight erupted between two men over a pack of disposable masks.

Keeping to the shadows and with an eye on the overturned trolleys, scraps of paper and glass fragments on the floor, Kim snuck from pillar to pillar, blending into the structures as best she could until the supermarket and the brawl was blocked from sight. As she rounded the corner, she rubbed sweat from her forehead and upper lip with the back of her sleeve, recognizing the tremor in her thighs and calves, a sure sign of exhaustion. Years of jogging and running marathons were beginning to fail her. What she needed was a day of total rest but until she had Emma somewhere safe, she'd crawl on her hands and knees if she had to.

Footsteps thundered up from behind and she shrank against a store's glass window, swinging around and ensuring her back was to the wall. But the pensioner couple were too fixated on hightailing their trolley out of the center to so much as glance in her direction. The white-haired old lady held a cricket bat close to her chest as if preparing to lash out at any moment while her bald, elderly partner, clad in striped pj's and bedroom slippers, pushed the trolley.

Her heart eased its frantic beats as she fished out her water bottle and took a small mouthful before stashing it once more inside her green shopping bag.

A young mother about seventeen, with dyed purple hair to her shoulders and a nose ring, squeaked a trolley into view, a toddler perched in the baby seat. Both wore Panthers caps on their heads and the girl kept throwing glances over her shoulder as if expecting to see someone behind her. Kim walked over and effectively stopped her by standing in front of the trolley as she held out her phone, showing the last photo she'd received of Emma. "Excuse me, have you seen this girl?"

"Um, not sure."

A muffled crash resounded through the building and Kim's belly fell away. She tacked a forced smile onto her face and waggled her phone to regain the girl's attention.

The little kid knocked his cap off and Young Mum paused to pop it back onto his head. The toddler sucked vigorously on his fist and stared fixedly at Kim with big blue eyes. "Might have—if it's her, it was ages ago. She in trouble?" Her gaze fell on Kim's stolen uniform and she stepped backward, dragging the trolley with her.

"She's missing—and she's my daughter." How strange it felt to actually say those words to another person, even a stranger. Kim's chest swelled beneath her shirt and she cleared her throat.

The girl's frown deepened, as if she thought Kim was lying. But it could be the uniform she didn't trust. Kim wasn't sure whether she should fess up or run with being an officer of the law. Maybe she should show the girl she was one of the good ones instead by offering a makeshift mask made out of the bandages in her first aid kit. She closed her mind on the sickening memory of how she'd hauled a dead policewoman out of the car and stripped her of her clothes. Not the actions of a good person. She'd left that poor woman with little more than a blanket covering her stiffening body. No—no more wasting time. Young Mum would have to fend for herself. Finding Emma was all that mattered. "Have you seen her?"

"Could have. Harry and me went into a baby changing room a coupla hours ago. There was a girl and boy inside there when we went in but then they left. The girl had dark hair and was coughing real bad. I think she went into the loo next door."

"Which changing room?"

"Lower level. Near the Ally shop." The girl pushed the trolley forward a few paces.

"Thank you."

"Whatever." Young Mum sent another narrow stare over Kim's uniform, lingering on the green shopping bag before turning away.

No way to tell if the girl was lying because she didn't like cops but what she'd said made sense. Ally was one of Emma's favorite shops. Kim hurried along the wide walkway, making sure she kept plenty of space between herself and the looters, until she eventually found the escalators leading to the lower level and the parking lot. Hands on the rails, she took one step when a hand came down hard on her back and pushed.

No time to think. No time to react. She pitched forward, head-first, wrenching her arms with a sharp thrust of pain until she released her hold on the rails and kept falling. Agony splintered inside her head when her jaw made contact with the steel steps. Her shopping bag slipped off her shoulders to tangle around her right wrist, the first aid kit jolted out and tumbled down the escalator. Someone hoisted her up by grabbing a fistful of her shirt, pulling it free of her belt.

"Where is it?" growled a furious male voice as he shook her violently and her bag fell onto the stairs. The man let go and she plummeted forward again, but this time she managed to shift her arms in front of her face and landed on her knees.

She had no idea what he wanted but she didn't intend to wait around to find out. Struggling to orientate herself, pain pulsed throughout her body. Kim moved forward, forgetting where she was and slid down the next steel steep, scraping skin from her knees, shins and elbows even through the drill cotton of the police uniform, tearing the material. Sniveling and gulping, she crawled onto the next step, then the next, seeing double of the steps and escalator sides. His hot breath blasted over her back as, laughing, he kept pace with her, the escalator shaking with every heavy step he took.

His tattooed hand landed on the rail beside her, with a loud smack. "Give it to me. Now!"

The next level was coming up fast. She had to get to her feet. She had to run! She shuffled herself upright, lurched forward, jumping the last couple of yards, wobbling on her heels until she wrenched off first one shoe and then the other. She found her balance and heard his grunt of surprise. Then she was on firm ground, stumbling forward. Swaying. *Got to get out of here.* He was right behind her.

She pushed into a run, the fastest run of her life, racing down the walkway, finding her rhythm, despite the burn in her chest and the fire in her damaged body. The thought of her daughter having to face someone just as nasty or desperate gave wings to her feet. *Find Emma. Find Emma.* The words ping-ponged inside her head as she ran. On and on. Down the wide dimly lit walkways until she'd outpaced him, and he was a long way behind.

Stopping, she scrabbled around to face the direction she'd come and turned on the flashlight. The wide beam moved over the shop fronts, catching a woman in the act of heaving a brick through a window. The woman's mouth dropped open as she froze then she scuttled off into a dark pathway between two rows of shops. But so far, no one else. No crazy, bad-ass man chasing her.

She hooked the flashlight back onto her utility belt, her hand trembling so much it took her several goes to get it secured. Then she stood listening, dragging in ragged breath after ragged breath until her racing heart slowed to its normal speed. Her bag was gone and along with it her first aid kit and water. She could have done with more paracetamol to dull the throb of pain pulsing over her face and body. She adjusted the gun digging into her chest, tucked her shirt back into her belt, then slipped her heels onto her aching feet. There was Ally, the dress shop Young Mum had mentioned, and a Stereo/HiFi store up ahead. The murmur of voices drifted out through the wide-open cage doors of the tech store. More looters.

But there above a narrow pathway on the other side of the store was the restroom sign.

After checking the walkway for any would-be pursuer, she headed to the restrooms. She was running out of options—Emma had to be there. The thought of searching an entire city was enough to make her scream and smash something. Every nerve was tingling as she pushed open the door to the ladies' room, and the world around her shrank until only this small room, and whoever might be inside, existed.

She swept the flashlight over a row of vanities and closed cubicle doors and came to rest on a small figure shielding their face from the glare.

The figure scrambled into a kneeling position, hands reaching for the numerous shopping bags scattered on the tiles. "Who are you?"

She shifted the light over the pretty young girl's long dark hair and face and grabbed the closest vanity for support as her knees wobbled. Though the odds had been solidly stacked against her, Kim had followed her heart to this tiny room, to find the person who mattered most in the world. "Emma. Is that you?"

"Maybe. Who are you?" The girl stood, hugging her leather handbag close to her chest, bags hanging from her arms.

"It's me..." How could she say those words? Her heart pounded as her mouth dried. "I'm Kim Walker. Your mother." She moved the flashlight revealing her face.

"Seriously?"

"Yes." She smiled, her skin turning clammy as she waited—hoping, wanting, needing some sign from her daughter that her previous absence from her life could be bridged. "Are you okay?"

"I can't believe that you're really here."

"Yes—here I am. I went to your apartment first but you weren't there, so I went to your school. One of your neighbors said you left this morning in your school uniform." A lifetime ago. So much had happened.

Emma's confused expression vanished as her chin jutted in a pugnacious manner. "Um, stalker much? What are you doing here?"

Kim tightened her sweaty grip over the flashlight, nausea

churning in her belly. "The mobile networks are down so I drove to Sydney to check on you." No need to make a song and dance about everything that had happened to her along the way. "I take it you lied to Natalie about school."

"Mum—Natalie is my mum, not you. So what? It was only a little fib. I intended to be home before her and then there was all this commotion. People running about. Cops everywhere and the next thing I knew, they turned off some of the lights and shut the doors." Emma made no move toward her. Her young face had hardened.

Kim didn't know what she'd expected, but faced with her daughter's lack of enthusiasm at seeing her for the first time in eight years, she was daunted. Maybe even diminished, like she was insignificant in Emma's life.

"What happened to your face? There's blood everywhere. And your clothes are all torn. You look awful."

It was like a knife thrusting inside her heart, but she hid her expression by moving to the paper dispenser, ripping off a few sheets and proceeding to dab at her cut mouth. "Long story." She stood the flashlight upright on the sink and ran the tap. Cupping her hands, she drank and drank. Wiping her face with another paper towel, Kim turned around and leaned against the counter, wanting to sink to the floor and sleep forever, wanting to close her eyes against the open hostility radiating from her daughter.

"I'm not interested anyway. Again—why are you here?" Emma kicked a shopping bag.

"To make sure you're safe."

Emma snorted. "You're not doing a very good job of it then."

"Hey!" Kim flung a hand toward the door. "What's happening out there isn't down to me. And I wasn't the one lying about going to school. You here by yourself?" Grabbing the flashlight, she pushed off from the counter and hobbled down the line of cubicles, shining the light inside each one and checking no one else was in the restroom. Young Mum had said she'd seen a girl matching Emma's description with a boy, but the cubicles were empty.

"I am now."

CHAPTER FOURTEEN

ANAYELI ALFARO. SACRAMENTO, CALIFORNIA

Anayeli's brain wasn't functioning optimally. Master Sergeant Kassis had made a great show of taking Anayeli into custody with martial efficiency, but as soon as Kassis and the helicopter pilot had gotten Anayeli back into the same exam-room-cell she'd been in before, things had taken a complete one-eighty. Ever since, Anayeli had been trying to jam together the puzzle pieces of what she already knew with what she'd learned from Kassis—Fatima, the woman insisted she call her—and Darren, the helicopter pilot. She ran through it all again as she lay in the dark of her tent.

It took almost no brainpower to understand the situation outside had gone from bad to worse. Way, way worse than when she'd first gotten Ernesto admitted to the evacuation center. It wasn't just the fires—there were bugs now, too, according to Darren. Some kind of orange-eyed cicada, which weren't even supposed to *be* in California. Worse, they were toxic. And they were multiplying, in spite of the smoke and the fires. "On the chopper, the lab coats were saying one

She flicked the light over her daughter's face. Emma squinted and turned aside.

"Where is he?" She moved over until she stood a yard away, ensuring the light was no longer in Emma's eyes but sufficiently close to see the tears well.

"He left me." Emma's voice dropped to a mumble. "Everyone was told to leave and there was this big rush to get outside. I was knocked over and trodden on. Then my asthma flared up and my inhaler wasn't cutting it. Some lady helped me to my feet, and I found Shane. We went into the babies' changing room to wait until I got my asthma under control. But then he said he couldn't hang around any longer. I guess he got scared."

"And left you alone. Asshole."

"Huh! Like you should talk!"

She wanted to explain but Emma's tight face made her doubt she'd listen. "He's not worth wasting any time over. Forget him."

"That's rich coming from you. You're just like him—anyone that holds you back or isn't exactly what you want when you want, you dump them. Including me."

Shaken to her core, she held out a hand. "Emma, it wasn't like that."

Emma knocked her hand aside. "I don't care anyway. Are there many people outside? I want to go home—to mum. My mum. My real mum." She picked up her shopping bags and stalked toward the door.

"Wait! Don't open that door."

Too late. Emma pulled open the door.

touch is enough to kill you. I had to fly right through a swarm of them."

Anayeli shifted but couldn't get comfortable. The door to her tent was zipped from top to bottom. She'd checked it ten times or more. There was no way *anything* could get in, but the image of those bugs danced in her imagination, robbing her of any calm she'd drummed up.

But even more horrifying was what else Darren had said: on the flight to the evacuation center, they'd received word the President of the United States had come into contact with the toxic cicadas. "He's dead." Darren's voice had been matter of fact, but his calm hadn't stopped Fatima from gasping and grabbing hold of Darren's arm, or Anayeli from blurting out, "No. *Imposiblé!*"

But it wasn't impossible and Anayeli hadn't misheard when Colonel Silver Fox had addressed the VP as 'Madam President.'

"The Vice President was sworn in on the flight, but by the time we landed, she had a bloody nose. That respirator she was wearing was at least in part to hide it. If she doesn't make it, it's only a matter of time before the government fragments, and if that happens..." Darren glanced at Fatima, who nodded. He had his arm around her, supporting her. Anayeli remembered the way Fatima had gone straight for him, once he'd disembarked from the chopper. They were clearly more than colleagues.

"It's getting bad here, already. Soldiers from my unit went missing last night." Fatima's face had gone ashen. "Just disappeared."

"They were hauling bodies out in refrigerated trucks, but I don't think any of them were dressed in National Guard uniforms." Anayeli's news, as much as it worried Fatima, hardly mattered in the face of what Darren had relayed. If the highest government officials were dying and the toxic bugs and ongoing fires had already overwhelmed the country's emergency response, then there was no help they could count on. If the bugs came—and Darren said they would —the evacuation center wouldn't be safe for anyone, no matter how they were housed. The tent Carlota and Bailey Rae were in would offer zero protection. The dogs would be goners. Who knew how Mama would fare? Ernesto was the only one who might be all right—

except there was the matter of the blood draws and weird test results and whether anyone would stay to run the evacuation center if the government disintegrated.

"I need to find my soldiers. And you need to find your mother. We need to figure out if it's safe for us to stay. If it's not—" The uncertainty hung in the air, as dense as the smoke outside. "If things are falling apart, we need to know, so we can get out of here." Fatima had been on the same wavelength as Anayeli was. "We need you to learn what the delegation is really doing here, how bad things are, and report back."

"Why me?" It didn't seem right that all the burden, all the danger of investigating whatever was going on, should rest on Anayeli.

"If either of us starts hunting around, it'll be noticed." Fatima glanced at Darren again. "And we can't afford to jeopardize our careers for nothing more than a suspicion. Not with the baby." The look that passed between the two had clinched it: Darren had to be the father of the baby Fatima was carrying. "But investigating *is* your career..."

Anayeli never should have announced she was a reporter. But it did give her certain protections, if she were to get caught. Assuming there was still a functioning government. She'd told herself that at least a million times ever since she'd made the deal with Fatima and Darren. "If I find information that proves it's not safe here, promise me you'll get me and my family out. Promise you'll take my family with you—on your chopper—" From the way Darren shifted, she saw she'd guessed right. If Fatima and Darren decided to escape, they were doing it in the helicopter.

Fatima had promised. Anayeli's family would have a spot on Darren's chopper. Anayeli hadn't asked about the dogs. She'd cross that bridge when she had to—*if* she had to. Once she'd found Mama, they could figure out what was next. Together. It sure as hell wouldn't involve an evacuation center. Mama had been right about it being too dangerous. Maybe it wouldn't involve Fatima and Darren either. Anayeli barely knew them. She had nothing to prove they were trustworthy.

Still. Options were good. Sid had been right about that. So

Anayeli would put the plan she'd made with Fatima and Darren into action. Maybe she should have told Carlota and Bailey Rae what she was doing. But after Fatima had released her and she'd snuck back to the tent, the only thing she'd wanted to do was watch the girls eat the food she'd brought and go visit Cricket and Roxy. She'd still had the slab of dried out ham Slumpy had given her and watching Bailey Rae laugh when Roxy licked and licked and licked her hand even after the meat was long gone had been worth it. She hadn't wanted to spoil that tiny happy moment with worries over what she was going to do. Instead she'd told Carlota she'd be getting up early again to check on Ernesto. That she'd be looking for Mama was left unsaid—Carlota restrained for once.

It was hard to gauge the time, when it was perpetually dusky thanks to the smoke, but Anayeli thought it was very early morning. In the darkness she changed into the uniform Fatima had given her. If Carlota happened to wake up, she wouldn't really be able to see. It would be better if the girls had plausible deniability about what Anayeli was about to do, in case she got caught.

Her disguise—thanks to Fatima—was simple: A National Guard uniform which, in conjunction with her black wristband, would enable her to move quickly and freely anywhere in the evacuation center. She pulled the uniform out of the backpack Fatima had given her and slipped it on over her regular clothes: the more options the better. She used the gauze and ointment Nurse Kerry had slipped her to make a clean bandage for her hand, and fitted a fresh mask to her face. Then she slowly slowly slowly unzipped the tent's door flap, notching the zipper one tooth at a time to avoid making any noise that might waken the girls. Finally, she was out.

"*Te quiero mucho.*" She mouthed the words as she zipped the tent closed—her voice too quiet for the girls to hear. But she would know she said it, no matter what. And maybe the sentiment would lodge somewhere in their subconsciouses. Then she hefted the backpack onto her shoulders and was gone.

No one stopped her, no guard did anything more than glance at her as she moved through the Orange zone, across the pavement where Darren's chopper sat, and into the hospital. As much as she wanted to check on Ernesto, she went instead to the ward Fatima had directed her to on the fifth floor—the isolation ward. "It's where the most sensitive patients are. In our briefing, that's where the Colonel said the delegation would be doing morning rounds."

Mama hadn't been sick, not when Anayeli had last seen her—Two days ago? Three? She'd lost track. But maybe Mama would be there too. It was one place Anayeli hadn't been—either she'd find Mama, or she'd cross it off her list of places to check.

The stairwell which had been crowded the last time she'd used it was abandoned, her every footstep echoing. She moved fast, but there was nothing to hide the things she didn't want to see—a child's shoe, bloodstained. A streak of something dark along the wall. Stains on the cement floor. A wristband, ripped in half. Bandages crumpled and crusted. Grimed masks. Even the dim, generator-run emergency lighting wasn't enough to obscure the evidence that the hospital staff was overwhelmed.

Each time she passed one of the doors leading from the stairwell back into the hospital corridors, there were shouts— "Go go go!" and "Please help!"—mingled with wordless cries and the wet, rasping-gagging sound that meant someone was dying. Or there was simply the slap of running feet or the squeak of rubber soled shoes on linoleum floors, the clatter of gurney wheels, sobbing. Even at this hour, whatever time it was. Each noise sent a spike of adrenaline through her, but the doors to the stairwell never slammed open.

"*Corre* Anayeli! *Corre*." It became her mantra as she ran up the stairs. She had to keep moving. She couldn't stop.

Her breath was coming in hard gasps by the time she hit the fifth-floor landing. She wasn't that out of shape—it had to be the impact of the smoke. Maybe the air filtration in the hospital wasn't so good. Or maybe another night spent in the tent had done its damage.

She stood on the landing, her hand on the door's push bar, trying to catch her breath. Steeling herself. There was no noise on the other side—just dead quiet. Her stomach did a twisting flip, a nauseous feeling oozing from her center out. "Just more adrenaline." Her own whisper was a comfort. "You've got a uniform. You belong. No one knows any different."

She pushed open the door.

It was like walking into a library—that same kind of living, breathing hush, that told of human activity *somewhere*. Every door was closed, and not a single one opened as she strode down the corridor—chin up, shoulders back, arms and legs swinging. There was nothing at all to pinpoint where the ward she wanted was, nothing to differentiate one door from the next, until she passed an intersection with another corridor. The one branching off was a dead end, a large, blue-tinted window at its end. But what lay there just beyond the mouth of the corridor made her stop in her tracks.

Soldiers.

There were two wearing the exact uniform she wore, slumped to the floor, M16s in their laps. Two more flanked a doorway partway down the corridor. And beyond them two more were slouched on either side of a window. Sleeping.

One soldier's hat had fallen off, and another's jacket lay twisted next to him. The instant she saw them she knew: she needed those things. When she found Mama, she could outfit her in the hat and jacket, and it would help them escape. She had to snag them.

She crept closer, trying for some combination of stealth and confidence, so no one who saw her would find anything to rouse their suspicion. The soldiers were all so still, sleeping so heavily it seemed miraculous.

Except there was blood. It had been there long enough it had congealed, but not so long to have lost its reddish color and gone brown. Her hands flew to her mouth, but still a squeak escaped. The first soldier was young—about the same age as Carlota—but whether his face was still rounded with the last of his baby fat, or if it was swollen, she couldn't be sure. His lips though—they had ballooned so much they'd cracked, and his tongue—

"Please... please..." She pressed her fingers to his neck. The skin was too firm, too rubbery. There was no pulse, no matter where she put her fingers.

Every nerve fired, telling her to bolt, but she couldn't turn away. Each of the sprawled-out soldiers looked the same. Swollen lips, protruding, purpled tongues.

"No pulse. Why is there no pulse?" She checked every single soldier, somehow finding whatever switch inside her turned off her revulsion. There was not a single flutter of life. Instead, it was only the evidence left behind that could tell the story of what had happened. An older soldier, perhaps this unit's commanding officer, crumpled alongside the doorway, chin drooped to his chest, one hand at his throat. Around his wrist, a pink band. Like Fatima's. Not a single one had a mask, not even pulled down to his chin—"But they shouldn't have needed masks. Not inside. Unless—"

She pulled up her own mask, then checked the window. There was no way to open it, and no evidence of any leak. Outside, the murk had darkened, so thick she could see something swirling through it—lots of somethings. "The cicadas?" But it couldn't be. Whatever it was— particulates, probably—was too small to be bugs.

There was nothing she could do for the soldiers, and no time to take down their names. Instead she picked one—the oldest, the officer—and hooked a finger on the chain holding his dog tags. "Ibrahim Jackson." She would give that name to Fatima. Maybe it would mean something to her. Maybe she would know what unit this had been.

Then she took Ibrahim's side arm—something Fatima had refused to issue her— and one item from each of the other soldiers. She chose the least bloodied items: the hat that had first drawn her attention—a name written inside. The jacket that had been torn off in a panic. A partially eaten ham sandwich like the one Patrick had brought her, the same as Slumpy had given her for the dogs, was jammed in its pocket, she shoved all of it into her backpack

From somewhere in the main corridor, a door made the snick-clunk sound of opening and then closing. Footsteps echoed down the hall. Someone was coming. There was another snick-clunk and voices reverberated through the empty corridor, growing louder. She froze.

"Move Anayeli. Time to go." She couldn't be found standing in the middle of dead soldiers.

She took the only option available: the door the dead soldiers must have been guarding.

She didn't know what she was expecting—a ward full of patients?

—but it wasn't what was in the room. The space was set up as a lab—its counter tops lined with microscopes and beakers and test tubes and vials and machines she guessed were centrifuges. In the center was a series of long tables, with double rows of coolers arranged down each side, identical to the ones she'd seen outside near the refrigerated trucks. Samples.

"*Qué es esto?*" She pried the lid off one, fingers shaking. Instead of skin samples like she was expecting, inside were vials, like the one Rumbly-Tumbly nurse had taken from Ernesto. Rows and rows of blood-filled vials, each with an orange label. She slid one out. It had a series of numbers and notations, but no name. The same with the next one, and the next. The real question was why these vials needed guarding. In the next cooler, the only difference was the labels were blue. The third cooler was full of green labels. She had just opened up a fourth cooler to reveal yet more vials, these with purple labels—*purple!*—when a shout erupted outside.

Her first thought was that she'd been wrong about all the soldiers being dead.

"Sir! Come quick! Hurry! We need medics!" It was a male voice but in a matter of seconds, it was drowned out by more voices, more shouts, more footsteps as the alarm was raised. The dead soldiers outside must have been discovered. She was screwed. She had no excuse if she were found in the lab, with the dead soldiers' stuff. And her way out was blocked.

She tamped down the lid to the cooler. She could stay put, or try to slip out and use the commotion to cover her. But then what? Her heart thudded as she tried to decide. She hadn't learned anything useful. Hadn't come any closer to finding Mama.

There was a metallic clunk behind her. She whirled, heart in her throat. An adjoining door had opened, one she hadn't even noticed —*You need to pay attention! It's the small stuff, Chica!* Sid's voice barked at her from somewhere in her memory. But she had no time for advice from her now-dead boss, because several National Guard soldiers and the Colonel were rushing through the door. There was nowhere to hide, and she couldn't risk being noticed so she just stood where she was, taking up what she hoped was the wide-legged stance of a soldier on guard duty, praying in the commotion no one would notice her backpack and her mask would be enough to conceal her identity.

"Move! Now! Go!" Colonel Silver Fox issued the orders, but still Anayeli stood. Professional Polo, one of the Matreus officials from the day before hurried behind Silver Fox, dabbing at his nose with a bloodied handkerchief. He stopped to cough, clogging the door so that the other Matreus Polo shirt and the lab coats had to squeeze past. More medical staff spilled through the door. The former Vice President, now President was nowhere to be seen. Maybe she was being housed somewhere else, somewhere safer. Wherever that was.

Safe was the last thing Anayeli was. If Silver Fox or the Polos recognized her that would be the end to all her plans. She needed to find the isolation ward, but if the delegation had been meeting in the room beyond, she wanted to see what was in there, too.

"Soldier!" It was Silver Fox. He caught her arm, his eyes cutting to her backpack. She kept her eyes forward, willing him not to recognize her or ask her what was inside her pack. "What's your assignment?"

She had no idea what the proper response was, but the last thing she wanted was to be forced to go along with the delegation, out into the hallway. "Here, sir."

His eyes were on her face, burning into her. Her heart stuttered. He didn't have time to consider her so closely, unless he knew who she was.

But then he gave a crisp nod. "Carry on. I need this area kept secure!"

She didn't know if she was supposed to, but she saluted. "Yes, sir!" It was all she could do to keep steady on her feet, the instant his hand left her shoulder. But if the delegation had been meeting in the adjoining room, that was where she needed to go. Before she even moved in that direction, a nurse pushed open the door and guided the VP-now-Prez through the lab and toward the corridor. Two more nurses hurried out, rushing to help the first nurse. The door to the meeting room swung in its arc, paused for just a moment and swung back.

Anayeli only just reached it in time. She threw a glance over her shoulder—the lab had cleared. She was alone.

The room beyond wasn't a meeting room at all—it was the stuff of nightmares. Inside were beds veiled with heavy plastic sheets that hung from the ceiling. Each bed was occupied, people coughing and crying out. Next to the door, a blood covered mop leaned against the wall, beside a bucket full of bloody fluids.

She pushed through the plastic sheeting surrounding the nearest patient and it was all she could do not to recoil. The person in the bed—a woman she thought— had features so swollen they were indistinct. The woman moaned and turned toward Anayeli.

"I'm so sorry, I can't understand—"

Tears—at least she thought that's what they were, they were tinged pink—dripped from the woman's eyes.

"Can you tell me again?"

The woman's lips were cracked wide, her tongue swollen and protruding—she was suffering from the same symptoms as the soldiers outside. She spoke slowly, her mouth barely moving. "More drugs."

"Okay. I'll find a nurse." She backed out of the plastic sheeting, tears pricking at her own eyes, her stomach roiling. The woman moaned again and she wished there was something—anything!—she could do. But of course, there were no nurses. They'd all gone out into the corridor to attend the already-dead. They would be back— soon. She didn't have much time.

Her hands shaking, she turned to the cabinets lining the wall where the door was. She yanked the first set open. There were several packages of masks scattered on the shelves and a folded rectangle of plastic that turned out to be a protective gown. She took those, plus a face shield that had been left on the counter. She yanked out all the drawers. Only the last one had anything useful—more of the plastic ID wristbands everyone was wearing. If she and Mama and the girls needed to escape, those would be useful. She grabbed a handful in every color—orange, blue, green, pink. No purple. She didn't see a single band with the color she was certain Mama's had been. Where the hell were they keeping the people with purple wristbands?

She jammed the wristbands and extra masks into her backpack, then donned the face shield and plastic gown. None of the staff that had spewed out of the room had been wearing any of it, but she couldn't afford to mess around. Mama was counting on her. So were Ernesto and Carlota and Bailey Rae. Fatima too. She couldn't afford to get sick.

She stalked down the aisle, keeping her feet busy to drown out the crying from the first woman she'd checked on. She hadn't found any painkillers. She looked in on another patient. The man's eyes were swollen shut. "Sir? Can you tell me how long you've been here?" He moaned and she couldn't tell if he was awake or crying out in his sleep. He thrashed, flipping himself partway over, his arm flapping. On his wrist was a pink wristband, just like the soldiers' outside, just like Fatima's. Except his had red stripes on it, like the wristband Ernesto wore.

The third patient was no more responsive to her questions, and she didn't have time to waste. She pulled back the sheet covering the man and found his wristband. Pink with red stripes. "Okay. Yours is pink. That other guy's was pink. Is everyone's pink?" She wished she could ask. It would take too long to check every patient to be sure.

The next three patients all had the same pink wristband. Which meant probably they all did. Which meant Mama wasn't in this ward. It wasn't enough information though, and the noise outside—it had died down. She needed something more to take back to Fatima, and she needed it quick.

"Where are the medical records?" It was another question none of the patients she checked could answer. But the records were there, hidden in plain sight inside a binder, like the one she'd found in Ernesto's room. There was one zip-tied by its rings to the foot of each bed, so she couldn't take it with her, not without cutting the zip ties. That would draw too much attention. Instead, she flipped the pages. This time she knew what she was looking for. She wanted a toxicology report, to compare it to what she'd seen in Ernesto's.

"Here it is!" At her exclamation, the woman in the bed jerked. "I'm sorry. You should rest. I'll be more quiet."

She ran a finger down the report until she found a value that was crazy high. It was the same one as Ernesto's. She ripped the paper from the binder's rings. Maybe it would be missed, but it would take longer to be noticed than if she took the whole binder. She shoved the paper into her backpack. She didn't know what that high value meant, but it was a clue. It was the evidence she needed to show Fatima, and then to show the world.

It was the same with each toxicology report she found. The same value was always high. She scanned the other information. The top of each report she looked at had a number that started with NG on it. If it weren't for the fact the place was crawling with them, she wouldn't have guessed it meant *National Guard*. The ward was full of soldiers. Only Fatima would know if they were from her unit.

She'd just set her backpack on the ground and unzipped it when there was a noise from the outer room. The delegation must have returned. She shoved the third toxicology report into her backpack—this one for Fatima to look at, the others for Anayeli to keep—and managed to heft it onto her back and straighten back into guarding position just as the Matreus Polo Shirts came back inside.

Behind them came a doctor in a stained lab coat, a stethoscope around his neck. "You see what's happening—if we don't ramp up testing and do another round of treatment on the subjects in the hospital at large *now*, we're going to have a dire situation on our hands."

"Seems to me, Dr. Thomas-Schmidt, we already do." Young Polo forced the words out, then dissolved into coughing.

Professional Polo shirt, looking decidedly wrinkled, took a step away from the younger man. "We really need to increase the testing on the asymptomatics. That's the only way we can figure out what the protective factor is. Once we have that, we'll have a fighting chance..."

The asymptomatics? That was definitely not anyone Anayeli had seen. Short of searching every room on every floor, she had no idea where to find them. But there was only one person she knew who hadn't coughed once, who hadn't seemed at all fazed by the smoke.

Mama.

CHAPTER FIFTEEN

DR. DIANA STEWART. MATREUS HQ, CHICAGO, ILLINOIS

Back in her apartment, Diana sat in the window seat looking out over the city. The day was murky, whatever light there was fading into darkness and rain, the fog which wreathed the city began to glow a dirty orange here and there where fires were burning again, the skyscrapers poking through it like dark islands in an ominous sea.

There were no sirens that she could hear; probably the rioters were taking cover from the weather, or the police were.

Her confrontation with Bryce had left her shaken. "You've done nothing but cause pain for years." His words echoed on an endless loop. "First thing I'll do once my father isn't here to protect you any more, is fire you."

"You can't fire me if I quit first." For all her bravado, the truth gutted her. Victor had *never* protected her. She saw it so clearly, with the benefit of hindsight. She had to get back the thumb drive with all her files on it. It was still there, stuck in Dan's computer.

Whether she could still retrieve it before anyone noticed remained to be seen.

She moved over to the sofa and turned on the TV to break the silence. It just showed static. Someone must have forgotten to connect it, and with her ribs still painful, she didn't care enough to go crawling behind the set. She turned it off again.

The front door's lock clicked, and the door opened to reveal Garrick, just putting a keycard back in his pocket. "Hey! Di. Thought I'd check in on you." He threw his jacket over the back of the sofa. "Just as well. You look as rough as a badger that got dragged halfway over the state on the underside of a freight truck."

"You have a keycard?"

Garrick moved past her and opened the fridge. He took a couple of beers out, opened them and handed one to her. She suppressed a flinch and the urge to duck, but he just held the bottle until she took it.

"I've been thinking about your kids."

Diana kept his gaze, determined not to let the hope show in her face. One smile too many and Garrick would know she was playing him.

"You wouldn't have just left them in the path of the fires without..." He set his beer down. "You must have had some idea how to meet up with them if something went wrong?"

She'd had a plan, but he wasn't going to hear about it from her. She shrugged. Best if he thought she was the same woman he'd bullied and pushed around, all those years ago; easily swayed, not in charge, *feckless*.

Garrick shifted further down in his chair. "Well, with those kids out of the way, you're free to get on with anything you want now." The cruelty came so easily to him. She could barely believe she'd married the man. "Seems like the fire burned our house in Berkeley down, so staying here while we get it fixed up doesn't seem a bad idea. It's not the Waldorf Astoria, but there are generators and running water and they're not charging us, so I guess we shouldn't bitch about it. Besides, you'll want to get on with your sciencing."

Garrick was right about one thing, she needed a place to 'science.'

She picked up the bottle of beer to take it back into the kitchenette, but it was covered in condensation and slipped out of her hand. The bottle shattered. She jumped back and yelped, hopping awkwardly. "Damn it all!" She grabbed at the counter, nearly slipping on the splatter of blood that dripped from where a shard of broken glass pierced her foot.

Garrick grabbed a towel, lifted her over the glass and dumped her on the sofa. Sitting on the coffee table, he took her injured foot and wiped away the blood, wrapping the towel around it. "Okay, what's this all about? There's more going on than you've told me." He didn't wait for her answer. "You need to get that seen to. I'll be right back." He went into the bedroom and she heard him talking on the phone; then he returned. "The nurse is on the way up."

"Thanks."

He sat on the arm of the sofa beside her.

Alarm bells went off in the depths of her mind. He was being kind. That always ended badly, always.

"Let me take care of you, babe. I want to make it up to you."

She brought her injured foot up close and opened the towel, taking a look at the gash in the side of her sole.

"You know you don't have to be alone. That was always something you did to yourself." He sat forward and took the towel out of her hands, rewrapping her foot as the blood started to ooze again. "I wasn't the one to walk away from our marriage, and I never stopped thinking about you."

She leaned her head on the back of the sofa wearily. "Why do you keep coming back, Garrick? What do you want from me?"

He set her foot down carefully on the table. "I don't want anything *from* you. I want *you*. You're mine. You've always been mine. You and I, we belong together. You know that as well as I do. I know you wanted to live this high flying life, and go down in history for fixing all the world's problems, but it seems to me that you haven't fixed anything. You were used by your employers, your inventions never came to anything, and now they've thrown you away like a gum wrapper. But you aren't unwanted and you don't need to be lonely. I'm here for you, and I always have been. You know that, right?"

He took her hand, and for a moment she remembered how sweet it had been at the beginning, how good they had been together, and she wanted that again. But there'd been violence and cruelty, real harm. What she didn't say, in spite of the words bubbling up, was, 'You beat me, Garrick. You broke my collar-bone! That's not what you do when you love someone.'

He went and filled a bowl of water, and set it on the table. He knelt on the floor in front of her and wiped the blood from her foot, his touch gentle. "After you left, it made me do a lot of thinking. You were the best thing I ever had in my life, and I'd driven you away when all I ever wanted was to protect you. It made me take a good look at myself, and think good and hard about how we ended up apart. I got myself into counseling and to anger management courses. It took a while, but I came to understand how badly I treated you. I realized that maybe it would be for the best to leave you to make your own mistakes and live your own life, if that was what you wanted, but now... I can't stand back and see you get hurt anymore, Di. I just can't."

The emotional whiplash was too much; he was playing her. She had to hang on to that. The charm always evaporated, leaving control and cruelty in its wake. *Think of Jesse. Be smart about this, Diana.*

He stood up and walked to the window, agitated, then turned right back and crouched on the floor beside her, so her face was almost on a level with his. "Whatever happened between us all those years ago is ancient history. Maybe it's time to give our marriage a second chance." He waited for her to answer, but she couldn't fashion a plausible reply.

He went on, "In your own time and at your own pace, of course. All of this has come around real suddenly, I know, but I swore to myself that if I ever got the chance I'd try again, try to make up for how I treated you before. And this time it's going to be different. I can't help but protect you, but this time we work it out with words, even if it gets frustrating when you won't listen to me." He laid a hand on the side of her face. "How about we start fresh, with a clean slate? No strings, no demands, just as friends if you like. You want to talk, we can talk. You need time alone, I'll wait for you to call me.

But know that whatever else you do, however bad you feel, there is someone who loves you, and I'm only downstairs if you need me. Okay?"

Diana couldn't move. She had to make him believe there was a chance, that she was on his side. She leaned in and brushed his lips with hers.

A knock at the door startled them apart.

"Come in!" Garrick went back to sponging her injured foot as the door opened.

"Lord above, what have you done to yourself, Doc?" Patti bustled in with a bag slung over her shoulder. "That's a lot of blood right there."

"She stood on some broken glass."

Patti waved him into silence. "You did a great job clearing it up, darling, but I'll take it from here. Why don't you go and watch some football or something?" She grinned as he hesitated. "I am perfectly qualified to see to your good lady. Go amuse yourself, why don't you?"

He stood up and dropped another kiss on Diana's forehead. "Do you want me to stay?"

No. Diana hedged. "I've got work, Garrick."

"Then I'll go. Coffee tomorrow? I can bring it up if your foot is painful. About ten?"

She nodded. "Thanks."

He waited another moment as if he expected her to say something, and when she did not, he grabbed his jacket and left.

Patti knelt down to look at Diana's foot. "He's not bad to look at, your husband. Always did have a soft spot for the rugged type."

"Ex-husband."

Patti winked at her. "Doesn't look very ex to me. He lining up for another run at it?"

"Hmm..." She searched for words. "He was hard to live with." She didn't want to say too much to Patti. Loose lips and all that. The nurse clearly had the hots for Garrick and people under the spell of their own, personal chemistry could be very chatty. "Or could be, fifteen years back."

"The pair of you would barely have been kids then, surely?" Patti dropped the shard of glass into a saucer and pressed a dressing on Di's foot to staunch the blood that welled out.

"I suppose. It didn't feel like it at the time."

"A man can change a lot in fifteen years," Patti checked under the dressing. "And he's a good-looking guy. You shut him up in here with a thousand office chicks hungry for a bit of rugged goodness like him...? Whoo, he's going to get snapped up if you leave him alone too long."

It was as if Patti had been sent in as Garrick's very own press agent. Diana knew she had to tread carefully. "He's not perfect, not by a long way... but then neither am I. And you're right, neither of us are who we were all those years ago. Older, sadder, wiser maybe, but different, definitely."

"I hear you, but I'm just saying. He's not going to stay single for long!" The nurse gave her an exaggerated wink, then laughed. "He was so *gentle* when he brought you in, stroking your hair and whispering in your ear. I had you down as newlyweds, he was so attentive!"

The door to another conversation opened in front of her. "Patti, when they gave me the sedative everything got weird. I thought I was in danger and... well... bad things had happened that I couldn't explain." *Bad things like Garrick telling me he'd killed Sam and Jesse, those kinds of bad, bad things.* "Could that have just been the sedative? Might it have made me remember things wrongly?"

"Honey, they brought you in through the middle of a riot. It's scary enough sober, never mind when everything is all surreal with drugs. I'm not surprised it freaked you out." Patti put a new dressing in place and unrolled a bandage. "Can you hold that for me please?"

"Sure." Di leaned forward.

"Don't worry if it leaves you a bit vague and confused for another day or so. Your body has more chemicals washing around in it than it knows what to do with. You'll be as clearheaded as ever soon enough." She brought the last of the bandage around Diana's foot and fastened it. "Now, this is just to keep the dressing clean and in place. The wound is deep but it will heal over quickly enough if you keep it clean and dry, and at least it's toward the side of your foot rather than in the middle of your sole." She pushed herself upright. "Well, that's it for me. You gonna call that stud of yours back?"

Diana fiddled with the edge of the dressing. "No, not now."

There was a click and suddenly everything went dark.

"There go the lights again." Patti sat on the sofa. "Afraid I'm going to be in here for a little while longer."

Diana got up and hopped, cautiously with one hand on the back of the couch, then the wall, to the window. The only lights she could see were the fires. "It's not just us." She slid the window open as far as it would go—only an inch or so—but enough to listen. There were shouts and screams, and a few moments later, shots.

"Another brownout?" Patti whistled. "I sure hope the guards are keeping those guys out of the plaza. It gets ugly out there whenever the electricity dies, and if the rioters were to break into the Tower here, it'd get a lot nastier real fast. They really don't like the Matreuses."

There was not much else to say, so they sat in silence in the dark, listening to the sounds of increasing chaos in the streets below.

CHAPTER SIXTEEN

CLAIRE MOONE. RAINFORD, MERSEYSIDE, ENGLAND

The only benefits to her six-hour incarceration were that it had given Grouse and Plank in the SUVs time to rendezvous with the rest of them at the police station, and for the police to finish organizing the evacuation of the town. Sitting in the front seat of one of the blacked-out Range Rovers, while her team finished securing the motorcycles, Claire watched the unusual hue of the sky. A blackness, deep and starless, had expanded and filled the horizon. Threads of fire ravaged any higher ground, casting an orange glow that only served to highlight the horror overhead. Rolling white clouds to the east reflected the red ribbons of taillights, as people evacuated their homes.

The sun rose, but barely cut through the gloom and her bottle of water did little to ease the scratch in her soot-filled throat. To keep her nerves at bay, she opened the cover of the mission briefing she'd left behind when they'd first split up the team. A picture of her father, Hunter Moone, stared back at her. His codename, Artemis, had been given to him during his time in military intelligence.

Her own codename was on the document. *'Freya' and team to retrieve 'Artemis.'* And yet, so far, she'd failed at her objective.

"Might as well say *Claire, go and get your dad.*"

Mickey slid into the seat beside her, then handed her a coffee, poached from the police station lobby. "Didn't catch that, boss."

"Thanks." The heat of the cup warmed her hand. "Just reading the mission brief. We should have been there within an hour of getting our orders."

"Yeah, but they wouldn't let us have a chopper, so we did what we did. The police didn't exactly help. We wasted six hours on those clowns and their paperwork." He took a sip and wrinkled his nose. "This one's yours. No sugar."

Her team knew her well. The six of them were only apart when the mission required them to be, never otherwise. They were a fighting unit, all the time. Even though they were her brothers in arms, her *family*, she was responsible for them, in the way she might be for a pack of hunting dogs. She kept them fed and watered, made sure they were well rested, and gave them purpose. She drained the dregs from the cup. "Get them ready to roll, Mickey."

He rolled down the car window, stuck his raised arm out and made a fist. When he pumped it up and down, the lights of the first and last SUV blazed, their engines started with that growling roar made by a cold V8. He turned the ignition key. "Ready, boss."

She hit the microphone of the radio. "Roll out, Grouse."

Artemis was less than twenty miles away. There were no obstacles between her and him, save the awkward dynamic between a father and daughter.

The backroads were clear, the police having funneled everyone onto main roads for the evacuation, and they made good time. A quick sprint on a narrow road took them through the town of Bickerstaffe and the last thousand yards uphill to an old windmill. It was set back from the road, with secluded private grounds. Other than the high main structure, there were two small brick equipment sheds. Large thorny hedges and tall, evergreen cypress trees kept strangers at bay. The front gate was of solid timber, hung between sturdy stone posts in the middle of a rough and weathered wall, in part hidden by the trees and bushes.

The three cars stopped. Claire stepped out and walked to a small keypad, punching in the familiar six digits that sprung the mechanism to life.

"Lights are all on, ground and upper floors. Front door's wide open. Grouse, out."

It wasn't what Claire expected. "Proceed with caution. Two-One-One." She gave the tactical code for them to move in pairs, one man lightly armed with another in support.

Parking in a line, at an angle with each other, the team used the cars for cover. The drivers drew their sidearms and moved to the building, spreading out as they did. Claire grabbed a submachine gun, tugged out the stock and provided fire support from the back of the line of cars. He might be her father, but the open door had her on edge. *Someone* might be waiting for them.

Mickey leaned to take a look through the lounge window. "Looks like there's been a struggle. The place is a mess."

"Move in." She stepped forward, gun raised. Ahead of her, her partner swept his pistol through all possible sightlines, before moving over the threshold. He went deeper into the building, so she moved to the door. Checking the movement to her flanks, she nodded to Nerd and Trigger, indicating they should all advance.

Shouts of "clear" echoed through the rooms. Treads on the stair squeaked as weight went on them. More confirmations came from upstairs. The home was empty.

Claire felt a cold chill run through her. "Check the outbuildings. Stay in your pairs." The way things were scattered didn't look as disordered as someone who didn't know her father might think. Books were in topic sections. Newspapers had their own pile. One or two had toppled. It was hard to say if there had been a struggle or if things had simply fallen as the stacks had grown too tall over the years.

"What's this stuff?" Mickey raised one foot, placed it wider, then moved his other, until she could see what he was standing on. "It crunched under my boot."

They were food pellets. She'd seen them before. "Is the back door open?"

He popped his head around the door to the kitchen. "Yeah. Wide open."

"Okay." She took a stride over a discarded bath towel, then slipped past Mickey and through the house. "On me. Hold back though."

To the rear of the wide kitchen window, there was an area of decking that was home to an L-shaped group of outside sofas with a table. She followed a small flight of steps that took her down to an immaculate lawn. Laid into the grass, flat stepping-stones offered a path to a large ornate pond. The calm of the water reflected the darkness of the smoke clouds above. White, orange and silver shapes flashed past and curved their silent way through their world.

There was a long-slatted seat tucked behind manicured shrubs. A pair of tan brogues and grey flannel trousers gave away where her dad was sitting. His arms were motionless, palms up on the bench, and his head lay to one side.

"Daddy?" She didn't try to keep the worry out of her voice. Mickey was only a few steps behind, but he wouldn't fault her for addressing Artemis that way.

His posture remained the same. "Just resting my eyes, Della." It was what he said when she was a child and she caught him snoozing.

The relief changed her tone from 'caring' to 'carer.' "Have you been asleep here all night?"

"No. No. I popped down this morning. They have to be fed, you know." He leaned forward with a sigh. "What's going on? I had a call. Had to feed them, before we go anywhere." He raised himself from the bench.

"Have you had breakfast, Dad? We could *all* do with a bite to eat, before we leave. We'll put the kettle on." Mickey got the hint, returning to the house ahead of them.

"Oh. I think a cup of coffee would be good. There should be some cake in the cupboard, if you'd like some. French Fancies, I think." He wasn't as tall as she remembered. He didn't stand as straight and his shoulders weren't pinned back like they used to be. His age was telling, as his military bearing began to fade. To anyone else, his presence would still be imposing but Claire could see the small changes, even if she hadn't spent much time with him over the past two years.

"I have to take you to the cottage, Daddy. They've called a meeting of Lazarus." With him on the stones, she walked on the grass at his side. A single glance from him and she stepped onto the stones behind him.

"Good girl. Yes. It's a real concern. The fires we have here are the same as the ones in Australia and The States. It's becoming quite a threat to humanity. I'm not surprised the PM called for the group to get together."

He inhaled, pulled his shoulders back and marched inside the windmill with purpose. "What's all this? Have you men ransacked the place? Look at the state of it all."

Plank was the one closest to him. "It's how we found it, sir."

"How you... Really? Good heavens." A bewildered look flashed across his face, before stern concentration replaced it. "Mugs are in that cupboard. There's tea, coffee, and sugar in the caddies. You chaps can work a kettle? Milk is in the refrigerator."

"You know some of the men, don't you, Daddy?" The way she addressed him made Nerd glance around. Catching sight of it, she explained. "This is *Artemis*, Hunter Moone, my father."

Artemis responded. "Are you testing my memory, my girl?" He grinned at her, then pointed at each man in turn. "Mickey, Trigger, Grouse, Plank. Not met this new chap. And you only brought half the squad?"

"Yes. Just the six of us." Indicating with a wave of a hand, she introduced the one he didn't know. "The new man is Nerd."

"Ah. I can understand that. Do you like eclairs, Nerd? There are a couple in the fridge."

Grouse raised his hand to show the one he was half-way through eating. "Not anymore."

It was early for them to be having what might be considered a 'tea break,' but keeping a good humor and having everyone relaxed made it easier for her father to trust them all. In other emergency situations, even mock exercises, Artemis had been quick to argue, truculent to the point of disruption and untrusting of those sent to escort him. When Claire was on the mission, it was much easier, but the thought she'd been given command of the Paladin unit just to manage her father was one that pricked at her integrity.

Mickey finished his coffee. "I'll get your *go bag*, sir." He'd done the run with Claire enough times to know where Artemis left everything.

"Is it time to go, already?" The older man smiled, watching the team gobble down and drink what they could, before their commander had them on the road again. "Don't rush, chaps. Della won't be happy if you choke on those cakes."

"With my first name, my codename, and you calling me Della, I'm surprised they know who I am."

"Claire Adele Moone, none of these men need to doubt the one name they can all call you." She wondered what he was about to say, as there were too many possibilities, some of which would be the sort of comical twist he liked. Others would be spiked with his brand of insensitivity.

Grouse didn't give him time to make the joke. "Boss. We call her boss."

Artemis smiled. "No doubt."

She couldn't tell if her father was being ironic.

Mickey returned with a mid-sized backpack. The man was meticulous, and ready for whatever came next, even if the living room of the windmill looked like it had been bombed. For a brief moment she considered raiding his cupboards for non-perishables they could take with them, in case they had another rough day like the one before, but she quickly dismissed the idea. It would only upset her Dad and she didn't have time to deal with any unpleasantness.

At their vehicles, he attempted to get into the front passenger seat, next to Mickey. She made a joke about celebrities being chauffeured and opened the rear door for him. There was no chance she was letting him sit up front, for her to be relegated to a back seat.

For the first few minutes of their journey, leaning forward

between the front seats, he gave them instructions on how to get to the motorway without using the usual and very busy intersections—the traffic there was bound to be even worse if other people were watching the billowing smoke clouds. When he'd exhausted the six or so possibilities, he settled back into his seat and started to twiddle any knobs or controls he could find. "This button says it's for my window, but the dashed thing doesn't operate anything."

"They're all off, Dad. We can't risk anything happening to you. We've got to keep security tight and stay alert."

"Ah, yes. You do that." He leaned his head back onto the head restraint. "I'll take a nap."

Mickey looked over at her, having checked their passenger's eyes were shut. Speaking with enough volume to carry to Claire, but not to the back seats, he spoke in a soft tone. "He's getting older. He was much more with it, last time we did this."

He was right. Artemis was aging and it had begun to show. It had been two years since the last Lazarus gathering. Although it wasn't a live mission, the government used the excuse to run through the procedures and protocols for the management of apocalypse level events. Considering the scale of what was happening globally, it had been a well-timed exercise. Artemis wasn't so altered since then that he couldn't do his job, just slower and that little bit less sharp. It happened to the best of men and now it was happening to him. At least he'd have one last mission to call his own, that was a kind of grace in itself.

Compared to the day of chaos they'd had getting there, the journey was going smoothly. They ran north on the A59, through Burscough, with Nerd calling out their route from the third car, managing to avoid routes clogged with ordinary citizens fleeing the smoke. Artemis roused, hearing the voice on the two-way radio. "That's very accurate navigation."

Mickey responded. "It's Nerd, behind us. He's got real time traffic and satellite imaging, so he can plot down to a couple of feet on the ground. We tried SatNavs, but they're not that smart. Not as smart as Nerd, at least."

"He may be smart, but how's he getting us onto the motorway, coming this way?" Claire heard her father's tone of superiority from behind her head, where it always had been when she did her homework.

She didn't have an immediate answer but couldn't ignore the question. "We trust him. He knows the parameters of the operation and he always comes up with something."

A turn was called against the 'no entry' signs that identified the road as being 'one way' and not in their favor. They sped along without questioning what they'd been told, reaching the boundary road of the Charnock Richard motorway service station.

Mickey chuckled as he heard Artemis utter the words a child might, when they left home unprepared for a journey. "I need to go to the toilet."

Claire pulled the microphone handset to her mouth. "Pull over at the main block. We're taking a bio-break. Trigger and Nerd to escort Artemis."

She leaned on her door, pushed it open, then pulled herself off her seat and out of the Range Rover. Taking the handle of the rear door, she opened it like a chauffeur would, standing tight against it to keep it steady while the passenger exited. Her father stood at her side, looked at the two men who came to the car, then acknowledged their presence. "Yes. You're going with me, aren't you?"

The trio went inside, the doors slid closed behind them and Claire took a deep breath. "Mickey, if he says 'Are we there yet,' I'll scream. Remind me I'm not allowed to shoot him."

Standing in a safe place on the other side of the car, Mickey grinned. "Boss. You're not allowed to shoot him."

"Funny. Very funny. Remind me, if he says it, though."

Ten minutes passed. Grouse, Plank and Mickey stood at ease, conserving energy. Claire checked her watch. "It doesn't take this long to go to the loo. I'm going to see what they're up to."

She marched to the automatic doors, scanning the little shop within for signs of her father.

Inside, Trigger walked toward her. "He's been a while, boss."

She flicked her hand at Nerd, sending him into the men's toilet.

He returned within seconds, shaking his head from side to side. "Not in there."

Her body tensed. Trigger stepped back a pace as she growled. "You *lost* him? You lost my dad?"

The two men looked somewhat sheepish, both speaking at the same time. They fell silent, before she got a full explanation. Nerd risked her ire. "Er... Boss... He's behind you."

Artemis looked to be unconcerned, carrying three bags of candy. "Thought we could have some of these in the car, for the rest of the trip."

He'd somehow found the good stuff, even though much of the store had already been picked over. Again Claire wondered if they should stock up on some more essentials—more water, more ready-to-eat, non-perishable food. But there was none of that left in the shop, and regardless, the Range Rovers were packed with supplies, and the safe house they were headed to would also be well-stocked. Those kinds of concerns were outside of her purview. She focused on what was in her control.

Her father pointed. "I see the media are having a feeding frenzy with all this. It makes people panic. I swear they do it for some sadistic pleasure. It's certainly not for the public good."

On every screen in the rest stop, there were images of homes burning, fire crews battling against raging flames, and crying children clinging to their parents.

Claire didn't have time for a discussion about the freedom of information. She agreed with him, anyway. "Everyone, back in the vehicles. Prepare to roll out. Nerd, get us a solution. We need to get moving. Things are going to get very serious, very quickly."

CHAPTER SEVENTEEN

DALE CURTIS. OUTSIDE LONDON, ENGLAND

All Dale could see when he closed his eyes was Terri. Terri lying motionless on the hospital bed. Terri convulsing—flatlining, for goodness sakes!—while he stood like a frozen lump, doing nothing to help her. Terri begging him to go and find their son. He sat up and scrubbed at his gritty eyes. For the umpteenth time he checked the digital clock on his bedside table which glowed: 03:54. It was hopeless, he was wired and couldn't shut the noise down in his head. Her entreaty, the last words she would ever speak to him: *Find Brandon. Bring him home.*

Kicking off the covers, he stalked over to the desk and fired up his laptop, opening a browser and tapping in: *Flights to Billings International Airport, Montana.* He'd get the girls safely to his parents' place, then go off in search of Brandon. But there wasn't a single flight available on any site. He punched in BZN. Maybe Bozeman still had flights available. His parents could drive, meet them at the airport. Nothing. It was ridiculous, there had to be some flights available, but each search turned up the same result. Great Falls Intl Airport, Glacier Park Airport, Missoula, no seats available.

A lump rose in his throat. Dale drummed his fingers on the keyboard for a minute. He couldn't give up. He changed his search for flights to the USA, Open airports. An article popped up on the closure of what appeared to be all International airports in the Western States. That wasn't going to stop him and the twins. They'd get there one way or another. He racked his brain. There had to be somewhere they could fly—and then the kids' godmother's face popped into his head. Ingrid. Terri's best friend. Maid of Honor at their wedding. She would help.

He punched in *'flights to Chicago,'* and sure enough: seven seats available for a 14:00 departure. There was no time for hesitation. He booked three outbound flights, no return tickets. There was no way of knowing how long it would take to find Brandon: two days or two weeks. A fresh bout of energy surged through him, as he checked in online. Anything to save them time at the airport. He typed in his name, the girls'—but when he got to the passport details field he paused. Terri had always kept on top of their important documents—his throat tightened. One more way to miss her.

He shoved out of the chair—no time to waste. He crept downstairs to avoid waking the girls and gingerly opened the 'document drawer' in the Welsh Dresser, their passports all neatly stacked to one side, everything in order. His eyes stung. Such a small thing his wife had done, that he'd never thanked her for. Never appreciated. He swallowed hard.

Back upstairs, he typed the passport numbers in with their flight details. First step done. Next he packed, trying to plan for every contingency. By the time he finished, the bedside clock read 5:17. Exhausted he collapsed back into bed. He was going to follow through on his promise to Terri and save Brandon from whatever debacle Jeremy had gotten him into. A peculiar phrase that Terri had enjoyed teasing him with crossed his mind as he drifted toward sleep, "I'm happy-sad."

He was half-awake, the room filled with the warm light of morning when he instinctively rolled over, toward Terri. But the emptiness on her side of the bed, the cool sheets against his skin jolted him from his waking fug. The world was not as it had been, his heart was not at peace. He opened his eyes to the stark reality of the empty space where Terri would have been. A cold dread gripped his heart and washed over him. He didn't bother dashing the warm, fat tears coursing down his cheeks as he cursed himself.

He should have done something proactive. He should have stopped Terri from leaving for work. If only she had agreed to quit—he would do anything to change the course of events that had ended in his beautiful wife's death. He turned his face into the pillow to stifle the noise he was making. The last thing he wanted to do was wake the twins. Maybe they had managed to get some sleep. Or maybe they, like him, had been consumed with thoughts of their mother. The memory he returned to over and over was the first time he'd seen Terri, when she was Jeremy's girlfriend; vibrant, full of promise, with that laugh that somehow put everyone at ease. Then that laugh had vanished, when she was pregnant and abandoned, vulnerable and beautiful. Dale had instantly warmed to this amazing woman, disgusted at his brother's cavalier behavior, discarding her like a piece of old gum. Making her laugh again had been his sole mission, at least at first.

The thoughts tumbled though his mind like a slideshow on steroids. Wooing her in Montana, taking her on hikes through the mountains and on road trips. Then travelling back to her native UK and taking up his position with Cambridge University, Brandon's birth, Terri falling pregnant again, almost immediately, with the twins. Footsteps creaked on the landing. The bathroom door hinges squeaked as it closed and the lock shot home with a click. He eased out of his reverie and back into his bleak, Terri-less reality.

Forcing himself out of bed and into the clothes he'd laid out earlier, he caught the girls in their room, huddled together at their desk. He needed to get the twins onside and they had a heap of stuff to organize. When he knocked on the door frame, they turned in unison, both red-eyed, their faces drained of all color. They hadn't slept much either.

"Girls you need to pack. We're flying out to Chicago today. I want to get Brandon over here as soon as we can."

Jojo leapt to her feet. "No! We're not going to the States!"

It took all he had not to shout back. "We went through this yesterday JJ, this isn't up for debate, we're getting Brandon back and we're going together."

Jojo's shoulders dropped and her chin dropped to her chest while Kitty smothered a sob, their grief lancing his heart. He softened his tone. "Girls, your Mum is gone and our lives are never going to be the same again. It's tough now and I'm afraid it's likely to get tougher. I'd really love to take whatever time we need, but Mum asked me to bring Brandon back." His voice cracked. "Will you help me?"

Kitty's chair scraped across the floor, too loud, too painful. They stood side by side, Kitty's eyes smouldering, JoJo's jaw set. Then they whirled, turning their backs on him.

"Pack. Please." Dale didn't know what they were up to, but he didn't have time to find out. He needed to plan. They were going to the States and had to be prepared for any eventuality. He had no idea what was going on over there, but if the airports were closing, it was bad. Try as he might, he couldn't truly pack for every possible scenario, but with enough money, they could get whatever they needed. It wasn't like they were going to some uncivilized backwater.

He went over the figures in his head. How much they had in their savings. How much they might need. If they took a week to find Brandon and bring him back—flight, cars, hotel, food—£10,000 should cover any costs. But then there were the "what ifs."

"Dammit. I'll just empty our account." Yes, £50,000. It was everything they had, but it should be more than enough. If his dad had taught him anything, it was that cash was a necessity in a disaster. He'd have to make the withdrawal at the bank branch.

He shouted up the stairs. "Girls!" There was no response. He raised his voice. "Girls! I'm off to the bank to sort some stuff. Get ready, our flight leaves in a few hours."

Silence was his only answer. He headed out to the car, hoping they were packing. He needed them to be packing.

With the BMW's windows down and the warm breeze washing

over him, the streets slipped by, as if he were on autopilot, his mind filled with a cacophony of emotions wrestling for position. Brandon. The girls. Terri. Always Terri...

The metallic, slamming jerk of impact to the hood snapped him back to attention. His car slammed to a stop, the airbag punching into the space between him and the steering wheel, the seat belt cutting across his chest. Dale cursed aloud; this was the last thing he needed. He fought the airbag, shoving at it until he had enough space to move. He unstrapped himself and leaned in toward the glove compartment, yanking out the insurance documents—more documents Terri had always kept in order—and stepped out of the car, approaching the sedan that had hit him, steam rising from his own vehicle's hood, some fluid dripping from hers.

A lady threw open her door, thunder on her brow as she pursed her lips at him, a shower of crumbs falling from her lap as she stood.

"Listen Ma'am, I'm sorry, stuff happens. Here's my insurance details. Get your people to call mine, I'll accept full liability." Dale held his papers out in front of him, like an offering of peace. He just needed to get going, as quickly as possible.

The woman narrowed her eyes as she clung onto the side of her car. "What the hell is wrong with you?"

"Ma'am—your nose—" A trickle of blood snaked toward her upper lip. She dabbed at it with her fingers. "You just ran a red light into moving traffic. Have you been drinking?"

Heat flushed over his face at her scathing tone. "What? No! Look, I have a plane to catch and stuff to sort out—can you just take my insurance details, and we can be about our business?"

The woman took her cell phone from her waistcoat pocket, her eyes boring into his as she scrutinized his face, her nose still bleeding as she poked at her cell, making a call. *Like Terri's nose*—but he couldn't think about that. The woman was talking to someone. "Yes, police, I want to report a collision, intersection of Gordon Road and Baker Street, Enfield. Yes, we'll stay here."

She cupped her hand around the mobile and turned her back on Dale, perhaps thinking that he couldn't hear her, but there was no mistaking the words.

"I think this guy might have been drinking—" The woman let out a little cough. "He went straight through a red light, and now I've got a bloody nose!"

"I wasn't drinking! I—my wife—" His voice wavered. He wasn't going to bare his grief before a stranger. Throwing his hands in the air, he turned and walked to his car.

"Where do you think you're going, mister?"

Her shrill voice grated on his nerves; did he have to explain the obvious to this obnoxious creature? "I'm going to move my car to the side of the street ma'am. It's currently causing an obstruction and traffic's backing up.

Not prepared to pander to the woman's paranoia, Dale slipped into the driver's seat and moved the battered car to the side of the road, the engine temperature warning light illuminating before he'd even reached the curb. Stepping out of the car he went around the front end. Instead of steam, there was fluid pooling at his feet. Great, the radiator was cracked. His car would need to be towed and he'd have to make arrangements to have it repaired. Two more things to add to his to-do list and no time to spare for any of it.

He'd just arranged for the towing company to meet him at the bank when a police motorbike pulled up to the other driver, whose car was still blocking the lane.

She was flushed, tears rolling down her now puffy cheeks, a handkerchief at her nose. She was already launching into her story before the officer had even gotten off his bike. "I had just gotten scones, those gluten-free ones, at that new organic place—" She waved a hand down the street somewhere and it was all Dale could do not to tell her to cut to the chase and hurry up. "They grind the seeds into flour right in front—" Dale shot the officer a look. Neither one of them had time for her saga.

"Ma'am. The accident?"

"Right. Okay. I'd just left *Tea & Teff*, that's the name of the place—and I was driving into the junction through a green light and this idiot pulled out in front of me. He must have run a red light. I had nowhere to go, and all my scones are ruined." She gestured at the crumbs smashed into the seats. "And look at the damage!" The woman wobbled on her heels and sank back into her car, her face gone pale. It was quite the performance. "I don't feel so well. Are you going to breathalyze him?"

"Yes madam, I'll be asking both of you to take a breathalyzer. Now, would you drive your car out of the junction and pull it over on the left, just beyond the BMW, so we can free the traffic?"

Dale suppressed a smile as she bristled at the suggestion she would be breathalyzed too and the seeming effrontery of this policeman telling her to move her car. Her tears dried up, as if she had forgotten that she was crying, but her nose was still bleeding. Turning her back on the policeman she shot a filthy look at Dale, got in her car, and slammed the door before breaking into another coughing fit. Something niggled at his brain. Something Terri had told him about the seeds she'd slipped in, before— But it made no sense he'd be thinking about that. The woman looked nothing like Terri, acted nothing like her. He had to get to the bank and get home and packed and to the airport.

The policeman was all efficiency in getting both parties to blow zero and ensuring that the insurance documentation was in order before announcing that both parties should provide the other with their details and he'd be on his way.

The woman still sat in her car, a blood-soaked handkerchief at her nose.

"Are you going to be okay, ma'am?" Dale didn't think she looked well enough to drive. In addition to her nose, as she took the paper where he'd written his insurance information, her fingers were puffy and swollen. That couldn't have been caused by their fender bender.

"I'll be fine, no thanks to you!" She had to clear her throat just to say a few words, and Dale was reminded again of Terri, those last minutes with her, how she'd struggled to get those final words out.

"I apologize for the trouble." His worry was misplaced—a reaction to his grief. And he really needed to be on his way. He turned away, pressed the button to lock his car, and headed on foot for the bank.

The hush of the bank was a welcome reprieve. He went directly to the customer service desk, where a young man not much older than Brandon sat. "I need to speak with the branch manager."

The boy pressed his lips into a straight line. "I'm sorry, but he's not avail—"

Dale checked the time: 10:15. The flight was scheduled for 14:00, he was cutting it too fine.

"Look. Mick is a friend and I need someone who can help me now! I have flights in four hours, I need to free up several tens of thousands of pounds and it can't wait until this afternoon. Now who can help me?"

The bank clerk blushed and fumbled with some papers on his desk. "I'll see what I can do, sir."

As the bank teller disappeared through a door marked, 'Staff only,' Dale stalked after him. He stood, barely able to keep from tapping his foot as one minute passed, then another. He didn't have this kind of time. He wasn't even sure yet how he'd get back home. He rapped on the door sharply. Aware he was drawing stares from around the building, he focused on the door and knocked again. The door opened inward, the flushed teller moving past him to attend to his desk, leaving a perplexed looking bank manager in the door frame. "Dale, I was in a meeting mate, this isn't like you, what's going on?"

Every eye in the bank was trained on Dale. He couldn't tell Mick about Terri—not in front of all these strangers. "Can we"— he gestured toward the staff area— "go somewhere private?"

His brows creased with worry; Mick led the way to an interview room at the side of the building. "How can I help?" Mick motioned to an armchair.

Dale sat heavily, the words he had to speak sitting like an anvil in his stomach. He hadn't told anyone but the girls what had happened, and now he didn't know how to begin. "Mick—" His voice wobbled but he forced himself to continue. "Our world has been turned upside down. Terri—she—" the lump in his throat was so painful, he had to stop. But his promise. Brandon. There wasn't time to waste on emotion. "Terri died yesterday, totally unexpected."

"Dale buddy, I'm sorry to hear— I just— I don't know what to say." Mick looked truly shocked, but there wasn't time for shock. He had to get through his story.

"Brandon is stuck in the States with his 'dad' and they're in trouble. Anyway, I promised Terri I would bring him home, so I'm taking the girls over to get him."

"Dale. The news from over there is—hell, more than half the country is in trouble. Not just your ordinary American trouble, but 'bring the house down' trouble. They're descending into anarchy. And now there's the fires in Wales..."

He ignored Mick. "That's why I want to make sure we're covered for all possible contingencies and I need to draw £50,000 in traveler's checks."

Mick shot him a startled glance, then turned to type something into his computer. After the smallest of pauses, then more typing, Mick gave a tiny, apologetic headshake. "Look man, I can understand why you want to bring Brandon back, but you don't have £50K to draw."

A roaring filled Dale's ears. He must have misheard. "What are you talking about? I reviewed the account three weeks ago. We have £50K."

"Sure Dale, you did." Mick spoke slowly, as if Dale were a rabid dog or a wild creature. "But, Terri transferred £10,000 to the girl's business account."

Mick might as well have been speaking gibberish, for all the sense it made. "What business account?"

Mick's expression was just as confused as Dale felt. "To pump-prime their online boutique." Mick's voice faltered. "I thought you were in on it."

All the girls' whispering sessions over the last few weeks, Terri's late nights, her fury when he'd suggested she quit her job. It all came back in a rush. He glanced at his watch. There was no time for this. No point in being angry. Terri was gone. The girls—he'd deal with them later. There wasn't the luxury of time, they needed to get to the airport. He adjusted to the new information. He had £40,000. It wasn't so different. He had good credit. Surely a loan—

"Mick, I need £50,000 in travelers' checks, how do we do it?"

"We'll need some solid collateral, a loan against your house, for example." From his tone, it was clear Mick didn't like the idea. He lowered his voice. "And—what about *arrangements for* Terri?"

"I just need a solution, Mick." He hadn't saved Terri, and he damn well wasn't going to fail Brandon, too. "I need to get my kid back."

"Even if we can get it arranged, you can't carry £50k into the States with you. The maximum anyone can take into the country is $10,000."

"But there's three of us—"

"Right. The girls. So if you and each of the twins carry $10,000 each, that gives you $30k. You'll need to wire the balance to someone in the States. You've got family there, haven't you?"

"I do but we're flying to Chicago—Terri's best friend is there. Her details are already in our account, she's the one we always send a couple of grand to when Brandon's visiting his Dad, just in case we need to call in a favor." There was the question of the exchange rate, but Dale was already burning through every nerve in his body. Any more *faffing* and he was afraid he'd lose it. "Give me $30,000 in travelers checks and wire whatever is left over to her." Once they were at the airport, he'd liaise with Ingrid, sort out the details of their arrival, and what they'd need.

"Sure, but Dale, take some time to think about the options here, I mean traveler's checks, really? There's better…"

He was trying to stay calm, but everything inside him was too big and clawing to get out. It took all he had not to shout. "Mick, I haven't got time to stop and consider options, our flight leaves in a little over three hours. I need it sorted now!"

Something in his tone must have registered. Mick put out his hands, making a placating gesture. "I'm printing off the contract for the loan now." He jabbed at his keyboard and from somewhere down the hall came the whining buzz of a printer. Mick clicked his mouse some more. "You have an Amex card, so we can sort your Traveler's Checks out in £1,000 denominations. I'll have them authorized for collection at the Bureau de Change at the airport. "And just fill out one more form for the wire before you go, and I'll get those funds over to"—he paused just long enough to find something on his computer screen—"Ingrid today."

It felt like a lifetime before Dale had signed and filled out the paperwork. The tow truck hadn't arrived, so he called in another favor, dropping the BMW's key in Mick's palm before climbing into the customer service clerks' hatchback, Mick having secured Dale a ride home.

After an even longer eternity, they pulled up outside of Dale's house. The place looked empty. Abandoned. Lifeless. He thanked the kid driving but even as he climbed out, he almost wanted to get right back in and tell the kid driving to keep going. But that made no sense. The girls were inside. It was still their home, even if Terri was—

He jogged up the walk, and pounded up the front steps, throwing open the front door. He half-hoped there would be suitcases in the entryway, but there were none except his own. "Girls?" The house was too quiet. If they had gone back to sleep— He called up the stairs. "Girls!" Still nothing. "Are you packed? We're going to need to leave, I've already called for a cab." At least he'd managed to do two useful things on the ride home: arrange the cab and email Ingrid, advising her of the wire transfer, asking her to hire a small RV they could drive to Montana, and pick them up at the airport. Hopefully he'd hear back from her before their flight took off, but with the time difference. He couldn't think about it now. And if the girls weren't ready and they missed their flight, all his arrangements would be for naught. "Girls!"

Relief surged through him when he heard the slide of a kid getting off the bed, the padding of feet.

Kitty came thudding downstairs, her face pale and drawn. She carried two rolling suitcases and had two small backpacks slung across her back.

"Where's your sister? The cab's going to be here in 15 minutes."

"She's gone to the post office. We had some orders that we finished yesterday, so she's just making sure that our customers get them." She must have seen thunder in his expression. Her voice hardened. "It can't wait until we get back!"

"Post office?!" Heat crawled over his cheeks and neck. He checked the time, again, and swallowed everything else he wanted to shout. He had questions. At the top of the list: just *what* exactly had happened to the money Terri had given the girls. But none of it mattered. Not when they had a flight to catch. "When did she leave? When's she coming back?"

"Dad, calm down. We've closed our online store for the next week. But if we leave without fulfilling these orders, we'll get bad reviews and that would bury us."

Bad reviews. Their brother was in trouble, their mother was dead, and they were worried about bad reviews. The explosion inside him mushroomed.

A key turned in the front door and Jojo entered, a defiant set to her chin. Dale took a long look at his daughter. There had been enough tension over the last twenty-four hours to last a year. This wasn't the time for confrontation. It took everything in him, but he walked over and took Jojo in a hug. "I'm glad you're home." He shot a glance over to Kitty. "And thank you for being all packed." The atmosphere warmed and Kitty joined them, throwing her arms around them both.

There was a pounding knock on the door and they all startled. "The cab." Dale brushed a tear away from his cheek. "Let's go get Brandon back, girls!"

CHAPTER EIGHTEEN

SAM LEARY. I-70 WEST OF RUSH VALLEY, UTAH

Driving a semi-tractor with its trailer was nothing like Sam had imagined. The thirty-foot trailer weighed him down. The winds pushed against the cab and buffeted the trailer and Sam over-corrected as the invisible force blew the vehicle from its lane. The steel and chrome bumper scraped along the concrete barrier, spitting sparks in a plume as if it were a mini firework. He spun the wheel in the opposite direction, over-correcting and veering back toward the middle of the freeway. If it weren't for the wide stretch of road that ran in a straight line, he'd have driven into the ditch miles ago. As it was, it was a small miracle he'd made it down the hill on the jouncing dirt road leading away from Bill's place and onto the Interstate.

Jesse sat, belted into the passenger seat and propped up on blankets so that he could see out the windows. He'd asked about Henry when he woke up, and Sam told him the facts. The boy had cried and then been angry Sam had lied to him, his demeanor changing from agreeable to stubborn. Ever since, they'd travelled in silence, the boy only looking at Sam when he said they were going to see Diana.

Sam white-knuckled and stiff-armed the steering wheel, the struggle to keep the vehicle straight a constant battle he was forever losing. He shifted back to the slow lane, but another gust of wind shoved the semi toward the shoulder. There was a steady buzzing from the right tires, the rumble strip vibrating the entire cabin, but he stayed where he was, more or less.

The highway markers that were posted every so often on the side of the road had long since disappeared, but he was certain he was on the right route. Still, something itched the back of his mind. He'd been digging around for its source for what seemed like hours, but as he rounded a sharp turn it hit him. Skateboard Lizzy had said there were people robbing trucks and something about damaged lollipops. The markers might have been what she was referring to. If that was still the case, then somewhere close by would be a policewoman.

Sam didn't want to break the rules, but if there was an officer who intended to pull them over and rob them, she'd have to wait. He didn't have time to deal with another Stacey. Unsure whether Lizzy's warning was real or not, he sped up. The engine roared. There was a slight bump, and numbers flickered on the digital readouts. The dash indicated that the automatic transmission had just shifted into thirteenth, and the metal beast quieted to its normal purr. He was the master of a ten-ton monster, directing it down the interstate at sixty-five miles an hour. He had no idea why the road was so clear. From what Skateboard Lizzy had said, he hadn't expected it to be—but he wasn't going to complain.

A car passed him, blaring on their horn, then cutting right in front of him. Cars were few and far between and he preferred keeping his distance. Another car pulled along his left side and when he tried to shift right to avoid brushing sides with them, Jesse let out a yell.

"No, don't! There's a truck!"

Sam craned his neck, trying to use the sideview mirror that wasn't adjusted for him. Sure enough, a truck had come up on his right, keeping pace with him. He was boxed in. It wasn't normal driving behavior for anyone in their right mind, but no one moved, except where the wind pushed them.

The tight feeling inside him grew the longer the caravan escorted him. And then, just as they rounded another curve, he caught sight of a police cruiser on the shoulder. A moment later, blue and red lights flashed in his mirror, their authoritarian blaze hard to look at for more than a glance or two. It must've been the group that was stealing from semis. No way was he falling for their trick. He stepped on the gas.

Outrunning a couple of trucks and a car should've been easy, but as Sam increased in speed, so did they. Each vehicle kept pace, speeding up and slowing down, so that they were always directly in front of him, right beside him. Jesse looked nervously at Sam and pointed out the front window and Sam leaned forward. There was something dark on the shoulder of the road about half a mile ahead. He was staring at it, trying to figure out what it could be when the truck on his right bumped him, shaking the semi. So they wanted to play hardball. Well, he could do the same. "Hold tight, Jesse!" As he said the words, he braced himself, gripping tighter to the steering wheel.

He took a breath, then veered to the left, mashing the semi's body into the white truck on that side. Sparks flew as the vehicle ground up against the barrier, but Sam was relentless. He had to be. He pushed the semi closer, smashing the white truck, while the truck on his other side body slammed into his front bumper. The impact jolted him so hard, he lost grip of the steering wheel just as another gust of wind buffeted the cab.

The truck on his left dropped behind and the police car disappeared from his mirror. Now was the time to run for it.

Jesse was turned in his seat, craning his neck. "Go Sam! They're coming back!"

Sam floored the gas pedal, and the engine screamed as the RPMs red lined. The semi lurched forward, outstripping the cars that harassed him.

"You did it!" Jesse's fingers clutched the arm rest.

A sense of pride surged through Sam. He'd escaped. He'd kept them safe. But he urged the semi faster, wanting more distance.

"Oh no, oh no!" Jesse's voice climbed with urgency. "Go faster, Sam! There's two of them!"

The engine whined under the strain—he'd max'ed out its capacity. Another impact jostled them from the right side. From the passenger's mirror, both trucks pulled out and swung inward for another strike. The dark spot on the road grew larger, resting on the left shoulder of the interstate, and he could tell it was at least a mile long. As long as he kept the wheel straight, he'd avoid it.

Twice the trucks rammed him, Jesse screaming each time as they buffeted the cab on his side. Sam's pulse hammered as they raced along and he fought to keep in the center of the road. In less than a minute, they reached the dark spot along the shoulder. It was rock. Someone had lost a bed full of gravel along the interstate.

The white trucks slammed the semi again, pushing him closer to the road hazard. Sam fought the steering wheel as the trucks pushed him onto the shoulder and into the debris.

The front tire caught, pulling the semi off the road and into the gravel and no matter how Sam cranked at the steering wheel, he couldn't wrest the semi back onto the road. The front end sank up to its running boards and the front of the vehicle collided with the concrete barrier. More fireworks sparked from the steel bumper and with no traction, the semi skidded to a halt. The engine chugged, then chugged again and died. In less than two minutes, the gravel had arrested the travel of a ten-ton missile that was barreling down the road and turned it into a roadside exhibit. They were trapped.

"What do we do, Sam?" Jesse's eyes were full of fear and Sam didn't know how to answer. He had no weapons, no way to defend himself and the kid.

With their prey stuck deep in the rock, the vultures skidded to a stop and whipped around, their engines racing as they returned to where Sam sat, stalled. The four vehicles that had harried him parked in formation, blocking him in even further.

Every vein and artery in Sam's body was ready to burst with the pressure of the blood pumping through him, as each driver got out, along with their passengers—eight in all. The police officer, a woman, took the lead while the other seven fanned out behind her. There was no doubt this was the group Lizzy had warned Bill about.

All the thieves wore gas masks which disguised their faces, but it was easy enough to imagine what kind of people approached. Two of the men behind the policewoman had tattoos up and down their arms, while another wore a duster and cowboy hat. Three wore the clothing typical of mechanics and the last wore a dingy pinstripe suit. He carried a cane and kept himself separate from the others. It was a mob borne of desperation and necessity. When they reached the semi, they surrounded the sides in a half circle while the policewoman stood at the front in view of them all. She motioned for Sam to come out.

There were no weapons to speak of, nor were there any signs of aggression other than the fight to push him off the road. Jesse grabbed for Sam. "Don't go, please."

Sam unbuckled his belt and turned the key in the ignition until the engine stopped running. "I'm afraid I don't have a choice. These people have made it so we can't go anywhere." He made sure his mask was secure around his face and clambered out of the semi.

As soon as he stepped onto the gravel, one of the tattooed men was there—but not to take Sam into custody as he'd expected. Instead, the man pushed past, onto the cab's running boards. Sam whirled and jumped for the door, but he was too late. The tattooed man had already climbed up to take Sam's place in the driver's seat.

Jesse screamed for Sam, but the tattooed guy slammed the door in Sam's face, deadening the noise, and then locked Sam out.

Only then did the others run up, grabbing Sam's arms and twisting them behind his back, before he'd managed to turn to face them. The cold metal of handcuffs bit into his skin as they clicked around his wrists. He pulled, twisting and turning, but they had him.

"Let's take a look at the kid." The second tattooed guy reached over his shoulder and wrenched him around so Sam was facing the rest of the squad.

They stared at him in his clown outfit, looking him up and down.

Tattoo guy circled around behind him. "Don't know what the fuss is about. He doesn't look all that special."

Pinstripe shot his cane up, using the end to prod at Sam, slowly dragging the polished rod down his shoulders until he reached the bandage on his leg. He tapped it with the metal end of the cane and Sam cried out. It was like someone had shoved a needle into his calf, pressing it right through the other side.

"You have the semi—what else do you want? Just give me the kid and let us go! I promise we won't bother you." Sam didn't know what else to do but beg.

Someone slapped the back of his head. It was the policewoman, and she leaned forward until he could see her eyes behind the face shield of the gas mask. "Keep it up and there won't be a boy to let go. Behave and I might let you see him."

Pinstripe pushed him into the back of the cop car and closed the door as Sam struggled into a sitting position. He leaned against the window, hoping to glimpse Jesse, but the only thing visible was the semi he'd stolen backing out of the gravel. Tattoo arms #1 must have put Jesse in the sleeper. When the truck was back on solid ground, it rumbled to life and the four vehicles that forced him off the road flanked the semi as it rolled past.

"Where are you taking us?" There was silence from the front seat. He squirmed some more, fighting against the handcuffs. They bit into his wrists, chafing. He flopped backward against the bench seat and rested his head on the headrest, dejected. He didn't understand what these people wanted, but at least they hadn't hurt him or Jesse.

The flat terrain of the interstate morphed into hills and valleys the further west they went and, without warning, they veered off the interstate onto a dirt road. Dust kicked up into puffs of fine grit and soon the caravan vanished in a cloud. The car jounced over potholes and dips. The shocks needed replacing. They hit something large, and the car dropped. Without a seat belt, Sam bounced off the roof of the car and smacked against the passenger window and things went blurry. After an hour of being thrown around, the ride smoothed out and the dust settled. Mountain ranges loomed on either side and the terrain was sparse of plant life.

Instead of one straight line, the caravan spread out, so each vehicle drove side by side toward a huge mirage. Wavering through the haze were, odd domed and triangular shapes jutting from the ground at haphazard angles, spread out for half a mile. It took another thirty minutes, but as they drew nearer, the trick of Sam's imagination took on sharper edges as the shapes became more solid. It wasn't a mirage at all, but rather a city of tents.

The policewoman pulled her gas mask off, wrapped a coiled headset over her ear and pushed the earpiece inside. "Burning Man, this is Fire Marshal. Come in." She paused for a few seconds. "Copy that. Five returning to base with two guests." She pulled the earpiece out and let it hang, clipped to her collar and slid the mask back over her head.

As they reached the perimeter of the camp, the semi veered off, taking a path opposite the others and rounded the back side of a large circus tent. Sam leaned forward, chin propped on the back of the seat. "Hey, where's that tattooed hooligan taking the kid?"

The policewoman parked the car and turned around. Her voice was raspy and alien. "It would be wise, Sam, for you to treat everyone here with respect. To continue name-calling will be to your detriment. The first name you better get right is mine. It's Belle."

Sam clamped his mouth shut and rocked back against the bench. The strange woman knew who he was, which didn't make any sense. When he didn't say another word, she motioned for his hands and he thrust them forward. Belle pulled a necklace from underneath her shirt, a handcuff key dangling from the end. She freed Sam and got out of the car as pinstripe opened Sam's door and offered a bow before falling in line behind Belle. They marched toward a tan tent and Sam followed.

Stepping through the canvas tent door, its heavy cloth flap hanging at an angle, he was greeted with what he could only describe as a low-tech scene out of science fiction film. Men and women worked in the small rectangular area, stationed at tables with steno paper, writing blocks of text from pages covered in dots and dashes. The cowboy hijacker sauntered inside, his spurs jingling. He'd removed his gas mask and peeled off his duster, replacing it with a vest. The man must have had circulation issues to wear something so warm in a desert.

People came and went, all of them dressed in outrageous circus-like get ups. Sam had no idea what he was looking at, but it wasn't civilization and it wasn't chaos; something new had grown up in the desert.

In the tent's hustle and bustle, Belle steered a thin man toward him and the two stopped on the opposite side of a table. She pulled the gas mask off and untangled her hair from the rubber straps. "Relax, Sam. There's no smoke here. The masks are for show. If a person can't see your face, then the faceless become an enigma and a living nightmare, only bested by the person's imagination." She tossed the mask on the table and prodded the thin man forward. "This is John. He's our communications expert."

John offered Sam a trembling hand. "Pleasure to meet you, Sam. Are you an entertainer?" He lingered on the blood on Sam's pants and shirt.

Belle slapped the back of John's head and sucked her teeth. It was the most annoying thing a person could do other than drag their nails against a chalkboard. Sam liked this woman less and less, and he hadn't liked her to begin with. She pushed the communications expert behind her and folded her hands in front of her and addressed him like a child. "Now Sam, what is it you do for a living?"

He smirked, but it was lost on anyone since he still had his clown mask on. As if he could explain what he did. He pulled the mask off and scowled to look his most intimidating. "I'm an entomologist."

Belle's eyes lit up and clapped her hands. "At last, someone who can help with the bug problem." She reached out and tugged on his rainbow shirt, bringing the blood-soaked portion to his sight. "And the blood is from your dog Henry, right?"

Sam choked and bit his tongue. She was an intelligent, heartless creature and he hated her. It was obvious that she knew a lot more about him than she let on and intended to show him she was the one with the power. He lowered his eyes to the table. "Correct."

Belle threw out her bottom lip in a pouting motion and patted the top of his head. "I'm so sorry. The best way to get over the death of a loved one is to keep occupied. I want you to help John with building something that can help with the cicadas." She swept out of the tent with much pomp and circumstance, leaving him speechless.

When Sam was sure Belle had left, he turned to John. "Where are we exactly?"

John ushered Sam over to the table with a map of Utah on it and circled the desert under Salt Lake City with chalk. "Somewhere in this vicinity. No one but Belle and her sons knows so anyone that tries to escape ends up dying of thirst and picked clean by the animals out there."

Sam stooped to get a better angle of the map and scanned the names that were printed on it. "A rather unlikely scenario."

John frowned and led Sam outside to a round wooden post that was sunk into the sand and supported by metal fencing stakes. A partially stripped corpse hung from the post by its limbs as a crow flew to the cadaver's shoulder and perched. It cawed, warning the two intruders that the body was his to pick clean and proceeded to peck at the body, plucking off a chunk of flesh before flying off.

Sam backed around the corner. He was alone in a strange settlement, where his jailer knew him, but he knew no one. Jesse had been whisked off to who knew what fate. His transportation had been taken, and with it the hope of reaching Diana in a couple of days, and he was stuck in the middle of the wasteland with no way out. His nightmares were coming true.

CHAPTER NINETEEN

DR. DIANA STEWART. MATREUS HQ. CHICAGO, ILLINOIS

Patti and Diana sat in the darkened lounge of the penthouse flat, waiting for the lights to come back on.

"The whole city's gone dark apart from the fires." Diana shivered. "I don't think I've ever seen it like that before." The lights came on, flickered, and went out again.

"They're firing up the generators. That isn't good." Patti sighed. "I guess they think the brownout is going to go on for a while." The lights came on and stayed on this time, though not at full brightness.

"Thank goodness." Diana relaxed. "The idea of trying to evacuate the building down thirty floors of stairs in the dark? I'm not exactly afraid of the dark but those stairs make me dizzy. I'd pitch over the handrail and still have time to write a will before I hit the ground."

Patti snorted. "Did you think it was a coincidence I decided to stay right where I was until the lifts are back on?" She stood. "But now I'll head back to my own floor. You kiss that delicious man of yours from me, okay? And if you do decide you don't want him, you send him down to me. My mattress is pretty snug but I'd find room for him on it somehow!"

Diana smiled. "Thank you for your help, Patti. I appreciate it." She saw the nurse out of the door and closed it behind her. Patti's words echoed in her head, and she was suddenly reminded of the first time Garrick had ever kissed her, and just how electrifying it had been, especially for a Plain Jane like herself to be noticed by the hunky athlete. It had been so good at first. And then, not so much. He wanted her, which was all to the good, but no matter how she reacted to him—and if she was being honest with herself, she did, at the physical level—she wasn't going back to him. Ever. She locked the door and wedged the chair under the door again, just in case of unexpected visitors. Particularly ones who had managed to get their own keycards.

She watched the orange flickering of firelight flare up in spots across the city and brewed a coffee. The steam from her coffee curled upwards in the sunlight, and she weighed whether to go down to her office or wait in the penthouse flat. But when Bryce had kicked her out, he hadn't specified how long she should actually stay out. Besides, she had data to find and a thumb drive to retrieve.

Finishing her coffee, she showered—carefully, one foot held away from the delicious warm water—dressed and slipped back to her own desk. It was still early in the morning, and the floor was empty, so she let herself into Dan's office. She fired up the computer and started copying files. There should be a little while before her colleagues turned up, but people started early at Matreus Inc. She started with her own folder, and once her FeedIt files were safe, dragged other subfolders onto the thumb drive. It took time though, and she wanted to be finished and out of there as soon as she could. If Bryce caught her in there again, he'd know she was up to something.

A squeal of rubber against rubber: the elevator doors. She froze. She'd reported it several times. The thought jolted her. A week ago? Two? It felt like an eternity, before chaos and death had descended on the world. A pang of longing for that quiet little existence shot through her like a cramp, but she did not have time for such indulgences.

The lobby door closed, and voices wafted down the corridor. To her relief they faded as the occupants went to the other end of the floor. It was past 7 a.m., and most of her colleagues were at their desks by 8 a.m. even in normal times.

She dragged and dropped file after file onto the thumb drive, but it was taking way too long and she could not afford all the delay. She went up a couple of levels and started dragging whole directories in.

The door squealed again.

She dragged the last directory across, but it was a huge one and instead of dropping into place, it brought up a dialogue box with a progress bar. She tapped her fingers on the desk, as the bar dragged itself along: and then the voices from the lobby caught her attention.

"Really, Father?"

Diana got up and peered out the door. She'd know Bryce's voice anywhere. Victor stumbled in, looking hungover and crumpled as if he had slept in his clothes.

"It's bad enough that you turn up in public looking like a drunken hobo, but I won't let Anna see you like this! She worships you for some damn reason. You're a disgrace!"

Bryce ushered him along the aisle between the desks. The pair of them would walk right past Dan's office, and after yesterday, Bryce was bound to check and make sure it was empty. She returned to the desk, and as the progress bar edged forward, she hit "Cancel." She didn't dare just pull it out and risk corrupting the other files.

"It's not what you think, Bryce, I just slept really poorly..."

She yanked out the thumb drive and stuffed it in her pocket.

Bryce's voice was quiet, but seething with rage. "You stink of whiskey and your eyes are so bloodshot there's hardly any white to be seen. I don't care how much you embarrass yourself but when you embarrass the company, that becomes my affair. And if you want to see your granddaughter, you'd better go shower and try to look less like the pathetic drunk that you are. They're on the way up from the gate now."

"Fine!" Victor slurred, and there was a clatter of chairs as if he had stumbled on his way out.

Diana turned off the monitor and dragged the chair around the desk, so that when Bryce stalked past, she was out of sight. But he slammed the door open anyhow. "You! Clearly you didn't get the message last night! If I see you in this office again, I will throw you to the rioters, regardless of what my drunk of a father says!"

"Just getting the chair and—"

He slammed the chair backward, catching her in her healing rib. She doubled over.

"Leave. Now. The chair stays here." He grabbed her arm and shoved her out of the door, so that she tumbled across the corridor and just caught herself on the cubicle wall, her foot stinging twice as much as her ribcage. "Johnson? Where's Johnson?" A burly, shaven-headed man hurried across to him. "Give me your master key."

"Yes sir." The man watched, poker-faced, as Bryce locked the door.

He handed the key back. "This is Dr. Stewart. I'm locking this office. If you see her even looking in this direction, throw her off this floor."

"Yes, sir."

The lobby door slammed open to reveal a woman in a dress which hugged her figure so closely it had to be tailored to her. She strutted in on four-inch stilettos, the sunglasses on the top of her head holding perfect waves of blonde hair back off her sculpted face—coiffed and clean and poised to a degree that should've been impossible, given the chaos roiling the city. The woman scanned the floor, her expression softening to something a little more human when she saw Bryce. "There he is, Anna." She had a Mediterranean lilt to her voice.

From behind her there was a squeal. "Daddy!" A small, brown-eyed girl carrying a plush bunny thundered across the floor to Bryce, who knelt so she could fling herself on him.

"Hey, pickle." Bryce laughed, and twenty years of sourness melted from his face. "Did you have a good journey?"

"There were lots of people shouting outside, Daddy. Did they know it was your birthday?"

Bryce tugged at a strand of her hair gently. "Something like that, sweetie."

The perfect woman swayed along to them with the practiced gait of a supermodel. "Hello darling. Are we interrupting something?"

"No, Selena. Dr. Stewart here was just returning to her accommodation." Bryce's voice stayed neutral as he hugged his daughter, but his expression did not.

Selena looked Diana up and down. "You're Diana Stewart?" Her eyebrows rose. "Not what I expected at all. I see what you mean, Bryce. Baffling." She turned and walked in the direction of Bryce's office. A quiet whistle came from the cubicle where Andrew, the intern sat gawping after her.

Bryce stood, lifting his daughter into his arms. "You may leave the office now, in case you'd missed that hint. If you must, you may use the lab on the 12th floor. At least I won't see your damned face there."

"Daddy, you said the D word!" Anna scolded.

"I did, darling, didn't I? That was very naughty of me." Bryce turned to walk away, and the plush rabbit fell to the floor.

"Daddy, stop! We need Benjy!"

"We'll get him from your bag when we get into the apartment, okay?" He did not stop.

"But Daddy—!"

"It's here; it fell on the floor, Bryce." Diana bent to pick it up, clutching at her ribs, and held it out to the child as Bryce paused. "Sorry, I mean Mr. Matreus. Here."

Anna took the bunny, big brown eyes peeping over her father's shoulder. "Thank you."

Diana smiled. "You're welcome."

Bryce stalked away.

"Ma'am?" Johnson gestured to the lobby.

"Doctor, actually." It was a feeble riposte but all she could manage. Patting her pocket, she checked the thumb drive was there, and limped away.

She headed back to the apartment to find Garrick banging on the door, a holder with two cups of coffee in his free hand. "Diana! Do you want this damn coffee or not?"

She hurried from the elevator. "Sorry, Garrick."

He set them on the side. "How's your foot?"

"Hurts, but you know, there was stuff to do." She limped into the apartment and took the tepid coffee. "I need to sit down now. Thank you, that's really kind."

"What were you doing in the office?" He drained the last of his coffee and lobbed the cup into the sink in the kitchenette, dropping onto the sofa beside her.

"Bryce has turned up, and his family. He has a daughter..." *Jesse's age.* She couldn't bring herself to say his name though. She took a gulp from the cup.

"Bryce Matreus is here? Guess he won't be staying in the dorms with the rest of us."

She snorted. "Hell, no. It's just a guess, but I bet the family have the rest of this floor and the one below us. The rooftop garden is shared, not that I'd ever go out there."

"There's a garden?" Garrick got up and peered out of the window. "Where? How do you get to it? Show me."

"I wouldn't feel right. It's the family's private place."

"If this apartment has an entrance to the garden, they can hardly bitch at you for using it." At the other end of the room there was a door to the balcony. He tried the handle; it squeaked open. "Come on. I want to see what's going on in the city."

"I don't want to make Bryce any angrier than he already is." Diana racked her brain for something that Garrick might listen to. "And my foot is pretty sore. It'd be nice to sit and chat for a bit."

Garrick shook his head. "So, you're fine to go wandering around the office but you can't be bothered to come out on the roof with me? I came up here to bring you coffee and catch up, but you were at work, just like always. I wanted to do something nice for you. You knew I was coming, and you still wandered off and left me standing here like a fool." He shrugged. "Well, that puts me in my place, doesn't it?"

"You know I didn't mean it like that." The words spilled out of her, and adrenaline pumped through her veins. *Don't make him angry. Never make him angry.* She'd been wrong—even for a second—to think he'd changed. He hadn't. He was the same bully he'd always been and whatever sweetness or kindness he'd shown her was a front.

He was already striding to the door. "It's fine, Diana. I guess I should have known that there was no point even trying if you never cared for me anyhow—"

"Wait." Her brain cycled through a million permutations, landing on a single thought: she needed him. Not in the sense he thought. She didn't need a husband, or a lover. She needed a guard, a shield, a protector. She'd discovered an enemy she barely knew existed. Bryce didn't merely despise her, as she'd previously thought, he actively hated her and meant to do her harm. The man at Matreus' helm simmered with a controlled rage. She knew well how devastating rage with intent could be, but unlike Garrick, Bryce had real power. He would consider the death of thousands of innocent people "collateral damage," a sacrifice he'd be more than willing to make. And he had a very specific, very directed hatred of Diana herself. No one would even notice if she disappeared—*apart from Garrick*. For that reason alone, she had to keep him onside, if only for a few more days. Once the rioting died down, she was out of there and no looking back. She reached for Garrick's hand and let her finger trail across his palm. "We can go and look at the garden if you like."

He didn't move, standing with one hand on the door handle but his eyes glued on her. "Your foot is obviously too sore."

"It's fine." She forced a smile. "Come on, we'll see what's up there. I've never looked."

"If you're sure." He let go the handle and went back to the balcony, gesturing for her to precede him. "Wow, the view from up here is something, isn't it?" He flip-flopped on a dime, the rage burning off him in seconds. Charming Garrick was back, all smiles and winks and wanting her to trust him.

Diana hated heights; just the thought was enough to make her head spin. She edged back against the wall. "We're so high." She was careful not to look down.

Garrick had no such scruples. He leaned out over the parapet.

"From here the protestors look like ants all scurrying around the entrance. If you fell from here, you'd end up spread over the entire plaza. That'd take a bit of cleaning up!" He chuckled. "Come on, let's see what's around the corner."

The balcony was not wide, but it led to the main roof garden. Wanting to be further from the edge, Diana hurried after him and into a pretty area of potted trees and shrubs, a little water fountain and a rooftop bar. She limped toward the pool and dropped onto a bench. Her hands were shaking. In the middle of the garden, it was terrifying but manageable, but being by the railings vertigo made her dizzy and nauseous; not the thought of how high up she was, so much as how far below the ground was, and how fragile a barrier there was between her and that horrid drop.

There was a splash. Anna, Bryce's daughter, was building a little wall of pebbles in the fountain. She looked up at Diana. "Hello."

Diana stood. "Hello. Anna, is it? Are you out here on your own?"

The child cocked her head on one side. "Mama went in to get a hat."

Diana suppressed a shudder. Bad enough being out here as an adult. To leave a child where she could clamber over the parapet and fall was just irresponsible. "Perhaps you ought to go in too?"

Anna shook her head. "Daddy is cross today. I wanted to play with my Barbies but he said I was making too much noise, so I had to come out here."

"Look at that smoke! I don't know what's on fire, but it must be huge!" Garrick was not paying attention. He was leaning over the edge, looking out over the city.

Diana shivered, though it was hot. "Please don't lean over the railings, Garrick. It's not safe."

"What are you talking about? It's fine." Garrick grabbed her arm and pulled her to her feet, steering her right to the edge. "There, see? The smoke's coming this way real fast. It doesn't look right." Diana strained away from the edge, but he put an arm around her shoulders and pulled her closer. "What are you, six? I bet the little girl here has no problems standing close to the edge, do you missy?"

Anna smirked. "No. It's just railings."

Diana could hardly hear past the buzzing in her ears. She was stiff as a board, unable to get further away from the roaring void below her. Garrick was holding her off-balance, but he was all that was between her and a thirty-five floor drop to an agonizing death. Her chest was so tight she could barely breathe.

"What's that?" Anna turned to look as something buzzed past her head.

Garrick recoiled from the parapet. "Hell no!" He let go of Diana and backed toward the apartment.

Diana stumbled backward from the edge, hit her bad foot on something and fell back to the floor, banging her head. Everything went white and she lay limp, her heart pounding in her chest and her palms sweaty. After a few thundering heartbeats, her vision faded back in. She sat up. She was terrified to go back along the narrow balcony into her own apartment, but she was more afraid of being up here with the fall whispering to her.

Something else dropped to the ground by her head, buzzing. Anna skipped over to look. "It's a bug. My friend Lucia is afraid of bugs. This one is really big. I'm going to call him Harold."

Diana's heart skipped a beat. *A bug?* She scrambled to her feet. "Anna, that's a cicada. Back away from it, quick."

Anna glared at her. "You can't tell me what to do." The buzzing got louder, and more cicadas zipped past. One fell in the water fountain. "Oh no, that one's drowning. Quick, we have to help him!"

Before Diana could move, Anna reached in and picked up the cicada, then screamed and dropped it.

Bryce appeared at the door. "Anna? What—?" He saw Diana. "What the hell are you doing to my daughter?"

"Cicadas!" Diana panted.

"Quick! The swarm's coming across the city!" Garrick reappeared, dashing across the roof garden to sweep up the shrieking child whose hand was puffing up already.

Diana limped after them. "Get inside and close the doors and windows."

Selena hurried out onto the roof, scowling and hissing. "What did you do to her?"

"It's an oily residue. Wash it off with soap and water, quick as you can," Diana urged. "Quickly, dammit!"

Bryce handed the child to Garrick who hurried after Selena. Then he stepped forward, almost nose to nose with Diana. "If she is seriously injured, I will make your life a misery, until the day you die. Get out. You will not be allowed out of the apartment unless you are accompanied. You're not welcome here."

"I couldn't stop her." Diana passed a hand over her face. "I may be able to neutralize the toxin. I'll start now." She waited for him to step out of the way so she could go inside, but he didn't.

"What part of 'You are not welcome here' was unclear?" He pushed her back a step so he could shut the door. "Go back to your own rooms. You're not setting foot in here." As the buzzing intensified outside, he turned the key in the lock, put it in his pocket and walked away without a second glance.

He had locked her out. Diana was stranded on the precarious roof garden, with an unthinkable drop on all sides and the oncoming swarm blackening the sky, like Death coming for her.

CHAPTER TWENTY

CLAIRE MOONE. CHARNOCK RICHARD, M6, LANCASHIRE, ENGLAND

There was a vibration on Claire's right thigh. Reaching into the pocket, she extracted her personal cell phone, amazed it still had service. She'd missed three calls and there was a text saying she'd received a voicemail. She activated the screen. She didn't recognize the number, but it was the same one for all three calls. Whoever it was, they knew her private number, so it belonged to her closest circle of contacts. That, or it was a consistent misdial by someone panicking. Either way, she selected to go to her voicemail.

First message: "Hi. Not got much time." She recognized the voice. "It's Frobisher." She'd known him far too long to know he wouldn't just be calling to say hello, if he didn't have time to talk. "I've been hired to deliver an unusual cargo. There's a company moving some of those cicadas from the US to other parts of the world. Taking some to Africa. Couldn't call sooner, as not much signal at sea. Some went missing. I've been able to trace one ship. It's heading to the Port of Liverpool Deep Sea Terminal. You got that? Don't let them dock or land their cargo. Keep them off the coast."

She'd heard there were massive swarms of cicadas in the States and Australia, but they weren't native to the UK, so she'd seen no immediate threat. "The ship is called *Maid of Morning*. It's Chinese registered and in international waters. That's all I've got for you. Good luck finding it. Stay safe."

She pressed repeat and gave the handset to her father. "I have something you need to hear." As he listened to it, his mood changed. Processing the information transformed him. When he handed the phone back to her, he *was* Artemis. "Action it. Do as you must."

"Yes, sir." Her thoughts were as clear as she expected his to be. "Nerd, the nearest airbase is RAF Woodvale. See what they've got that can be fueled and ready to go, by the time we get there. See what you can get on the *Maid of Morning*."

As they rolled out, Artemis voiced his thoughts. "The idea of a cicada swarm on home soil is not one I've spent time thinking about. Our physical geography, being an island state, protects us from such things. These insects are being transported on purpose. They're being weaponized."

From what Ron Frobisher had said, her father was perhaps being over-dramatic. *Some* of the insects were on a boat, far out at sea. They were being transported for unknown reasons, yet Artemis had to see it as being purposeful, threatening, and a weapon. She had to see things with a more pragmatic view; stop ship at sea. Problem solved.

Claire could either use the radio to contact Command, or she could use her phone to call the only person she ever answered to. Intercepted, an uncoded broadcast to either could cause a political incident with China. She would have to keep details to a minimum, until she had access to a secure connection.

She knew the phone number by heart. She made the call to *Charlemagne*. Inhaling, she settled her nerves with each ring of the call. His voice was calm and clear, which helped. "Hello, Freya. What do you need to tell me?"

"Sir, we will be delayed delivering Artemis. A very pressing matter has come to our attention. It requires our immediate and thorough response." She hoped that was enough for him, for now.

"Very well. Give him my regards and Godspeed with the matter at hand." The line clicked and went silent.

Looking around at Artemis, she could see his scowl and darkened eyes. "Dad, the PM sends his regards."

Distracted, he didn't seem to be too concerned with the kind wishes. "Yes. Fine."

They headed east, toward the coast and the ominous clouds of smoke. The roads were busy, but traffic was heading in the opposite direction. Mickey concentrated on the road, watching the car ahead, pushing hard around the curves and corners. "If we keep going at this pace, we'll be at Woodvale by the time the RAF get a helicopter up and over to us."

Nerd's voice came through the speaker. "They've a C-130 Hercules on standby. It will be fully fueled for us. Told them we're on a coastal survey."

"Good man. What else?"

"Nothing on the boat, boss. Still trying."

The Hercules would give them a platform from which they could skydive, with enough fuel to patrol for several hours. They would have to find the ship, track it, and wait for it to be under British maritime jurisdiction. Anything else could be considered 'piracy on the high seas,' according to the Admiralty. Wars had been started with less of a spark. As far as Claire was concerned, if they stopped the ship before it became a threat to the nation, it didn't matter who the thing belonged to or where it was floating.

In the back seat, Artemis unclipped his seatbelt. Claire knew the sound and turned to get a clear view. Spry for his age, he twisted his body and climbed onto the seat. He knelt facing the rear, leaned over the back of the seat and began tugging something.

Claire was alarmed as the course of their vehicle changed and he was thrown from side to side. "What are you doing, Dad?"

"Just getting..." They bounced on a pothole in the road. With clear relief, he dropped back into his seat. "... Got my phone."

"You could have said; we'd have stopped. Or you could've used mine."

"We've important things to do. No time to stop." He clicked the seatbelt back into place. "Charles Grey's number is in my phone. I must speak with him, to get things in motion."

Claire's pitch rose. "You're going to speak to Gandalf *now*?" She turned to face forward. "Signal out here might be poor." Not like that would stop him.

She was intrigued to know what the conversation would be, given the new information she'd presented him with.

"Hello, Charlie-boy. Yes. Likely... Hold on." He placed his hand over the phone. "When are we likely to be in Patterdale, Claire?"

There wasn't anything definite she could say. "Depends on when we find this ship and what it's carrying. Could be a couple of days."

"We should be there tomorrow, Charlie. How about you? Ah. Make sure you stock up. It was supposed to be a level three scenario. Yes. I know. Were you updated about this ship Claire has been told about? Good. Devastating. Level two. Yes. If we're lucky. Can we liaise with the US? They've had these insects for generations. The CDC must have something by now. Good. I'll leave that with you, Charlie. No. Tomorrow. Bye for now."

For all that she'd heard them speak often, it was the first time she'd heard them discuss *Lazarus* business. Only they understood the difference between Level Three and Level Two. If decrementing meant worsening, that left one level. The entire situation was more dire than she thought. There was no indication of such severity in the public announcements that had been made by the Government.

"Boss?" It was Nerd.

"Go ahead."

"We've got the *Maid of Morning*. She's in UK coastal waters, twelve miles north off The Great Orme, Llandudno, heading east."

That was some good news, at least. "Good work."

"More, boss. The vessel is not communicating. It's on course to dock at Liverpool, but the Coast Guard has not been able to contact the crew."

"They've gone dark? That's a concern. We need that Hercules on a runway with the bay open. It has to take off when we roll onboard."

"I've checked the map of the airbase." Nerd understood the possible take-off scenarios. "It's going to be on runway two-six. The weather is currently fine, but there's a storm moving quickly over Anglesey."

Her mind went quiet. "Have them set up Forward Ops at the Coast Guard station on Crosby Beach. Artemis will require an armed escort. We'll leave him with the RAF. Have them arrange a secure vehicle."

The theoretical twenty-minute drive was not without incident. Cars pulled out from sideroads, desperate to join the stream of traffic leaving the coast. On the narrow rural roads, the unpredictability of panicked families made progress slow, halving their speed, doubling their journey time.

Frustrations were at their most obvious when a Ford Transit van drove head on at the team's lead car, on the wrong side of the road. When the Range Rover did not yield, the driver blared his horn and flashed his lights, as though it gave him some right of way. The two vehicles came to a standstill. They were no more than a yard apart.

A tall, muscular man in his thirties threw the driver's door of the van wide open. He jumped out then leaned deep into the cab, from where he retrieved an alloy baseball bat. He was clear. He wanted the SUV out of his way.

Keen to keep moving, Claire prompted, "Grouse. Use the blues."

"I've got this, boss." Trigger shoved the door open, swung his legs and got out. Slamming it shut, he strode forward, blocking the advance of the menacing thug. They were the same height, but the soldier looked to be the less bulky of the two. The van driver grasped the bat in both hands and took a swing as his target came into range.

Trigger took a step forward, into the path of his assailant and spun around, pushing his back into the guy's chest. Raising his arm, he put it between both elbows of his would-be assailant, avoiding any impact and controlling all movement. With a twist and a bump, the metal weapon was released, and the larger of the two men tumbled to the ground.

Trigger towered over the supine bully-boy. Although his words were not clear, the ferocity of his shouting had the man recoiling. The guy scrambled to his feet and scurried back to his vehicle.

Trigger returned to his seat by Grouse, carrying the baseball bat. The van sped backward, turning hard onto the sidewalk along the lane, ensuring there was enough space for the SUVs to go past. Before pulling forward, someone in the lead car turned their blue flashing lights on. The convoy of three hurried on, using their pseudo-police authority to move through yielding cars at the junction that took them onto the Formby Bypass. The highway was just as busy as the smaller roads. Driving along the wide sidewalk and cycle path at the side of the four-lane highway, they sped to the entrance of the airbase.

An armed guard stopped them at the security barrier. Wearing his RAF blue-grey wool tunic, the guard stood forward to halt the lead car, weapon at the ready. A second guard moved to the driver's side of the Range Rover, where Grouse wound down his window. They exchanged words, before the guard retreated to a security hut.

"Don't. Just don't. Just get on with it." Claire blew through pursed lips as the barrier went up.

Grouse drove far enough into the compound for all three of the SUVs to get inside, before he waited for instructions. There were no immediate ground markers for runways, but they couldn't miss the huge C-130, it's belly deep and the wings low to the ground.

"Car one and three, get aboard." Claire scanned the flat expanse of land beyond the hangars and the control tower. Putting the microphone down, her tone softened. "Follow them in, Mickey. We're not driving onto the Herc until Artemis is secure."

The plane's four powerful Rolls-Royce T406 turboshaft engines droned at idle. Four more RAF guardsmen stood to the side of the rear loading ramp as the first two SUVs rumbled up. Claire got out and had to shout to be heard. "Where's the transport for Artemis?"

Their sergeant answered. "We've got an FV432, over there, ready to go."

An armored personnel carrier complete with caterpillar tracks was not what she had in mind. "You can take the Range Rover. Keep him in it. Keep him safe. He is the most important VIP you've ever had to guard. Do not doubt this."

"Yes, Major." He saluted. "We've been briefed."

She was happy enough he understood that, even if she, her team or any SAS unit, never used rank or acknowledged an officer. "We'll have to take *all* our gear out of the back."

Nerd and Plank ran down the ramp. "Need help, boss?"

Opening the rear of the SUV, she spoke to her father. "These guys will guard you. You're going to the FOP." She clipped her weapons to her belt and webbing, with practiced ease.

"Yes, my girl. Be safe. I'll see you after your jaunt." He turned and walked away. No kiss. No hug. No sentimental goodbye. Just a smile and that tone that said, 'I know you've got this under control.'

Submachine gun in hand, backpack on and shouldering her parachute, she marched onto the transport plane, side by side with her men. *Jaunt?* She was surprised how quaint he could make a blind operation sound.

She stowed her gear and strapped in, giving a thumbs-up to the flight crew. Green lights turned red. There was a rumble from the rear, as the ramp rose to close. Before it was shut tight, the buildings of the airfield slipped by. There was a hiss from the hydraulics as the flight deck was sealed, then only the vibration and noise of the engines being throttled up.

When the plane levelled out and the 'fasten seatbelt' sign was no longer illuminated, Claire moved to the rear of the car in which Nerd had been travelling. "What have you got for me?"

He moved to the side, showing her a 3D render of the *Maid of Morning*. "Got the blueprints and schematics from Lloyds. She's a decent size. There's a quick briefing about the bugs."

"Great. Yes. Looks like one of our favorite scenarios." The rest of the team gathered around her. "We're going in fast. Daytime HALO. Stick with our pairings. Grouse and Trigger to the bow, landing here. Clear the hold and take engineering." She tapped the screen with her index finger. "Plank and Nerd amidships for the crew quarters. Me and Mickey at the stern. We'll go for the bridge. We know these *cicada* things are ridiculously toxic. Be careful when making any contact."

"Any questions?" She was pleased there were none. "This is a hostile situation. Expect resistance. We do not know how many enemy combatants there will be, but the crew will all be of fighting age. Be sure of your shot if you have to take it. Gather as much intel as you can." Clapping her hands together, she marked the moment as she always did. "*Allons-y!*"

She checked the seating of both filters on her Avon M50, pulled her bangs from her forehead, then pulled the rubber straps tight over her head. Standing beside Mickey, she raised her hand, made a fist high above her head, then stuck out her thumb.

Amber lights flashed around them; the rear ramp opened. Red lights went to green and she walked off the edge of the platform and began her descent.

There was no way to know what awaited her team. The *Maid of Morning* took shape below her. The container ship had been running silent for hours. It was either aggressive and bold, or arrogant and stupid. Freefalling at one hundred and twenty miles an hour, she would discover which, within sixty seconds.

CHAPTER TWENTY-ONE

DR DIANA STEWART. MATREUS HQ, CHICAGO, ILLINOIS

Diana stared out across the roof garden, the cheerful colors of the flowers bright against the dark cloud of cicadas surging toward her. Pulling her jacket off, she made a hood of it and dashed across to the opposite wall, dodging the buzzing, bumbling creatures that were already starting to strip the bushes and plants of their foliage. Her breath was coming in short gasps and she could hardly take air in through the thick material of the jacket she clutched around her, but she couldn't tell how much was panic and how much the toxin they gave off.

She was brought to a stop by the sight of the narrow little balcony to the guest apartment. Safety was not far but it might have been a hundred miles away. Garrick had made her look down thirty-five dizzying stories to the tiny plaza below and she couldn't unsee the abyss just a brick's thickness away. It made her dizzy and afraid. She tried to make herself move forward, but her feet were frozen to the ground.

The buzz was louder now, almost deafening and she couldn't possibly survive out on the roof in the middle of a swarm. There was no one to help her get through it though: she would have to cheer herself on. It wouldn't be the first time.

"You have to get inside, dammit!" she muttered. She turned her back resolutely to the drop and closed her eyes, clutching at the sun-warmed roughness of the wall in front of her and trying to blank out the staggering fall that yawned behind. It helped, a little, and she shuffled, one terrified inch at a time, toward the door into her apartment.

"Heck!" Something bounced off the hand clutching her jacket over her head. She cried out, as the skin of her knuckles began to itch and then burn. But she'd taken an unwary breath, and her cry tangled into a cough immediately. Her ribs screamed in agony, adding to her fear; if her rib re-fractured enough to puncture a lung she was dead.

For a moment it was all too much, and she just wanted it to stop. "Don't you dare, you coward!" But a traitorous thought whispered that if she gave in to the dreadful allure of the edge and let herself pitch headlong over the side of the building, it would only be a few seconds of terror and then she would find oblivion. What did it matter whether she lived or died? Jesse and Sam were gone, and Jane likely burned to death in the fire; there was little else that mattered.

But the pain of the cicada burn was intense. It broke through her paralysis, demanding attention. Her breath caught in her throat, and she bent double, coughing until she could hardly move. If it was the toxin, she'd be in trouble if she didn't get inside. The main part of the swarm was just sweeping over the rooftops and up the side of the building toward her.

Diana forced herself to get moving again and edged further along, concentrating on the pressure of her free hand on the warmth of the wall and the burn of the toxin on her fingers, and breathing so lightly it made her dizzy. "You don't get to... take the easy...way out. You have... a lot of mistakes to ...make right. Starting with Anna—" But with her next step the wall disappeared in front of her and she cried out, and fell... onto carpet.

"Get in here, will you? You of all people know how dangerous those things are." Garrick whipped the door to the balcony shut behind her.

"What? How did you—?" She rolled onto her side and sat up, cradling her injured hand. She limped over to the sink and lathered her hand with detergent, rinsing it off with cold water. It stung like hell and was already starting to blister up.

Garrick shook his head. "Look, I get it. It's hard when you mess things up that badly. I'm doing my best to cover for you here, but it isn't easy. You're supposed to be the expert. But I wouldn't call that keeping people safe. You've gotta be more careful, especially with kids." He stomped on something. "Ugh. Bugs."

"Wait. We need to trap them." She ran-hobbled-hopped to the cupboard, and grabbed a stack of tumblers, upending them onto the cicadas that crawled and blundered drunkenly across the carpet. "I need samples."

"Well, if that isn't you all over." Garrick wiped his boot on the carpet, making no effort to help. "Work lights you up like a candle, when nothing else can. Never mind the rest of us."

"I'm good at what I do." She slammed down the tumblers over two more. Outside, the cicadas pattered and bumped on the windows, but not in such numbers as at the farm. She stored that information away for later when she had time to think about it. "I hope the protesters managed to get inside when the cicadas came. To be stuck outside in the plaza with no protection would be carnage."

"You owe me an apology." He stepped over the tumblers to prod her in the chest. "That went bad, real bad, and even if it hadn't, it would've been embarrassing, walking into their private garden like that. Mr. Bryce wants to keep you locked in your apartment for good, and only let you out under guard!"

"What?"

"He thinks you deliberately let his daughter hurt herself, and it was pretty hard to persuade him it was an accident." Garrick helped himself to another beer from the fridge. "I fixed that, though."

Dismay rose in her chest. "What did you do?"

"I said if he made me your guard, I'd make your life miserable. He agreed."

Diana turned from the sink to hide her smile. It was galling that Bryce wanted her life to be "miserable" but perfect that Garrick was now, officially, her guardian.

"I know, it's not ideal. But I couldn't stand the idea of some stranger being told to keep you in line. I know you, Di; you'd mouth off and get yourself in trouble in the first half hour. I just want to keep you from hurting yourself anymore, and to protect you from Mr. Bryce, and this is all I could think of to help. There is one thing though."

"What's that?" She went to the icebox with a bowl and filled it full of ice, which she piled on a dishcloth. Bundling it into a parcel, she set it against the blisters, and gasped at the pain as it made contact.

"I'm gonna have to act mean to you if there's people about. Don't go getting all sensitive about it; it'll be for show, but if I don't, he'll replace me with someone who'll really hurt you. And Mr. Bryce don't care how they do it." He took a long swig of his beer.

"Right." Diana held the icepack against the back of her hand. The whole situation was surreal, but with Garrick in her corner—bossing her about, mouthing off, being faux-mean—she might have enough cover to do some real 'scienceing' as he called it. "I'll be back in a moment." She slipped into the bedroom and called down to her lab, two floors below. "Diana Stewart here. I've caught a couple of cicadas and I need some sample boxes. Can you have someone send them up please? Thanks."

Garrick came into the bedroom as she straightened. "This place is very fancy. A TV that big, you could see every last person in the stands in a hockey game. Have you tried it?"

"Just static. The signal's out."

He moved up close behind her and reached up to massage her

shoulders, and the back of her neck. "You need to relax a little, hon. Your shoulders are tight as piano wire."

A smile curled her lips unbidden as his hands moved on her back. She stood, eyes closed while he worked on her shoulders. It was one thing he'd always been good at. She wasn't sure she was happy to have him in her bedroom, but as his fingers smoothed her muscles and unknotted all the kinks in her tired, tight spine, everything apart from the pain of her hand faded into the background

When his lips brushed the back of her neck, she nearly dropped the ice pack on the floor, and a thrill of fear and need ran through her. It had been so long since she had been with someone. She'd allowed her work to take over her entire life, and it had been a sterile, lonely existence. The need for physical intimacy hit her like a sledgehammer. But it wasn't going to happen with Garrick; *never again with Garrick.* She turned away, trembling, as he slid his arms around her waist. She tried to pull away; he did not loosen his grip.

But to her immense relief, the door intercom buzzed. "Dr. Stewart? It's Andrew. I have your sample boxes out here."

"Thanks Andrew." Garrick let her step away and she hurried to answer the door. "The cicadas are under those tumblers. Could you box them up for me please?"

"Sure." The intern took a pair of tweezers from his pocket. "What would you like me to do with them?"

"Can you prep a lab on floor twelve?" Diana shifted the icepack on her hand. "One of Mr. Bryce's staff will need mine. I'll be down shortly."

"Yes ma'am." The intern bustled off.

Garrick lingered in the bedroom door. "They can spare you for a half hour or so, surely?"

"They probably could but..." She searched for an excuse to get out of there, then showed him her blistered fingers. "It's getting worse. I don't know if the toxin has been absorbed into the skin or if it would rub off and blister you, but I don't think you'd enjoy finding out."

He scowled. "Guess we're going to the lab then."

Bullet dodged. By the time she had got to the lab, all four of her fingers had swollen to the size of hotdogs. Garrick left her there and wandered off to the cafeteria to find something to drink. Diana called Patti, who brought down a selection of treatments.

Patti bustled in with a bag, set it on the table, and started to pull bottles and jars from it. "I have an antihistamine cream in case it reduces the swelling, a painkiller to ease the pain, calamine lotion, Aquaphor, you name it. I've checked in on Miss Matreus and her hand is a mess. For now I've given her painkillers and an antihistamine, but if we can find anything better, now's the time for it."

Diana picked up a ball point pen. "Well, it's on four of my fingers. That gives us four test sites. I've washed them all with dish soap and water, and hopefully Bryce washed off Anna's hands too. Choose your top four treatments and let's see how it goes."

The process of painting the ointments onto her cicada-burns was painful enough to make Diana's head swim, but Patti was calm and steady.

Then Diana wrote on each of her fingers. "Antihistamine cream here, calamine on this one, aloe vera; and this is the one we washed with alcohol. There's some ice in the freezer."

"Let me put on a membrane, to make sure it doesn't burst." Patti opened a paper packet and peeled the backing off a clear film which she stuck over the blister. She rummaged in the fridge for ice, and put it in the samples bag Diana had set on the table. "Now, I need to go check in on some of the others."

"The others?"

"A couple of the guards. I dread to think what happened to the protesters. There was no cover out there, and we're not allowed to bring them inside." The lights flickered, and then steadied again.

"Generator on again? That's pretty long for a brownout isn't it?"

Patti shook her head. "The electricity never came back on. We've been running on generators for a while now. So long as the pipeline is running we'll be fine but Dr Evans was saying that the pipeline is dependent on the pumps running, so if the electricity goes down over a wider area things might go downhill fast. As for what's happening beyond these walls... well, I only know what the gateline staff have told me but it's not pretty. Even in here they're talking about cutting down on food portions if the city doesn't sort itself out soon. There's no food to be found and people are desperate. Things are getting dangerous."

Diana went to the window, trying to see out across the city but her view was blocked by the other buildings. They were past 'dangerous' and well into 'hazardous' territory.

"Why do you think the Matreus boys stay thirty-five stories up, hey? So they don't have to have any idea of what's going on outside." Patti packed up her bag. "Sit in the cafeteria and listen to the stories, Doc. It's gone bad outside, very bad. It's a good time to be in here. They called out the National Guard yesterday to enforce a curfew, but only half of them showed. It's been an eye-opener to see the city fall to pieces in such a short time. And that was before the cicadas. What's happening out there right now doesn't bear thinking about."

On one of the lower roofs there was a movement: a group of youths were scattered about, several lying sprawled in unnatural positions. One boy was pulling himself along toward a second who was lying motionless in a pool of blood, and a third was kneeling next to him, pulling the dead man to him in a hug. She peered downwards, trying to look down to the plaza but couldn't see the ground.

Patti put her bag strap over her shoulder. "If it gets too bad out there, it'll get difficult in here. At least here we have running water, power, AC. Who knows what it's like in the city. Of course they all want to be in here, with the luxuries we've got. And if something happens and they break through the barricades...." She whistled. "There's a reason I'm working to keep the gateline guards patched up, and only part of it is because it's my job. Now, keep an eye on that hand of yours, and the minute any of those creams looks like its making a difference, you let me know?"

Garrick wandered back, beer in hand, as Patti left. "What are you doing?" He reached over her shoulder and picked up a flask, lifting it to look at the label. "What's this stuff?"

"Careful!" She jumped backward from it. "Put that down, gently!"

"Why, what's it gonna do?" He grinned, sloshing the liquid around. "Explode?"

She backed away further. "It's hydrochloric acid. It will dissolve your face right off your bones."

Garrick set it down carefully and backed away. "Why would you even want to mess with stuff like that? No, don't answer me; I don't care. I'm not sitting around here for hours on end watching you mixing up death juice. They've got last season's hockey on the TV in the cafeteria. I'm going back to watch that. Call them when you want to leave. They'll give me a yell." He left the empty can on the side of the sink and left.

Diana set the flask back on the shelf, turning it so the label, 'Distilled water' was at the front. *Small pleasures.* Then she got on with her analyses of the creams on her fingers.

It took a few hours to make any difference, and Diana wanted to know more than just how to treat the cicada burns. She analyzed each lotion for its active ingredients, and noted them, starting a pictorial record of her blistered fingers with the webcam on her computer, each picture marked with the time. She filtered out the active ingredients of each of the creams Patti had left her and added them to one solution. She thickened it up to a smooth consistency so it could be smeared on. Then she left it to cool.

She took a basic barrier cream, smeared some on her forearm. Then she took a pair of tweezers and extracted a live cicada from its box. "I don't think either of us are going to enjoy this," she told it, "but one of your lot just injured a little girl on my watch, and I need to know what eases the burning best. This is going to be the quickest way."

The insect creaked and chirped, wriggling so she nearly dropped it. She swabbed it with a Q Tip before replacing it in the sample box. Then she smeared the toxin on her arm, gritting her teeth against the pain. She made two stripes on her bare skin, and another over the barrier cream. Two angry red stripes came up at once on her unmedicated skin, but the barrier cream seemed to block the effects of the third stripe of toxin.

She waited for a few minutes for the reaction to develop. It was excruciating, but science required sacrifices and she was ready to make them. She washed off the barrier cream and one of the other stripes of toxin with detergent, and the last stripe with a solution of alcohol, and let them dry naturally. Finally she smeared some of her ointment over half of the two remaining stripes, leaving the other half of each free as a control patch.

The ointment didn't ease the stinging much: but after another hour, the half of the cicada burn that had the ointment on it was considerably less raised and painful than the half that had had no cream on at all, and it was free of blisters. The alcohol seemed to have washed off more of the toxin than the detergent, but both were considerably better than not washing it off at all, and Diana's ointment seemed to make far more of a difference than any of the individual cures.

It was only a start, but it was a promising one, and given that it had ameliorated her own burns with no apparent ill-effects, it was time to bring Anna some relief too.

Of course there was no sign of Garrick. When he got watching the hockey—even on repeat, even if he'd seen the same game a hundred times—he'd be there for hours, especially if he had beer and a few likeminded fans to argue with. However, Diana had no intention of hanging around while he finished his beer, his argument, or more likely, whatever match was playing. Anna was in pain.

She left Garrick to his sports bonanza, took her ointment to the penthouse, and asked the security guard to take a message in to Victor.

He hurried to the door. "Di, what are you doing here?"

She explained briefly, showing Victor the markings on her arm. "I wanted to make sure Anna got the chance to try the cream if you and Bryce are happy with that level of testing—"

He took the flask. "Thank you. I'll try it on her now."

Diana leaned back against the wall. She was exhausted, and her own apartment was on the opposite side of the lobby. She wanted to go back and sleep, but she needed some reassurance that the cream was helping the little girl. Then high-pitched shrieks sounded.

Bryce shouted "What are you doing? Get that stuff off her. It's hurting her!"

Victor started speaking but Bryce cut through again. "You did what?? ...I'll deal with you later. Where is that witch now?"

Diana hurried toward her apartment, but as she reached the lobby door it slammed open and Garrick strode in, his face like thunder. "Thought you could sneak away from me, did you?" He grabbed her arm and twisted it painfully, and that was how Bryce found them when he erupted from the family apartment.

CHAPTER TWENTY-TWO

CLAIRE MOONE. IRISH SEA, 12 MILES NORTH OF PRESTATYN, NORTH WALES

With her crew all down safely, Mickey covering her, and her first round loaded, Claire commenced with the dangerous part of their mission. She slipped over the side of the steel roof of the ship, found purchase with her feet, then dropped to a crouch on the walkway at the side of the superstructure. Raising the MP5 to look down the sight, she checked forward, to her rear, then over the side to the deck below. There was no crew activity. Nobody had seen them coming. In silence, her partner lowered his body to her side. She knew he was there, but he put his hand on her shoulder to indicate he was ready to move.

Crouched, she edged around a corner, bobbed her head out and peeked. It was clear for them to go to the door of the ship's bridge. She moved beyond it to look in through a side window. There were two men in dark blue fatigues inside at the control desks – one at

Primary Navigation and the other beyond him at Radar. Slumped over their consoles, they didn't move.

That was when Trigger called over their short-range radio "Bodies. Three dead crew on the bow."

Plank reported the same. "Two dead, midships. No sign of weapons fire. No wounds, but blood from their noses and mouths."

Nerd added, "Looks like they were trying to get in a lifeboat, trying to get off the ship."

Claire was on the hinge side of the door and Mickey had the firing angles. Concentrating, she turned the wheel of the locking mechanism until it could go no further, then leaned back to use her bodyweight to move the bulk of the oval door.

Mickey moved through the portal, she followed. He went right and to the rear of the room, so she went forward and left.

The two crew she'd seen were dead. On the floor, in the middle of the control room, she saw the polished boots and well-ironed trousers of a uniform. It was an officer.

"I've got the captain over here, boss." Mickey pointed his gun downward and twitched the muzzle. "Dead."

"Engineering, secure." Not a shot had been fired and the first report was in. "The engines are at one-quarter speed. No crew alive. Several bodies. Blistered skin."

"Crew quarters secure." Both teams had reached their goals. "They're all dead. Same. Blotchy skin."

Claire added. "Bridge secure." To make it clear they had control of the ship. "Search for any live crew. Assume there's an active pathogen. Don't make physical contact."

"Too late. I just rolled him over." Mickey was squatting at the side of the captain's body. With a gloved hand, he'd searched the cadaver's pockets and unclipped a set of dangling keys. "His face is just a mass of lesions and puss. His hands, too. Something's infected them all."

"It's hard to say how long they've been dead, just by looking at them." She took a deep breath, reassuring herself nothing was getting through her filtered respirator. "I'm glad we're wearing masks. The stench must be terrible."

Mickey offered to toss the keys to her. She declined. "You can keep hold of them. You've already touched them." She wasn't being squeamish. It was a practical choice. There was a pathogen. She had no idea how it had been transmitted to the crew, even the ones on deck. "You know the drill."

"Yeah. I'm the guinea pig." Behind the visor of his mask, he raised his eyebrows. "Anything happens, if I feel sick or disorientated, I'll tell you."

They descended a metal staircase, going a floor lower in the accommodation block. A door at the rear took them into the captain's ready room. They could have been stepping into an accountant's office from the 1950s, were it not for the round windows, the charting table, and picture frames displaying knots of all kinds.

The captain's diary lay open on the broad wooden desk. She grabbed it by the corner, spun it around and read the date. "Last entry was two days ago. The crew were nearly all dead. Officers and the day watch were alright." She flipped back a page. "Some sort of outbreak. Anyone infected should have isolated, but they were running scared."

She ran her finger down the lines then moved it in a diagonal over to the previous day's entry and continued to scan the writing. "They got an instruction to move the insects from where they were stored. Some guy called Marsalis was responsible for them. He was supposed to put them in a container. He opened the container too soon and died. The cicadas escaped. They tried to catch them, but the things flew into the ventilation system."

Mickey was caught between the horrific deaths they were discovering and a dark admiration for nature. "Cicadas? Plural?"

"Apparently." Reading the more recent entries again, she was concerned. "They didn't see a correlation between the insects and the sickness."

"So, one guy dies after opening a box with some cicadas in it." Mickey began trying keys in the filing cabinet. "They escape and people start dying, but they don't think the insects are the problem?"

Claire hadn't finished reading the page filled with notes. "Some of the crew went down with respiratory failure, which made it seem like they'd been exposed to a chemical spill. Those who attended them didn't have problems breathing. But the ones up top got it from stuff they touched or were handed—their skin blistered, then they died. Secondary contact."

"Have we altered course?" It was Plank. "We've got a problem."

Claire returned to the Bridge. Hard rain hissed on the glass of the windows, cutting down visibility. Evening was falling. She could pick out the lights of the ship and those of the coast. Looking to her left, fires were the brightest thing she could observe through the oncoming storm.

The Radar console was beeping and pinging. She couldn't see what the alarms meant, because of the dead sailor slumped over the screen. She put a boot against the corpse's hip and eased him off the chair. Mickey was right behind her and took care of the second crewman at Navigation, forcing him to the floor with his crewmate.

Beneath the smears of bloody discharge streaked down the controls of the panel, a pattern appeared every time the radar beam passed around the circular screen. It was a regular shape, five connected diamonds made by three rows of dots – five, six and five. Each time the light on the screen passed the cluster, the pinging happened.

Plank called out, before opening the external door to the control room. "Friendlies incoming."

Nerd raised his arm, pointing a finger through the front window. "We're heading straight for that coastal wind farm." That made sense of the shapes she'd seen. "We're right on top of it. We're going straight through it."

Another shout came, before the last two members of the team joined them. "They've set the autopilot. It'll be coded and locked in." Mickey was joined by Grouse. The former Special Boat Service man, he knew his way around things that sailed. "This storm's pushing the ship and it's not been set to compensate. I can see about overriding things in Engineering."

The console showed their projected path at current speed. "Get to it, both of you." They had less than ten minutes to alter course. "Did we find any surviving crew?" The answers were negative. All the crew were accounted for. All were dead. "Don't touch anything you don't have to when you're down there. If you've got gloves, put them on."

Each member of the team had a sharp mind and a complimentary set of skills. Nerd was the most adept at electronics and communication. He would put himself into that role, whenever it was required. "Want me in the Radio Room, boss? It's all working. Only one dead guy in there."

She nodded. "Let Control know what we've encountered. We'll want the Coast Guard and RIB support. We're not getting airlifted in these conditions."

Dragging a map across the charting table, she found their general position. She wasn't interested in the coast or their bearing. Contours showed the depth of water. The rows of turbine blades that made up the windfarm were visible, sitting on an underwater shelf. "Mickey! Drop the anchors!"

He moved from one set of controls to another. "They're on either side. I can drop the portside from here. If you want all of them, do starboard over there, too."

"Hold, while I check with Grouse." She put her hand to her neck, to activate her throat mike. "How are we doing with the engines? We're ready with the anchors."

"Just got here. Will... shutting them down... as I find... overrides." The Scot's voice crackled as the signal broke up. "Whatever... don't... wait... drop... anchors."

"Dropping the portside anchors." Mickey pressed the big button on the panel marked 'Release.'

Yellow lights flashed at the bow. Seconds turned into minutes. Nothing happened.

The winch motors of the elevator at the back of the bridge whined into service, startling Claire. There shouldn't be anyone taking the elevator, but the panel of lights for each floor showed activity. Claire signaled Mickey to cover from the port wing. She remained central, giving her an immediate kill shot. The elevator arrived with a ping. The doors opened with the thinnest crack. "Friendlies incoming." They hadn't used it to go down, so they retained the element of surprise.

"Hi, boss." Trigger was first through the door. First to see the muzzle of the weapon pointed at him. "It was quicker than taking the stairs. There's a lot of stairs."

Claire lowered her weapon. "Assholes."

Grouse grinned and saluted. "Sorry, boss. Didn't mean to give you a heart attack."

"Report?"

"We had to shift a few bodies down there, but we got control of the engines. I put them in 'Stop.' We'll drift until I change course on the autopilot, but it's integrated with the ECDIS, so it shouldn't be a problem."

"It's okay." Mickey gestured at the console. "We dropped the bow anchor on this side."

The Scotsman took fast paced strides across the space between the door and the control panel. "I said don't drop the anchor. When did you—"

The ship lurched sideways, the hull groaning under the immense pressure. In a violent twist the entire accommodation housing shook, throwing them all off their feet. Waves rose high, cascading over the entire vessel, swamping the open deck and washing bodies into the sea.

Shouting came over their headsets. "What the hell's going on? We've just been smashed against the walls down here."

"Are you both alright, Plank?" Claire pulled herself up on the nearest piece of equipment, steadying her stance to allow for the spin of the ship.

"Yeah, boss. A bit bruised. Nerd's been on to Command. They're sending boats." There was a muffled conversation she couldn't quite make out. "They're asking what's happened. We've suddenly changed course and they're wondering why."

The slewing stopped. "I've raised the anchor, again. Don't drop them in deep water in a storm." Grouse stepped around the portside control module, over the festering body of the crewman who had been at Navigation and took his empty seat. "We need the engines to slow down before we hit the windfarm. It put us side on to the storm, which increased our drift toward the turbines. We'd have been alright anchoring, but not while we're still moving."

Striking a button on the console, he took control of the ship's course. As the waves calmed, so did Claire's mind. The toxin was from the cicadas. There was enough evidence of that danger from the US. They'd wiped out the entire crew in a matter of days.

"I want the shipping manifest and the location of the guy who had the bugs. We've got to bag as much evidence as we can." She was putting them all in peril, but she led the way down the stairs. "Keep at it, Grouse."

There were as many containers lining the hold as there were on the deck above, in the storm. "Find me Marsalis. He was the one handling the insects."

The team split up, weapons no longer drawn, to check each of the crew. They were not difficult to identify, with their pictures and names on a card around their necks or clipped to their clothing.

The confines of the narrow walkways were maze-like. When Trigger found the corpse they wanted, he radioed but he couldn't give a precise location, so he back-tracked to meet her and took her to it.

Talking to the dead man, she asked a question he couldn't answer for her. "Which were you going to?" She surveyed the owner details and container numbers. All the doors were still sealed, their security tags unbroken. Except one. Lifting her phone from her pocket, she took a picture of it. "We're *not* opening it."

A static hiss came from her earpiece. A voice garbled something she couldn't decipher. Trigger tapped the side of his head, as if to clear the sound. They were too deep inside the hold, surrounded by metal that inhibited the signal. Running, they found a set of ladders that would take them to the upper decks.

Between floors, she could see along the corridor that ran the length of the vessel. Inertia dragged her boots away from the rungs. Her reflexes tensed her hands to grip hard, as she was pulled forward, off the ladder. She dropped, aware that Trigger was below her. She didn't hit him and managed to stay on her feet. The sound of a thousand clanging church bells rang around them. The entire body of the ship groaned. A shockwave rippled toward her, distorting the gangway and walls, until it hit, knocking her to the floor.

Hands grasped the chest plate of her armor, pulling her from the ground and her eyes flew open. "C'mon, boss. Wake up." Trigger steadied her on her feet, pushed her toward the steps and up onto the rungs. "Get going. I'm right behind you."

Flames lit the night. Even as the rain lashed down, the open deck was somehow ablaze. As the two of them emerged from the hold, the mast of a turbine dragged containers past them and off the ship, into the sea.

Claire stood, exposed to the night sky, looking at the ship's bridge. There was nothing they could do in the face of the storm. Wounded, Trigger stumbled at her side. Blood poured from a gash on his neck she hadn't noticed when he'd helped her up. He put his hand to it to stem the flow. "That bloody hurts." She watched his eyes as they darted from place to place. He coughed, as though clearing his throat.

Through the mist of bouncing rain, she saw four shapes running from the accommodation module. She could see her men.

Again, Trigger coughed. His eyes were fixed on hers. "I'm done, boss." There was no appeal or uncertainty. She couldn't imagine what he was feeling, but she believed he knew. "It's like a fever, everywhere." He tore his mask up and off his face, revealing the waxen hue of his skin. Blotches appeared on his cheeks and his lips blistered. When his knees buckled, Grouse put his arms out, making a grab at his partner.

"Don't touch him!" Claire's sharp words made him retract the support he was offering. "He's infected. He's already dead."

Lifeless, the soldier's body slumped backward, slamming against the rail of the stairwell. They watched as he slid over the edge and fell.

"Throw the ladder over the side." She had to keep them safe. "They'll pick us up." She had no way of knowing where the Coast Guard or support boats would be. If they weren't close, her team would suffer the same fate as Trigger and all the ship's crew.

CHAPTER TWENTY-THREE

KIM WALKER. SYDNEY, AUSTRALIA

There was no mistaking the venom in Emma's voice—she hated Kim and wanted nothing to do with her. But walking away from her daughter for a second time could never be an option as far as Kim was concerned. All she had, and all she could cling onto, was the driving need to ensure her kid was safe. Nothing else mattered. And as long as she drew breath, she'd do whatever it took to ensure nothing ever threatened her. At least then she'd have done something right for her little girl.

The washroom door clanged shut with a din that echoed and made Kim wince. She rushed after Emma, who stalked along the wide walkway inside the World Square Shopping Complex with her nose in the air. "Don't go that way."

"Duh...The escalators lead to the main entrance." Emma kept on walking, shopping bags banging against her denim clad legs with each long stride.

"I had a run-in with some man. He pushed me down the steps. He may be waiting there to see if I come back."

"That explains the blood."

Blood. Barry. The woman at the gas station. Luke. The people dying in their cars, in the streets outside the complex. "Slow down, Emma. We need to find a different way out of here and a safe way to get to your apartment."

"Mum will pick me up." Emma shuffled her shopping around and dug into her cross-body leather handbag.

'Me.' Mum will pick ME up. Not us. "Don't bother checking your phone. There's no signal, I've tried multiple times. Is there another exit?"

Emma whirled around, bags swinging out. "What is it with you?"

"There's a full-scale riot going on at the main entrance."

"How did you get inside?"

Did the girl have to debate every single thing she said? "Listen. We need to get out of this place. Now. Any ideas? And you're going to have to ditch that shopping. It will slow us down."

"No way. This is my new outfit for the school dance. And, I've got Mum's birthday present. I'm not ditching any of it." Emma's voice rose with each word.

"Stop yelling. Someone might hear us." Kim swept her flashlight down the long pathway keeping the beam as low as possible to avoid detection. The area was devoid of people, although shouts and the breaking of glass sounded in the distance. And...were those footsteps coming toward them?

"Then stop telling me what to do!"

Heart juddering painfully in her chest, she tilted her head. "Emma. Shush for a moment."

"I don't want you here," screamed Emma. She broke into an awkward run, her shopping bags smacking against her legs as she headed toward the escalators.

Kim raced after her, sucking in the pain from her blistered feet and bruised body. She reached out, grabbed Emma's arm and dragged her to a stop. "We..."

"There she is!" The shout came from a young man with a retro, flattop hairstyle rounding the corner.

Kim had never seen him before in her life but there was no mistaking that gravelly voice filled with pent up violence. She wrenched the shopping bags off Emma, tossing them onto the floor then grabbed her arm. "Run!"

"My shopping!" But Emma didn't pull away from her.

They charged back the way they'd come. Footsteps pounded on the tiles behind them. Louder. Gaining ground.

Kim didn't waste time turning to check. "Which way?"

"I don't know!"

From a side pathway ahead of them, two young men dashed out, fanning across the walkway effectively cutting off their escape. Another figure shifted in a nearby shop's shadowy entrance.

They skidded to a halt. Pushing Emma behind her, Kim whirled to confront Flatop Hair Man. "What do you want with us?"

"The gun."

"What gun?" Kim tried for a bluff.

"So much for keeping me safe," Emma scoffed, but her voice wavered and her fingers brushed Kim's back as she held onto her belt.

"See for yourself. There's no holster."

He backhanded Kim across the face and pain exploded and she saw stars. "Where is it?"

She stumbled, bumping into Emma who squealed and jumped sideways. Spitting blood and gathering her reeling senses, Kim shook her head. "I stole this uniform. There was no gun."

He raised his hand again and she lashed out with the flashlight, smashing it down on his wrist. Bone cracked. He screeched as he yanked the flashlight from her grip with his other hand.

One of his followers grabbed Emma, hauling her around the waist and pulling her backward. The other hesitated as if unsure what to do. Screaming, Emma tried to twist out of his hold while he laughed and groped at her chest with his other hand.

Kim had to get Emma away from them. She shoulder-rammed the leader, causing him to stagger. It was all she needed. But she couldn't pull out the gun now. She was too close. Instead, she whipped off one of her shoes and stabbed the heel into his cheek feeling the slight push-back of bone, then the steel stiletto cut through muscle and tissue.

Blood spurted. He let loose another high-pitched scream and fell back, clutching at his ruined face.

The other young man stepped forward and punched Kim in the belly. Bent over, she gulped for air as she reeled back, swinging her shoe wildly while he danced out of the way and laughed.

"Get lost, Ray. She's mine." Bellowing, Flatop rushed forward, tackling Kim around her ankles and she plunged onto hard concrete. Pain streaked up her tailbone and along her spine.

If he got on top of her it would all be over. He had ten times her strength. Squirming and wriggling, she got one leg free and drove her bare foot into his windpipe. He lost his grip and she army-crawled until she could scrabble onto her feet and lashed out with her stiletto, over and over at his head, his shoulders, his arms. Moaning and blubbering he curled his body on the floor, trying to protect himself with his hands. Breathing hard, she pierced his shoulder with her shoe three more times for good measure. The heel flew off and tumbled onto the floor.

Emma reared her head backward, ramming into the nose of the man holding her. Swearing, he kicked the back of her left knee. She cried out.

Kim pulled the truncheon off her belt and whacked him about the head over and over until his hold on Emma loosened and she broke free. Shrieking and swearing, he brought his hands up to protect his face while Kim kept pounding him.

Emma slammed her booted foot into his groin, yelling, "Loser!" He doubled up, crying.

The young fellow who'd punched Kim backed away, eyes wide, hands in the air while Flattop began to pick himself up off the floor. "You're both crazy."

Kim tossed her battered and bloodied shoes aside. "Worth every dollar. Come on! Run!" She grabbed Emma's hand and together they took off down the dark walkway back toward the escalators and the main entrance.

"Who are they?"

No time to answer.

"Get them!" From behind them came vicious swearing and the slapping of feet over concrete.

Running wasn't going to work. That bozo and his mates would hunt them down until they had possession of the gun and taken revenge on two girls who'd gotten the better of them. She was flagging fast and she hated the wheeze rasping from her daughter's lungs. She tugged Emma to a halt and dropped the truncheon. "To hell with this." She'd been against the use of unnecessary force her whole life—eschewing guns—but this was different. This absolutely fell into the 'necessary' category. Wrestling with her shirt, she dragged out the Glock. Hand wobbling, she aimed in the general direction of the rapidly approaching young men and pulled the trigger. Nothing happened. She tried again. Nothing.

"Seriously? Give me that!" Panting, Emma wrenched the gun from her, chambered a round by pulling back on the slide until it was all the way back and let it go. She took aim, her feet apart, her free hand bracing the arm holding the gun: the stance so smooth and easy it looked instinctive, practiced. Emma fired a shot and the men ducked, diving for the pillars. She must've aimed into the air above the men's heads. They reeled backward, cursing and sending uncertain glances at each other. "One more step and I'll shoot you in the chest."

Muttering they shifted back into the shadows, their footsteps fading. But they were waiting. The only way to escape was forward.

"Let's go. We'll use the escalators and find a way out on the next level." She scooped up the truncheon and set off again. Pain radiated up her legs with each step and blood seeped onto the floor from her bare feet, causing her to slip but she wasn't stopping.

"You're limping."

"As I said before, long day." She tried a shaky smile and a little of her heartache soothed away as Emma gave a nervous giggle.

They took the escalator steps two at a time, to the ground floor, breathing hard, and barely one hundred yards away were the glass doors of the main entrance where a massive crowd of people jostled and fought.

"We made it!" squealed Emma, punching the air, handbag banging against her hips as, she danced on the spot.

Kim grinned. But her smile died as the muffled roar outside grew louder. She whirled from her frantic search for an exit just as the rioters swarmed, breaking through the line of police. They surged over the fallen bodies and attacked the glass doors, snarls twisting their mouths, and weapons in their hands. Under their onslaught, the glass cracked, and an instant later, shattered. The mob flooded inside while great, thick clouds of toxic smoke blasted through the opening.

"Put your mask on!" Kim ordered as she and Emma fled onto the escalator and then kept running until Kim judged they'd placed sufficient distance between themselves and the crowd of desperate people. Following Emma's lead, they headed in the opposite direction to the Liverpool Street entrance hopefully leaving the threat behind. But there was still the matter of the gang to evade and she kept one hand gripped around her truncheon while the other rested above the pepper spray she hadn't even realized she had attached to her belt until Emma had pointed it out.

"Something's burning." Kim sniffed the air through her mask, turning her head this way and that as if somehow that would help her work out where the danger was coming from. But there was no glow of fire. Power was down or cut off in this section of the shopping complex and she'd lost her flashlight in the fight with the gang over her stolen gun. A faint, weird orange light filtered through a fixed window farther along the walkway of ground level.

"Duh. The place is full of smoke." Emma took another suck of her inhaler before shoving it into her handbag and adjusting her cloth mask over her mouth.

"No. This smells different. More like electrical, which tells me that there could be a fire somewhere in the complex."

"I'd be home by now if it wasn't for you. You were the one those crazy people were after; you should never have come here." At least Emma didn't stop walking even if she hadn't stopped complaining.

Kim winced as her bare foot came down on a discarded steel fork, but she set her jaw. "No, you wouldn't. You were hiding in the loos, waiting to be rescued."

"Like you're my hero." Emma snorted, tossed back her long hair, then patted the Glock she'd stuffed into the waistband of her jeans. "You think being here like this, makes you my mum? No way."

Emma's shrill tone cut through her aching head. "How about we discuss that later?"

Huffing, Emma increased her pace, quickly outstripping Kim's hobble. She had to do something about her feet. If she continued like this, she'd be down to her bones. "Is there a shoe shop on this level?"

Emma squinted through the thin fingers of smoke at the shadowy shops. "I think Glue Store is down that really dark walkway. They have sneakers and joggers. And there's a great dumpling place close by. I'm so hungry."

"Same." Lifting her arm, Kim wiped her stinging eyes with her shirt sleeve. "Then, I'm thinking if we can get down to the parking lot, maybe we can boost a car."

"This way then." Without commenting on her proposal to steal a car, Emma set off, hurrying ahead as if she couldn't wait to be rid of her.

Kim couldn't blame her. Entering her life again after all these years and without so much as an invitation. She'd make the same decision again. Even if Emma never smiled at her or called her mom, she'd be there in a heartbeat. If there was anything she'd learned these past terrible days, it was that she'd do anything to keep her daughter safe.

Toby's last words echoed inside her mind—*'Don't die alone,'* and despite the warm, smoky air, an icy shiver streaked over her bones. Three days earlier, her biggest concern had been whether her next delivery would arrive on time—right at that moment it was finding something, anything to wear on her feet. And please, please, some pain killers.

"I can hear voices. I think they're coming from the next shop." Emma stopped and taking a tissue from her handbag dabbed at her watery, red-rimmed eyes.

Plucking the truncheon off her belt, Kim stepped around Emma and crept forward, straining her ears. "I don't want to hang around. Follow me and be as quiet as possible."

Not speaking, they passed the shop where flashlights lit up the interior and the looters worked their way through the shelves. They kept moving. It wasn't until they were outside the Glue Store that Kim thought they might be safe—for the moment. The glass door had already been broken and she waited a few seconds until she was satisfied there was no one in the shop. "Okay. Let's go but be quiet."

Emma pushed past. "No. You stay here. Your bare feet remember? There's glass everywhere. Tell me your size and I'll grab some shoes and socks."

"Emma, no."

"Don't worry. I'll be careful. I've got a gun." Emma grinned then stepped over the remains of the door.

She told her kid her shoe size and watched as she pancaked herself against the wall and disappeared into the shoe store. After scrutinizing the walkway behind them, Kim crossed to the dumpling store which had already been raided, judging by the shattered glass counter. But she did find an empty water bottle which she filled up with fresh tap water from the mini-kitchen, and a pork dumpling in the small fridge. She crossed back to the shoe shop and waited, her ears peeled for sounds of anyone approaching. Each second ticked down like a time bomb. If her daughter didn't reappear in the next minute she was going in after her. She had moved to the door when Emma stepped over the doorframe, boxes in her hands.

"I've got three pairs of sneakers half a size larger than you asked, plus a bunch of socks. I reckon you may need several pairs to cushion your feet." Emma shook the boxes. "And I found some goggles for our eyes."

"Thanks, you're a star. Here, I found you something to eat." Kim handed over the water and dumpling. Plonking herself on the ground, she used one of the socks to wipe off the blood and blister pulp as best she could, all the while tears streamed from her eyes and she had to hold in her scream. Once finished, she covered her feet with the remaining pairs of socks. While Emma put on her goggles and then devoured her dumpling, Kim tried on the first pair of shoes. "These are perfect." She tossed aside the other shoes and stood, as she slipped the goggles over her eyes. "I saw a sign a few storefronts back to stairs going down to the carpark."

All the way to the stairs and down to the parking level, Kim's senses remained on high alert. But no one accosted them. The distant crashing and shouts and yells indicated the action was taking place on the upper levels. Perhaps the looters had moved out of the shopping section and into one or all the hotels that made up part of the World Square complex. Whatever those thugs were doing, she didn't care, as long as they were as far from Emma as possible. A few overhead lights lit up the parking level. Only four cars remained. She tried handle after handle, but all were locked, and she had no idea how to gain access, let alone start a car without a key.

"Now what?" Emma took a swallow of water before offering the bottle to her. "You dragged me all the way down here for nothing."

After taking a few sips of water, Kim gave the bottle back. "There's a bike rack. Come on." She charged off, fresh energy flooding her veins. Finally, something was going right. She was going to get Emma home safe.

"It'll take forever, to cycle home," whined Emma as she popped the water bottle into her handbag and pulled out her mobile. Holding it high she walked around checking for a signal. "Dad, where are you? I need you to organize a car for me. I don't want to ride a stupid bike."

Kim bit back her retort as she jogged over to the steel racks. Emma had been through a lot already. She was no doubt tired and probably frightened, although she suspected Emma would rather her nails be pulled off her fingers before she'd admit it to her. "Any luck getting a signal?"

"No." Pouting, Emma stuffed her mobile into her handbag then shoved her hands into her jeans' pockets.

Walking along the racks, Kim inspected the bikes. "There's five here that aren't locked. Can you ride a bike?"

"Hello. Of course I can." Emma marched past and chose one.

"Excellent. Come on." Kim adjusted her mask more securely over her face then mounted a black road bike. The exit ramp was ahead, easy to discern in the gloom due to the glow of faint light depicting the opening. "Keep close and don't take off your mask. Do you know how to get to Milsons Point from here?"

"Well, duh."

"Okay, you lead the way." She hesitated then added as Emma flashed past her to get in front. "Listen. You're going to see a lot of people in trouble out there. Some will have blood on them, some may even die in front of you. But remember, whatever you do—don't stop."

CHAPTER TWENTY-FOUR

ANAYELI ALFARO. SACRAMENTO, CALIFORNIA

Anayeli slammed through the door leading onto Ernesto's floor. She barely registered the chaos now—the blood-soaked gurneys lining the corridor, the soiled linens piled outside doorways, the sleeping people slumped against the walls. It was all the same and all horrible and none of it touched her because her every nerve was already overloaded with blinding rage.

They—Matreus, the government, Anayeli wasn't sure which—were using the evacuees as test subjects. That much was clear. The undisputed fact of it jolted white-hot fury through every one of her synapses, making her move fast.

"I need to see my br—I need to see Ernesto Alfaro *ahorita*. Right now." She wasn't talking to anyone in particular, and no one—not any of the dazed evacuees, not the nurse hurrying with her arms full of soiled bedding or the one wadding up old bandages, turned her way or even looked at her as she barged down the corridor toward his ward. That was fine. She just needed it known she had come for her brother and there was no stopping her.

She'd seen the coolers full of blood vials—identical to those Nurse Rumbly-Tumbly had taken from Ernesto. That was proof enough Ernesto was being tested on, somehow. She needed to make sure he was fine before she went searching for Mama. Because she'd heard the Matreus doctor, Dr. Thomas-Schmidt, saying they needed to ramp up testing on everyone, and the Matreus Professional Polo suggesting more testing on the 'asymptomatics'—but she hadn't seen a single truly asymptomatic person yet. Not in the orange zone. Not in the green, or blue, or pink, or any of the hospital wards she'd visited. She had to find where they were keeping them, because that had to be where Mama was. Mama alone had shown none of the symptoms everyone else exhibited—no bloody nose, no coughing, not even the slightest wheeze. But first—Ernesto. Get him safe, and then Mama.

But she couldn't get through the door to Ernesto's ward. There was a gurney blocking it, and a nurse—the helpful nurse, nurse Kerry—hovered over the patient who laid there, sobbing. It was the sob that made Anayeli's heart stutter. It was the blood—so much blood, soaking the bottom half of the sheets, dripping onto the floor—that made her feet stop. The body on the gurney didn't stir.

"Ern—!" Her brother's name died on her lips. Nurse Kerry didn't look up, her shoulders heaving now with sobs. Anayeli had to control herself. She couldn't ask what was going on and risk being recognized. She had to keep her disguise—no one could know it was her dressed in a National Guard uniform or there would be far too many questions. If she was going to keep her mission to find Mama, she couldn't afford to reveal herself—she couldn't allow Nurse Kerry to see her.

Two orderlies dressed in full protective gear—full-face respirators, white gowns, gloves—came out of the ward.

"We have to take her now." The taller of the two put a hand on Nurse Kerry's shoulder. The woman nodded, stepping back from the gurney. The two orderlies pushed it forward and Anayeli's stomach clenched, a wave of nausea radiating from her middle.

She stepped forward, timing herself so that the gurney and the orderlies would pass between Nurse Kerry and her, keeping her hidden from view. She had to see who was on the gurney.

The pale face on the pillow was familiar—but it wasn't Ernesto. It wasn't anyone she could place—just a sandy-haired girl with a strong nose and even features. An echo of someone she knew. A doppleganger, maybe. For the first time in hours, Patrick floated into her thoughts. That was who the girl reminded her of.

Whatever relief she'd felt at the *not* Ernesto realization was immediately replaced with another wave of nausea. The girl on the gurney wasn't her kin, but that didn't mean her brother was safe. It meant Patrick's daughter—if that's who the young woman on the gurney was—was possibly in trouble. It had been hours and hours since she'd last seen Ernesto, longer since she'd seen Patrick. Anything could have happened in that time. Ernesto could have been wheeled away and she wouldn't know. It was entirely possible that Patrick had no idea what was happening to his kid—if that was in fact his little girl. She would see with her own eyes that Ernesto was safe, and then she would go looking for Patrick, to make sure he knew where his daughter was.

Nurse Kerry still stood in the hallway, wiping her eyes with the back of her hand, watching after the gurney. Anayeli pulled her hat down low, and mumbled "'Scuse me," making her voice deeper. Nurse Kerry didn't even look up as she squeezed past and yanked open the door.

A frazzled looking nurse with a creased brow and arms full of supplies bumped into her, not even thanking her for holding the door open as she rushed out. "We need you back inside," the woman was saying to Nurse Kerry. Anayeli hurried away.

Ernesto was right where she left him. Alive. Asleep. Her baby brother's eyes were closed, his breathing slow. She threw a glance over her shoulder, then went to his side.

"Ernesto?" She took his hand and pressed it as she waited for his next inhalation. His breathing was too slow, his eyes stubbornly shut. When at last his chest rose with another breath, the air rasped through his lungs, punctuated by a high-pitched wheeze. Maybe he was off the ventilator, but his lips were tinged blue. He was better—just not better *enough*. But he seemed peaceful and she didn't dare wake him. She gave his hand the smallest of squeezes and went straight to his charts binder. It was exactly where she'd last seen it.

Acting for all the world like she had every right to do what she was doing—*which she did*—she opened the binder, flipping to the most recent pages. There was a new medication listed as the last entry—a different one than she'd seen on each of the charts she'd looked at on the ward full of the sickest patients, the National Guard soldiers. *Ibrahim Jackson* she recited, making sure she still remembered the dead man's name so she could tell Fatima about him and the other soldiers she'd found upstairs. So many dead. She shook her head to clear that thought. It would only lead to a tumble of bodies, of faces, of things she didn't want to remember.

There were more toxicology reports in Ernesto's binder. One of the values had gone up—the same one she'd seen in all the charts she'd looked at on the pink ward. *Agriosphodrus dohrni* toxin Ado-1. It didn't make sense when they were in a hospital with filtered air unless there was some other way patients were getting exposed to more Ado1—like maybe Matreus urging doctors to expose their patients as some part of their rounds of testing and treatment. If Ernesto's values kept going up, he might be moved to that same ghastly ward she'd just left.

But he was okay for the time being. His values for Ado1 were nowhere near as high as the patients on the pink ward—yet.

Ernesto sighed out a long breath—no wheeze this time. "Are you awake?" She thought maybe he was, but instead of opening his eyes, he rolled onto his side.

With a quick glance out into the ward—everyone still busy—she tore the toxicology reports from the binder and shoved them into her backpack. She would have to move quickly, while Ernesto was still stable, before Dr. Thomas-Schmidt began whatever "ramped up" testing the Matreus Polos had been insisting on.

She couldn't risk bending over Ernesto to give him a kiss, so instead she took up his hand again. *"Te quiero mucho."* Maybe she imagined it, but she could have sworn Ernesto's mouth curved upward in the slightest of smiles. Then she turned and was gone, marching out of the ward like she was on a mission. Which she was.

She barged into the neighboring ward with her chin up and shoulders back. Confident. No nonsense. "I need to see Patrick." She made it sound like a general announcement. Like an order. None of the nurses even looked her way. "Patrick! Now!" She tried barking the words like Silver Fox would and kept moving. If no one would tell her where he was, she would just look at every patient in every bed. She ripped back a set of curtains. The patient in the bed—a woman—barely stirred.

"Ma'am—you can't—" A hand landed on her arm. It was a grim-faced, soft-spoken nurse, a vial of blood in her free hand. Orange with green stripes. Anayeli made a mental note of it.

"Where is Patrick? I've got orders—" Her stomach lurched as another soldier stepped through the door onto the ward. If she got found out now...

"He's down there, last bay on the right, but—" The nurse pointed and Anayeli was gone before she finished whatever she was going to say.

She shoved her way through the curtains. She was going to need whatever privacy they afforded. The man seated in a hard plastic chair next to the hospital bed—empty—jerked his head up out of his hands. Patrick. "Hey! What are you—" His face was haggard and grey-tinted, except for the gash that marred it. He had dark smudges under dull, red-rimmed eyes without a spark of recognition.

But there was no time to explain. She snatched at the binder left zip-tied to what must've been his daughter's bed, already stripped.

"What are you doing? Those aren't yours!" Patrick was on his feet, knocking into a tray table, still holding a partially eaten meal.

"It's me! Anayeli!" Her voice was low enough no one else would hear it.

"Anayeli? What are you—?" His shoulders sagged, the fight gone out of him.

She turned the pages of the girl's chart, wondering why it hadn't been taken along with her, but grateful it hadn't.

"They took her to surgery. To amputate her arm—" A shudder went through the man and he swallowed hard. "She didn't make it..."

The curtain twitched the other side of the bed and a man peered in. "Aww, Patrick, no. Say it isn't so."

Patrick clamped his hand over his mouth, but it did nothing to hold back the wrenching sob that broke from him.

The stranger invited himself into their space, one hand on Patrick's shoulder, the other held out for Anayeli. "Jeremy Curtis. My son was in the next bed. We've been holding each other up."

Anayeli shook his hand, searching for the words to comfort Patrick. 'How did she die?' and 'Was she coughing?' and 'What color was her wristband?' were all precisely the wrong things to say, even though they were burning holes in her brain.

"They won't let me see her." The strangled words, terrible as they were in themselves, raised alarm bells for Anayeli. "Too dangerous..." He trailed off. "Like I care anymore?"

Anayeli wasn't a parent, but she'd lost so many in such a short time, she felt like she ought to know what to say. Unlike Patrick, his daughter's death only made her want to try harder, dig deeper, understand more. Something rotten was worming its way through the wards, something that Matreus was orchestrating, and she *had to* find out what it was.

She eased her way out of the shrouded cubicle and snuck to the next bed. Patrick's buddy, Jeremy, had said his son had been in that space. Another fatality? She helped herself to the tox report, trailing her finger down the values.

The patient's name was Brandon Curtis and his values were almost identical to her brother's.

The curtain behind her swished open. "Do you have news? An update?" The man's face was creased in worry. "My son." He pointed at the chart. "He went up for surgery at the same time as Caroline." His voice had dropped to a whisper. "They told Patrick she slipped away before she made it to anesthesia, but they wouldn't tell me squat about Brandon."

Anayeli's blood ran cold. She pointed at the tox report. "Right there. That value. My brother was tested for that same thing Ado1.

So were all the patients in a ward I just came from, where all the sickest people are."

"She was taken to surgery." Jeremy wrapped his arms around his middle, not quite a hug, but not folded arms either.

"Has your son had any symptoms of smoke inhalation, Mr. Curtis?"

"Jeremy. Call me Jeremy." He shook his head. "No. None."

Anayeli shook so hard, a bell might've been rung inside her. She ripped the tox report from its binder. "Where did they say they were taking him?"

"The surgical ward. They told me to stay here and they'd—"

Anayeli's eyes landed on the tray table. There was a ham sandwich on the tray, a few bites taken from it— just like the one she'd found in the jacket she'd stolen, and the one Slumpy had given her. It was identical to the sandwiches Fatima had first given Patrick, a lifetime ago. Next to it was an orange wristband with green stripes, cut in half. "Who was eating that?"

"It was meant for Brandon—"

"They're not taking him to surgery."

"Yes, they told me—"

"If they were feeding him, then they're not taking him into surgery. Not any time soon."

Jeremy staggered backward and sank into his chair.

"No. Get up. Get up right now. We have to go. We have to get him."

Still Jeremy sat.

"What color wristband did they put on him?" Anayeli pulled at his arm. He didn't budge.

"Pink." It was more moan than word.

"You have to trust me. Get up." The man was as good as frozen. "*Ay Dios!* I need you to listen to me, and I need you to trust me. I know where they took him, and we can stop whatever they're doing." Jeremy was shaking his head, a stricken expression on his face. "If I'm wrong, then at least we'll know I'm wrong, and if I'm right..." She didn't want to say what it meant if she was right.

Something in her tone pushed Jeremy to stand. She grabbed his arm, just like the soldiers had done to her when they took her into custody. "Come with me, sir!" She made her voice loud as they pushed through the curtains. Jeremy lagged, still stunned. She pulled him faster. Only when she'd gotten him out the door, down the corridor and to the stairwell—just as bestrewn with ugliness as before, just as deserted—did she relent.

"I'm going to run. I need you to run too, or we won't make it. They have a head start, but they have a gurney to move." The elevators weren't working, she knew that much. The two orderlies who'd taken Jeremy's son would have been forced to use the stairs, just like they were.

She took the stairs up, two at a time, urged onward when she heard the echo of Jeremy's footsteps following after her. Her legs burned and she called "C'mon!" unsure if it was more for Jeremy or for herself.

At the fifth-floor landing, she grabbed at Jeremy's arm. "I've got a plan. Just follow me."

As soon as she opened the door to the corridor, they saw them. The orderlies, approaching the same dead-end hallway that led to the pink ward. There was a new pair of guards at the mouth of the corridor. They had to stop the orderlies before they passed those guards.

"Stop!" Though her voice was the same one that she'd used on her family days ago, it didn't work on the soldiers the same way. They kept walking. Jeremy sprinted ahead, easily outpacing Anayeli. Not the plan she wanted to shout, but she was running too.

"Brandon Curtis! Brandon Curtis!" Jeremy's voice was a panicked bellow.

"Dad?" Even from the other hall the worry in the boy's tone was clear. Jeremy's knees buckled, and he staggered, then somehow caught himself and managed to keep upright. He was at his son's side, gripping the gurney before Anayeli could catch up.

"That's my son! Stop!" He kept saying the final word over and over, but by the time Anayeli reached them, the orderlies had at least listened.

Anayeli squared her shoulders and waved the tox report in her hand. "There's been a mistake." The orderlies and Jeremy all turned to stare at her. "He can't be placed on this ward. New results just came back—"

"We have orders—"

"Yeah." Anayeli's voice was a whip crack. "And I have new orders. This patient is not suitable—he can't be brought onto this ward." She was making it up as she spoke, with no idea whether it would work. "We're supposed to take him elsewhere, until his Ado1 level stabilizes." It sounded good. Official. Science-y.

"How's your leg?" Jeremy tugged at the bloodied sheet covering his son.

"Dad, don't—" Brandon propped himself up on his elbows, his voice the whining teenager tone she recognized from her sisters—sister—when their mother was embarrassing them.

"I think it looks worse, don't you?"

Anayeli wished Jeremy would shut up and leave his son be. Just for a minute. They didn't need to complicate the situation. But Jeremy went right ahead and pulled the covers back, revealing a leg swollen and an angry gash closed with staples, the skin bulging around each one. It was gruesome, but to Anayeli's untrained eye, definitely not amputation worthy.

"We'll take him from here." Anayeli made her voice louder and stepped forward, hoping to distract the orderlies from what Jeremy was doing, from what he was saying.

"Dr. Libby will take a look at it, as soon as we get him to the new ward." Anayeli made her voice hard and willed Jeremy to stop talking. "We need to take him there now. Get that leg examined. Get a new sample."

The shorter orderly stepped away from the gurney, seeming all too happy to comply.

"Who did you say you had orders from?" The taller orderly kept his grip tight on the gurney. Anayeli knew this kind of guy. She had met a hundred just like him. The kind of guy who didn't believe any orders, if they came from a woman.

She straightened and lifted her arm so her black wristband would prove her special clearance. Then she levelled a glare at the orderly, her voice a steel spike. "Colonel Wilson. Directly."

The man stepped off. It was amazing, the power of the right name. It was the exact opposite of the impact her own name had on people.

It would have been nice to have the orderlies help in getting Brandon to where she wanted to take him, but she wanted them gone. "You're dismissed." Still the power of the Colonel's name was conferred on her. The two men turned; went back the way they'd come.

Anayeli pulled at the gurney before the orderlies were even halfway down the corridor, dragging Brandon away from the stairwell, the opposite direction from where they actually wanted to be. She just needed to put more space between them and the orderlies and the guards on the pink ward.

"Where are we going?" Jeremy dragged against Anayeli as she turned down another corridor, identical to the guarded one, except it was empty. But she was determined and they did not stop until they were beneath the same window looking out over the same bleak sky.

"We can't take him back to his old ward, but Fatima—Master Sergeant Kassis—has a secure room. We'll take him there." It was the only thing Anayeli could think to do. They'd get Brandon safe, and then she would figure out how to get Ernesto out.

"But look—" Jeremy pointed at the angry wound down the length of his son's leg. "He's too sick to just stop treating him. He needs to be in the hospital."

"Fatima can help us arrange care." Anayeli had no idea if Fatima could really do what she was promising, but it was the best alternative. The only alternative. She had to make Jeremy understand that. "If the Matreus people are going to keep testing, we can't stay—"

"Wait! Matreus people are here?" His voice was suddenly bright, excited. The exact opposite of the dark, oily, sludgy feeling Anayeli had, every time that name crossed her lips. "That's great news! My sister works for them! Did you hear that Brandon? Maybe we can get a message to your auntie and she can help us understand what's happening or get us a flight out of here—or least get word to your mum!"

"That'd be nice. Mum's probably worried—" Brandon's voice was hoarse.

"Your sister works for Matreus? In Chicago?" A switch flipped, turning Anayeli from National Guard Impostor to Reporter Anayeli. "What's her name? Can I talk to her?"

Jeremy furrowed his brows and eased away from her, as if taken aback by her intensity. "She's not that important." He went from shaking his head as if he was trying to clear away some confusion to shaking it as if he was saying an outright no. She'd gunned too hard. "She's not a scientist or a doctor or anything—and she's based in Sydney anyway. I just thought, if there are lines of communication open, she could get word to Brandon's mum—"

Anayeli's brain whirled. Young Polo from the Matreus delegation had mentioned a 'Natalie from Australia.' Taylor Muckenfuss had said some specialist was coming—from Australia. And now Jeremy was saying his sister worked for Matreus in Sydney. It was all too neat, the ducks lining up too perfectly for it to be a coincidence. But Jeremy had gone all wary on her, and pushing wasn't the way to build a source. Still, maybe if she just asked what his sister's name was—or maybe Brandon would let slip what he called his auntie.

"What's your—"

There was a roaring rush from outside, so loud it rattled the window in its frame and drowned out Anayeli's voice so thoroughly she couldn't even hear herself ask the question. Brandon's hands flew to cover his ears, but Anayeli dashed to the window. Outside, barely visible through the smoke, small dark shapes flew, smacking into the windows, leaving smears of bug guts.

"*Dios mio*! What is that?" Neither Jeremy or Brandon seemed to hear her. "Gross!"

But the bugs smashing themselves into the windows wasn't what was making the worst of the noise. Something else flew higher, big enough to cast a fleet of shifting half-shadows on the pavement outside. Then, in unison, a torrent of something bright red spewed out of the sky. Anayeli had watched enough news reports of the fires that had plagued California to know exactly what it was. Flame retardant, being dumped from air tankers. And it meant only one thing: The fire was coming.

CHAPTER TWENTY-FIVE

DR. DIANA STEWART. MATREUS HQ, CHICAGO, ILLINOIS

Bryce thundered down the corridor toward Garrick and Diana. "What did you do to my daughter?" He grabbed her and shook her until she was dizzy. "Did you tell my father to put some cream on her?"

"I told him to give it to you and explain—"

"A good lawyer could leave you with nothing, suing you for assault." He leaned so close that his coffee-breath gusted in her face.

"But it will help. I tested it on myself." She held up her arm, but he ignored it. "Give it an hour, please Bryce. The stinging wears off quickly, and in an hour if it hasn't helped I'll leave the building quietly, I swear."

He ignored it. "She's screaming. I don't think it's helping as much as you think."

"It stings. Victor didn't warn her? Oh poor Anna..." Diana

suppressed a flare of anger. "Look. Look at my arm. That's the difference it makes, the difference between this part and that part. Look!"

Bryce took hold of her arm so tightly it hurt, but she did not back down, and he scrutinized it. "One hour, no more, and only if the sting has worn off by the time I get back to her. If it doesn't make a difference to her burns, I'll shove you out the gates myself." He turned and strode back to the flat, leaving her shaking.

Garrick hustled her away. "What the hell, Diana? Are you trying to embarrass me? I told you to call me before you left!" He marched her back to the apartment, but to her relief, he hurried back to whatever he had been doing and left her to herself.

An hour or so later, there was a knock at the door. Diana was still slumped on the sofa, a cup of tea going cold on the table beside her, but she limped over and opened it.

"Victor?" She hobbled back to her sofa. "Is this wise?"

He followed her inside. "This is Diana who made the cream that made you better, honey."

Diana trod on the painful part of her heel and nearly fell over. "Victor! You didn't!"

"Of course I did." Victor brought Anna over to her. "Anna wanted to say thank you herself. The cream made it sting a bit at first but then it made it better."

The little girl held fast to Victor's hand, but she smiled tentatively.

Diana sat on the arm of the sofa. "May I see your hand, please? I was very worried about you."

Anna held her hand out. The palm was raw and shiny, but not blistered, and it wasn't the angry red it had been at first. "It doesn't hurt so much now."

"I'm so glad." Diana stood up again. "Isn't it a bit late for her bedtime, Victor? Bryce won't be happy—"

She stopped. Anna was scratching her cheek and suddenly the gesture reminded her so much of Jesse that her heart cramped in her chest. She bit her lip and turned away to hide the tears welling up in her eyes. "I'm glad I could help you, Anna." She cleared her throat.

"And glad you feel a bit better, but you should really get back now." She sniffed.

Victor came forward and turned her around. "Are you okay?"

She nodded back at Anna. "Jesse...."

He looked blank for a moment, then understanding flashed across his face. "Jesse is the farmer's kid, the one you were looking after? Oh Di, I'm so sorry." He put his arms around her and she wanted—*needed* that father figure she'd always seen in him, so she turned into the hug and rested her head on his shoulder, fighting back the tears. Perhaps it was foolish to hope that Jesse was alive; Berkeley had been burned to the ground. It would not be a good place for a child. But at least she'd helped one kid; that counted for something.

"Things are so difficult at the moment." He stroked her hair.

The door slammed open. "Well!" Bryce sneered. They sprang apart. "As if I needed it confirmed."

"It's not what you think, son—"

"You tell me every time that it's not what I think, and it always is. But that you dare to bring Anna into the middle of this!" Bryce bit off the sentence and called to the bodyguard, "Have someone tell my wife they're here."

A shout, and then running footsteps sounded along the corridor. Selena stalked into the room and threw her arms about her daughter. "Anna, there you are! We were so worried!"

"Take Anna back to bed," Bryce stood back and held the door open. "I'll be with you shortly."

Selena stood, holding Anna's hand firmly. She sneered at Diana and hurried the little girl away.

Diana walked into the kitchenette and sat on a stool at the breakfast bar. She had an idea that this was about to go ballistic and she wanted a clear path to the bedroom should she feel the need to get away and lock herself in.

Once the door closed behind his wife, Bryce paced to the window and back, his jaw clenched. He turned sharply and went to stand nose-to-nose with his father, a leaner, more furious copy of Victor's easy good looks. "You will not take my daughter anywhere without my permission again. You will not take her anywhere, but most especially *not here*."

Diana found herself in agreement which was an odd sensation.

"She's my granddaughter!" Victor objected.

"She's my daughter, and I have firsthand experience of just how incompetent you are as a parent." Bryce turned his back on his father and strode over to Diana. "You. Your cream has some merit at least. You have a week to perfect it."

"A week? But—"

"One week." He went back to his pacing. "If we can come up with something that treats cicada-burn effectively it could mean big money. The Pentagon would pay through the nose for something that would protect their people on the ground. It could cover a lot of the money we've lost from the Texas projects."

The Texas projects? Nothing Diana had heard of. But Bryce was hoping to monetize the cicada cream, instead of working to distribute it as widely as possible? She bit her lip. Now was not the time to antagonize him anymore.

Victor must have caught her expression. "Really, Bryce, we can't just keep this for the military—"

"You're right. Everyone will pay top dollar for this. Hospitals, logistics, pretty much everyone." Bryce pulled his phone out and hit the record button. "The Army and the National Guard can cover the logistics. We can sell it online. We can make 500% profit on this at least. More, even."

Diana frowned. Things had been in chaos even before she'd arrived, and that was days back. She didn't know how far the fires and cicadas would have gotten, but she wasn't under the impression they'd dispersed. But then, sitting pretty there in the luxury penthouse, it was easy not to see how bad things were outside, even to someone not trying to ignore it. But he was so focused on the profit, perhaps that was all he could see.

He was still dictating. "Who will dare *not* buy the one thing that protects them when the sky is black with swarms of cicadas? We can corner the market, at home and abroad, if we get this manufactured soon enough."

"You can't do that." Diana had not intended to speak out, but she couldn't stop herself. "Make it patent-free, generic even. Everyone needs protection from cicada-burn, not just the people who can afford it."

Bryce turned on her. "This is not some charity, lady. We have a workforce to pay. There is no magic money that appears in the vaults every full moon. You want to give this away? Then you better be ready to explain to fifty thousand workers why they're losing their jobs. We sell it, we make a profit, people keep their jobs, families can put food on the table, everyone wins."

"Food? What food?" Diana gestured out the window. "Have you seen what it's like out there? There's no food."

"Oh I know all about it. The riots out there are because there is no food, no running water, no power, no phone signal... It's a warzone." He leaned right in. "So you'd better hope we let you stay here, eh? How far do you think you'd get, like that? You can't walk, never mind run. So, have a hard think about your priorities, because I will kick you out that gate and listen for the screams with a light heart if you cross me one more time."

He was in absolute earnest. This was no bluff; if she gave him the excuse he would throw her to the wolves in a split second. The spoiled kid she knew had matured into something much darker. She shuddered.

"Bryce!" Victor paled. "I know you're angry but there is no excuse to be so..."

"So what, Father? So *ruthless*?" Bryce turned his back on Diana and she slid out of the stool and around toward the bedroom door, leaning against the wall. "Didn't you always tell me how you were rich because you were a ruthless player and didn't let anything get in your way? Didn't you boast of buying out family company after family company and stripping them of assets? Didn't you tell me that Grandad's achievements were nothing compared to what you would do for the company?"

Victor loosened his collar. "Yes, I did say that; but that was companies, not people, and I came to understand—"

"Didn't you tell me that it was only the weak who were too

cowardly to do what they should? And only failures who let people get in the way of profit?"

"Bryce, I—"

"I'm what you made me, Father. I'm what you could never be and always deluded yourself you were. I'm ruthless and successful and I will not let you put this company at risk for one sad, middle-aged gold digger."

Diana had seen Victor's gold diggers with their fake eyelashes and sultry pouts, silicone breasts artfully spilling out of miniscule bikinis. The thought that she, "Dowdy Diana" would fit that mold? In any other circumstances it would have been hilarious. Now, not so much.

Victor was still gaping after Bryce's insults, but he straightened to his full height and squared his shoulders. "That is a totally inappropriate way to speak to me. You'd better apologize right now."

"Really, Father? You're delusional. Can it be that you haven't yet realized you're obsolete?" Bryce walked forward and prodded his father in the chest hard. "You're a dinosaur, yesterday's news. You're certainly not an asset—haven't been for years. You were useful as a smooth-talking face for the company, when Grandpa was getting too old and I was too young but now? I'm an up-and-coming business leader. We don't need you to press flesh and schmooze at business summits anymore. You're a liability. You're expendable. So I'm going to give you a choice. Her or me."

"What?" Victor fell back a pace.

Bryce stepped forward with him, keeping the pressure up. "You can stick with your whore, and I'll kick you out together. Or, you can leave her to her fate and come supervise the Teff project while I deal with the other issues. Your choice."

Victor gaped like a goldfish. He was backed up against the sofa and couldn't retreat any further. Bryce had him trapped in more ways than one, and Diana shivered again as Bryce watched the conflict on his father's face with an expression of fierce satisfaction. He was like some caricature of 'the selfish businessman,' but flesh and bone, and large as life. He might sound like a cartoon character—with all his bluster and bravado—but Diana was struck by the fact that he might be one of the most dangerous men she'd ever encountered.

"Huh!" Bryce pursed his lips and stepped away, and in that moment, Diana knew he had won. She leaned her head back against the wall, drained. The tables had turned completely, and Victor was not on the winning end of that dynamic any more. It could only go downhill from here-for Victor and for her.

"In case it wasn't clear cut enough…" Bryce went to the door and leaned out, calling up the corridor "Davis."

Footsteps, and one of his bodyguards appeared. "Yessir."

"Shut the door behind you." Bryce went back and leaned on the island, between Diana and Victor. "Call the gateline. We want to speak to whoever's in charge."

Davis took out his radio. "Gateline? Davis. Who's on tonight?" There was a hiss of static.

"Ford here. Just me. It's quiet at the moment so I sent Benny on his break. He's exhausted." The voice seemed vaguely familiar, but Diana couldn't place it.

"Ford, I have Mr. Bryce and Mr. Matreus here. Mr. Bryce wants a word."

"Happy to oblige."

Davis held out the radio to Bryce who took it. "This is Bryce. Question for you, Ford. Have you been outside the gates at all over the past few days?"

"Yes sir. We've made a few sorties, looking for supplies."

"What's it like out there? Don't sugar-coat it, we're looking for facts."

An audible sigh. "Sir, the men are exhausted. At first people were protesting, not rioting, but now they have no food, water, or medicine and they're desperate. It's dangerous out there, and getting worse."

Bryce paced over to Victor and kept talking. "Have you found much in the way of supplies?"

"Not this past day or so, sir. Food, meds, bottled water—it's all been taken. We have enough in the gatehouse to keep us going for a few days but it's horrible to see the children, sir. Bad enough turning the adults away but to see hungry children and not be able to help."

"If I find out that anyone has been giving away supplies, they will be kicked out immediately," Bryce snapped. "We are not here to feed the hungry."

"Noted, sir."

"So if we were to send our good friend Doctor Stewart here out into the city, unarmed and unable to walk far, what would you say her chances were?"

"Slim to none, sir!"

"And what if she went with a friend, an older man like my father, say?"

Victor loosened his collar.

Ford did not answer for a moment. "Sir, nobody should be out there now. It's not safe. We're starting to get groups attacking us, coordinating their plans, sir. This place is a beacon for trouble—"

"And that is why we employ people like you, Ford. We don't want to get in a war with the locals but we're keeping you well fed and heavily armed just for this. Heavily armed, Ford. Do what you must to keep this tower safe. Do *whatever* you must. Is that clear?"

There was an appalled silence. "Yes sir, it's very clear."

"You may return to your post." Bryce handed the radio back to Davis, who left silently.

Victor looked at his shoes. Diana waited. It did not escape her that this was supposed to be hurtful to her too. The old man was fond of her, sure, but if he had to choose between going out to danger and possible death with her or maintaining his own safety and position by standing aside when Bryce finally chose to kick her out of the building alone? He would choose his own safety, even at the cost of hers. Diana knew it; Bryce knew it. It seemed that the only one who was taken by surprise was Victor.

Victor turned his back on Bryce, leaning both hands on the kitchen counter, his head down. The muscles of his jaw were tight and his hands slowly clenched into fists. Then he slammed both fists on the counter hard enough to bloody his knuckles. It made Diana jump.

"Well?" Bryce demanded. "How long do you think you'd last out there, Father? Or are you going to stay here and work for me?"

"I'll stay," he mumbled. "I'll work on Teff."

Bryce gripped Victor's shoulder and turned him around. "I don't think your whore here heard you, Father. Tell her she's on her own."

Don't do it, she willed him.

Victor swore under his breath. "I'm not coming with you. Outside, I mean. I'm staying here. Working on Teff."

Knowing it was coming did not make it sting any less, but she'd be damned if she'd let Bryce see it. She let her expression soften. "As you should. You have more staff than me, and the rest of your people need you."

"You'll make the cream for Bryce though. You must, Di, and then he'll let you stay."

Ha. She doubted that very much, now he'd broken Victor. She was running short on friends. "Well, it seems I have a formula to perfect." It came out catty. She bit off the rest of that retort. It wouldn't help anyone if she was thrown out. She needed to perfect the cream, to protect herself as well as others.

"I'll leave you two alone." Bryce paused at the door. "Don't try to leave this room, Stewart. Davis has orders to check in with me before allowing you to set foot outside the doorway, and he's authorized to use whatever force he needs to. People are dying in droves outside and the police were the first ones down. One more body won't even be noticed. There's no one coming to save you. There's not even anyone left to try and identify you, apart from my father. This tower is my own personal domain, and my power is absolute here. Remember that when you're giving me that insolent look."

Victor slunk over to the sofa and dropped onto it, fiddling with the cushion. "You don't need to threaten her. It's not like she has anywhere to go. Her apartment went up with the rest of the city."

"What?" Diana froze. "My apartment? It's gone?" She limped to the sofa and sat before her knees gave way. "Everything?"

Victor passed a hand over his face. "I thought you knew. There's nothing left of it, nothing at all. The whole building is ashes."

She blinked, trying to take it in. Her clothes and furniture – not that those mattered, really. The really biting losses were precious and irreplaceable: the one tattered photo of her father and mother together, with her as a baby. The photographs of her at University when life had been bright and promising. Her old journals.

She bit her lip hard, refusing to cry with Bryce in the room. "Oh no...." The last things she had to remember her little brother by, stored carefully in a box under the bed. A picture of her with Charlie when he was a baby. The tattered old blanket that had been his comforter. A picture he'd drawn for her.

He was gone now, really gone. She had lost Charlie for good, and the grief ripped her heart open again. Her chest was too tight to take more than quick little breaths, and she dug her fingernails into her palms and concentrated on slowing her breaths to keep from hyperventilating. "It's all gone."

Bryce snorted. "Better make sure that cream works. Because if, or rather when, I kick you out it's nothing but soot and ash for you." He closed the door behind him and they heard him walking along the corridor, whistling as he went.

CHAPTER TWENTY-SIX

CLAIRE MOONE. IRISH SEA, 12 MILES NORTH OF PRESTATYN, NORTH WALES

Retrieving Trigger's body was too great a risk and even if there had been time, it was outside the operational parameters for their mission. Claire had to be hard-assed about it, denying Grouse his request to go below. "Get down and wait for the Rib. We can't lose anyone else. Go!" They would mourn their fallen comrade later.

Securing a second ladder of wire and alloy steps, Mickey waited for her. She made a cutting motion toward him, shaking her head. She would wait until the other four were on their way down, before she'd move. Flames flicked and danced between cargo containers. She pulled her gun to her shoulder, watching for threats. "Not as if I can shoot a swarm, but we might as well be prepared for anything." She laughed at her own grim assessment. It'd make a good story. Some day. As long as her team—those who remained— made it off the boat alive.

She leaned over the siderail, shifting her weight to see over the edge. Mickey was halfway down. Plank was at the bottom of the first ladder. A rubber dinghy came in, bumping the side of the ship, steadying in the swell of a wave. The driver leaned over, gave his hand to the descending soldier, and pulled him aboard. A second dinghy came in below. Mickey was ready and jumped in at the front. It peeled away from the position, as the first boat swerved, then zig-zagged away from the ship, the driver slumped strangely over the controls. Hit by a wave, it turned back, then ran hard along the metal hull of the *Maid of Morning*, which was headed straight at the base pylon of the damaged wind turbine.

There was a white-hot flash. A pressure wave slammed into her, twisted her torso, and knocked her off her perch. The force of the explosion tore her from the rail and flung her out into the nothingness of the night. Weightless and in the dark, she fell. The sea smashed hard against her back, almost a solid mass, as she hit the surface. The cold water snatched her breath away.

The back of her head ached, but her limbs were still attached, and her right hand had a tight grip on the MP5. She was grateful for that. She flailed about in the choppy water, but Nerd and Mickey were there, reaching out to her. With no ceremony or sense of propriety, they grabbed at her wherever they could get a solid purchase, dragged her onto the slatted wooden floor of the inflatable boat, then fell back.

As the engine of her rescue boat idled, she heard the other boat's engine whine. Grouse was still on the ladder. Plank, inexplicably at the controls, steered the boat up to the ship. He got close, then cut the power. In the swell of a wave, the boat rose until it was as high as it might go. With ease, the big Scotsman stepped from the precarious stepladder onto the safety of the rubber raft. Plank engaged the outboard motor once again, as did her driver, and the two boats sped over the water together.

They swept and swerved between the turbine towers of the windfarm, moving east with as much pace as the 1,000 horsepower Ribs could deliver. Almost the exact moment they left the container ship, the rain subsided, the storm broke, and the sea calmed. It was typical

British weather, at its worst when you needed it to be fine, fine when you no longer cared what happened.

"Are you hurt?" Yelling above the noise and through his mask, Mickey leaned toward her, bounced and jittered by the motion of the boat riding over the surface. He unclipped the gun that was dragging at her side. "Is your back alright? Arms tingling? How's your neck?"

"Stop fussing. I'm fine." It sounded wrong to shout that back at him. He was too anxious. There had to be something else troubling him. The loss of their fellow soldier, their comrade in arms, their close friend. "Trigger saved me. He pushed me up the ladder when the fire caught us."

"He's stupid like that." He tried to make a joke. "I mean *was* stupid." It fell flat.

The other boat came alongside. "Why's Plank driving their boat?"

"The guy who was driving collapsed onto the controls and the boat went haywire."

That explained the erratic driving.

"Plank pulled the guy off the seat. Dead. Blood coming from his nose and mouth. Like the others. The body went overboard." He shrugged. What else was there to say? The sea was a cruel mistress.

Claire pressed her back against the inflated side of the rubber dinghy. Their driver was wearing goggles and a face covering, but no PPE. His hands were bare to the elements, open to any contact pathogen.

Nerd was as close to the middle of the boat as she was. Trigger was closer to the bow. "How near to the driver have any of us been?" They indicated it was no nearer than where they were.

Careful to keep her footing, she put her feet flat on the decking, curled up and into a crouching ball, then pulled herself along the rope that ran the length of the side.

Close enough to shout at him, she got his attention. "Do not touch any of us. We're toxic."

He raised a hand to the side of his head and tapped his ear. He couldn't hear her properly.

Sweeping her hand across the boat between the two of them, she drew an imaginary line. She pointed at him and his side of the line, then at the three of them and theirs. "Do not cross this line."

He kept one hand on the wheel, but turned to face her, so he could look at what she was indicating.

Jostled and jolted, she drew her pistol, held it aloft for him to see it. His eyes flicked to the waving weapon. It kept him in his place. Using it, she drew an invisible line across the bottom of the boat and mimicked a vigorous, "No."

His eyes were wide as he pulled himself back onto his chair. He looked scared enough not to move or get close to her and her men. She couldn't be sure if he understood there was an ongoing threat, but at least she was keeping him at a safe distance.

She slumped against the side of the boat again, next to Mickey. "I've no idea how this stuff kills. We're going to have to work it out."

Mickey looked puzzled. "What?"

"Nothing. How long before we're on shore?" There was no quick solution. Prestatyn, Talacre Point, and even the beaches of the Wirral were burning. Crosby was their logical destination.

He pointed to the other occupant. "Ask Nerd."

"About forty minutes, at this pace." Still carrying the radio gear on his back, he slid across the slatted floor. He held the far side rope but stretched to get close enough to be heard. "What was that with the other chap?"

"Need him to keep a safe distance, in case he inhales anything." She gestured up and down her body. "We've got that poison all over us."

"Oh, right. Command have been on. They want to know what's happening."

"What have you told them?" There was no point in her repeating anything he'd reported.

"They know what's happened to the ship and the windfarm. Told them we have a lot of intel and that we lost Trigger."

"We need a full decontamination suite to be set up." He acknowledged her instruction. "Whatever it is, it killed the driver of the other boat."

"Wait... what?" The puzzled look in his eyes. "You think that's what killed the guy?"

"Yes. Of course." Her picture of events was missing something. "Why?"

"Our driver grabbed your feet when we were hauling you aboard. And he's still alive and well."

She nodded. There was data, but no analysis. That would come later. "Report all that to Command."

Nerd dropped back to his side of the Rib, talking and listening for several minutes. Their mission was done. They were a man down for it. As hard as it was to lose Trigger, her feelings would not affect her ability to command the team. She'd activate a reserve. There were always twelve on standby, waiting to join the elite group, to be one of her hand-picked team.

Skin contact. From nowhere, the thought hit her. Trigger had touched his throat, taking the toxin to his skin. It couldn't have been that. The drivers had both made direct skin contact with her team but only one of them was dead. Plank got aboard his boat first. Grouse had no trouble getting in. Neither did Mickey. Nerd was fine, as Mickey would've helped him. She'd been in the water. She'd been pulled aboard.

Standing, she hailed the driver once more. Making a new gesture, cutting her fingers across her throat, he got the message. Plank saw her standing, moved closer and killed his engine too.

They were still far from the shore. She couldn't estimate the distance, but the driver would know. "How far out are we?"

"About four miles." He looked over as the second boat bumped against theirs. "It's about twenty minutes on a calm sea."

"Can you swim?" She realized she was asking a sailor. "I mean, can you swim five hundred yards in your gear?"

"Sure. But... We don't need to swim."

She was the ops commander. She didn't need to explain herself. "Take us that close, but no further. We're swimming in from there." She looked to the others. "Mickey, go in the other boat. Nerd, signal Command. Tell them what we're doing. They have to quarantine the boats."

The boat driver shouted to her. "What's the problem?"

"I can't figure out why you're not dead." His eyes widened. "You held my legs, when they brought me aboard."

"I was wearing gloves." He pointed to the pair, lying by his feet. "They got water in them, so I took them off." If you hear hooves, think horses. The answer was obvious, but it didn't help her understand what they were up against.

She sat opposite Nerd, and kept the boat balanced with her weight. The idea of having them all swim in didn't appeal to her. She'd already experienced the cold of the North Sea and didn't relish getting back in. But given how many questions she had, there was no alternative.

With the shore in sight, the pilot cut the engine and Claire plunged herself into the water. It was even colder than before, and the waves were harder to swim against. They'd left their weapons and equipment on the boats. It was difficult enough to swim wearing a respirator, without the extra weight dragging them down.

The driver called out. "Stop swimming!"

Claire tread water, her head bobbing beneath the crest of a wave. She kicked hard. Her toes dragged against something solid. In the lessening of the wave, she extended her legs until her toes found the soft surface of the seabed. The men—all of them taller than her—had stopped swimming, electing instead to drag themselves through the surf toward the shore.

Searchlights sought them out. In the brilliant beams, shadows reached out to them across the waves. Medical technicians wearing hazmat suits splashed into the ankle-deep waves, ushering them forward, funneling them into separate tents.

Claire allowed herself to be steered, happy to be out of the frigid, frothing waters. She stepped behind the heavy acrylic curtain and readied herself to be hosed down before she took her armor off. Another spraying came with another layer. When she was naked, they kept spraying. At least it was warmer than the sea. The water subsided, and a curtain opened. Beyond it, powerful lights illuminated a tunnel that took her to another tented room, where towels and a dry uniform awaited her.

Someone patted the fabric of the tent. "Knock knock." It was Mickey. "Are you decent?"

"Nope. I can be a right bitch at times." She waited for him to comment, but he said nothing. "Thanks, *pal*. What do you want?"

"I went back to the Ranger. Your phone's pinging like mad. I brought it for you."

"Actually, you are a pal." She pulled back the curtain that was supposed to be a door and held out her hand. "Thanks."

The screen showed she'd missed another cluster of calls from the burner Ron Frobisher had used. She hit the button for her voicemail and waited for the number to be dialed.

"You have two new messages. Message from..." She ignored the sequence of numbers and waited for his voice. "Hi. I'll make this brief. Can't talk here." There was a lot of background noise. She couldn't make out where he was, but his voice was clear enough. "Did you get that ship? How many bugs did you find? There are two more crates not accounted for, not one. Got that? Two."

A chill ran down her spine. She put it down to the cold of the sea, rather than anything to do with fear. She wasn't scared of spiders or insects in general. She didn't have any idea what a cicada even looked like, other than a sort of grasshopper or maybe a cricket. She'd have to Google them to know more.

"Me again." She'd listened to the outro of the first message and the intro for the next. "From what I can tell, there's some sort of plan to get the things breeding. If that happens, the UK is doomed. You have to find those crates. I can't get any support from the US, so you're on your own." That wasn't much of a surprise. "Good luck. I hope we get through this one, but I really don't feel good about it, even if we do. Will call if I get any more intel."

It seemed he'd tried to sound up-beat at the end of a doom-laden voicemail. He'd given her a lot to process yet offered her nothing in the way of concrete answers. While she'd been masquerading as a teacher, she'd learned a lot about the impending apocalypse from the children. She'd heard about the bugs and fires in the States, but those things were far away. When the fires started in Wales, there wasn't much political flapping about the situation.

When it suited Downing Street, Wales was another country, a holiday destination.

As she walked from the makeshift changing room to the command center tent, the freshness of the night air chilled her lungs. She could just make out the crashing of waves. They were so small, a mile distant over the expanse of floodlit sand before her. The burning ship was visible on the horizon, lighting up the towering spires of the turbines. More than one was smashed and broken over the vessel. At sea, it was the only thing ablaze. On land, the coast was a thin ribbon of fire. Smoke loomed over everything to their south.

"Looks like it's just you and me, boss." Mickey grabbed two bottles of water from a well-stocked refreshments table. He tossed one to her.

"Cheers. Yep. I bet they're washing behind Plank's ears." She twisted the top off then took a long drink.

Grouse was heard, before he was seen. "Those showers were too warm for my Hebridean hide."

Plank walked in, then Nerd. He sat at the closest computer and booted it up. "Do you want me to update Lazarus, boss?" Nerd's hands were poised over the keyboard.

"Inform Artemis. He can relay the information."

"We've got to find two more crates of those bugs. When we get the information from decontamination, we've got to analyze all the data we can retrieve, extrapolate and identify anything we can. It's the only way." She handed each of the three men a bottle of water. "Hydrate. Eat. Make sure you're ready. We don't know how far down this rabbit hole we're going."

Nerd jogged back to their tables. "Boss, we've got a problem. The old man they've got in the command tent isn't Artemis. He's just some local. He's really not happy."

"Old man? We left him in the Range Rover *with* the RAF. What do you mean *some old man?*" Her brows furrowed. She had to keep him safe and deliver him to Lazarus. The country could not afford her to fail the mission. She stormed through the command center. Her voice boomed, getting everyone's attention. "Find him. Find Artemis, now!"

CHAPTER TWENTY-SEVEN

ANAYELI ALFARO. SACRAMENTO, CALIFORNIA

Anayeli was as good as her word, delivering Brandon and Jeremy directly into Fatima's care. It wasn't easy, being crammed into a room not much larger than a utility closet—especially not with a gurney and four adults—but they were at least away from prying eyes.

"I'm telling you, my folks will welcome all of you. Us. All of us." Jeremy was making promises like there was no tomorrow; his folks had a ranch, far from civilization, somewhere in Montana, self-sufficient, blah-blah-blah. She needed to get to Ernesto before the cockamamie plan they were concocting was activated. If she understood Fatima's boyfriend, Darren, correctly, he was going to sneak them out of the compound under cover of night.

She'd never seen a device quite like the one Helicopter-Darren set less-than-carefully on the exam table. It might as well have come straight out of the Closet of Obsolescence for all she knew. Except obviously it wasn't obsolete.

"Use it. Radio your folks right now. Prove this so-called family compound exists." Darren pushed the device closer to Jeremy, prodding him.

"I'm happy to try, but I'm telling you, anyone who shows up with me and Brandon will be—"

"I want confirmation. Now." Darren wasn't messing around.

Anayeli made for the door. Whatever negotiations were happening between Jeremy and Helicopter-Darren didn't concern her. She'd already made her deal with Fatima. She'd delivered the information—the evacuation center was not safe—and she needed to get her family. She didn't care where Darren flew them, so long as it was away from the evacuation center and the fires. Anywhere would be better as soon as her family was all together again. If it happened to be at Jeremy's family compound, that was so much the better, because maybe she'd convince him to let her talk to his sister Natalie and she'd still get her story about Matreus and hold the company accountable for the lives they'd destroyed. But that was last on her list of things to do. She had to get her family first.

Darren stepped back and blocked her path. "No one's going anywhere until we have a plan. Not until he makes contact."

Jeremy was fiddling with the radio on the exam table, static and then voices filling the small room. But if she didn't get out of that room, five minutes ago, Anayeli was going to explode. She caught herself rocking back and forth and made herself stop long enough to find Fatima. She stood just behind Jeremy, between the wall of cabinets and Brandon's gurney. Brandon was, blissfully, asleep. Anayeli locked eyes with Fatima, sending her own secret message over the airwaves. *Please. Let me go to Ernesto. Let me get my sister. Help me find my mama. Please.* She put every ounce of frantic desperation into the silent message.

Fatima gave her a curt nod. The static from the radio spiked, then evened out into words. But it was strings of numbers Anayeli didn't recognize, phrases she couldn't understand. It was English, but it didn't make sense. And Jeremy didn't say anything, just stood there listening to the jibberish.

Except at last "10-4 Good Buddy. Shiny side up," came through the speaker. That's when Jeremy opened his mouth, following right on the heels of whoever had just finished speaking. "Break one-seven for Big Moose. Big Moose, Mama Moose got your ears on?"

They waited. Long enough to make Anayeli want to scream. Nothing but static was coming from the radio.

Until there wasn't.

"10-4 Big Moose here. Over." The voice was gruff, somehow weathered, and something about it made Jeremy wince and Brandon stir.

"Buckling here—"

They all leaned closer to the radio, as if that would make it easier to hear whatever answer came back. The radio crackled. Someone said "Break one-seven—" but then that same gruff voice came through the static-y fuzz.

"10-4 Buckling, what's your 20? Over."

On his gurney, Brandon leaned on one elbow, grimacing as he edged himself upright. "Is that Gramps?" It was the most bright-eyed Anayeli had seen him, the way she imagined Ernesto would look when she finally managed to get Mama to his bedside. Her knee jiggled.

"Can I go now?" She turned to Helicopter-Darren who crossed his arms against his chest. Resolute. And way too big for Anayeli to push past. "He's made contact. What else do you need for proof?" Darren didn't answer, just stared straight ahead at Jeremy who had just said something about Sacramento.

"Oh honey, you've got to get out of there! The fires! Is Brandon —" It was a woman's voice this time, cutting through the crackling airwaves. Mama Moose, maybe.

"I'm here, Gran!"

But there was another voice coming through the static—a different one than before. "Break one seven—"

Jeremy kept talking, right over Brandon, right over whoever the other voice was. "We gotta put the hammer down and get to the Home 20. Extra hands okay? Over."

"Mash your motor Buckling and get to the Home 20! Over." It was Big Moose again.

"10-4. Over and out."

"Be safe hon—"

But Jeremy turned the radio off before Mama Moose finished talking. "That confirmation enough, Darren?"

"I didn't hear any kind of confirmation. Just a bunch of code talking."

Jeremy ran his fingers through his already mussed up hair. "I had to use code—you heard other people breaking in on the line. Extra hands, the home 20. That's the confirmation. I asked if I could bring extra hands—extra people—and my dad said mash your motor—he said hurry up and get home. It's fine. We'll be fine there." Brandon groaned and flopped back on his pillow, his eyes squeezed shut.

Darren looked anything but reassured.

"Ow. I shouldn't have sat up." The boy took in a hissing breath, held it.

Jeremy lowered his voice. "We'll be fine, so long as we get what we need to keep him stable." He tipped his head toward Brandon.

Anayeli's mind raced. Jeremy hadn't told his dad how many extra hands. He hadn't specifically said she and her family could come to the compound. He'd only made his deal with Darren. And her deal with Darren and Fatima was only that they'd get her and her family out of the evacuation center. She had to make herself indispensable. To all of them. "Let's you and me go, Jeremy. We'll get whatever supplies—whatever Brandon needs, we'll get my brother and—"

"No." Jeremy's no made her go to trembling. She needed this to work. "I can't leave him. Not now. I'm all he's got—"

"Okay. Tell you what. I'll go on my own." Jeremy was nodding before she'd even finished, agreeing. "But if I do that, then we're coming to your family's place. Ernesto and me and my sisters and my mom. Okay? Do we have a deal?" Without help there was no way she could move Ernesto in a gurney down all the stairs. But she'd figure it out. Somehow.

"Of course!" Jeremy's tone was emphatic and somehow surprised. As if he thought her family coming along had been a given the whole time. But nothing was ever a given.

"Okay. I'll get a nurse to help—I know just the right one." A trickle of relief washed through her. She had no idea if Nurse Kerry would agree to come with her, but they were going to need help. "She and I will get the supplies Brandon needs and—"

"Look. I don't care what y'all need to do to get ready." Darren uncrossed his arms. "I've got clearance to take-off with the Matreus delegation tomorrow, noon sharp. That clearance'll buy us time once we take-off. My chopper normally fits twenty, but with two hospital beds, we're looking at room for maybe twelve. That's it. It's going to be tight. And either you're ready when I take off, or you aren't. I said I'd take you if that place was someplace safe for us, too. I guess—" His eyes were locked on Fatima's.

"We trust you." It was Fatima who finished—or stopped—whatever Darren was going to say. Anayeli didn't trust anyone, not after what had happened on the river. But she didn't have any other option that was any better. "We trust that Jeremy has a place for us. All of us."

But Anayeli had what she needed. Jeremy had said *of course*. "I've got to go. I'll be back here with Ernesto as soon as I can."

This time Darren stood aside. She was already out the door when Fatima's voice came from behind her. "Wait. I'm coming too."

Anayeli whirled, the kindness making her eyes sting. "No, Fatima—"

"Yes. We'll get your brother, and whatever he and Brandon need. You can't do it alone. Okay?"

"Okay." But Fatima wasn't looking to Anayeli for the answer. She was looking at Darren.

"'Tima." Darren's arms were back to being crossed. "The baby—you shouldn't—"

"We'll be quick. I've decided."

Just like that, with those firm words, Darren stood down, shaking his head. "Woman..." But he didn't move to stop her.

"You get supplies. Water, food, some blankets. Enough for ten people for however long it will take us to fly there. Plus some extra. Put it in packs so we can carry it easily if we have to." It was easy to see why Fatima was a good soldier, why she'd risen through the ranks. She took charge, and suddenly, there was order and efficiency in the chaos. Darren nodded, but he didn't move. Not until Fatima squeezed past him.

His arm snaked out, hooking her around the waist, pulling her to him. "I love you, woman. Don't you forget it."

"Don't you either." Their eyes were locked onto each other, in some secret communication. Then he kissed her—just once, and fast—and released her.

"More than anything, Darren. Now let's go." Fatima's tone was the same one she used when she was giving orders, and she never looked back. Instead, she charged down the hall toward the stairwell, Anayeli following in her wake.

They went straight to Ernesto's ward, not a single word having passed between them. When Anayeli pulled open the door to his room, someone else was already trying to open it from the other side—Nurse Kerry.

Behind her, Ernesto was propped up in bed, his face even more pale than last time she'd seen him. But awake. There was no time to waste. "Nurse Kerry! Stay, please. I need to talk to you." The woman nodded, her expression going wary as she took in Anayeli's uniform, and then Fatima's. Anayeli ignored that, and herded the woman back inside Ernesto's room, Fatima following right behind her.

Anayeli went straight to Ernesto's side, took up his hand. "Hey *cabroncito*."

He wore a wan smile. "Why you dressed like that?" He pointed at her National Guard uniform, then leaned toward the edge of his bed, taking in Fatima, who was hanging back by the door, blocking it, keeping Nurse Kerry confined.

Anayeli switched to Spanish. "No time to explain. I promise I'll tell you everything later, but right now I just need you to trust me and go along with whatever I say, okay?"

"Okay." He drew out the word, making it long so his suspicion was clear.

For Nurse Kerry's benefit, she went back to using English. "This is Fatima"—she hooked a thumb toward the woman. "You can trust her, too. She's got some new orders for us." They didn't have their story worked out, not really, but she hoped Fatima had figured out something to say that would lend credibility to their evacuation plan.

"That's right." Fatima's tone was even more clipped, more official than before. When she spoke, she directed everything toward Nurse Kerry. "No doubt you've heard the reports about the fires advancing, and now the cicadas too. As a precautionary measure, the Colonel is planning to move a select few patients—" Fatima trailed off. But Anayeli had an answer at the ready.

"To a Matreus test site." She wasn't sure this would lend any credence to Fatima's story, but it gave them wiggle room. And judging from the look on Nurse Kerry's face, they were going to need a lot of wiggle room to convince her of what they wanted her to do. "He's going to be part of a special trial. To help other patients with the toxic smoke symptoms."

"That's right." The look Fatima gave Anayeli skewered her. It was the kind of look Mama would give in church when she wanted her children to shut up that very instant. Anayeli shut up. They should have talked about what their plan was, what they were going to say.

"So. What I need from you is a list of the medications this patient is currently receiving and what he might need to make the trip. And I've been authorized to ask you to accompany Ernesto—"

"Asked? Or ordered?" Nurse Kerry was frowning and had taken a step away from Ernesto's bed, away from all of them. Fatima hesitated.

"Asked." Anayeli interrupted before Fatima had a chance to say anything. Nurse Kerry had told her 'we're still in charge here' and Anayeli was pretty sure the woman wouldn't take kindly to being ordered to do anything.

"At my regular pay?"

It was evident from the way Fatima's expression went somehow flat and bitter that she hadn't considered the idea of pay. Anayeli hadn't either. But she wanted to interrupt, to tell Nurse Kerry the truth—that she had to come if she wanted to stay safe, and that she would give her every penny in her meagre savings account if she would just help them. But she held her tongue and Fatima went on. "Regular plus overtime."

Nurse Kerry stopped backing away, but her expression hadn't brightened. She was going to say no, and then they would have no nurse. Ernesto needed a nurse.

"And another patient of yours—the one who went to surgery earlier?" Anayeli would never forget the way her heart had stopped, to see Nurse Kerry sobbing over that gurney. She'd been so certain it had been Ernesto on the gurney, but it wasn't—

"Brandon?" His name was immediately on Nurse Kerry's tongue, and that was when Anayeli knew they had her.

"He'll be coming too. His surgery was delayed."

"He's keeping his leg?" Nurse Kerry's expression had lifted. Either she was on board, or she was a really great actress. Anayeli gave a nod. "Oh, I'm so glad! I couldn't lose another one."

Damn. Patrick! He'd been so kind and Anayeli had almost forgotten he existed. They'd find room for him on the chopper. Somehow. Right?

Fatima was all business. She had no time for gushing and relief and instead stayed in command mode. "We need you to prepare Ernesto to move to the quarantine room we've set up for the patients being moved to the test site, but first we need to organize the supplies to keep them stable."

"Oh, I couldn't do that. That's for Dr. Libby to organize. Or whoever the attending physician will be—"

"No." Fatima's voice brooked no argument. "This is top secret, and Dr. Thomas-Schmidt said only nurses we can trust. She"—Fatima hooked a thumb at Anayeli—"vouched for you. Not everyone is being evacuated. We fear when word gets out, there will be mayhem. So we need you to keep this all quiet while we get everything in place. We'll need you to come with Ernesto and stay with him and Brandon in our secured room until it's time to evacuate."

Nurse Kerry's expression had gone back to doubtful, her forehead creased with worry lines. And she'd stepped back again. "How long?"

Anayeli hadn't expected these kinds of questions at all—Nurse Kerry wasn't as simple as she'd thought. But of course, the woman must have her own family, her own friends to get to. They'd been stupid not to account for that—

"I'm not at liberty to discuss that. Soon enough." Fatima's answer was not one Nurse Kerry liked, apparently. There was a long silence.

"Both those boys would be better here, in a hospital."

"We're determined to do this." Anayeli said it without any pause, so there was no room for doubt. "There's no other choice." It was as close to the truth as she could come without giving away too much.

Just as the silence stretched past discomfort, Nurse Kerry took a pen from her scrubs pocket. "I'll make a list."

For each of the minutes it took for Nurse Kerry to write out the supply list in hand, Anayeli cursed herself for having left the tox report back in the safe room. She should know better by now to always bring everything of any use with her. But there was no time to go back for it. There was still so much she had to do.

Instead, the moment Nurse Kerry handed over the list and turned to prep Ernesto to move, Anayeli used the pen she'd snuck from Ernesto's chart and made her best attempt at forging the scrawled signature she'd seen on the tox reports, the same name Fatima had dropped. *Dr. Thomas-Schmidt*—the doctor she'd seen talking to the Matreus Polos—across the bottom of the supply list. Hopefully the forged signature would be enough to convince the Head Nurse to give them the items on the list. There was nothing to do but try.

Her heart was floating somewhere in her esophagus when she and Fatima stepped up to the Nurse's station. Anayeli slipped the paper across the counter. "We need these supplies." Then, as the Head Nurse looked over the list, without quite knowing why, Anayeli added, "For the Asymptomatic's ward."

The Head Nurse's head snapped up. "Why would the purples need anything?"

A *llorona* wail reverberated through Anayeli's core. The Asymptomatics. The purples. *Mama.*

She was so stunned; she was rendered speechless.

Fatima took over. "We've ramped up testing—on orders from Matreus and Dr. Thomas-Schmidt."

Anayeli found her voice and used it to test the connection that was screaming inside her head, the wristbands and what they meant. "The purples aren't asymptomatic anymore."

"If they've got symptoms..." The Head Nurse shook her head. "They'd better not bring them in here or the rest of us are really going to be in trouble." Her answer confirmed Anayeli's theory. *That's* what the purple wristband had meant. Mama had never had any of the Toxic Teff symptoms. And if Matreus really was ramping up testing, that meant there was only one place to find Mama: wherever wasn't *in here*. Anayeli could hardly keep her feet rooted to the floor and had to grip the counter to keep from dashing for the stairs. Ernesto to the safe room first. Then—

The instant they'd wheeled the supply-laden cart away from the Nurses' station, she put a hand on Fatima's arm. "I need you to help me. Once we get Ernesto to the safe room, can you get my sisters? I have to go find my Mama. I think I know where she is."

CHAPTER TWENTY-EIGHT

SAM LEARY. THE GREAT SALT LAKE DESERT, UTAH

How anyone found their way around the camp's chaos was beyond Sam, and that boded ill for his desire to find Jesse. The tent city held a myriad of dwellings organized to maintain a three-foot distance between structures. A spoke-wheel path ran from the center of the settlement to its perimeter, every five or six tents.

John guided Sam down the hard dirt path, staying on his left side and a step behind with a hand on his back. It was Belle's express wish that Sam explore the area to get a better idea of the layout so that he could protect the people living there from the cicadas. They skirted a piece of re-bar driven into the ground with a rope tied around it. Its bright orange synthetic line led to one corner of a light brown canvas tent. Sam tapped at the metal stake with his toe. It didn't move. "These stakes look pretty serious. Do you get storms to warrant these precautions?"

"I'm not entirely sure how fast the winds get because we don't have a gauge, but I'd estimate some dust storms have whipped up to fifty miles an hour or more. Probably more, now that I think about it. Knocked over one of the semi-trailers sitting on the outer perimeter and treated several tents like kites. We anchored everything down after the first storm." John plucked at a taut line and it twanged like a bass string.

Sam bobbed around another tie down and wormed through the row of tents. The walls on either side of him were a variety of white canvas, blue polyester, and yellow nylon with a bit of green splashed here or there. Most tents were for singles or couples. Dammit. That meant Jesse was being held somewhere else. "Why aren't there any children?" He stopped at an intersection across from a porta potty as four workers cut through the space, blocking the way with two, twelve-foot metal beams, giving the toilet a wide berth. The wind blew into Sam's face, pushing the aromatics of the plastic toilet toward him, and he wrinkled his nose. No wonder the workers avoided it. The stench of its heated contents alone would be enough to keep an entire crowd from passing too close.

Covering his face with a handkerchief, John watched the workers delve deeper into the maze of tents. "Children and families are farther in, at the center of the city. Belle likes to keep them safe, but if you ask me..." He glanced around and lowered his voice. "They're prisoners here like the rest of us. Used as motivation for those who might get ideas of going on strike or trying to escape."

"Certainly people can leave if they want to. Once they finish their job, right?"

John returned to watching the men as they reached a wall of tents, maneuvering the beams so that they wouldn't crush a fiberglass pole or rip through fabric. "It's like Hotel California."

Sam shook his head. "Hotel California?"

"You know? The song! You've checked in, but you'll never leave. Anybody who finds out about this place is too great a risk to allow to leave. Belle can't have people telling others there's safety and food here." The four workers took a right. "Come on, let's see what they're building." John crept to the corner, peeked, and waved his hand. "It's clear."

Sam followed and they slunk past four rows of tents until coming to a poorly made replica of the Eiffel Tower. It was diminutive in stature, made of metal bars and beams of varying thickness, and at the top held a platform surrounded by glass. Every edge and joining surface was welded together, the thick, bumpy welds not inspiring confidence that the person who'd built the tower knew what they were doing. Sam knocked on the support leg in front of him. There was a hollow thud. The thing must weigh over a ton. God help the person who was on or under it if it ever toppled.

John grabbed the first bar of the structure and started climbing.

"I'm not sure you should be doing that. It doesn't look sturdy." Sam pushed on the ladder-like supports but it didn't budge. He must not have had enough weight to move it.

John continued to climb until he was halfway up the tower and looked down at Sam. "We do this every day, are you chick—" He snapped his head up and swiveled his head west. His hair ruffled in the sudden breeze, which turned into a stiff wind, plastering it to his forehead. "Sam, get up here now!"

A dust devil whirled through the valley of tents, followed by a harder wind, snapping their edges in undulating waves. After fifty tries at getting a sound out of the flexible leather rope, he got a terrific crack out of it, and a lash across the knee which cut a gash in his skin. The sand pelted the bandage on his leg and the bullet wound throbbed with pain. His entire calf cramped to the point his foot wouldn't rotate, and he dropped to one knee. He grimaced at the ache as sand struck at his face like sandpaper and he spit out the accumulated grit, clamping his eyes shut against the onslaught. The wind might help keep the desert safe from the toxic smoke, but inhaling dirt could be just as bad. He pulled his shirt collar over his nose and dug his fingers deep into the muscle, working it until he could move his foot up and down.

When he stood, the only visible thing was the tower leg and ladder. Sand pelted his body, and a canopy whipped over his head. He should get climbing. He didn't want to be a target for something he couldn't see, and being under the tower wasn't an option. Unsure how long the storm would last, he grabbed the first slanted bar and wedged his foot into the base. Hiking his other foot higher, he pressed it against another slanted post. His shoe slid down until it was under enough pressure that it stopped and he leveraged his body higher. As he worked his way up the sandblasted side of the fake Eiffel Tower, his shirt slipped off his nose and a gust shoved dust and sand into his nostrils. He sneezed and choked on the grit, letting go of the higher support. Using his fingers to close one nostril, he snorted with little effect. The dirt and sand filled his orifices faster than he could empty them. The only way to breathe was to reach the top enclosure. He kept climbing.

His heart pounded and his lungs threatened to burst as he pulled with his arms and pushed with his legs. He was suffocating, unable to draw in a breath without inhaling the sand that came with it. Spots flashed in little bright pings of light in front of his eyes and darkness edged his peripheral vision. Without air, he'd pass out soon. He reached for the next bar, grasped nothing, and tumbled forward into empty space.

He crossed his arms over his head to protect it, tried to relax his body, and muttered the only prayer he knew. "Our Father, Who art in heaven..."

He wheezed at the impact, what little air he had escaping from his lungs as he bounced, and landed on his side, wobbling up and down. A net had caught him in midair. He laced his fingers through the diamond weave, clutching the safety netting to keep from bouncing around. He wheezed again, coughing, and sucked in a scant breath. It was enough oxygen for another few seconds.

"Sam! Sam? Belle's going to kill me if you die!" John's voice was thin and garbled.

Sam pulled in as much air as he could without the dirt. "Net!"

Metal clanged overhead, and the safety net bounced, sending him airborne for several seconds. The meshed material enveloped him a second time, and he rolled toward the weighted side. Unsteady footsteps crossed over the diamond netting and hands grabbed hold of him. He struggled to his feet and wrapped an arm around his savior.

Swaying as they crossed to the edge of the netting, they clambered onto a platform and up a set of stairs into the enclosed glass area. The volume dropped at least ten decibels, and John placed a wet rag into Sam's hands. He ran it over his face and cleared out his eyes and nostrils, heaving in a few great gulps before collapsing on the ground.

When he'd regained his composure, John handed him a canteen of water. He took a swig to wash the sand stuck in his teeth.

"Thought I'd lost you when that dust devil came up. Once the sand starts, it takes a while for things to clear out. But this is one time Belle can't blame me for not sounding the alarm. I was doing something she told me to do."

Sam wiped the last of the grit from his eyes and sat at the glass wall, the sand pelting the windows. The tower swayed in the storm and he held his head as the earthquake like effects made him dizzy. "How long do these things last?"

"The shortest was two minutes, the longest an hour. That was when the trailer tipped over."

A couple of minutes later, the wind swept the rest of the airborne sand and dirt from the area. Sam got to his feet, roaming from window to window, watching as people emerged from the tents and buildings he was supposed to protect. From above the tent city was a dartboard: five concentric circles radiating out from geodesic domes at the center. The men who'd passed them earlier were already getting back to business. They'd reached the construction site and were using a hand crank to lift the beams into place near the top of one of the unfinished domes. A man scaled up its side with a tank that looked like a fire extinguisher on his back and bright blue flame came from his hands. It sparked and sputtered as he moved it across two beams.

John steered him toward the western set of windows. "I didn't realize Belle had started the dome project back up. Best to not let anyone catch you looking at that."

Sam took a swig of water from the canteen. The liquid washed the rest of the dust from his throat. "Why? I thought I was supposed to get a view of the entire city?"

"You're not allowed anywhere near the domes or the fourth circle.

Belle's order. Besides, this was the only place available to get out of the storm." John pointed west to a large circular tent on the fringe of the city.

If it hadn't been for the elevated radial antenna at the top of its flagpole and the extra cabling draped over its top and sides, along with the many satellite dishes guarding it like an area fifty-one film, the multicolored circus tent would've been a welcome sight. From their angle it looked more like the Borg had lost their ship and rummaged through a bunch of space garbage to create a makeshift craft.

"That's my workplace. It's on the front lines, so to speak. Now you have a better idea of what I'm dealing with." John swung his arm north. "That tent is the one you were in yesterday." He opened a side door, and they climbed down the tower.

As they descended, Sam caught sight of the ruffle of camouflage netting to the east. On the ground, he paced around the perimeter, measuring out its base. "Where did you get all this metal?"

John didn't answer. Instead, he pulled Sam down another pathway.

Flustered at the sudden lack of response Sam stuttered. "Well, where does it all come from?"

Four people banded together carrying baskets full of wet clothes. They stopped and hung shirts, pants, and an assortment of socks on a makeshift line.

John ducked under a sweater and took a right, Sam hard on his heels. "Best I can tell, Belle and her boys have been stealing from any place they can, especially semis. The one they drove when you arrived makes at least five. You know that area to the east behind those camouflage nets?"

Sam nodded and perked up. If there was anything of value to help him escape, he wanted to know everything his captor had to say.

"That's where they keep the goods they bring back from their raids. After the first storm, they parked all the vehicles and trailers over there."

They approached the plastic toilets and Sam held his breath until they passed. He was glad he didn't have to live anywhere near one of the foul boxes stationed around the city. They passed four more rows of tents before standing in front of the monstrosity he'd seen from the tower. He counted the minute hands on his watch face. "It took us eleven minutes to reach the outer tents. I don't suppose you have an idea of how big this place is in actual square meters, do you?"

John shrugged his shoulders. "Why keep track when we keep expanding our boundaries?"

Sam didn't even have time to develop the next question before John slipped through the tent's opening.

Inside the sixty-foot dwelling were more tables, like the first tent he'd entered when he arrived. There were paper maps, tools, a station set up with a spotting scope, and an old-fashioned hand cranked warning alarm. Most everything was analog, and he loved it. Since he and John were the only ones there, he picked up a compass that lay on one of the maps, walked outside, and faced true north. An outcropping of rocks sat two degrees left of it and another due east. He had two landmarks he could work from. All he needed was to locate their position from Interstate 80. He returned to the table and scanned the maps. A large red circle filled an area about half an inch in diameter in the desert, somewhere between Salt Lake City and the salt flats. They were definitely in Utah, arid without a single plant in sight.

John pulled a pencil from behind his ear and leaned over the table. Its graphite tip marked a spot on the west side of the red circle. "This is where our camp was before the cicadas hit. They swarmed, ate what little there was, and were swept away with a windstorm. We know they'll be back, it's just how disasters work. My problem is how to get them to go somewhere else." He turned and dug into a box behind him, and pulled out a small black rectangular box, a speaker from a phone, and headphone cables. He dropped the box onto the map, its digital readout and buttons facing upwards. It was an audio recorder.

Connecting the speaker to the recording device with the stripped cables of the headphones, he checked the batteries and pressed the play button. The screech of the cicada blasted through the crude radio assembly. The sound crackled and John adjusted the wires, making the signal clear again before stopping the recording. "This's the best I have. The noise of the swarm." He turned his back on Sam and put the recorder away. "We have two problems. The first is the expansion. The domes being built at the center of the city are supposed to replace the tents, but Belle continues to move them to the outer perimeter once a dome takes their place." He returned to the table with a steno pad and his pencil. Sketching a crude topographical map of the city, he drew arrows from the center out, highlighting places with triangles. "I keep telling them that's more area to protect against the cicadas, but Jerry says the tents will act as a deterrent, because there's more area to cover and the bugs won't fly over all of it. Of course, that makes no sense."

"Who's Jerry?" Sam waited until John looked away and slipped the compass into his pocket. It could aid him in his search of the city if he ever got enough time alone.

John scribbled on the map, adding details of the command center and the storage depot on the east side. "He's the buffoon that Belle put in charge of building the domes. She gave him the official title of contractor, and it went straight to his head the first day on the job. He's only gotten worse as the dome project continues."

"I'd like to meet this Jerry. Can we go to the center of the city?"

John shrank, his posture slackening until he looked like a hunchback. His eyes narrowed. "You'll meet that snake soon enough. Besides, I've told you you're not allowed past the third ring of tents."

Another rule from on high that Sam had to circumnavigate. He traced the crude drawing with his fingers. It was so much easier to remember when he added physical activity to the process of memorizing things. He'd have to find another way to get John to help him or else he'd have to go around him. "So what was the second problem?"

John moved Sam's hand out of the way and marked a set of tents on the north and west side. "The second, which effects the first, is infrastructure. We keep taking on more people and they consume more space and supplies. Soon enough we won't have what we need to run my plan even if I succeed in getting the cicada repeler to work."

Sam crawled under the table and pulled out a crate, crammed with tech that he presumed had been stolen. He pulled out a tuning fork. There must have been a musician in the camp. "What was your idea for getting rid of the cicadas?"

"To blast them with some sort of dirt, sand, or powder. They fly away from the dust storms, so why not create an artificial one? But Belle and the others keep taking the radiators and fans from me, so I'm left with no good way to fling the material mechanically."

Sam struck the fork against the side of the table and placed it on the top. The wood vibrated with a low-pitched g and filled the tent with the soft note. He smiled and struck the fork again. It was a starting point. All he needed was John to review the idea. "What if, what if we created an ultrasonic sound generator based on the recording you got?"

John chewed on his cheek, evident by his dimple on the left side. His vacant expression was one of extreme concentration. He sat for several minutes while the fork continued to send vibrations through the wood. "I suppose the idea's to drive them away from the camp and around the perimeter of the city with the right frequency. In order to do that, we'd need several points throughout the vicinity and that would require at least four generators. I'm not sure Belle will go for it, but it's worth a shot."

The sounds of engines revving came from outside the tent. John rushed to the opening and threw the flap wide. A row of car's snaked through the desert. "Why now?" He rushed to a scope and peered through it before grabbing the hand cranked alarm and started pumping the handle.

Sam covered his ears at the screeching wail and moved out of view from the tent flap. "Who's that?"

John continued to crank with one hand and pushed Sam in the opposite direction. "Run for the camouflage netting. Tell Belle, marauders are coming."

CHAPTER TWENTY-NINE

DR. DIANA STEWART. MATREUS HQ, CHICAGO, ILLINOIS

"Di..." Victor still couldn't look at her.

She didn't answer. Sitting forward, her head in her hands, she didn't have the capacity to deal with him.

"Di, please. There's nothing I could've done. My father's brainwashed Bryce and now he's... I don't know what he is. I've never seen him like this before. I can't risk him throwing you out and I couldn't think of another way to pacify him—"

"No." That sparked her anger. "You can't risk him throwing *you* out, Victor. Don't you *dare* claim that you're doing this for me, or for anyone but yourself!" She erupted out of the chair and strode across the room, almost reveling in the extreme pain in her heel.

He rocked back in his seat as if she'd slapped him. "I had to. I have to balance Bryce and my father, and that means I can't always do what I want. You don't get it, my father has *literally* poisoned Bryce's mind. He's made him the ruthless creature you saw—"

"Yes, and why was it your father that formed him?" She leaned her head against the window watching the sporadic fires that lit the darkness of the city below, the glass cool against her skin. "He's your son, Victor. How much time did you spend with him? When did you show him what was important and why? Did you ever even try to persuade him to make his own mind up? Or were you busy playing on the yacht?"

"The yacht—?"

"Don't try to answer, I know exactly how much time you spent on that bloody yacht." She wanted to cry suddenly, partly from betrayal but mostly from sheer unadulterated fury, at herself as well as him. "I heard what Bryce said. You knew what you were doing with this project from day one. Or if you didn't you should have. All this death and destruction, Victor, and you made me a part of it. It goes against everything I ever stood for, weaponizing this, but you got me involved anyhow. We are responsible for each one of these deaths, don't you see? You, me, the company, the team. Why would you do that to me? I don't understand."

The couch creaked as Victor stood. "It wasn't supposed to be like this. It started off for good, just like you wanted. But then it started to go wrong, and I couldn't stop it. It just happened. The cicadas, the fires... we're doing our best to get them sorted out, but you must see that we can't admit that we're involved. We'd be sued into nonexistence."

"By whom?" She straightened. "People are dying all over the country, and while half of the West Coast is in flames, Bryce is counting his profits." She was so tired. "It makes me sick. You make me sick. Get out." She watched his reflection in the window.

He opened the door and hesitated. "You'll make the cream, right? The salve? We need it, Di. It will save lives."

She laughed, more bray than peal. "You heard Bryce's ultimatum. 'Make the cream or fall prey to every criminal out there.' Not much of a choice, really. I'll keep working on it. For now. It might buy me a few more days to heal before I get sent to my inevitable demise."

She didn't turn to face him. After a second, the door closed, and she heard him exchange a few words with Davis. When the sound of his footsteps had faded and the lobby entrance had opened and closed, she relaxed. She locked the apartment door and wedged a chair under it then limped into the bedroom which she also barricaded shut. She dropped into bed fully clothed and was just reaching out to turn off the lamp when something occurred to her. "What do the fires have to do with us?" But though she racked her brains into the early hours and even dreamed about it, neither her dreams nor the morning brought her any answers.

She was drinking a coffee strong enough to etch glass when the door grated against the chair she had wedged under the handle.

"Diana? Let me in, dammit!" Garrick. As if she hadn't enough to be dealing with already. But he was the only ally she had, even if he was something of a two-edged blade, so she shifted the chair away and let him in. He sniffed. "You got coffee? The cafeteria's out."

If it was as bad as it sounded in the city, that would only be the first of many things. "Plenty in the pot." Sooner or later, the Tower's supplies would run low; Bryce wouldn't hesitate to get rid of anyone he didn't need then. And there were a lot of children and families eating at his expense right now. She shuddered.

Garrick poured himself a coffee. "You embarrassed me yesterday, sneaking out of the lab without me. I'm here trying to keep you safe and you're not helping. What did you think you were doing?"

She took a sip of her coffee before she spoke. "Trying to help a child, Garrick. It was important. And I couldn't find you."

"I was right there, Diana, right there. I get that you couldn't be bothered to look for me but if you'd had the courtesy to call I would've come with you." He burned his mouth on the coffee and swore, reaching into the fridge to top it up with milk.

Her mind was clear, no lingering effects of the sedative, no matter what nonsense he spouted, she was sure of the *facts*. She wondered if he'd always tried to gaslight her, and if so, how she'd ever listened to him; but right that moment she had no time for his nonsense. "I need to go see Nurse Patti, or have her come here. Can you sort that out or do I need to talk to whoever's on the door?"

"I'm drinking my coffee." He slammed the fridge so that the

bottles in the door clanked. "I'm here to guard you, not be at your beck and call."

Diana suppressed the urge to roll her eyes. "Fine. I'll talk to them."

Davis was outside, talking to a tall man with curly black hair. "Ma'am, you know I can't let you leave without getting permission."

"Dr., please." Diana smiled at him. "Or just Doc is fine if you prefer." The second man? She knew him, but she couldn't think from where. He was an odd contrast to Davis; he had an open, friendly face though his smile had turned into a carefully neutral expression when he saw her. "Davis, I could really do with seeing the nurse. If Bryce prefers that I don't go downstairs, that's fine but in that case I'll need a workstation in here. My laptop screen is too small to be of much use with the sort of data files I need to be using. I'll need at least another screen, and a full PC would be better."

"Let me check in with him, Dr. Stewart. I'll let you know what he says."

"Thank you."

Davis unhooked his radio from his belt and walked away a few steps to make his call.

She glanced at his companion. "I'm sorry, you look familiar, but I can't place you at all. Have I met you before?"

"Yes, Doc. Illinois." He held her eyes for a moment. "Ben Ford. I went to the farm with you."

She still couldn't place him. There were many farms that had been testing FeedIt in Illinois but he didn't look like a farmer. "Nice to see you again." It would come back to her, or it wouldn't. "Davis, let me know about the nurse, please. I need the dressing on my foot changed. I don't want it going bad, and it's quite painful to walk on."

"Yes ma'am- sorry, Dr." Davis nodded at his companion. "I'll be going off-shift shortly, but Ford here will take over."

"So long as someone tells me at some point, that's all good." She smiled at Ford again, wishing she could remember where she'd met him, and went back inside.

"Really, Di, I would have spoken to them if you hadn't been so impatient." Garrick drank the last of his coffee. "And your coffee's too strong. I forgot you like it like that. I don't know how you can drink that swill."

"That's a luxury compared to the stuff we normally get in the labs." She sat at the desk by the window and turned on her laptop, logging into the intranet. "I'm going to spend today researching. I probably won't go out of the flat apart from seeing the nurse. If you have better things to do, I can always get Davis to radio you if I need to leave."

"Oh, I'll stay here." He sat on the sofa and flicked the TV on. It showed static but he flicked a few buttons on the control, and the screen went black. The words "INTERNAL NETWORK FEED" appeared and then with a jolt of noise the screen faded to the permanent reruns of old hockey games that were all that were on the Tower TV system. "After yesterday's stunt I realized I'm gonna have to stay a lot closer to you. Besides, you have coffee."

"I need to work, Garrick."

"So work." He shrugged. "I don't care. I'm not here for your thrilling conversation, am I?"

"I can't work with the TV blaring." It was a bizarrely familiar argument, as if they'd suddenly leapt back to the old days.

"Don't be so stupid."

"Can you at least turn the volume down—?" Once upon a time that growl would have cowed her, but she wasn't twenty anymore, and she had to stop herself from sliding back into that person. She picked up the remote, turned off the volume, then took the batteries out and handed it back.

Garrick flushed red. "What the heck, Diana?" He lunged half out of his seat, snatching the control back, but she did not allow herself to crumble.

"You've watched this game about seventy two times. I've heard you quoting the commentary verbatim. You don't need the sound on, and if I don't work, I'll be thrown out of the Tower and you with me."

That stopped him. "What? Thrown out? Don't be so ridiculous!"

"Talk to Davis, Garrick. I don't care whether you believe me or not, but I'm not about to get thrown to the wolves because you want to watch the hockey game a seventy third time." She went back to her computer and started to record the details of the salve and the results she had seen on her own arm and Anna's.

Garrick got up and went out. Voices in the corridor told her that he was talking to Davis. When he came in again, he approached the desk. "Give me the batteries, Di. I'll turn the damn thing off if you need to work that badly."

Really? That would be a first, from him. She took the batteries from her pocket and held them out.

He took them. "Look, this is a good place to be right now. It's safe, there's supplies and electricity and stuff. From what that Ford guy says, it's madness out there. Whatever you need to do to stay in here, you should do it. Going out there would be a death wish. Stay here, eh?"

She bit back the many replies that leapt to her tongue. "Busy, Garrick."

"Yeah, of course." He turned off the TV and lay down on the sofa.

Before long he was snoring, but that was a sound she'd long since learned to tune out. She focused in on her work, and quickly became lost in it. When the tap finally came on the door, Garrick snorted himself awake and sat up, blinking.

Victor came in, studiously not looking at Diana. "Where do you want the PC?"

"Here." She took her laptop from the desk and stood out of the way.

A tech guy brought in a trolley and started assembling the computer. "They need your PC where it is, apparently, so I brought a spare one from one of the offices. You may have to reset your preferences." He plugged in the keyboard and mouse, attached the various network cables and turned it on. "There you go."

Victor was still hanging about. "I hope that gives you what you need. Patti will be along shortly."

"Thank you, Mr. Matreus."

He winced. "I'll leave you to it, then." He didn't wait for an answer but hurried out of the apartment, the tech guy following.

Once they'd left, Diana sat down at the PC and frowned. The

keyboard wasn't the cleanest – clearly not hers – but there was a sticker on the computer itself that she recognized. Where had she seen it? The mystery was resolved when she hit the key and the log on screen came up, though. The name and password self-populated; DANIEL JENSON.

"Dan?! Holy—" *Yes, that Dan. The one who tried to kill me.* She sat back in her chair and considered what this might mean, the computer. Victor, it seemed, was trying to throw her a bone so that she'd stay and do her work. He'd been there when Bryce discovered her in Dan's office but he'd been drunk. Did he mean her to have access to Dan's work, or was it a mistake?

Who knew? But his motivations were irrelevant. Now she had Dan's password she could access his main files, but if there was something he was hiding, it would be just like him to keep it on the drive of his own computer. She opened it up and checked; she'd hit paydirt.

If Bryce found out, he'd take the computer straight back, so she needed to take the opportunity to look while she could.

Behind her, Garrick was already sawing logs at the ceiling.

Dan had access to another area of the company drive, which was password protected. Knowing how lazy he was, she input his logon password and was not surprised when it worked. There was a whole drive of files on FeedIt which had been hidden from her. There was some sort of reference to a previous trial in Australia. She looked at the date. That would have been about the time of Ed's death, before they'd promoted Dan to take his place as her boss.

There was a chilling note that Ed had been stirring up trouble, and a final note: *Issue resolved. New recruitment in place.* She plugged in her thumb drive. It was a terabyte, but she was still afraid not everything would fit on it, so she saved as much as she could and zipped the files, then saved some more.

Another file talked of experiments she was unaware of, a whole project based in the company buildings in Austin, Texas. This had been Bryce's project, and though an initial glance through the work involved seemed innocuous enough – it was some sort of high-yield crop – there was a whole file of notes marked "Management eyes only" which referenced meetings with buyers. She didn't recognize the names, so she searched a couple and found herself looking at police reports and newspaper pieces. Some had little in the way of search results at all; but several did and the sort of names which came up were enough to tell her what markets Bryce was chasing. It was nothing domestic and, as far as she could tell, it was nothing legal. She copied that, too.

She went to get herself another coffee and stood looking out of the window at the charred wreckage of the city below. The sky outside was dirty, almost brownish. She didn't know how much of the city was still burning but somewhere there must be an inferno to generate this sort of haze.

Voices, and a tap on the door. Patti came in, coat on and carrying a backpack. "You need your foot dressed, best get it done now. They've told me I'm leaving in the next group."

Diana held a hand up to shush her, and nodded at Garrick. Then, with some reluctance, she beckoned the nurse out onto the balcony, leaning her back against the door in an effort to stay away from the edge. "What's going on?"

"You know they said everyone should bring their families in?" Patti's clipped whisper was full of fury. "That was so they have the staff they need. Supplies are starting to run short, and the Matreus boys have called time on so-called 'unnecessary personnel.' The employees are to stay but the families have been told to leave, and it's been strongly hinted that the families' safety is dependent on the employees staying."

"The families' safety? But—"

"There are a lot of guns in this building, and the sort of people the Matreuses have employed are not the sort to hesitate just because it's a child at the other end of the barrel."

Diana leaned back against the wall. It was exactly as she'd feared, only it was happening sooner than she'd expected. But she had to keep focused. "I need to make sure they all know how to make the salve, regardless of Bryce's plans. Why are you leaving though? Surely they can't have so many medical staff that you're expendable?"

"Maybe not, but apparently medical care isn't their highest priority."

"Shoot." Diana sank her head in her hands briefly. "Okay. Okay. I need to think. There has to be a way to stop this."

"The first two floors have been cleared already. There's nothing you can do when someone has a gun in your face, and it won't help anyone if you die for a principle." Patti looked at her watch. "I have an hour, no more. We should sort out your foot. I'm not sure they have anyone medically trained when I've gone." She ushered Diana back into the lounge and went to her backpack, which she unclipped and took out a clean dressing, disinfectant, and antiseptic wipes.

Diana sat back in her chair while Patti removed the dressing, cleaned the wound, and re-dressed it. She was in a nightmare, caught up on the wrong side of everything she held dear. The company she'd spent her youth on was corrupt, working for wrong. Victor was a spoiled, weak, rich guy who had destroyed her reputation to keep his alimony to a minimum; it had all been about money.

She was done. "Patti, can you give me twenty minutes?"

Patti checked her watch. "I can, but no more."

"If you can find another backpack, fill it with whatever is going to be most important out there. Then we'll go to the lab and shag ingredients for the salve." She stood.

Patti caught her arm. "We? Are you mad?"

"I found out some secrets. If they find out what I know, I'm dead. My only chance is to run, right now." She held Patti's gaze until the nurse nodded, and then hurried into the bedroom. She rummaged through the wardrobe and emptied it of the few clothes that might be practical, which she stuffed in a pillowcase. She eased her feet into the trainers they'd given her, and came back out into the kitchen, where Patti had been going through the cupboards grabbing the teabags, the unopened bags of coffee, anything that looked light enough to carry.

Patty stuffed the food in her rucksack and straightened. "Ready?"

"What should she be ready for?" Garrick drawled. Diana turned to find him standing behind her, hand on his holster. "You aren't going anywhere, darlin.'"

"I—I—" She backed away, but he followed her until she was backed up against the counter with a clink of glass. Something fell and rolled as she leaned backward, fear coursing over her shoulders like cold water. There was nowhere else to go, and his eyes had that angry sparkle that meant real danger. "Please, Garrick, don't…" But he slapped her, hard.

The metallic taste of blood in her mouth kicked her adrenaline into overdrive. She grabbed the beer bottle from the counter behind her and smashed it across his temple.

Patti cried out.

Garrick dropped to the ground.

The apartment door flew open with a bang, and the guard shouted "Don't move, or I'll shoot!"

CHAPTER THIRTY

CLAIRE MOONE. IRISH SEA, 12 MILES NORTH OF PRESTATYN, NORTH WALES

Claire threw back the canvas door and stepped from the command tent. If she stormed into the VIP section, she might scare the old man they had mistaken for Artemis. She stood before the two armed guards posted either side of the unzipped doorway. With the calmest disposition she could muster, she entered the other tent.

The space was more like the living room of a house. There was a table full of snacks, a refrigerator and gas-powered space heater. An older gentleman sat on one of two chesterfield sofas. An army captain in urban camo sat on the one opposite. A coffee table separated the two.

He rose to speak. "Sorry, Major. We thought he was just confused. He kept saying he didn't know why he was here. Wanted to see someone in charge. We told him he was, but he got agitated and we couldn't calm him enough to…"

"It can wait, Captain." She relaxed her face, so nothing of her anger showed. "We'll talk later. Dismissed."

"Yes, ma'am." He marched out, without another word.

Claire put a smile on her face. Their guest needed to be reassured. "Hello, this must be terribly confusing for you." She could see the doubt and anguish in his body language and facial expression. "The men here thought you were someone else."

"I keep telling them I'm Colin Baker, from the Crescent. They thought I was making it up. Kept calling me *Arty Miss*. I thought they were being sarcastic about my oil paintings." He blurted out all the things he must've been trying to convey to those who hadn't listened. "They kept telling me about a ship and bugs. They told me someone had died. I don't even know the man. I told them I want to go home. They wouldn't let me go home."

Coming closer, she squatted by the table to be less threatening. "Hello, Colin. I'm so sorry."

"Who are you? Are you going to let me go home? Can I go home now?"

"Yes." She leaned on the table, smiling, feigning relaxation. With any luck her presence was a comfort rather than a source of more agitation. "I'm so sorry they didn't understand. I'll have someone take you home, to make sure you're safe."

"What's going on? Why are there all these soldiers and police? Is it because of the fires in Wales?" He was starting to add things up and get his own answers. "Are we in danger, here?"

She couldn't confirm or deny, but her smile didn't change. As angry as she was about her missing father, she knew that the confused gentleman with her might have some information about how the mistake happened. Remaining calm and friendly, she engaged with him. It was the quickest way to find out what he knew. "Were you out for an evening stroll, Colin?" Out at sea, they'd been in a storm. On land there was the smoke that was blotting out the stars. But people were strange creatures of habit, leaning on their routines when life got uncertain.

"Yes. I always take a stroll on the beach in the evening." His panicked tone was subsiding.

"Where were you when they brought you here, Colin?" Claire used his first name to keep him relaxed and engaged.

"I was along the beach, just at the end of the parking lot." She knew where that was.

"Did you see anyone else on your stroll." His own words, mirrored, would prompt him best.

"Oh, yes. Old Mister Martland, walking Bruno. I always see him. He says an evening walk is what keeps him going."

For a moment, her heart raced, then froze. "Did you meet any strangers this evening, Colin?"

"I did, indeed. There was a very well-spoken man. Quite tall. Looked a bit confused. Never seen him before."

It sounded like her father. It had to be. "Where was that, Colin?"

"Oh, I was at the end of the footpath from The Serpentine. It was on the promenade, by the ramp down to the beach. He was very polite."

Nothing was open at that time of night. "How long ago was it that you saw him, Colin?"

"They brought me here a few minutes after I saw the tall chap."

She gave him a partial explanation. "They were confused, Colin. They thought you were him."

He sat back on the seat. "I don't know why. He was much taller than me and he sounded like he was from down south. A military man, by the looks of him."

"Would you like something warm to drink, before you go home, Colin?"

"I can go. You're letting me go home?" As he stood, he fixed his gaze on the table of drinks. "Warm, you say? I'll take that bottle of Jura with me, to calm my nerves after all this malarkey."

She rose, walked to the refreshments and wrapped her fingers around the characteristic, almost hourglass bottle of the single malt whiskey. She'd known what it was since she was a child. It was all her mother would drink, until she could drink no more and fell asleep. As comforting as it would be for Colin, it was disquieting for Claire to touch it.

"Someone will walk you home, Colin. Thank you for your help. I'm so sorry that we caused you all this inconvenience."

Taking the bottle from her, he smiled. "This will be compensation enough."

She gave him her last smile of the long night, then stepped outside the tent. The two guards were given their marching orders, escort duty. That done, she wiped her falsely pleasant expression from her face in favor of her usual sternness, went to get her team, and then they all jogged to where the vehicles of the camp were parked.

Their SUVs had been returned to them from the Hercules. None were locked, so she opened the rear of the first one she got to. They were laid out the same. She popped a catch, lifted a lid, and pushed her fingers between the foam and the cylindrical monocular she needed. Her fingers knew the shape of it. Without looking, she switched it on and activated night vision. When she knew it was working, she took a walkie-talkie and clipped it to her belt.

Once the team was similarly outfitted, she gave her orders. "You two, with me." Mickey and Grouse equipped themselves as she had. "Plank and Nerd, take a car down to Waterloo, check the main road then come back up the beach and sweep north. He's between here and there."

She ran from the parking lot through the village of tents and onto the promenade path that ran south along the edge of the beach. "Grouse, check here. Sand, sea, inland over the dunes."

Mickey ran with her to the path where Colin had seen Artemis. At the top of the ramp that led down to the beach, she gave him the same instructions. On the sand, they separated. With three hundred yards between them, she looked out into the blackness of the night. Behind her, over small dunes, the glow from the streetlights and houses of Blundell Sands lit the chilled coastal air. As she looked out across the sand to the retreated sea of low tide, there was nothing so comforting. The sound of waves told her they were there, but too far away for illumination to reach them. Pinpricks of color were visible on the horizon, the navigation lights of ships.

As she raised the monocular to her eye, those small dots became exaggerated flares of light as the electronics began to compensate and contrast the image. Clicking another button under her finger, she changed to thermal imaging. It was a shock, even though she knew what was out there.

Registering the heat of the fires running rampant on what land she could see, the towers of smoke that rose on the thermals they were creating, the device showed her how much of her world was on fire. Australia and the Americas were suffering worse, but at that moment, the only person she was concerned about was her father. It was hard for her to balance the fact he was her father, with the importance of him as a problem solver for the Government. As Artemis, he was even more important to the world, than he might be as her dad. Whatever his role, she had to find him.

"Nothing here." Mickey reported in as she swept her view north, toward him. His body glowed in the eyepiece, like some psychedelic vision. "Moving south."

"Roger that." She scanned the other way. There was no evidence of anything alive on the shore. "Moving south."

Even in the night air, a healthy body should remain warmer than the environment for a considerable and detectable length of time. There were no anomalies of any kind, no warm spots or hints of heat, other than the burning land beyond the blackness of the sea.

"We've driven through Waterloo. No pedestrians. Moving north." She could see the headlights from the SUV as she heard Plank's voice. "Wait. Nerd's spotted something. We're going onto the beach."

The beams turned from the tarmac path of the promenade out toward the sea. She raised the eyepiece and swept the horizon. The dark shape of a tall man came into view. He was standing to attention, but there was no heat signature from him. That was why she'd missed him. She switched back to night vision. He didn't register as anything at all. On thermal again, there was another shadowy figure in the distance. The more she looked along the shoreline, the easier it became for her to pick out even more strange men.

"We've got a clear sighting. We think it's him." She watched the Range Rover ride over the undulating sand. It half disappeared in a gulley, before jumping over a rise. "He's half a mile out from you."

The taillights became more visible than the rest of the vehicle as it sped across the wet sand of Crosby beach. Fountainous arcs flew up where they crossed shallow lakes of trapped sea water and then the massive SUV was nowhere to be seen. She looked down her scope for it, but it had vanished. The Victorian seawall at the edge of the beach would give her a better perspective. She ran back to it, clambered up and pointed the monocular to where she'd last seen activity.

"What's the situation out there, guys?" Mickey ran to her along the wall. "What's going on?"

She raised her hand and pointed. "Out there. I can see them. There's a massive depression in the sand. They're out of the Rover. They're with someone. Can't make him out, but it's got to be him."

"We've got Artemis."

It was all she wanted to hear. "Great work, guys." Relief washed over her. The lights from the SUV shone over the beach as they rose to a visible position, making the other standing figures of men appear from nowhere. "Who are those men out there? Why don't they show up on thermal imaging?"

Mickey leaned his shoulder against hers. "They're an art installation."

"They're a what?" She hadn't heard of such a thing at sea.

"An art installation. A hundred cast iron statues of nude men, all standing and looking out to sea. It's called *Another Place*. It's by Antony Gormley. It's really famous. Are you sure you haven't heard of it?"

"That's what it is? *That's* the Gormley people talk about?" She stopped watching the car drive over the sand. "I didn't know it was like that. I thought it was on the shore, not out there."

The Range Rover drove up the ramp from the sand, coming to a halt beside where they stood on the parapet. Claire jumped down and opened the rear door. Her father sat on the far side of the bench seat. Shuffling across, she kept her temper and remained silent. Mickey got in behind her. Unlike Artemis, who took up the whole seat, with his leg pressed against hers, Mickey kept his hip against the door.

The tension in the SUV was palpable in the silence. Her men

kept quiet. It was for her to say something, but in her frustration, she couldn't find words.

Artemis spoke first. "I've always wanted to see that."

Like a trout rising for a fly, she took the bait. "See what?"

"Another Place." His words infuriated her. "It's a lovely sculpture, evocative of those who've come and gone from Liverpool over the years."

"Why would you go to *see* it, in the middle of the night, in the pitch black, when we're trying to stop Armageddon?" She exaggerated, her tone was sharp, bordering on aggressive and she knew it. "Why, Dad?"

"I've never been so close. I thought it was a good opportunity to go for a stroll."

Claire stared ahead. There was such a gap in their perception of the situation. She was the cutting edge of the knife, the tip of the spear and aware of the clear and present danger threatening the entire nation with pandemonium. *In theory*, he was responsible for making decisions that would get that same nation through the harshest scenario imaginable. She'd lost a member of her squad, a good man, a friend and someone she relied upon to be there at her side. He was busying himself wandering off to see an art installation.

She didn't want to look at him, but she had to brief him on the new information she'd got from Ron. "There's another two crates of cicadas not accounted for."

"I see." He raised his head and stared at the ceiling of the SUV. "More potential attacks. You'll have to investigate. Go through all the data you retrieved from the *Maid of Morning*. See what correlations there are with other vessels, perhaps of the same shipping line."

If there was one thing she hated, it was being told to do what she was already doing. Even though she'd already chosen that logical course of action, she acknowledged his instruction. "Yes, sir."

The car pulled up. She followed Artemis, as he got out. The two guards from the VIP area were waiting for their arrival. "If you'd like to come this way, sir, we'll make sure you're warm and comfortable."

She walked behind, until he went into the tent. When they came out, she put her hands on her hips. "If he so much as steps one foot out of that *bloody* tent, I swear I will break you both. Is that understood?"

For whatever being broken meant to either of them, they acknowledged there were to be no more mistakes.

Back with the team, she grabbed the scraps of paper that were left on the middle table. The others were already looking through logbooks, note pads and other paperwork that had been brought from the ship. The decontamination team had dried things off and made certain they were 'clean.' The effect of the pathogen was so rapid, they must have been effectively sanitized, as nobody was dying.

Nothing jumped out as obvious to Claire. They needed to pack up what they had and take it with them. Whatever it was they might discover, they still had to complete their original mission. "Pack up, guys. Call in an airlift. We'll need to be picked up on the beach, before the tide comes back in. We need to take the Range Rovers with us."

Mickey put the ships log down on the table. "Oh, crap. You know how Artemis feels about Chinooks."

"Yep." She closed her eyes in a long blink, running the conversation through her mind. "It's going to have to be that though, we need all our gear. Call one in. I'll tell him, when it gets here."

By the time the characteristic sound of the twin rotors could be heard overhead, the darkness of the night sky was once again yielding to the coming dawn. The team was assembled; SUVs packed and parked side by side, away from the village of tents that had been erected to accommodate their emergency effort.

Grouse smiled at Claire. "Best go and get B.A." Her cheeks tightened as she grinned in wry amusement at the 'A-Team' reference. He emphasized the point by saying, "Ain't gettin' on no plane, fool." It was fortunate her father's fear was well known by her team, as it was an added burden they helped her surmount.

Claire paused outside the tent where Artemis had been sleeping. His sudden appearance at the door shocked her. She took a step back.

He stood rigid, his arms pinned to his side. "No."

"We've got to. It's the only way we can transport you to Patterdale quickly and safely."

"Safely? In one of those things?" He raised his foot and stamped it down in an almost petulant exhibition. "The Second of June, Nineteen-ninety-four. Z. D. Five Seven Six. Do I have to remind you, Claire? We lost the heads of Special Branch and a third of the Antiterrorist team. Fourteen, we lost. All in one of those *contraptions*."

She knew the details. He'd told her often enough. "Get in the car, Daddy. You won't need to get out of it. We'll be in the air for twenty minutes and you can sleep. I'll be there with you. You'll be safe."

On exercises, they'd had the discussion about helicopters before, but this was the real thing. Time was being lost. People in Wales were losing their homes and who knew what else. Those still alive were scared, fleeing in herds, trampling over the land, looking for safety. Claire and her team had to stop the bugs, before there was nowhere left for humans to run.

CHAPTER THIRTY-ONE

KIM WALKER. SYDNEY, AUSTRALIA

Legs pumping the bike's pedals as fast as they could go, Kim followed Emma as she led them through the city's smoke-filled streets. A bundle of clothing piled high lay right in the middle of the road. Emma went to swerve around the mound but as the distance closed the truth was revealed. Not a heap of discarded clothes but rather a jumble of bodies stained dark with blood.

Emma's bike wobbled as she looked over her shoulder, eyes wide behind her goggles. "Are they... dead? What's going on?" Her voice quavered.

"Yes, I'm afraid so, kid. It's the smoke from those bloody fires. If you thought it was bad inside the shops, it's nothing to what's been happening outside. Remember what I said. If you need to stop and use your puffer, give me a signal. I'll check to make sure no one is close to you and *then* we'll stop. We don't want anyone stealing our bikes. Do you still have the gun?"

"Well duh." Emma patted her bag.

At least she'd been correct in her assessment of her daughter—Emma did have juice. And she'd need every ounce of her cheeky resilience to come to terms with what she'd seen and heard. But it wouldn't be long, and Emma would be safe in her adoptive parents' apartment. All Kim had to do was get her there in one piece.

"Keep the gun hidden." She waved Emma on and they continued down streets where sirens and alarms continued to wail, past stationary vehicles with ominously motionless occupants, and past pools of blood hardening on the ground. Not once did her daughter cry out or slacken her pace. It was as if she had no intention of stopping now until she was home.

The smoky clouds covering the night sky gave the city a creepy feeling. A few more hours and a new day would be born and with the sunlight would come hope that the nightmare would soon be over. Sounds were muted as if the smoke was smothering all life on the streets. Occasionally, blue strobe lights flashed briefly in the darkness indicating the presence of a police car as they wound through the city, but she didn't suggest they stop. Explaining away her stolen uniform would take some doing and she wasn't that convinced the police could help. Between the fires and the riots, they were surely overwhelmed.

As they rode along a smoke-filled street of narrow terraced houses, a figure staggered out of a dark garden, hand outstretched as if reaching for Emma's bike. Crying out, she swerved, and Kim shot forward to get in between her daughter and the swaying man. Blood flowed from the poor man's eyes and nose and he tried to speak past more blood bubbling from his mouth, hand still clawing for something, someone to hold onto.

Emma slowed. The man collapsed to his knees, then fell forward onto his face, convulsing.

"Don't stop, Emma! Keep going!" Kim tugged at the girl's arm, urging her forward until, with a little sob, she wrenched her gaze away from the dying man.

After that encounter Emma didn't turn, didn't look, at any of the coughing and blood-stained people pleading for help as they emerged from the shadows or died on the road. She kept on pedaling and pride welled inside Kim at the girl's resilience.

How long they rode down dark streets, Kim wasn't certain but it had to have been at least two hours before Emma slackened her momentum and stopped. "We're almost at the Bridge. There's a ramp access up to the cycleway we can take."

It took some time to locate the southern side access ramp and Kim was soon sweating, her calves protesting with each push down on the pedals.

"Here it is." Emma stormed along the ramp which gradually leveled out to a cycleway that ran parallel to the train line and the roads leading across the Sydney Harbor Bridge to the North Shore.

The cycleway was wide enough for them to ride abreast and tall steel fencing encaged the pathway on both sides. The wind howled down out of the west, pushing against their bodies now that they were out of the relative protection of the skyscrapers. Ash flurries rained from the smoke-clouds. They pedaled down the cycleway, passing through the southern, granite-faced concrete pylon and the first of the arch trusses. No pedestrians. No other cyclists. Several cars and trucks sat abandoned in their lanes, doors open, while others had doors shut, the outlines of their occupants were dark shapes behind their closed windows. They could have been the only ones alive in the city.

A little way ahead was a pileup where a semi had rolled onto its side, blocking two lanes. A pickup truck had smashed into the cabin, crumpling the hood and shattering the windshield. The driver hung unmoving over the steering wheel while his radio played the haunting strands of a country-blues ballad. An insect of some kind crawled over his bloodied face.

"Spooky." A fit of coughing interrupted Emma and her voice was raspy when she continued. "What's with all the ash?"

"Maybe the fire's getting closer." A faint glow glimmered to the east while the reddish colored clouds to the west boiled and tumbled like they were inside a tornado. Kim's nerves tensed as embers blew toward them, skipping and whirling in the wind. She quickly brushed a tiny spark off her shirt. And leaned over to swipe off another that had landed on Emma's hair. "Go faster."

The closer they got to the rolled truck, the more her gut cramped. There was the distinct tang of fuel mixing with the acrid smoke stench.

More burning embers twirled from the sky, blowing past their faces, heading toward the truck and all that fuel flowing over the road.

"Go! Go! Go!" she screamed, giving Emma a little push on her back.

After one terrified glance, the girl responded putting her head down and pumping her pedals. She shot forward; Kim followed hard behind.

A tiny flame flickered over the utility truck's crushed hood, danced over the cabin roof and with an almighty roar burst into a conflagration that quickly engulfed the entire vehicle. The heat blasted toward them.

"Don't stop!" Kim screamed as flames rippled over the ground, gorging on the spilt fuel and climbing the sides of the fuel tank. The truck exploded, sending fire and force in all directions, punching into them. Crying out, she slammed against the steel cage of the cycleway, her left leg jammed in between the fence and her bike. Ahead of her, Emma fell, snarled her pant leg in her bike chain, and skidded along the concrete.

Another explosion rang out, rattling the famous bridge as if it was little more than a pebble in a blender. Shaking her head as if that would clear the fog and confusion, Kim pushed away from the fence, dropped her bike, and helped Emma to her feet. The bridge gave another gigantic scream of rending metal. "Get up. Get on your bike. You can cry later." Grabbing Emma under the arms, she hauled her to her feet and shoved her bike at her. "Ride, Emma. The bridge might collapse."

Gulping and sobbing, Emma moved. Kim climbed on her bike and then they were riding side by side, pedaling furiously over the cycleway that shook beneath their tires. Fear and adrenaline gave her strength as she encouraged her daughter to keep going.

Steel groaned and the bridge creaked. Far below swirled the dark, deep waters of the harbor, while above the 28-panel arch trusses swayed from side to side. Then an ear-splitting crack reverberated through the smoke. The path under them tilted. Downwards.

"The access ramp!" Emma pointed toward the newly completed ramp.

"Go!" Kim screamed, not even certain her daughter could hear her above the shriek of bending, breaking steel until Emma veered off the bridge and down the ramp. The girl fairly flew down toward ground level.

Kim flung one last glance behind her at the storm of flames and smoke consuming the iconic bridge, melting the steel girders and trusses. She took off and didn't stop pedaling until the ramp flowed out onto a grassed area. A horrendous squeal and grind of splintering metal assaulted her ears and she instinctively ducked as a massive splash came from the harbor.

Emma had stopped and was sucking on her inhaler when Kim drew up beside her. "The Bridge?"

Chest heaving, her muscles trembling, Kim squinted through her foggy goggles, then swallowed over the knot in her throat, refusing to accept the bridge she'd always admired was in ruins. "I can't tell. It's too dark and there's too much smoke. We need to keep moving."

After they'd shared the last of their water, she asked, "How far?"

"Not very. We'll be home soon." Her face whiter than paper, Emma pushed the empty bottle inside her bag. She pulled off her goggles then patted her watering eyes with a tissue. "Do you think those people in the cars were already dead before the explosion?"

"Yes. I'm certain of it." Kim had no idea, but she had no intention of adding to Emma's trauma.

Twenty minutes later, Emma slowed as they crossed an intersection toward a smoke-shrouded building that suddenly looked familiar. A woman called out for something—someone, the tone sharp-edged. A second later, a slim, well-dressed blonde, forty-something woman emerged out of the haze holding a flashlight. Natalie Shields. Kim would know her anywhere, even wearing a full-face respirator.

"Emma!" she called from where she stood on the footpath outside the posh apartment high-rise. The instant Emma pedaled up to her, Natalie strode forward. Tugging her goggles off Emma burst into tears as she was pulled into her adoptive mother's embrace.

Hopping off her bike, Kim leaned it against the wall, her palms clammy and her pulse rate firing up again. She hadn't thought a great deal about what would happen next. Her mission had been to get to Emma. Emma was safe and Kim had no idea what to do with herself. Even though the girl had been hostile and upset in turns, she hadn't factored in how hard it would be to walk away from her daughter for a second time. Pushing the goggles to the top of her head, she wiped her stinging eyes when a sharp stab of pain pierced her ribs. Gently massaging her aching chest, she swallowed over her scratchy throat, making a mental note that as soon as this madness was over, she would go to her doctor for tests.

Natalie released Emma and pulled off her own respirator. "Put this on and don't take it off until we're inside our apartment. Whose bikes are these?"

"We stole them." Taking off her cloth mask, Emma giggled then quickly wiped the smile off her face as if she'd suddenly remembered who she'd been with the past hours.

"We? Who is we exactly? And where have you been? I know you weren't at school because I phoned the principal several hours ago and was told that school was closed for the day."

Jerking her chin toward Kim, Emma scuffed her feet over the ground. "I was with *her* at the World Square."

"It seems you have a lot of explaining to do. Get inside, quickly."

Emma pushed her bike past Kim without a word, or even a glance in her direction. Kim might as well not exist, apparently. She blamed the smoke for the burn of tears prickling her eyes and pinched the bridge of her nose.

Natalie crossed over to Kim, hand held out. "And of course, you're Kim, I remember you although I don't quite know what you're doing here." Her brief smile held nothing but friendliness, but stress lines bracketed her eyes and mouth and a frown appeared as her gaze flicked up the street.

The smoke shifted to reveal an armored car approaching, moving slowly, then the vehicle disappeared in the smoke once more. The rumble of engines at first faint grew louder, then in the distance a tinny voice barked, "Stay in your houses. I repeat, curfew is now in force. Do not leave your homes."

Emma shoved her bike into the rack next to the front doors. "What's happening, Mum? There were dead people in the streets. Lying in pools of blood. I don't understand. And where's Dad? I want him." Her voice cracked.

"I'll explain later, Emma. Please put that respirator on and get inside the elevator." Natalie cupped a hand under Kim's elbow and shepherded her inside the building. "Come on up. You can't stay out here and besides you look tired."

She was more than tired—her limbs were as heavy as lead, pain radiated from every portion of her body, especially her jaw and shins, and her swollen feet were on fire. Sinking into a soft, comfy chair in an air-conditioned apartment where there would be no looters, no fighting, no danger, and her daughter would be safe—and nearby—sounded like heaven. She could consider her next move after she had rested. But her heart twisted. She didn't want to leave Emma. Certainly not until she'd discovered why the couple she'd entrusted her to had left her—a mere child—alone when all hell was breaking loose. "A shower would be good, if you can spare the water."

"I repeat, stay inside your homes," squawked the voice over the ever-louder growl of engines. "The city is in lockdown, effective immediately,".

"Of course." Natalie's lips thinned, as they crossed the foyer to where Emma waited with the lift open. Stepping into the lift with a decisive click of her heels Natalie tugged at her jacket revealing for a moment the employee ID she wore on a chain around her neck.

Time slowed as specific memories shifted into focus. People convulsing, dying, blood flowing from every orifice. That Matreus Inc. representative, standing beside the State Premier and the NSW Rural Fire Services Commissioner at the first televised news conference. Matreus Inc.—the company Natalie worked for; the company she considered more important than ensuring Emma remained safe inside their home, out of the smoke.

Heart thumping, her head pounding with unanswered questions, Kim staggered into the lift. Before the doors rolled shut, an armored tank jolted to a halt in front of the building and a troop of soldiers wearing full respiratory gear and carrying weapons marched past, the military cadence of their footsteps echoing with grim purpose.

Natalie punched in the floor number, pinning Kim with narrowed eyes. "You can stay as long as you like in our apartment, but Emma and I are leaving the city. We're going over the Blue Mountains to Bathurst."

"*But*... that's straight through the fire zone!"

The lift door opened. Natalie and Emma brushed past leaving Kim, gutted, as realization dawned. Emma was supposed to be safe with these people—the couple Kim had vetted so thoroughly years ago. The couple who was supposed to cherish and keep her daughter safe. She had never been more wrong in her life.

CHAPTER THIRTY-TWO

ANAYELI ALFARO. SACRAMENTO, CALIFORNIA

Anayeli waited until past midnight to make her next move, though the smoke had gotten so heavy there was no distinguishable difference between night and day. She'd already helped Nurse Kerry move Ernesto out of his ward, and it had been easier than she'd expected to wheel him to Fatima's safe room without attracting any attention—one benefit of the cascading chaos descending upon the evacuation center the longer and closer the fires raged. In the panic outside after the cicada swarm and flame retardant drop, everyone was being quarantined to their tents, which made her disguise especially useful. The only people out and about were the soldiers tasked with sweeping up and collecting the dead bugs that littered the parking lot. At least the flame retardant seemed to have immobilized the bugs that hadn't smashed themselves.

But Anayeli was done believing everything would go according to plan. There was no way she could entrust all of the most important things in her world—her siblings—to near strangers.

Her every instinct told her she needed to move fast, and she'd been pacing for hours, unable to sleep or sit, her body thrumming with an energy that vibrated through her every cell, with one message: run. *Corre corre corre!*

But there was one thing she had to do before she could go find Mama. She slipped back into the safe room from the hallway. Two faces whipped to hers, lit by a small lantern Darren had found for them and packed in with the other supplies they'd carry onto the helicopter at the last moment.

"Sorry, I didn't mean to interrupt—" She kept her voice low, so she wouldn't wake Ernesto, or Nurse Kerry, who was curled up on a chair, knees up, head drooped to her chest. With the two gurneys there was only the smallest of gaps left for anyone to squeeze through.

"It's all right." Jeremy's voice was rough, his head bowed close to Brandon's. They were having some kind of heart-to-heart, judging from the way Brandon swiped at his eyes and Jeremy's lips were pursed as if he was trying to hold back some strong emotion. Any other time, she would've turned right back around and given them their privacy. But she didn't have that luxury.

"I just need you to know it was never supposed to be like that." Jeremy patted his son's arm, the awkward comforting of one unused to dealing with other's emotions. "If I'd known, Brandon, I never would have—"

"Okay, Dad. Brilliant. Can we just... not, right now?" He threw a glance at Anayeli and then back at Jeremy, making her wish she'd stayed outside. But she couldn't. Instead she scooted between the gurneys.

"I'll be gone in just a sec—" She shouldn't have to explain herself, but she did anyway. "Just wanted to see Ernesto before I..." She almost couldn't go on, afraid that if she spoke what she was about to do, she would jinx the whole thing. "You'll make sure he gets on the helicopter, if I don't—" Her throat closed up on her, images swirling through her mind—Papa's face screaming out of the smoke, Luz's hand scraping past hers, just out of reach in the muddy river-water.

Her palm throbbed, a steady reminder of her failures. She would not fail this time. She could not.

"No one gets left behind." Jeremy's voice was low, but it was emphatic. Strong. She took what reassurance she could from it. She had enough time. She would get back before the handful of hours left before they all made their break for the helicopter were up. She would be the one—not Fatima—to get Carlota and Bailey Rae. She would be the one—not Nurse Kerry, not Jeremy, who would be busy enough with Brandon—to load Ernesto into Darren's helicopter. *Darren's helicopter.* That's what Anayeli was calling it. That way she could pretend not to think what flying in a helicopter stolen from the US military might mean for all of them. There was just *too much*. She had to focus on what she needed to do next: Save Mama.

She pressed a kiss to her palm—the uninjured one—and hovered it above Ernesto's heart, warmth radiating in the tiny gap between her skin and the sheet that covered him, his chest rising and falling slowly, no trace of a wheeze. Then she turned to leave.

"We're all going to make it out, Anayeli." The resolve, the confidence in Jeremy's voice made her eyes sting. "See you back here in a bit." He gave her what might've been a smile and she slipped out the door, praying everything would go as smoothly as Jeremy seemed to think it would. That's why she had waited until the middle of the night. It was the safest way to accomplish what she was planning.

"Please let everyone be asleep." She said it aloud, as if that would somehow send it to God's ear faster.

Out in the tent-filled parking lot, she glanced toward the tent where Carlota and Bailey Rae were hopefully asleep, then turned the opposite direction—she'd stopped by earlier, to tell them she needed to keep watch over Ernesto, and not to worry. She'd used her black wristband to sneak them out of their quarantine and they'd all gone to the perimeter fence. Cricket and Roxy had come dashing out of the bushes, Cricket licking their hands in turn through the fence and Roxy wriggling in non-stop excitement. Anayeli had almost burst into tears, but she'd managed to hold it together. She couldn't betray anything to Carlota. Like before, if her plans went awry, she wanted them to have plausible deniability about what she'd been doing. If all went well, she—and Mama—would get the girls later. And if it didn't... she wasn't going to think about that.

Anayeli moved quickly through the orange zone, then through the blue zone, not allowing herself to run, not bothering to hide. She moved through the night like she was one with it until she found herself before the gate where she'd seen the refrigerator trucks loaded with the dead. It had been open for the truck the first time she'd gone through, but it was closed, a heavy chain wrapped around the place where the double-gates met. In the glare from the single solar light that shone down on it, a padlock dangled.

But the padlock told her she was in the right place.

The first time she'd been at the gate, she'd been too sick over the piled human corpses to think about what the second gate, just beyond led to, but in the hours since leaving the Nurses' Station, she'd thought of it over and over. It was the only place in the evacuation center she hadn't investigated where asymptomatic people could be easily—and constantly—exposed to whatever was in the smoke.

She stepped into the halo of brightness the solar generator-powered light threw across the pavement, shuddering at how much it was like the night Mama was ripped from her family. But this time, no one was dragging Anayeli anywhere. There were no guards standing at the gate like there ought to have been, just someone slumped in a chair under the pop-up tent that had been erected just inside. A guard station, maybe, or perhaps a shelter intended to offer some meagre protection from the falling ash and bug swarms. She could just make out a humped shape, a person whose density gave them an even greater darkness than the surrounding night air, swirling thickly with particulates. "Sleeping. Like you wanted." Her own voice, in a barely audible whisper, gave her some comfort, made her feel less alone.

The person in the chair jerked awake. "Wha—who—" The soldier's voice was muffled by his mask. "Crap. Where's Rodgers? You here to relieve him?"

"No. Permission to pass through." She made it a statement, her voice firm. She had a story at the ready—but her tongue had stuck to the roof of her dry mouth. The guard didn't care though. He took in her uniform, nodded, and pushed to standing.

That was the thing about looking like you belonged—no one questioned you. Never mind that she had a backpack she'd stolen from a dead soldier slung across her back that gave away the fact she wasn't going out on guard duty, or that if anyone looked inside, they'd find the officer's gun she'd lifted, a spare camo jacket, toxicology reports, and all the wristbands—every color and combination except purple—she'd taken from the pink ward. Not to mention a few bottles of water, and freeze dried rations she'd managed to sneak from the stash Darren had amassed.

The sleep-befuddled soldier cleared his throat as he trudged toward the gate. She held up her arm as soon as he was close and flashed the black wristband.

"Granted." His voice rasped and he let out a little cough before pulling at his neck chain, drawing a single key from beneath his shirt and unlocking the gate, the heavy chain's clanking far too loud as he unwound it.

She didn't pause once he'd let her through. No sense in giving him more of a chance to get a good look at her or to start asking questions. Instead, she hurried across the space that had been occupied by the refrigerator trucks, headed toward where the second gate was located.

After the bright aura of the solar light, the night was even darker, the smoke even thicker. Splotches appeared before her eyes every time she blinked; her eyes seared from the light. She couldn't see the second gate at all, couldn't see the pavement, and there were no stars to orient herself by. She swayed; her equilibrium more fragile than she'd realized. She had to get to Mama. She hurried forward again.

The clanking of the chain behind her stopped and the night went too quiet, everything blotted and muffled, gauzed in cotton. The silence grew and she lost any sense of space and time.

She kicked something heavy and unyielding and not quite knee-height. She stumbled and tried to step over whatever it was—but instead of righting herself and finding the flat of pavement, she toppled onto a solid, yet somehow soft mass. She caught herself with her hands and shrieked before her brain even registered what she was touching.

Cloth, hair, a shape that could only be someone's nose beneath her. It was bodies under her knees, cold skin giving against her palms—the dead, left in a heap, waiting to be trucked away. She scrabbled over the lumped and uneven pile, panic turning her into every cliché she'd ever seen portrayed in a movie—the World War I soldier fighting his way through a logjam of dead bodies clogging a river, the poor unfortunate in a horror movie discovering her murdered friends.

Familiar eyes stared up at her—not Mama, not Mama—and she let out a noise more animal than human, bursting forward, kicking against slicked and swollen limbs, the metallic tang of blood and the putrid sweetness of decay rising as she struggled. She landed on her hands and knees, the hard, bruising pavement a painful relief. It hadn't been Mama she'd seen, but Slumpy, the woman she'd recognized from the line outside the evacuation center, who'd given her sandwiches for the dogs only a day or two earlier. But it wasn't Mama. It wasn't. Mama was alive. She had to be.

Anayeli stayed on her hands and knees, heaving deep breaths, unsure whether she was going to vomit or just needed more oxygen. In the dark, she must have veered closer to the hospital building, instead of the straight shot it should have been from one gate to the next. She raised her head, and there was the fence in front of her. She grabbed it, the wire biting into her fingers, her injured palm protesting as she hauled herself upright. She crabbed her way along the fence, working toward where she hoped the gate would be.

A harsh laugh rang out. "Bravo! You made it through the booby trap!" An indistinct dark figure moved on the other side of the gate, giving her a slow clap. She didn't like the tone of his voice at all. Or the idea that the bodies had been left in front of the gate on purpose.

"Yeah, I guess I did." She should've kept the irritation out of her voice—it wasn't going to help her get through the gate—but as the adrenaline ebbed, it was replaced with rage. The dead weren't some sick joke to be played on the unsuspecting. "Permission to pass."

Her strictly business approach was the wrong tactic.

"Oh, okay. It's like that, is it?" The guard's jokey tone carried an edge that twisted his words from friendly to creepy, tripping the same alarm that went off in her head when a knot of frat boys boiled out of a downtown bar and one peeled off to trail her out into the parking lot, raucous laughter following them both. She was going to have to navigate around this guy with extra care.

"Busy night is all." She gave him an electric smile.

He didn't take the hint that she was in a hurry and instead just stood there, arms crossed over his chest. "You need the testies?"

Gross. The guy was gross in every possible way—he'd disrespected the dead, dehumanized the living, and he was harassing her in the kind of just-under-the-radar, can't-you-take-a-joke way she'd been served her whole life. He couldn't even wait a beat before her lack of a response drove him on. "Get it? Not testes." He grabbed his crotch and thrust his hips. "Testies. *Test subjects.*"

Nothing had ever been less funny, but she giggled anyway—the please-let's-get-through-this-without-you-murdering-me giggle every woman knew intimately. "Good one." If she'd been her sister, she would've dead-panned the words so they would cut, but she kept a lightness in her voice, stroking his ego just enough, she hoped. Because he'd confirmed it—there were people locked back there, and she needed in.

"I've got orders from Colonel Wilson." The less the creep knew and the less she had to lie or make stuff up on the fly, the better. But for the first time, the Colonel's name didn't have the desired effect. The soldier didn't move. The gate stayed locked. "Inspection orders."

"Kind of a weird time for an inspection..." The guy's voice trailed off in a way that was somehow a threat.

"Yeah, well, weird times in general, amiright?" She gave another little laugh and a don't-ask-me-I-only-work-here shrug. She wished Carlota were with her. That girl would've ripped right through the guy's power trip. But her joke did the trick. He pulled his key out on its chain.

He held the gate open for her just enough for her to squeeze through sideways, her breasts squishing uncomfortably against the metal, the creep's eyes on her the whole time.

"Thanks!" She hated her chirpy voice, hated herself for thanking him for harassing her, but she still had to come back out the same gate. With Mama. She needed him on her side.

Dog kennels. That was her first thought as soon as the cages loomed out of the haze. But inside there were people. Women and children and men, curled up on the ground under foil blankets or leaning up against the fences. None of them were wearing masks or respirators, but there was no blood anywhere. No one was coughing. There were no tents, no cots, no chairs, nothing but buckets in each cage—totally illegal. But it was desperate times, an evacuation center hastily constructed in a parking lot. Many of the people were asleep, or else trying to sleep, but others were whispering. They went quiet and stared at her as she passed, wearing the sagging, blank expressions of the thoroughly exhausted.

"You got more food?" A lank-haired girl's hands reached through the wire toward Anayeli. The girl's clothes hung loose from her frame. Her wristband had purple stripes. "Getting kinda sick of them ham sandwiches..."

"Sorry. No. Do you know anyone named Maria Alfaro? I'm looking for her." It was the wrong thing to say, dressed in uniform the way she was. The girl's mouth went straight, her eyes hooded.

It was the same thing at every cage. Everyone was hungry. No one had seen or heard of Maria Alfaro. All the wristbands she could see were of different base colors—orange, green, blue, yellow—but they all had purple stripes. And every single gate was padlocked.

She hadn't come prepared for picking locks or cutting chains. All she had was her stolen gun, but the instant she thought of it, something niggled in the back of her mind. There was some reason why shooting off locks didn't work, besides the obvious danger to anyone nearby. She'd have to come up with something else, if she found Mama...

If.

At each cage, a little more hope washed out of Anayeli. Even though there wasn't a single person locked up who had symptoms of poisoning, there was no sign of Mama. No one who knew her name. When she asked one man how long he'd been there, he gave her a hard look. "Since the beginning. Like everyone else down here." But when she'd asked if anyone had gotten sick, if anyone had died, he'd gone quiet. Sullen.

The farther she went, the more gaunt the people looked. The longer they said they'd been there. She asked a beefy man who looked ex-military—short haircut, bad tattoos—what he'd been eating. "Dried out ham sandwiches. And bugs. From that swarm that flew over just before they sprayed the fire retardant." The woman at his side stepped forward. "Cicadas. That jackass out there said they were poisonous, but we've been eating them just fine."

Wait, what? She could barely process what she was hearing. They'd been eating *bugs?*

It was a damn humanitarian disaster. Perpetrated by the US government and the Matreus Corporation. The story of her career, if she'd still had a career.

A voice rang out, pitched high. "Anayeli? *Mija?*"

Anayeli's knees tried to buckle at the same time she told them to run. "Mama?" She stagger-sprinted toward the voice. And there she was. Her eyes were sunken, looking more like a skull's dark holes, but it was Mama, her curly hair matted after days in the river, followed by this prison. But she was alive.

The jumble of sounds and words that came from both of them was incomprehensible except for the emotion they contained, until finally Anayeli managed to find what she needed to say most. "I'm so sorry. I'm so sorry. I was so wrong."

"Ernesto? Carlota? *Mis cariños?*"

"They're good. Ernesto is okay—better. Mama, I have to go…"

"No! Anayeli!"

"I'll be right back." She hated every step she took away from Mama, down the long row of cages, more and more of the prisoners —because that's what they were, not just test subjects, but inmates— gathering at the gates, fingers clawed through the wire. There was only one way to get Mama out.

Her fury burned incandescent, more nuclear with every step, uncontainable. Her resolve was infinite by the time she reached the creep at the gate, and her gun was stuck in her waistband. She kept her hands behind her back, so she could grab it if she needed to.

"Hi there." Her chirpy voice made the creep startle. He hadn't heard her coming, or felt the rage seething off of her. "So, turns out I need to take some of the"—she hated the word but she had to use it—"testies up to the Pink Ward."

"Now?" He let out a little cough. "I thought we were supposed to be evacuating."

If she'd been struck by lightning, she couldn't have been more shocked. A mass evacuation would put every plan she'd made with Fatima, Darren, and Jeremy into chaos. They were going to have to move sooner, not later. But the guard was waiting for some kind of answer from her. "One last blood draw before we move. It was just supposed to be the healthy ones, but... they're all healthy, so..."

"Colonel Wilson only sent itty bitty you to take all those testies?" His skepticism was written in the angle of his eyebrows. She might have punched him for it, except the white of his mask had a dark spot in the middle. He let out another hacking cough, and the stain seeped larger. He was coughing blood. "I hate this thing." He pulled down his mask. "Doesn't even do jack."

"You should get inside, to the filtered air. I can do the gates..."

The creep shook his head. "They can't expect you to keep control—"

She shrugged and went for her weapon, hoping her face wouldn't betray what she was doing behind her back. Her palm slipped against the butt of the gun, her hand slicked with sweat. "Have you seen them?" She kept a laugh in her voice, because she didn't want to shoot him. She didn't want to watch him die. "I don't think any of them have energy to fight." But she did. She had so much fight in her. "Plus, I'm going to tell them we're going to the cafeteria and then to the showers."

The casual cruelty worked just like she'd hoped. The creep let out a guffaw that turned into a sloppy, wet cough. When finally he straightened, she was ready, her finger on the barrel, alongside the trigger. He was dying either way—from her bullet or the smoke.

But he pulled his neck chain over his head, the key dangling from it and she stayed her arm. He twirled the chain around his finger, as if he might spin the key off into the darkness. Then he smiled, his teeth tinged with blood. "I'm gonna go inside like you said. Check in with command." He whirled the key faster. "But man, I'd love to see their faces when the testies get to the needle room and realize you lied to them."

The key sang against the chain, jingling in the air as he released it and flung it at her feet. "Good luck with that."

CHAPTER THIRTY-THREE

DR. DIANA STEWART. MATREUS HQ, CHICAGO, ILLINOIS

Diana dropped the beer bottle, her heart pounding. Garrick lay motionless at her feet—surely he wasn't dead?

"Let me check him." At the guard's nod, Patti hurried over. She knelt, checked for his pulse and then pulled his eyelid up and looked at his pupils. "Not dead, just out for the count. Good job. He might be pretty but he's a real ugly customer."

As the adrenaline ebbed, Diana registered that the guard was Ben Ford, who'd spoken to her outside. He holstered his pistol. "He's not going to be happy when he comes around. What do you want to do with him? I can throw booze all over him and leave him in a corner somewhere if you think he won't remember?"

He hadn't hesitated to help, and suddenly she placed him. "You're the Sheriff. From Watseka, right? What are you doing here?"

"I was the Sheriff, yes; not anymore." He pursed his lips. "That's another story though. I was on the gate when they brought you in looking all kinds of beat up. I didn't like what I heard on the radio from Mr. Matreus, so I thought I'd check by and see what was going on."

She forced her shoulders to relax. "We need to get out of here. Can you help?"

"It's dangerous out there too. No supplies and a lot of desperate people."

"We'll have to chance it. We know how to make a salve that helps. Bryce hates me. He'll likely disappear us as soon as he's happy with the recipe."

"Sooner, maybe." Patti stood. "Your boy here is thick as thieves with Mr. Bryce, and that man enjoys his work far too much."

Ben pressed his lips together. "Even so, it's likely to be safer in here than out there."

Diana shivered. "This is not a safe place. Better we get out now, with whatever we can grab than find ourselves outside without any warning or any chance to collect supplies." Maybe that was an exaggeration, but Diana wasn't confident enough to assume otherwise.

"We should hide him, first. He's going to be a problem when he comes around." Ben slapped Garrick's face lightly; no reaction. "He's out for the moment though. Bathroom?"

"That way." Diana slipped into the bedroom and opened the door to the en-suite. "You'll get in trouble if they find out you were helping me. Be careful."

"If you two are leaving, I'll come with you." Ben dragged Garrick after her by the feet. "This is not what I signed up for, and it's getting nasty. Besides, if this is going to be more than a few days' upset, I want to get back to my daughter. Her mother isn't the sort to do well in a crisis." Garrick's head thunked over the ridge that separated the bathroom from the bedroom.

Diana took hold of Garrick's hands and prepared to lift him. "In the tub, I think, and then gag him. We'll muffle him up with blankets and leave the TV on as loud as we can; it might give us a little time before anyone can hear him."

"Wait." Patti looked at the flimsy office trousers Diana was wearing. "That suit will be rags in two days flat. His uniform is far more sturdy." Ben looked dubious, and she winked at him. "Don't worry, sugar, I'm a nurse. I'm qualified to undress him. Besides, it will slow him down when he comes to."

"It might be best to go back to the door, in case someone comes past," Diana suggested.

Ben handed them the handcuffs and hurried away. The TV blared suddenly with those damn hockey playoffs, and then the door slammed shut.

They had Garrick stripped to the underwear in moments, then clicked the handcuffs around his wrists, threaded between the grab-bars on the sides of the bath just for good measure. "That should definitely slow him down." He moaned and Patti straightened. "Come on, he'll wake any minute." They packed him with blankets and pillows to make kicking difficult, gagged him with a sock and shut the bathroom door behind them.

"Can you wear a size ten?" Diana dangled the boots she held. "Too big for me."

"Probably wise." Patti slipped off her flats and put on the boots as Diana changed into Garrick's uniform. There was another groan, then infuriated grunts and muffled thumps from the bathroom.

Diana started. "Guessing he's awake. Let's hope the TV is loud enough."

"Let's not leave anything to chance." Patti picked up a heavy glass ornament from the side table and went in. There was a mighty thump, and the noise stopped. She closed the door behind her. "Don't look at me like that. I didn't spend all this time trussing him up just to smash his brains out. I know how to hit someone *just* hard enough. Bought us another few minutes, is all."

Diana wasn't sure if she was relieved to hear that or not, but she returned to the kitchen and double-checked for anything else that should go in the pillowcase of belongings.

Ben opened the apartment door. "All done, ladies? Then let's go."

Knotting the corners of the pillowcase Diana hurried ahead to call the elevator, Patti close behind, while he set the apartment door to auto-lock behind them and yanked out the wire from the keypad.

Then the elevator arrived, and they all piled in. "Let's get going, before they figure out we're missing."

The elevator stopped and Patti got out. "There's another backpack in one of the offices down the hall. Give me your pillowcase and I'll add whatever meds will fit in and meet you in the lab, ok? It's better if you're not seen wandering around with luggage just yet. They all know I'm on the list so no one will wonder about me leaving."

"We're floor twelve East, Lab 7."

"Got it. Good luck."

"You, too." Diana stood back and Ben released the hold button. "I have a feeling we're going to need it."

At the twelfth floor, a group of people was waiting to get in. Ben shouldered his way through them, Diana followed.

"Doctor Stewart? What are you doing down here?" It was Andrew, the intern.

"My new lab." To her relief his puzzled face was hidden as the doors closed. "Dammit. That boy is really anxious to impress Bryce and if he hears I've gone, he'll go tell Bryce immediately."

In the lab, she phoned Patti. "All well?"

"I think so." Patti's voice echoed hollowly on the speakerphone. "Ben, there's another backpack. Will you be able to take it?"

"Definitely."

"I'll be down in a couple of minutes. Nearly done."

At which point Ben's radio hissed static. "Hey! Who's supposed to be on guard outside the penthouse? There's no one here."

"That's not good." Diana rummaged in the cupboard. "Make it quick, Patti. Like, now."

"On my way."

The phone went dead and Diana opened the bag she'd found stuffed in the bottom of a cupboard. "Could you hold this, please?" Ben took the bag and followed her as she went along the shelves carefully placing the jars of salve she had made into the waiting bag, followed by as many of the raw ingredients as she could find. Then she took her notebook from the side and photocopied the page with the ingredients. As the copier spat out copy after copy, she tore out the page and shoved it in her pocket.

Patti arrived in the lab and Ben worked the sack of salve into one of the backpacks, which he slung over his shoulder.

"Take these." Diana shoved a sheaf of copies at Patti. "We leave them everywhere we go." She grabbed the rest and walked over to the windowsill, just as the lab door squealed on its hinges and Victor walked in.

"Diana! What the heck are you doing?" he demanded. "You! Why didn't you check with Bryce before allowing her to leave the apartment?"

Diana held up her hand. "Sorry, guys, could you give us the room for a moment?" Ben and Patti edged out, waiting in the corridor outside. Diana leaned on the windowsill, staring out over the city. Then she unlocked the window and opened it.

"Well?" Victor demanded.

Diana picked up the rest of the copies of the salve recipe and dropped them out of the window. They swirled in the updraft, drifting in all directions like leaves in autumn. They would spread out over a wide, wide area.

Victor grabbed her shoulder and turned her around. "Di, tell me that wasn't what it looked like."

"That was me giving the rest of the city their chance, yes."

He went white. "What have you done? Bryce will throw you out just as soon as he hears—"

"He'll have to hurry." She walked around the desk, collecting the safety goggles, and stuffed them all in her pack bar one pair, which she hooked over her wrist. "I'm leaving now. He's already started throwing our colleagues' families out, and if I stay, that would be condoning his actions. Which, needless to say, I absolutely oppose."

Victor turned away. "Oh for goodness' sake. Of course he's not throwing out the families—"

"Are you so sure?" She picked up a small tub of salve and dabbed it on her hands and face, rubbing it in briskly. "Are you telling me you didn't know?"

"I don't know anything about it, and if it was true I'd veto it on the spot. What do you take me for?"

"What do I take you for?" She walked past him and opened the other windows wide, then came back and set her bag by the door. "Someone with a whole load fewer principles than I believed, maybe?" She glanced at Ben's worried face, looking through the glass of the door, and nodded at the bag, willing him to take it. Then she took Victor's arm and walked him to the back of the lab out of Ben's view. Behind her the distinctive sound of the door opening and closing quickly meant Ben had understood her cryptic nod. A glance over her shoulder confirmed the bag was gone.

"Look Victor, you need to rein this in. Bryce, I mean." She turned to the window, looking out over the ruined city beneath. "If you don't do something, he'll be telling you what to do for the rest of your life. He's not a good person and he doesn't like you much. If you let him take control now, you'll never get that back."

Victor fiddled with a cufflink. "It's not that easy, Di. I love my granddaughter, but I only get to see her if I—watch out!" He waved his arm as a cicada buzzed past him. "Quick, shut the windows! Cicadas!"

"Sorry, Victor. I opened the windows to let them in." Diana pulled the goggles on and unlocked the door to the storeroom behind her. "Get in there. It's sealed, so you'll be safe."

"Di, we have to leave!" Another buzzed past him, and he yelped as it brushed the side of his hand.

"Too late, I'm afraid." She pushed him gently back into the storeroom and pulled the door shut, locking it from the outside.

He rattled the doorhandle. "What are you doing?"

"Keeping you safe from the cicadas, not that you deserve it." She dropped the key. "I'll tell them to come find you when we've gotten out. You shouldn't touch anything; it will need a deep clean before you can use the lab again."

He banged on the window. "Dammit, Di, I trusted you!"

"And I trusted you and see where that has left us." She hefted her bag over her shoulder, ducking as another cicada buzzed past. "This is where we see if the salve works as a barrier cream, eh? So long,

Victor, and thanks for whatever you actually did for me. You should probably count this as my resignation. I won't be working my notice."

She slipped out into the corridor where Ben and Patti waited. "Let's go." They ran to the lift and got in. "Here, keep these goggles to hand. Soon as we get somewhere quiet, cover your face and hands in the salve. The cicadas are back." She handed over goggles and cream and the others stuffed them in their pockets and fell silent as the elevator stopped at the next floor and someone got in. Diana tensed, but it was one of the janitors, an ancient lady called Rose who had been there longer than Diana had. Rose shuffled in with her trolley and ignored everyone as she usually did; her sight was failing and she couldn't afford new spectacles to make out who was actually there.

Diana looked up at the display in the lift. There were four lifts, and only one went up to the penthouse, but that was where it was now, and as she watched, it started to move downward. Catching Ben's eye, she nodded up at it.

He nodded. They'd already discovered she was missing, and Victor hadn't brought her back so the manhunt would be on. Ben waited until Rose got off and they were alone in the lift again; then he took out his radio and turned it on again. "Control, where's the clean-up crew?"

"The clean-up crew?"

"Yeah, the cicadas are back and some idiot's left a window open on twelve."

Diana watched the floor numbers go down. 11...10...

"Office morons. Anyone hurt?"

"Not so far, but someone said they'd gotten into the stairwell."

"And it's not like we can evacuate the building. Okay, we'll evacuate twelve in the first instance and make sure the windows are closed. Can you do it?"

"They'd get me if I went in. You're gonna need PPE, man, and plenty of it."

Ninth floor, and two women got in.

"We'll send a team soon as we can get them suited. Cleanup, this is Control; suit up and get to twelve. This is an emergency."

309

The women stopped talking. "What's the emergency?"

Ben turned his radio off. "Cicadas on twelve, ma'am. Someone let them in. Pass the word to stay away from the stairwells, okay?" The women got off at the eighth floor and hurried away, muttering between themselves. "Not far now, ladies. How are you with stairs?"

Patti looked at Diana.

"I'll do what I have to. My heel isn't badly damaged, just painful." As well as her shoulder, which was a dirty yellow where the bruising was healing, and her ribs, which were cracked rather than broken but still stabbed at her. But that could not slow her now; Bryce would happily have them shot if he had to.

Ben stabbed at the lift button for the third floor, and turned the radio volume up again. "They'll check the lifts next if they have any sense. We'll walk the last bit." Commands crackled from several different sources, some looking for cicadas and others for Diana.

The lift doors opened, and they filed out; a crowd of men and women got in. "I actually *need* coffee now," a dark-haired woman was saying. "I live off the stuff. I'm already having DTs from missing the first two of the morning—" Her voice was cut off as the doors closed. Ben led them to the stairs and opened the doors, checking up and down before beckoning them in.

"Wait." Diana waved him over. "Let's add to the chaos. It worked last time."

He took out his gun and smashed the glass on the fire alarm, and sirens blared. Once again, Diana found herself in the stairwell with the sirens shrieking, and people began to spill out of the offices and go down the stairs to mill about in the lobby. By the time they got down, it was crowded and chaotic.

"Everyone go back! This isn't a fire, it's a drill, but we can't let you outside. The cicadas are out there." There were two men trying to keep control of the situation, but the crush in the lobby was getting tighter and tighter.

"This way, quick." Patti led them down the stairs into the basement garage where a bus idled. A man with a clipboard was checking people on and off. "Jeff, there's chaos following us. The cicadas have gotten in and the fire alarm's gone off and no one knows if there's a fire or not."

"Not my issue." The man pushed his spectacles up on his nose. "You can get on. You're on the list. Who are these people?"

"It will be your problem when all the staff whose families are about to be sent away on this bus realize they can't come with them." As she spoke, a stream of people ran down into the basement, and several came running toward the bus. A woman stood up, yelling "Harry! Harry! Come, quick!"

Jeff held a hand out. "If you're not on the list—"

A man—Harry, presumably—felled Jeff with a punch and clambered onto the bus. The man threw his arms around his wife. "Don't worry, Kitty, everything will be okay. I'm coming with you."

"He was the driver!" Patti yelled.

Others were running toward them now, and the families were yelling frantically. Harry fought his way forward as Patti and the others took seats. "I'll drive, if someone can open the gates."

"I'll do it." Ben left his bag on his seat. He grabbed the set of keys from the driver's belt and tossed them to Harry, then took the keycard and ran for the entrance.

"Anyone getting off, now's the time," Diana yelled. "If you get in trouble ask to see Mr. Victor. He'll help you." *I hope.*

There was a rush for the door as people tried to rejoin their families, and then a few groups getting back on as they found their missing members. Security guards erupted out of the stairwell. "There, on the bus! Stop her!"

Harry revved the engine. "Time to go!"

As the guards ran to cut them off, Harry floored it. He accelerated to the end of the row, smashed through the cars at the end and won through to the exit lane.

Ben skidded to a stop by the office and swiped the keycard. The gate screeched as they began to grind open.

"Wait for him!" Diana gasped and Harry opened the coach door, slowing so that Ben could catch up.

Ben put a couple of bullets into the card reader and then sprinted after the bus. The security guys were close behind him; one tried to tackle him, but he dodged and leapt up onto the bus' stairs. He teetered, unbalanced and Diana reached out to grab his hand; but there was a gunshot and he collapsed forward.

Diana grabbed at his jacket as the bus smashed through the exit barrier and out onto the streets. There were screams and shouts inside and out, and a flood of people ran out of the basement; but then fog descended on them, a black cloud, and the people outside started to drop and writhe.

The cloud got nearer; something buzzed and fell onto her hand, tumbling down over Ben's back and outside. She recoiled but dared not let go of Ben, who lay still. "Cicadas! Shut the doors and windows, now, or we're all dead!"

"I don't know how to! I can barely drive this thing!" Harry's voice was high and squeaky. Hoping that there was still enough of the salve on her hands, Diana batted away another cicada, and another. And then the main part of the swarm closed in.

CHAPTER THIRTY-FOUR

CLAIRE MOONE. PATTERDALE, CUMBRIA, ENGLAND

With each turbulent vibration, Artemis gripped the sides of the car seat tighter. Claire sat in the back seat beside her father. She'd been there when they drove onto the Chinook and remained for the flight. No words were spoken.

In front of the Range Rover, even though the space inside the cargo bay of the helicopter was restricted, the team sat together on boxes and equipment crates. Unlike her, they all wore headsets and chatted. They were informed of how the flight was progressing. They knew things Claire didn't, and it irritated her. She had to babysit her father, relying to some extent on the substantial soundproofing of the vehicle.

"Who is your choice to replace your lost man?" Artemis's question surprised her. Not only had he found the power of speech, but he was showing an interest in her team.

There had been no time to speak to anyone about it. As Paladins, the primary squad operated at an elite level. It trained against the very best all services had to offer. A second team existed, but they were never used for missions. They were the group of candidates from which a replacement would be 'promoted.' Known as Tenebrae or Shadows, they followed all the missions and scenarios, making sure they were conversant with whatever situation the squad was in.

"With Trigger's specializations and his field experience, there's only one Shadow who logically fits." Claire was intrigued to know how he would react. "I want to fill the role with Dancer."

"I see. It's entirely your call, of course." He sounded like he was leading to a 'but,' yet didn't use the word. "Feathers will be ruffled at you bringing a second female operative into the squad. But if Dancer fills the requirements, as you say, that is really all that matters."

Plank walked beside the SUV, tapped on her window and pointed down. He raised his finger to indicate one minute.

"We're on approach to land, Dad." She wanted to sound as reassuring as she could. "We're nearly there." She hoped the pilot was as careful with landing as he had been on take-off. She'd been explicit in her instructions, delivered by Mickey.

Her father turned his head to hers. Following his gaze, she looked outside. He pointed at the only visible mountain peak that could be seen in the fuselage window beyond. "Helvellyn." It was a trip they'd shared. "Do you remember Striding Edge, my girl?"

"I do. I remember the summit, too. All three thousand, one hundred and eighteen feet of it." She had never forgotten the view, seeing out to the sea and the entire range of mountains that gave The Lakes their home.

The big Chinook pitched forward. He shut his eyes tight and braced himself against the driver's seat. "I hope that means we're landing, not crashing."

Tree tops flashed by, close to the helicopter, but far from the rotor blades. What few rooftops there were in the village became clear through the foliage. Claire knew the field where they were landing. "There's the White Lion Pub. We're coming in behind it, close to the Beck."

Touchdown was so smooth it was imperceptible. The descending whine of the engines and slowing rotors gave the only indication they were no longer airborne. Mickey opened the driver's door and jumped into the seat. "We'll be out of here in sixty seconds, sir."

Artemis relaxed his death grip on the upholstery and sat back into the leather seat. "Good man."

Operating in 'good daughter mode,' Claire used the most soothing tone she could find. "We're taking you straight to the cottage. The road over the bridge is clear and the gate is already open."

"That's good. Grey said he was here, already. There'd better be some of that mead left. He said he'd bring a bottle, after last time." He chuckled. "We ran out."

The thoughts he expressed were more private than she expected. They weren't as congruent with the seriousness of the situation as Claire thought they might have been. There was something about it that didn't add up. In the immediate moment the flight ended, he'd gone from being somewhat terrified, to calm and relaxed. Even the moment he caught sight of the mountain top, he hadn't shown any signs of fear that they were in the Chinook.

"Are you feeling alright, Daddy?" It was hard to ask him, with the enormous pressure they were all under. "Is everything okay?"

He jolted up in his seat, as if something pricked him. "Yes. Why wouldn't it be? We've a lot to sort out. I know you have your team on it. Use any extra resources you need. If you want more manpower, more eyes to look at things, pull people from Command. If they query it, tell them it's on my orders."

He was focused again. She couldn't see anything wrong with his logic and would take what she needed, on his say-so. "Yes, sir."

The tires of the SUV made a rumbling noise as it descended the metal ramp of the massive lifter, before scooting over the short grass of a field that had been grazed by sheep until it was commandeered as a landing zone. The wooden five-bar gate that held them away from the road was opened and the three cars slipped out onto the road and left past the whitewashed brickwork of the pub.

Another left turn took them over the broad stream of the Beck. The wrought-iron rails that sat on either side of the bridge had been there for over a century. The gate to the gravel drive of the cottage was open and welcoming. It was all so idyllic, it was hard to believe that only a hundred or so miles away, fires were raging.

Their Range Rover came crunching to a halt in front of a double-doored garage, built a few hundred feet away from the house.

A gray-haired man appeared from a path between blooming flowerbeds. His clothes were *retro-stylish*; a thick woolen jersey of heavy knitted cable, with an asymmetric neckline. Gray baggy flannels and leather walking boots. The kind of thing an alpine hunt master might wear.

Before Mickey could get out and open the door for Artemis, the other man did so.

"Hunter! You old bore." He bellowed, as if there was fifty feet between them. "You took your time getting here."

"Charlie! You survived a whole night here without me?" Artemis stood a good foot taller than Gandalf. Their handshake was polite yet enthusiastic. "Tell me you brought it."

"I brought a few more bottles, this time. I think we're going to need them. Let's get inside. We've got everything set up. The bunker is warmed up and we're already talking to the CDC and the UN. The others will be here later."

Claire shuffled over, then leaned out to take hold of the door handle. Artemis left her, without any acknowledgement of who she was. It was strange, because she'd known Charles Grey since she was a small child. Then again, much as it would have been pleasant to be reintroduced, she had her own purpose and an ongoing mission. "Take us to the tent, Mickey. It should be where it was last time."

Driving up the lane, the three SUVs went between two gritstone gateposts and onto plastic tiling that stopped vehicles getting bogged down or churning the field into nothing but ruts. A complex of tents, antennas, and radio dishes spread over an acre of meadow. A pontoon bridge and walkway were under construction to link the control center with the landing and supply zones of the base. They arched over the water running from high in the valley to the south, feeding Ullswater, the local lake.

"Food and drink, fellas." Those were her first orders, on arrival.

They were already taking their equipment out of the vehicles, all but one of them. It was a poignant reminder they'd lost a colleague and close friend. It was the right time. She had to make her announcement. "This is going to be hard for us all, but I have to organize Trigger's replacement. We'll have time to drink for him and send him on his way when this is over. We can't let it slow us down."

"It's going to be tough." Grouse's growl was heartfelt by them all. "He's a hard act to follow."

"I've made my selection." They stopped hauling their bags and waited to hear who she'd chosen. "Dancer is the best fit, considering it was Trigger we lost." She was his counterpart Shadow in recent training exercises. Taking her would mean Claire wouldn't have to go through the entire selection process for another Tenebrae operative, and more administration work.

They looked between each other, nodding and mouthing her name. There was an acceptance of the choice. Any one of them could have raised an objection. They would have been heard and their reasons discussed.

"Dancer it is." She walked toward the communications tent. "She's going to have to get her arse here on the double." After a few strides, she put her hand into her tunic pocket, took out her badges and tapped them onto the Velcro that would hold them while she was on base. Her black uniform was no indication of her unit, nor did any of them display rank when on a mission.

There was no division for Claire or any of the Paladins, between duty and death. The certain commitment to both was an absolute requirement for the selection process. Any one of them could die in a given moment. Looked at dispassionately, all of them could be lost on a mission. They accepted death as more than a risk, it was a likelihood. Death or retirement from duty were the only two ways out of the Paladin team. If they were fortunate, they would be 'aged out' of the squad.

Losing a man to a poison, rather than a bullet, was something different. There was no immediate enemy, other than a swarm of bugs. The collision of the ship with the windfarm had been a complete accident, but Trigger was dead before the explosion that took his body. Someone would pay for that. Hopefully they had all the information they needed to work out who. The team could work on that before Dancer arrived. Claire needed them to do it, so they could have their vengeance.

The comms tent was situated in the middle of the array of antennas. It was small, containing computers and server stacks. A junior rank in his twenties wearing camouflaged fatigues typed at a keyboard. "Personnel only in here, love."

Someone was asking to be punched. "On your feet, corporal." Her tone was flat. Her immediate instruction caught him off guard. "Who's in charge here?"

He scrambled to his feet, with a puzzled look on his face. Another soldier appeared from behind one of the tall system stacks. "That would be me. He's right though. You'll have to..." His eyes widened. His entire body stiffened, and he came to attention, raising his hand to his forehead in a salute. "Apologies, Major."

"Send this message to Specialist Amelia Fontaine. Stirling Lines." She handed him one of her business cards. "Give my number, this location, and whatever she requests."

"Yes, ma'am. But..." He tapped the touchscreen of his computer console. "I can't do that without an..." He knew her rank, yet there was still a patronizing tone to his voice. It irritated her even more than the ignorance of the corporal. "Auth code is One Tango One Hotel Three X-Ray Eight."

"That's done." He leaned on the back of his chair, posing for her to admire him. "Is there anything else I can help you with, major?"

"Yes, there is."

He sat forward with a slight grin on his face. "And what might that be?"

She inhaled, filling her chest and pulling her shoulders back on purpose, ensuring she had his attention and admiration. "Call your wife. Make sure she's safe. And... Don't try to flirt. It makes you look like a lovelorn puppy."

His left hand slid to cover the wedding ring on his right hand, and he rose from the seat to stand at ease. The younger soldier smirked.

He was not going to escape her scathing tongue. "As for you, corporal, be more observant. Don't open your mouth, before you open your eyes. You'll look less like a muppet."

Embarrassment flicked through his cheeks, coloring them deep red. "Yes, ma'am. Thank you, ma'am."

She couldn't tell if either of them would change from her light roasting but pushing against the assumption that she was a low-ranking officer, rather than the person in command, was something she'd had to do all her life. "The moment there is a response, find me. Is that clear?" As they uttered their understanding, she turned to face the entrance. She marched out of the tent, into the fresh air of midmorning.

Crows cawed overhead. Trees swayed in the light breeze. Until her life as a soldier gave her more understanding of her father's work, the village and the surrounding mountains had been a charming holiday destination. It was where she'd taken a walk in her very first pair of shoes. She had so many fond memories of the place, before she learned of the true purpose of the Cottage. In some ways, nothing had changed over the years. The growing military encampment was just a few days old and in contrast with the quiet country setting, but it didn't alter or detract from the true beauty of the landscape.

Walking through another canvas portal, her senses sparked. A waft of burned fat brought a mouth-watering tang with it. Her stomach growled in hunger. "Where the hell have you horrible lot found bacon?"

Wedging half a sandwich into his mouth, Mickey glanced at Grouse. In turn, he looked at Plank. "The post office started doing bacon butties, boss. I saw the sign as we drove past."

"I've been gone five minutes and you're all scoffing grub down without me?" She raised her hands at her side. "Where's mine?"

Without a word, Nerd slid something across the table, between her and his laptop. A paper plate, covered with a crisp white napkin.

She revealed a greasy sandwich of toasted bread. A slice of thick-cut bacon poked from between the two sides. "Aww. I love you guys."

As she took the first tasty bite, there was a tapping noise behind her. "Excuse me, major." It was the signalman from the tent.

Grouse spoke, so she could continue to chew. "What is it, corporal?"

"Sir. The major's message was received and acknowledged."

The Scotsman waited for Claire to give him the nod, before speaking. "Very well. Dismissed."

"Wait," Nerd called out, making the soldier tense his posture even more than he had. "Take this cable back with you. Lay it as you go." He lifted a reel from behind his chair, took the plug at the end and located a socket on his machine. "I want a clean ISDN 30. Direct link."

"Yes, sir. I'll do that. Clean ISDN 30." He stepped forward, grabbed the handle of the frame and walked backward. He pulled the cable off as he moved, laying it in a small trench that contained other wires and cables.

When the soldier left, Nerd had a smug look on his face. "Saved me doing it."

Claire wiped her hands, then sat at the head of the long table. The layout of the tent was no different to the one they had at Crosby or any they'd used in missions or on exercises. Everything was where it was supposed to be. Taking hold of a manila folder, she opened it and thumbed through what few pages of intel there were. "Is this everything?"

"It's going to be enough." Mickey was ever the optimist. "We just need to go through it until we get what we need."

Plank stood, pulled a whiteboard closer and began writing. "We've got the *Maid of Morning*. Chinese registered vessel. I asked an old mate about that. He's captain of coastal boats, nowadays. Chinese ships, anything from the Far East really, come into ports in the south, Southampton, Portsmouth, Tilbury, not Liverpool."

"It's a deep-water port. The Maid's an ocean-going freighter, not coastal." Grouse sat forward and flipped back to the beginning of the ship's log. "It must be on a charter of some sort. There's nothing in here, though."

Mickey chimed in. "There's a note in the captain's daybook. Something about putting the cicadas into a container of fig plants.

That was what Marsalis was doing, before he died. He was taking the bugs to... to what?"

Nerd tapped and clicked. "I've got something. That ship was registered in China. Three sister ships, all built the same way. All Maid of something. Dawn, Morning and Evensong. Hang on... No... Two are in the South China Sea. Bollocks."

It was clear to Claire. "We need to know who chartered them and we need to know if they chartered any other vessels."

"Got that." Nerd continued his digital investigation. "It's a company called Arnet Holdings, though that could be an alias, a front of some kind? They've got twenty contracts through agencies. Six are bound for UK ports, at the moment."

Plank was writing everything on the board, drawing lines between elements of linkable information. "What cargo are they carrying? Do they have fig trees?"

"There are... Two... Only two carrying fig trees." Nerd shoved the mouse here and there, clicking it with his finger. One of the printers at the side of the tent came to life. "Got their details."

Claire could see the relief on the faces of her men. The information gave them an opportunity to stop the attacks. "Forward that stuff to Lazarus. Relay it to Team Two. Immediate tasking. We're *all* going ship hunting."

CHAPTER THIRTY-FIVE

ANAYELI ALFARO. SACRAMENTO, CALIFORNIA

Anayeli knew there was time. The light was dim, the hour early. The sun was a red disc low on the horizon, a faint glow just above the barest hint of an outline of trees. Even though everything—unlocking all the cells the evacuees formerly known as "the purples" had occupied, cutting off old wristbands, handing out new ones from her stolen stash—had taken longer than she'd imagined, she still had hours until Darren's scheduled flight-time. Every time her unease spiked with a surge of nausea, she reminded herself that even though she'd only intended to get Mama out and hadn't budgeted time for a large-scale rescue operation, she had wiggle room. Because once she saw them, leaving the other purples behind had ceased to be an option. But as the minutes stretched, her patience thinned. She didn't want to wait any longer to get through the last set of locked gates and bolt for Carlota and Bailey Rae. She wanted her whole family in Fatima's safe room two hours ago, ready to get on Darren's helicopter well before it was time.

"Listen up!" Anayeli used her commanding voice. "We're going to stay in line and go through these gates in an orderly fashion. A few of us at a time. So we don't attract too much attention." It was almost imperceptible, but the line of purples shifted and straightened. It was weird the way they listened, how she'd managed to keep everyone together all the way through the first set of gates and past the pile of bodies. Maybe the lie she'd told the long-gone creepy guard was true: the purples didn't have the energy to fight. She preferred to think it had more to do with the goodwill the purples felt toward her for getting them out.

Except one person—the skinny girl who'd asked for more food—didn't get with the program. She strayed out of the line, a hand on her hip. "Why don't you just open the gates and let us out?"

Anayeli's insides went tighter, as if her veins were being pressurized. She gripped Mama's hand and let out a sound that was half hiss, half whistle, her eyes fierce, her finger stabbing toward the girl's chest, laser-beaming fury straight at the girl's heart. "Back in line. Now. Or no one goes at all."

Anayeli waited. She had her gun in her waistband and the gate key around her neck, tucked under her shirt, the same way the creepy guard had done. Skinny Girl held her ground, still jutting out of the line.

"It's not up for debate!" Anayeli made her expression as flat and grim as she could before leveling a hard stare at Skinny Girl. The last thing Anayeli needed was for impatience to spread and grow into panic. Her every joint tingled with a terrible urgency—the same feeling she could only assume was making everyone else twitchy too—but she made herself project calm immobility.

Someone in the line raised their voice. "Get back in line!"

Skinny Girl glanced away from Anayeli, just a flick of her eyes to the crowd of purples, and that's when Anayeli knew she'd won. This round.

The girl sidled back into her place. But the order wasn't going to last. The longer they stood taking in the scene outside the last set of gates, the worse things were going to get.

Tension crackled through the air and more whispers from the line of purples reached her ears. A surge was building. In the hours since she'd moved through the evacuation center everything had changed. No one was asleep anymore. In the same open area where Darren's helicopter had landed and was still parked, rows of drab green and tan military transport vehicles massed, engines rumbling as they idled in a line that snaked out of the hospital parking garage. Soldiers passed boxes from one to the next, loading the vehicles with supplies.

Several soldiers hurried from the hospital, fanning out. The one nearest their gate shouted, "Move! Double time! Move, move, move!" He waved his arms. "The fire has breached the retardant! It's headed this way!"

Beyond the last set of gates out of the purple zone, the main camp churned with the frenzy of a kicked-over ant hill. Anyone well enough to move was moving. Masked refugees spilled out of tents, dragging children and blankets and their meagre belongings. Other soldiers took up the call, directing their own lines of refugees to "Move!" pointing them toward guarded staging areas.

It was clear to anyone with eyes: the evacuation the creepy guard had told her about was already underway, and it was less than orderly. In a world that was moving, she was asking people to stand still. It went against every instinct.

The creep had been right—she wasn't enough to control all the purples.

"*Qué está pasando*, Anayeli?" Mama squeezed Anayeli's hand, gripping hard the way she had the moment Anayeli'd thrown open the gate to her dear Mama's cell. There would be time for explanations, for more apologies later. Much later. Once the family—what was left of it—was somewhere safe. Truly safe. In Montana, maybe. But Anayeli couldn't screw up again.

She recalibrated her plan in a blink. She didn't owe the purples anything. She'd already done more than she'd intended and put her own family's safety at risk. No more. She yanked the key up by its chain and pitched her voice low. "Get ready Mama. We're going to run." She unlocked the padlock, threw the gate wide. "*Corre!*"

Anayeli bolted through the gate and sharply to the left, dragging Mama after her, out of the path of the charging purples. It was mayhem—anyone watching would be immediately suspicious. But no one was watching. No one shouted at them to stop. Still, Anayeli wanted to get as far from the purples as they could, praying the chaotic evacuation would be enough to conceal her and Mama. She pulled Mama through the gate into the blue zone, flashing her black wristband at the guard there, and pushing through the evacuees already waiting at the staging area.

"Carlota!" Mama cried, pulling away, as if she wanted to search the gathered crowd.

"No! She's not here! We've got to get to the orange zone!" It was slow going, with Mama pausing to search every face, calling Carlota's name.

"Mama! *Corre!* She's in the orange zone!" Mama's backward drag on Anayeli's arm eased and they barreled past a coughing woman, supported by a hobbling man. At one tent, soldiers were pulling several children out, lifting them into their arms before hurrying away. Pairs of soldiers used cots as stretchers to move the sickest blue zoners.

Anayeli and Mama were like salmon swimming upstream, battering themselves against rocks. Only when the gate to the orange zone loomed in front of them, did Anayeli realize Mama was sobbing.

"It's all right, Mama! Carlota will be here." It was too early for Fatima to have already come to collect the girls. She searched the faces of the people gathered in the orange zone staging area.

"Carlota Alfaro!" Mama's voice was a raw siren calling for her daughter, over and over.

"She'll be waiting in the tent! Come on!"

But when they arrived at the end of the row, in front of the tent where Anayeli had left Carlota and Bailey Rae, the flap hung open. Anayeli ripped it aside, peering in. The tent was empty, as if the girls had never been there.

Outside, Mama wailed, every sob Carlota's name, ripping from her throat. And then the barking started. It had to be Cricket, still waiting outside the evacuation center fence. Anayeli would recognize his bark anywhere—the sharp warning one. Another bark, lower pitched, joined the first one. Roxy.

Anayeli backed out of the tent, grabbed Mama by the shoulders, and shook her. "Stop it! Mama! It's okay." Her mother's eyes were red and puffy, her face streaked with tears, pain etched through every feature. "This is all part of the plan. My friend Fatima was going to get the girls if I couldn't—" The words caught in her throat. It was too early though. Even without any way to tell time, she knew from the flat red disc of sun. It wasn't time yet for Darren to be flying. "She must have taken them to our safe room to wait—so they wouldn't get caught up in all this!" She waved a hand at the seething mass of activity around them. Some people—maybe former purples who no longer had any trust in the troops running the evacuation—were climbing the chain link fence surrounding the evacuation center. Things were getting worse, just as she'd predicted.

"We'll get the dogs and go—"

"*Los perros?* Are you *loca?* We need to find Carlota!"

Anayeli didn't disagree, but the dogs were barking. And there was time. Cricket and Roxy had stayed faithfully outside, watching over the girls. Maybe they'd belonged to Farmer Josh and Sid, but they were hers now. The fire was coming and hundreds of desperate, hungry people were going to be roaming the city. None of her beloveds were going to be caught up in that madness.

"I'm not leaving anyone behind!" She wrenched her hand away from Mama's and ran along the fence line, for the gate. Cricket bolted ahead, ears laid back and wolfish, while Roxy bounded alongside. From behind her, Mama screamed at her to stop, but she pushed that aside. There was time. She knew there was.

The gate—the same one her family had been dragged through that first night—was unguarded and unmanned, and locked. That hadn't stopped a crowd—men mostly, but a smattering of women—from gathering at it. The group of maybe twenty were pulling at the gate, yanking it inward, then shoving it out, as if through sheer force of will they might break the chain holding it closed.

"Let me through!" Anayeli threw elbows as she fought through the heaving, shouting mass. It was a mosh pit on steroids and her borrowed uniform made her a target for foot stomps and shoves. "I have the key!"

The people in her immediate vicinity gave way as soon as her words penetrated. She went a few steps before she had to shout again. "I have the gate key!"

"Let the lady through!" A barrel-chested man let out a loud bellow and plowed a space for her, using himself as a battering ram.

When she'd finally wormed her way to the front and found the padlock, she had to lean into Barrel-Chest's sweat-slicked body, as he stood at her back, barely managing to keep her from being pressed into the gate.

"Stay back! Let her open it!" If Barrel Chest's words had any effect, she couldn't tell.

On the other side of the gate, Cricket's bark became a mix of bark and growl, and Roxy's hackles were up. And from somewhere, Mama's voice cut through it all, screaming curses at her. So much for being forgiven. *Later.* She had dogs—and maybe people—to save. Because if these people weren't going to get in on the military evacuation, they were better off getting out sooner, rather than later. Maybe they could get ahead of the fire and stay there. Maybe if there was anyone still left outside the fences, they could come in and get help. That's how she justified it to herself. Really, she just couldn't bear to leave the dogs behind. And besides, Bailey Rae needed Roxy.

It took several tries thanks to the crush of bodies behind her, but she got the key into the lock—it fitted the lock easily, went in smoothly. Except it wouldn't turn. She pulled it out again, then shoved it back in—still it wouldn't budge. "No. No no no." It was the wrong key. Of course one key couldn't work on every gate—that would be stupid. She tried one more time, pulled it out, shoved it back in. This time it went in one click farther. "Please *Jesus, Maria y Jose, hear my prayer.*" She twisted the key—and it turned, the padlock releasing with a pop.

Just like before, she threw the gates wide—but she couldn't get out ahead of the human tide, and was swept along with the rush, stumbling through the flood of people. She fell, hoping she'd helped save lives, instead of the opposite.

The dogs found her first, Roxy licking her over and over, before she could manage to find her feet. And then Mama was there, screaming in Spanish, calling her an idiot, a crazy girl, as she yanked her up and back through the gates, pointing toward the hospital. At the roof.

If Mama hadn't been pulling at her, she would have stopped in her tracks. It couldn't be. But a throbbing beat cut through and above all the other human and canine and mechanical noise, beating against her eardrums. No—

The whine of an engine revving for lift-off and the beating throb of the helicopter's blades were unmistakable. It was coming from the hospital roof. Where Anayeli was supposed to meet Darren, Fatima, Jeremy, and Brandon—but not yet! It was too early!

But it wasn't. Two figures darted across the roof toward the spinning blades of the helicopter—one taller, with dark hair streaming like banners behind her, the other shorter. "Carlota and Bailey Rae! We have to get up there!"

She and Mama bolted for the medical building, the dogs charging ahead, then dashing back, their frenzy just more of the same chaos already going on around them.

They had just cleared the orange zone gates—Anayeli's uniform and black wristband working its magic as she threw her arm up and kept running past—when shots punched through the noise.

She would have pancaked on the pavement—terrified like Cricket —but screams rang out, thin and high enough to cut through everything else.

Her sister.

She and Mama must have been hit with the same surge of adrenaline because they both charged the distance to the hospital. There was no time to waste to go see if anyone was still left in the safe room, to make sure Nurse Kerry had gotten Ernesto and Jeremy had managed Brandon's gurney. Instead, they barreled up the endless flights of stairs as if they were nothing, shoving through whatever people were in their path, the dogs behind them now, their barks echoing through the stairwell, helping clear it.

They made good time, as good as they could have ever hoped. But at the last landing, their way was blocked. Two guards stood in front of the door.

Anayeli had no breath with which to speak. She held up her wrist, exposing her black band. "I need... through... now. This woman... she needs—"

Before either guard could react, Mama yanked the gun from Anayeli's waistband and fired. There was the sickening thug of a bullet hitting soft flesh. A spray of blood. Both soldiers hit the floor and Mama fired again. More blood.

Anayeli didn't stop to see which one Mama had shot. If either of the soldiers lived. She leapt over them and shoved through the door, Mama hard on her heels, the gun still in her hand.

They were too late.

The helicopter was already in the air, disappearing into the smoke—too far gone to see them, let alone hear their screams. They'd been left behind.

"*Ay, dios!*" Mama dropped to her knees. "*Mis bebés!*"

But they weren't the only ones up there. Roxy and Cricket ran across the roof, to a slumped shape on the ground. Anayeli dashed after the dogs, afraid to hope, afraid to look. The gunshots—had they—?

It wasn't her sister or Bailey Rae. The shape was too big.

"Jeremy! Oh, *Dios mio!* What happened?" Anayeli knelt beside him, trying to avoid the creeping spread of the blood pooling around him. He looked pale—paler than usual. "Where are you hurt?"

He didn't answer, just flapped a hand like a half-dead fish flopping on the ground.

"Are you—Can you talk? Why are you here—Did everyone else make it?"

"The girls—Brandon... safe." Every word was an effort, half gasp.

"Ernesto?" She clutched at Jeremy's hand. "Stay with me. Where's my brother?"

"I couldn't—The nurse. Your brother—" Jeremy pressed his free hand to his side and let out a moan.

"No! You can't! Please. Get up—" Anayeli pulled at Jeremy's shoulders, trying to help him upright.

"Thompson Falls." His legs writhed as he forced the words out. "Get there. If, then dry creek. The end." Something like a breath escaped him, forcing out the next words. "You go." Then he was still. Heavy.

She jumped to her feet. Jeremy had only said the girls and Brandon were safe. She didn't even know what that meant, not really, but she had to assume they were on that helicopter, headed for Jeremy's family's place in Montana. That's what Thompson Falls meant. The rest of what he'd said, she had no clue about.

"Mama! We have to go down. The safe room—I think Ernesto is still there!" She didn't know what to hope, what was better. She had no idea how they would reunite with Carlota, how they could get to Montana. But none of that mattered until they figured out whether Ernesto had gotten on the helicopter or not.

Anayeli had no memory of getting back down the stairs or through the hall. Mama was with her, running and crying. The dogs were there too. Everything else, every face they passed—not Ernesto, not Ernesto, not Ernesto—blurred to featurelessness. She tore through a haze of numbness until the moment she threw open the door to the safe room. It was empty.

"No!"

There was only a purple binder—Ernesto's medical records—left on the chair where Nurse Kerry had been sleeping the last time Anayeli had been in the room. Nothing else. She snatched up the binder, her thoughts spinning. What could it possibly mean, if Ernesto's records were here, but he wasn't? Jeremy must have meant that he didn't get Ernesto out, but Nurse Kerry had, after all. And if Nurse Kerry had Ernesto, it could only mean he was caught up in one thing: the official evacuation.

Still Mama sobbed, Anayeli's gun in her hand. Anayeli snatched it, stuffed it into her backpack along with Ernesto's binder.

She couldn't think. She didn't know what to do. She only had the few meagre supplies she'd thrown in her backpack, thinking she wanted at least a few things, just in case. But this was beyond any kind of just in case she'd considered. Her brother and sister were gone. She and Mama had no other way out of the evacuation center, except whatever the military was planning.

"We'll get a car, Mama. Out of the parking garage. We'll drive to Montana. That's where the helicopter is going."

Mama didn't say anything, her face a mask of grief and stony anger, but she didn't resist when Anayeli pulled her back out into the hallway. The medical center was a madhouse of people scrambling around, grabbing supplies, wheeling patients, everyone trying to get out. But they had a gun. And the dogs. And a plan. A new plan.

Anayeli was shouldering her way through the door from the stairwell to outside when someone caught her free arm.

"Anayeli? Oh thank goodness!" It was Nurse Kerry. "Hurry! You have to get on the convoy. I already got your brother on it."

CHAPTER THIRTY-SIX

SAM LEARY. THE GREAT SALT LAKE DESERT, UTAH

The circus tent was coming down around Sam. He'd watched from the darkness of the door flaps, assessing, gathering data. Shadowy figures, lit by the headlights of the marauders' vehicles, had spilled out into the desert and run toward the settlement. One of them, a man with some kind of pry bar, had headed straight for the command center tent Sam was hiding in. But instead of barging into the tent and going after people, pry bar guy had laid into one of the tent's stakes. The metal twang as he'd attacked it had echoed in the vast emptiness of the desert.

As soon as he'd loosened the first few supports for the tent, two other men carrying a heavy chain had joined him. They'd used the chain to yank the rebar from the ground and the rope keeping the tent from collapsing in on itself. They moved with quick efficiency around the circumference of the tent, loosening a third stake, and then a fourth.

As the tent's material sagged inward and the center dipped down,

John cranked on the alarm. "You'd better get out of here, the whole things coming down."

"I've got an escape plan."

Another few strikes and the tent would become a ground cover, Sam and John two lumps beneath it. But Sam didn't want to be trapped under a collapsed tent. He'd rather take his chances in the desert. He crept out and let the flaps settle closed, the heavy canvas swishing. Headlights from the marauders' cars sped past, lighting up the pathway where he stood. He crouched, his throat dry as sand. The majority of the caravan was making its way further into the tent city, but they'd left behind pry bar guy and his chain-wielding pals. The last thing Sam wanted was to become a target. It'd be better to stay invisible, to disappear into the darkness.

Pry bar guy shuffled into sight, his tool slung over his shoulder. The man was skinny, but he looked strong in a sinewy, wiry kind of way, and as far as Sam was concerned, anyone bent on destroying instead of building was someone to avoid. He backed into the fading light of dusk, becoming one with his surroundings. The people invading the camp had provided him with the perfect distraction, and he was going to use it to find Jesse. His friend and mentor, Dr. Diana Stewart was counting on him.

John's hand-cranked alarm stopped and one of the marauders yelled into the quiet. Sam spun around as a tall woman, wearing cargo pants and a vest, carrying a baseball bat primed with sharp nails, pointed the weapon in his direction. Dammit, they'd spotted him. An SUV engine revved from the opposite side of the tent, and instead of collapsing, the circus tent moved. The vehicle dragged the tent, pulling its mass of cloth and metal with the chain. The antenna smashed into the ground, its rending spikes digging into the dirt. Sam bolted.

Panicked screams rose from the interior of the city, harsh in the evening air. He threw a glance over his shoulder, and in the glare of the headlights, he could make out the woman who'd spotted him. She was stalking him, swishing her bat back and forth as she moved. He tore down the path toward the Eiffel tower, its dark silhouette tall and stark against the stars.

Sam dodged left down a side path, away from the tower. His calf burned, slowing him down, and he dove behind a baker's tent. His pursuer must not have seen him because the woman jogged on, passing between him and a set of pup tents.

A whistle pierced the night air, growing louder as it neared his hiding place. With a light thud, something hit the dirt behind him and rolled foward. It stopped in a divot, rocking back and forth before it settled. It might've been a rock, except for the amber glow, about the size of a dime, on one side. It flickered, sparked, and, with a sizzle, grew brighter. Flame! He leapt away, ducking behind a plastic building—the porta-potty. Not good. He held his breath to avoid the stench, but before he could get any farther away, a blast of heat surged around the porta-potty and enveloped him. An instant later, the plastic toilet fell backward, throwing him onto his back. Liquid waste splattered across the ground and his feet as flame licked the side of the destroyed toilet. Sam pushed up on his elbows, his ears ringing from the blast. The entire side of the porta-potty was gone.

Those idiots were throwing homemade explosive devices into a city with families and innocent people.

There was another flash of heat and flame, followed by an explosion so intense, it caught the tent next to him on fire. Above the ringing of his ears, he heard a muffled whistling as another inbound explosive flew overhead. He stayed down until the missile passed him, then sat up. The plastic toilet melted further, gone in less than a minute. The contents oozed out from the holder, its waste on fire. There had to be enough methane to run a generator for an hour. The scent of burning sulfuric molecules, along with an enormous rush of barnyard, filled his nose, and his eyes watered. He needed to move. Fast. He gagged and coughed twice before he scrambled to his feet and ran from the lava like sludge.

He darted down another row of tents. In his headlong dash, he missed the corner and tripped over the line. He dropped, skidding on his knees and face-planted on the hard ground, the sand digging into his cheek, scraping at his skin. One knee bled and his eye smarted as he got to his feet and stumbled on.

People from the city scurried as more of the homemade bombs

dropped, screaming and calling out. It was a madhouse, and they blocked the way to the tower. He needed to see where the marauders had gone. He needed to know which path was safe to take so he could search for Jesse. Limping, he shuffled on, hoping that whatever was dripping down his leg was blood instead of sewage.

Another bomb whistled overhead and landed next to him. He hop skipped around another tent just before the force of the explosion threw him forward onto his hands and knees. The tent that had taken the blast flapped around him, burning and melting, dripping hot nylon onto his clothes. The heat sent him into a panic. He kicked at the fabric and waved his arms, freeing himself from the inferno, then rolled in the sand. The bubbling plastic came free, along with patches of clothing. His shirt and pants looked like swiss cheese. There was another thud as a new projectile hit to the side of him and he ran. It didn't matter if he was bleeding or his skin was singed. He may not get another chance to rescue Jesse. Pushing through the pain, he limped toward the tower.

By the time he'd reached the structure, three areas of the city were on fire. He struggled up the ladder, keeping his eyes on the platform above. His body zapped of energy as he rolled onto his back, breathing hard. Safe on the perforated metal, he snatched up the binoculars John had left there and took in the battle. The west side of the city was a hot zone, cars zipping left and right, tearing down tents and people if they didn't move. A couple of people in the bed of a flatbed truck were using a type of slingshot to shoot the bombs into the camp. If they had any sense, they'd have targeted select areas to drive everyone a specific direction. The creeps were firing at random.

The north wasn't as bad off, but they'd burned many of the dwellings to the ground and the first tent Sam had ever entered had been dragged across the flat dirt plain by an overzealous compact car. Further east, the camouflaged canopy rippled in a light wind and small wisps of green and orange light flitted in and out of sight. Something was happening where people least expected it. Sam slapped his forehead. Of course, a diversion—he should have thought of it sooner, given he was employing the same strategy. The intruders were making the most noise where they wanted all the attention while they robbed their actual target.

Sam climbed down the railing, limbs shaking as he reached solid ground. The monstrosity wasn't safe, even though he'd climbed it twice. Another homemade bomb struck the tower and glass exploded. He covered his head, ducked as low as he could, and scurried south, across a clear patch of dirt.

He stopped where the path curved around a bend. A line of tents blocked the way to a metal rib that reached high into the sky. He was in the second ring before the center of the city. From the right came raucous laughter, and he made for the line of tents. Three men ran past, holding bottles with cloth hanging out of the tops. Molotov cocktails! One marauder lit a rag, the material burning bright like a bonfire. When the flame expanded enough to reach the neck of the bottle, he threw it. It bounced off a tent wall and rolled back toward the man who'd thrown it, lighting his pant leg on fire. He jumped around, slapping at the hem of his jeans as the contents of the bottle ignited and exploded. The man screamed but his buddies laughed and kicked at their companion as he dropped to the ground. *Madness. Absolute madness.*

Sam ducked behind an awning as the two men passed by, carrying the third. They babbled like a trio of drunkards on their way to another bar. The city was being pilfered by the most inept thieves he'd ever witnessed. He shook his head and continued south, intent on finding Jesse.

The wind kicked up, throwing dirt devils through the small passages and temporary dwellings. He shaded his eyes against the dirt. Jesse had to be around there somewhere. Sam hastened to the first metal and glass dome house. It had to have been thirty feet tall and about the same in diameter. Unlike the Eiffel tower, which was made of scraps, the dome was uniform and sturdy, as if someone who knew what they were doing had constructed the building. Glass panes fit in each small triangle and a soft glow of chemical light eked out. He pressed his face against the glass, The dim interior was sparse. There were no kids, no toys. A man passed by and he sidled sideways out of view. It'd be best not to reveal himself unless there was a chance Jesse was there.

He ran to the next dome and hid behind the bracer. It was thick enough to hide his skinny body. A couple of kids flashed by the windows, just visible by the dim light. They pressed their noses against the glass, fogging up the pane with their breath. A parent loomed behind them. "Keep away from the windows. You know the drill."

Sam was in the right spot—the family quarters—but had no idea how to rescue a kid without causing a ruckus. He placed his hand on the metal girders that made up the exterior shell of the dome and followed it in the dark until he came to the door. It was a small thing, and the hinges groaned with their heavy, unoiled creak. He had to duck to enter and the door slammed shut the instant he let go of the handle. Four families snapped their heads toward him and gathered their children close.

Sam put out his hands to show he was unarmed and squatted down on his haunches. "Have any of you seen a boy called Jesse recently?" The families stared at him. "He's about three feet tall with brown curly hair and a scab on his face."

Recognition dawned in a father's eyes and he cast a glance around before whispering, "You mean the new boy. Arrived this week."

Sam's heart lurched, and he leaned forward. "That could be him. Any idea where I can find him?"

The father shook his head and wrapped his arms around two children in front of him, pulling them closer. "He's not in this dome, or the one next to us. We're not allowed to talk with the other families in those domes unless we're working the greenhouse. Sorry I can't be of more help."

Sam got up and reached for the door. "Thank you." Two domes down, and three to go.

The door groaned again as he pulled it open, and he dashed into the night. He'd gone maybe fifteen paces when the woman wielding the death bat rounded the dome and bumped into him. She cried out and fell to the ground. "Help, I'm being attacked."

Lantern light flashed from the south and the Cowboy appeared at the center of the domes, raising his light high as he scanned the area. Sam reached for the door. All he needed to do was run in and check for the child but the woman yelled again, scrambling backward. Sam withdrew. If he was caught looking for Jesse, it might endanger the boy and ruin his chances of searching another time. He hobbled northeast.

The sounds of the attack fell away as he entered the supply depot, which housed everything from food to machinery. No wonder the camp was being attacked. Not only did the mini city have semi-tractor trailers and power tools, they also had boxes of dehydrated food and barrels of water. Two generators were positioned side by side along the front of the cordoned off area. Extension cords that had to be at least one hundred feet coiled like serpents and lay on top of the machines. The tinge of oil and gas filled the air as he walked further into the storage area. "Belle? I've got news from John." There was no response. He walked to the other side of the storage area, following the trailer and a car. The place was deserted.

He wasn't supposed to be there, but there were too many supplies for him to go away empty-handed. The fires burned on and, in the distance, the yells of the marauders echoed through the night. There was still time, and he needed to look, or get out of there. He dug through a toolbox, producing a multi-meter, a soldering station, and chainsaw. He put them in a pile and shifted to the next crate of supplies.

There were explosives and ammo of all sorts, boxes of canned goods and freeze-dried food. He slid the box of explosives under the semi-tractor trailer, hiding it behind the wheel as best as he could. If he found Jesse, they'd need supplies, and maybe the small stash would go unnoticed until he returned for it. He added a box of canned fruit to his secret cache but as he pushed it forward, green and yellow lights flashed. Four men entered the storage area, and Sam scrambled to slide under the semi-trailer.

Each of the men was armed with either a hammer or axe. Sam held his breath, trying to be as still and quiet as possible as the men stalked through the supply depot.

The closest took a swing with his axe and Sam scooted farther under the semi-trailer. He'd played this game before. The axe plunged into a barrel, sticking, and the man yanked on it, pulling the curved weapon out of the container. Liquid spilled on the ground, filling the area with fumes.

While the men were intent on destruction, Sam edged to the other side of the trailer. Keeping behind the stacks of supplies, he scurried outside. He'd come back later for the things he'd gathered. Once he'd found Jesse.

Someone yanked hard on his shoulder. He toppled to his back and stared up into the eyes of the Cowboy who'd run him off the road.

"What are you doing here?" He stomped on Sam's bandaged calf, and a charlie horse froze his muscle.

Sam grabbed the cramp, squeezing at the knee to stop the pain. Through his teeth, he spat at his captor. "I came to... tell Belle about thieves." He pointed at the storage area.

Cowboy made for the chemical lights of the supply depot, drawing a pistol from his belt. Sam was desperate to get moving, to keep searching for Jesse, and the sounds of a scuffle were the perfect cover. But his leg gripped in a spasm that twisted the muscle in his calf. He couldn't move.

A gunshot rang out. Screaming replaced the heavy thumps of fighting from the supply depot and pounding feet hit the earth hard and faded away. Revving engines filled the air and then, when they'd faded into the night, all that was left was the crackle of fires and the call for a fire brigade.

The pain had only just started to subside into a numbness when Cowboy returned. Sam rolled to his back, and started. Belle stood over him along with Pinstripe Suit. The well-dressed thug prodded Sam with his cane and tapped his knee. It involuntarily jerked, and he nodded. "Looks like his reflexes are still good. Should still be able to work with the proper motivation."

Belle frowned and flicked her chin out. "Get him up. Take him to the new apartment and keep him there until daybreak."

Pinstripe squared his shoulders as Belle handed him a silver key with a black bow. "Come on science boy. No point in delaying the inevitable." He guided Sam along the perimeter of the city. Out in the open, parked where everyone could see, was the semi he'd stolen. Pinstripe opened the door and prodded Sam into the driver's seat. "Clean yourself up and don't think about escaping. The passenger side door is welded shut and I'll be keeping watch right here. People who run never make it to the interstate." He slammed the door and plunked himself down on a log within view of the front of the semi.

Sam moved to the bed and found a bowl of water and a washcloth, along with a small meal of dried fruit and nuts. He used the washcloth to dab at his wounds, and lay down, munching on the meager meal as the start of a plan percolated in his mind. He could use the tools and other equipment to create a diversion just like the marauders had and escape in the semi.

But first, he needed to find Jesse, and so far, there'd been no sign of him anywhere.

CHAPTER THIRTY-SEVEN

DR DIANA STEWART. CHICAGO, ILLINOIS

The bus rattled and bumped along the road, the windows covered in yellow cicada-slime. Diana and Patti had hauled Ben up onto the front seat and gotten the door shut before the main body of the swarm had hit them, and Harry had sent the bus careening away through the city until the Matreus guards and the swarm had both been left behind.

"Can we slow down?" Patti grabbed at the back of the seat. "I need to take a look at Ben's wounds without going out the windshield myself."

Harry looked in his mirrors. "Yeah, sorry. Adrenaline kicking in there. That better?"

"Thanks, sugar." She moved across and started to examine Ben.

Diana delved in the bag. "How badly is he hurt?"

"He's not bleeding too heavily. Well hello there Sheriff, are you back in the land of the living?"

Ben blinked, dazed, and struggled upright. "Damn, they really shot at us? Was anyone hurt?"

"Only you, big guy." Patti straightened. "Drop your trousers. I need to see to that leg." She grinned as he revealed his Batman underpants. "Stylish."

He blushed.

Patti examined the glancing wound on Ben's leg. "Nothing serious. It's not deep." She cleaned it, dressed it and tied off the bandage expertly.

Diana turned away to give him whatever privacy was possible. It was only then that she had time to register the destruction around them. The city was in ruins and the road was peppered with crashed cars, discarded shopping carts and bodies. The carnage combined old devastation and new. It all blurred into flashes of horror. The older cadavers were maggot-ridden, their flesh falling from their bones; an adult sized corpse with wispy hair, the face peeled loose to show the skull beneath, sprawled next to a tiny figure that was mercifully little more than a mess of fragile bones peeping out from under the clothing. The more recently dead were covered with a crawling, buzzing cloak of flies that rose and swirled and settled to feed again.

Abruptly there was a bang. Harry braked, but the bus skidded sideways at a crazy angle. "Tire blew out! Hold on!"

Everyone screamed. The skid ended abruptly in a deafening crash, metal screeching as the low wall by the road ripped the side of the bus as it rode up to beach on it. The impact threw Diana backward, but Ben grabbed her so she fell against the seatback rather than down the aisle. Several other passengers were flung onto the floor, and the air filled with shouts and sobbing. A streetlight teetered, then smashed down on the curb with a thunderous crash as the bus came to rest.

"Thanks Ben." Diana righted herself.

"Don't want to worry you, but the windshield's shattered to pieces," he murmured.

"No cicadas yet though. Hopefully we've left them behind." Diana pulled her jacket tight. "I've already got salve on. You stay here, I'll check outside."

"Yes ma'am."

She peered out of the gap in the window; there was no buzzing and the grey smudge of the swarm was behind them. She took a cautious breath; her throat did not burn.

"Safe?" Patti edged up behind her.

"So long as they put the barrier cream on. Hand out a jar or two." Diana limped around the bus. It had a broken axle and there was gas draining down the side of the mangled vehicle, forming a spreading pool. As she watched a trickle formed slowly edging down the toward... *Oh crap.* A fire. What in the—? Some hobo maybe? Or a family trying to stay warm?

Diana's shoulders went tight. "Guys, you need to get off, NOW! The bus is about to catch fire!" Faces appeared at the windows. There was a flurry of panic, and Ben's voice calmly issuing instructions. Diana ignored it. She had to divert the stream of fuel, or at least hold it up for long enough for the passengers to get away, but with what?

The trickle inched nearer to the fire, and she had nothing to use. The street was empty of anything except cars and—dead people. She ran to the nearest corpse and grabbed the coat, retching at the smell. She laid it in the path of the fuel, trying to absorb it, and went back for a sweater from the next one. The corpses were almost cleaned by maggots, so the clothes came off with a quick jerk. The sweater bounced along the ground, and she nearly gagged when she realized there was an arm still in it. She laid that the other side of the coat, and ran to the end of the bus. "Are they off yet?"

"A few more, and Ben." Patti called back.

"Get them further away, behind shelter, and call me when everyone's safe." Diana glanced back at the trickle, which was not soaking in but pooling around the wadded-up coat. "Be quick – I can't stop it!" She dashed back to the fuel, which was starting to ooze around and under the coat, and lined up the sweater behind it, then went for something else.

Two more jackets, and Diana was out of space. "Running out of time, Patti!"

"Everyone's safe! Go! Go!"

Diana sprinted across the road and the bus exploded in a fireball.

The blast slammed her into the wall, and the acrid stink of burning rubber made her cough. Heat licked out, intense enough that she shielded her face with her hands, and felt the skin on the back of them contract and sting as she turned away from the blaze. The bus was one great inferno in seconds, thick black smoke rising up and then falling to choke the street in great oily clouds.

"Diana! Diana, are you okay?" Ben grabbed her arm.

"I'm fine!" Wincing from the fierce heat on her back, she and Ben limped to the corner where many of the passengers were standing, dazed.

"Thank goodness!" Patti embraced her. "Well, I guess that's that for the bus. What now?"

"We still need to get away from Bryce and Garrick." Diana scanned the street for vehicles. She was daunted at the idea, and all the cars in sight had crashed or been burned out already. "There must be a working one somewhere."

The passengers dispersed. Most of those who lived in the city wanted to go home, as if their homes might still be safe. The rest formed little groups and disappeared until it was just Ben, Patti, Diana, and a woman with two tween girls. The woman was clutching her head, a trickle of blood oozing down her face.

Diana went over. "Hey. I'm Diana, and this is Ben. Patti here is a nurse. Do you need help?"

The woman shook her head. "It's a scratch. It's fine. Thank you." She wiped it away with her sleeve. "I'm Mary. And this is Izzy and Lettie. We need to get to Chicago Union Station—I've got to get to Texas. I had no idea how to get back but my brother works for Amtrak, and when he heard we were so far from home, he and a few others came up and arranged one last train." She sniffed, wiping her eyes on the back of her sleeve.

"We're not far from the station." Diana frowned. "When do you need to be there?"

"It leaves at nightfall, and there won't be any more trains after it. They've closed the lines. But my parents are in Texas, and they need us; it's our only chance to get back there."

"If we can find a car, we could make it." Diana bit her lip. "I have to get back to California. Will your train go in that direction?"

Mary wiped her eyes, her voice getting stronger. "My brother said it's the Texas Eagle route, which ends in California. We'll be getting off at Texas, but some of the others live further along, so I think it will go the whole way. If it can. Who knows anything anymore?" She stood, gathering the children. "You should come with us, on the train, I mean. There'll be a few families on it, but it won't be full, and you can get off wherever's nearest to where you need to go. Help me get to the station and I'll make sure they let you on."

Diana paused. Texas? There was some connection between Sam and Texas. She couldn't immediately remember what but in any case, getting out of Chicago seemed like a good idea. She turned to the others. "What do you think?"

"Texas is in the right direction for me." Ben picked up his rucksack.

"Let's go." Patti handed one of the others to Diana.

A few minutes' walk took them to a McDonalds. It was burned out and wrecked but some of the cars outside looked intact. After a few tries, Ben found an old van, with half a tank of gas, that he could hotwire. "Everyone in."

They set off, and in the back of the car the girls were soon arguing about something trivial, Mary and Patti chatting between themselves. Only the brittle tone of their voices betrayed them.

"Diana, are you going back to California?" Ben navigated cautiously along the obstacle course that was the street.

Diana leaned her head against the headrest. Garrick had told her so many lies and half-truths, she didn't know what she believed anymore, but it there was any chance—just the slightest sliver—that Jesse and Sam were out there, she had to find them. "I have to know whether they're alive or dead." She could barely say his name. "Jesse..." she croaked out and turned her face away, to better hide the tears.

"Jesse? Jonah's kid?"

Diana blinked tears away. "I promised him. I promised him I would come back but I don't know where he is. I left him with my friend, Sam." Sam Leary might be a socially awkward savant, but she was pretty sure he was a man of his word. He'd said he'd keep Jesse safe. If they'd made it past Garrick and his goons, he'd have made good on his word. There was only one way to find out.

Ben slowed to edge around the wreckage of a sports car. "Where would he go, this friend of yours? Would he take Jesse with him?"

"He wouldn't leave him. But his apartment was in the part of the city that was burned."

"Does he have family?"

Diana sat forward in her seat. "Family! Ben, you're a genius. He doesn't really get on with them, but he'd go there if there was nowhere else. I didn't even think of that! I'm so stupid. Sam's parents live in Texas, in a suburb near Austin. And I know their details!"

Ben nodded. "I'm headed to Austin myself, or at least a little way outside it. I know that Jonah reckoned his relatives lived near mine. We can travel together at least that far, if that suits. It might be safer not to travel alone."

"Of course. Thank you!"

"Your friend Sam, where do his parents live?" Mary asked from the back seat. "I can ask around once we get to the train. Some of the families are from that area, they might be able to give you directions. Can you write it down? We can give it to my brother; he'll know who to ask."

Diana rummaged in the glovebox, pulled out an old notepad, thought for a second or two, and scribbled down the address, then tore off the page and tucked it in her jacket pocket. Amazing how the brain—her brain, no longer addled by the meds or the pain of her appalling ex-husband's lies—could pull facts from the far reaches of its many, many folds. Sam had mentioned the connection between his street address and the periodic table—which was very, very 'Sam' of him—which was what had made it stick! She was so relieved she wanted to cry.

Mary leaned forward. "It's getting darker. Will it take much longer? We don't have long before it leaves."

Diana blinked away tears. "Hopefully not. We're not far from the station now. If the roads stay clear—"

Ben slammed the brakes on. "Sorry, guys." There was a series of cars ahead, smashed and burning. "We'll have to find another way through."

Movement caught Diana's eye: a group of men in uniform hurried into the street ahead. "Great. The first living things we see, and they're wearing Matreus uniforms."

Ben reversed and started to pull forward when an SUV swerved in from the main street. He jammed on the brakes. Diana was thrown forward in her seatbelt. She sat upright again, to find them hood to hood with the other vehicle and its driver.

"Garrick!" Diana froze. Her breath came in gasps, faster and faster as he saw her, recognized her. One eye was swollen and blackening already. His face twisted into a snarl and he threw the door open. Ben floored the accelerator. The tires screeched. The van leapt forward in a haze of acrid smoke, ramming Garrick's door shut. Dragging the SUV against the wall, the vehicle ground past, metal squealing against metal, then jolted free.

Diana twisted to look behind them, only to see the SUV door fly open. Rolling out, Garrick fired at the retreating van, shattering the back windshield. The children screamed.

"Down!" Patti yelled, and they ducked behind the seat. More shots clanged on the metal and crashed through the impacted glass, sending sharp-edged pieces flying like crystalline wasps.

The shots stopped. Diana glimpsed Garrick jumping back into the SUV. The wheels screeched; it jerked forward and smashed into a car, then freed itself and whipped around.

Diana braced herself on the dashboard, heart pounding painfully. Fear sent a surge of cold through her. He wouldn't give up, not after the humiliation of being left stripped and handcuffed in the bathtub. And if he caught them, he would show no mercy. "Now is not the time for a panic attack, dammit!"

Ben spared her a quick glance. Had she whispered it out loud? They swerved onto the main road and once on the straight, he reached for her hand and squeezed it. "Doc, help me. How do we get to the station without that jackass catching us?" The calmness of his voice steadied her.

With an effort, she slowed her breathing and let go of his hand, focusing on the route. "Duck into this road, next right."

Garrick swerved onto the road just as they turned, and followed.

Diana was calmer now, plotting their route like a chess player, the familiar grid of the city streets mapping themselves out in her mind. "Straight on to the lights, next left and right immediately after. There, you see? We'll have to go over the curb at the end." The van jolted across the pavement.

Another screech of tires, as Garrick's SUV overshot the street, braked and reversed crazily.

Diana braced herself against the dashboard. "The alley by that burned out truck—SUVs often get stuck there. Hopefully this shouldn't."

"This is gonna be close!" Ben accelerated into the alley. The girls screamed as narrow walls smashed away the wing mirrors; sparks fountained up on either side as the van scraped its way along the alley to the end, and eased its way out.

Behind them, Garrick's SUV came to a crashing stop, wedged in the entrance. He wound down his window and loosed a futile shot or two, but then gave up and reversed out.

"It'll take him two minutes to come around the other way." Diana pointed along the street. "That's the back of the station. At the corner there's a passageway. Turn in there, Ben, so we're out of sight." The van jolted to a stop in the passageway.

A screech of tires: Garrick was approaching. Diana waved the family on. "We can still make the train, but we don't have long. He doesn't know you by sight. Go!"

Mary and the girls dashed into the concourse. Diana, Ben and Patti ducked out of sight until the SUV shot by, then followed the others.

The station was darkening and mostly empty, the long wooden benches charred and every glass window broken. Bodies were huddled in piles; whether they were dead or asleep, Diana didn't want to know. She and Ben limped faster; the family sprinted downstairs to the platform. Patti reached the stairs, running on ahead.

Ben clutched at his leg and stumbled on the stairs.

Diana grabbed his arm to steady him. "It's bleeding again."

"Doesn't matter. Come on!"

They navigated the stairs slowly, descending into the disconcerting gloom below. The only lights were those on the train and the engineer's flashlight. He was standing in the last open doorway, arguing with Patti.

Patti waved frantically. "Hurry! They're leaving!"

"We're coming!" Diana gasped, but the engineer ignored her. He stepped out of sight, and Patti followed, scolding like a mother hen. There was a roar as the engines ramped up; the stench of diesel smoke filled the dark. "Ben, go!"

Ben sprinted to the door, and Diana followed, a hot rush of adrenaline lightening the heavy backpack she wore. Ben was clambering up the steep steps to board when there was a shot from the stairs. Diana ducked away as a bullet ricocheted past.

"Diana! Get yourself here right now!" Garrick stood silhouetted in the light of the concourse, gun in hand.

The train started to move; Garrick ran down to the platform. Diana jumped up into the doorway, to climb up the stairs but half the step fell away as she stood on it. "No!" She tried to drag herself up, but her bad shoulder would not take her weight, and she could feel her grip slipping on the handrail.

"I'm coming for you, Diana, and you're gonna regret you ever saw fit to raise a hand to me!"

Above the roar of the train's engine the clatter of Garrick's feet on the concrete came closer, and the train was moving so slowly. She gritted her teeth and made herself move one foot up to the next step, but the weight of the bag was pulling her outwards. The old familiar helplessness gathered like snakes in the darkness. She was going to fall, and this time Garrick was going to beat her to death.

"You got this, Doc." Ben took hold of the strap of her backpack and pulled. "Come on." His grip gave her the purchase she needed.

She launched herself forward and scrambled up the stairs onto the train, threw off her backpack, and lay gasping on the floor. "Thanks, Ben. I really thought—"

A hand clamped around her ankle. She fought to scrabble backward, knocking Ben over. He landed with a thud. Garrick forced the door wide open, wedged himself on the steps, and dragged her toward him. "You're coming with me. You're mine, not his. Mine!"

She writhed desperately, trying to kick free of his grip but still she slid toward him. She grabbed at the doorframe, but he hauled at her harder, pulling her toward the rushing darkness outside the train.

"You abuse me, humiliate me..." He gasped, barely able to get the words out.

She despised him with a sudden fervor. "*I* abused *you?*" Hot fury swept through her, and it burned all her fear to ashes. "No. All I have to say to you is 'goodbye.'"

It was like a red rag to a bull. He clambered up her, like a lizard grasping purchase on the tiniest foothold, and gripped her throat, squeezing hard. Black spots danced in her eyes. She wedged her arms into the doorframe, despite the burning pain from her shoulder, and swept his legs out from under him, jackknifing to kick at his head.

Losing his grip, he lunged at the rail with one hand and at her with the other. She pulled back but not far enough; he caught the front of her jacket and began to pull himself up into the carriage again.

"Doc! Here!" Behind her, Ben rolled across the engineer's flashlight, huge and heavy. She grabbed it and battered at Garrick's hand on the rail, but despite bloody knuckles, he clung on, legs swinging outside the train door. She struggled wildly and smashed it down on his head; there was a ripping sound and he fell into the darkness, knocking the flashlight out of her grip.

Diana fell back into the train, coughing. She rubbed her throat, trying to catch her breath.

Ben clambered to his feet and closed the door. "You're okay, Doc. He's gone now. You're okay."

Patti erupted out of the carriage holding a stiletto, heel outwards. "Where is he? Where's that jackass?"

Ben snorted. Diana nodded to the fading darkness outside, as the train finally pulled out into the dusk.

Patti glared at Ben, all outraged dignity. "I don't know what you think is so funny, Batman. You've wrecked that dressing. I suppose you want a new one now?"

"Yes, nurse."

The carriage itself was empty, apart from Mary and the children, huddled at the far end with a man so similar to Mary that he had to be her brother.

Patti began to change Ben's dressing as the train pulled around the corner, but glancing up, she stopped. "Oh goodness. Look at that!"

They turned to see Matreus Tower in the distance. It was wreathed in an orange glow that lit the sky, flame licking out the windows.

"All those people!" Diana could not look away. "Oh no—Anna!" A helicopter circled and headed off into the swirling smoke, lights blinking in the darkness.

"I suspect Anna is on that helicopter, and the rest of the Matreuses too. They'll be safe."

There was a glare of brightness and a projectile sped down and out of sight; then there was an explosion. A fireball rose around the tower.

"The propane tanks." Ben murmured grimly. "He had them target the propane tanks." No one had to ask who he meant.

The windows shattered, and slowly, ever so slowly, Matreus Tower began to crumble in on itself, collapsing floor on floor as it teetered and toppled. The middle floors buckled, tumbling backward in a trail of sparks and flames, while the lower half fell forward over what must be the plaza. There was one more great mushroom cloud of flames, and a muffled *boom* that rattled the train windows; and then there was only flame and smoke. They watched in horrified silence until the track curved, and the view was lost.

Patti broke the silence. "There's nothing we can do. Come on, girls, there's no one else this end of the train. Choose your seat and try to sleep."

Diana turned away from the devastation of the city. She suddenly felt as if she'd run a marathon. "I'm so tired. And we'll need all our strength to deal with whatever we find at the other end."

Ben got up and opened his backpack. "I just had a thought. You might find this useful, Doc. He passed Diana something blocky wrapped in a shopping bag; she opened it up to find a satellite phone.

"Oh..." She sat down. "Oh my." She started to dial; hesitated and reached into where her pocket had been, and found only ripped seams. Just one more loss among many. What did a tattered coat matter, when so many had lost their lives?

She turned on the phone and waited for it to find a satellite.

CHAPTER THIRTY-EIGHT

CLAIRE MOONE. PATTERDALE, CUMBRIA, ENGLAND

Claire brought her fists down hard on the table. "Are we sure these are the right ships?" Her voice was loud and carried her frustration into the wider camp. "Neither of them is bound for a UK deep water port. We don't even know if either are carrying the cicadas." She pushed her chair back and stood. "We're missing some vital intel here, chaps. Go through everything again. Start at the beginning."

Their entire defensive strategy was based upon the assumption that there were two crates of cicadas still out there, and that the creatures were being put inside a container of fig trees.

Claire cringed at the lack of real information. Whatever course of action she thought of, there was no guarantee she was right. "Why fig trees? They're not native to the UK, either."

Nerd knelt under the table. "That should do it." He stood up and clicked his mouse. A large flatscreen monitor came to life at the side of the whiteboard. "Ok. We need to watch this." He played a

YouTube video. "It's the lifecycle of the cicada. There was a good one with David Attenborough on it, but this explains why they are using fig trees."

They all watched in silence. The discussion began, the moment the video stopped. Plank went back to the whiteboard to scribble the main points that were raised. When they ran out of things to say about the bugs, he prompted them to recap. "So, we've got these main points. They're putting bugs in with the fig trees so they can lay their eggs. The lifecycle is a minimum of two years, but up to seventeen. There's no mention of them being poisonous in any way."

Claire slid back on her chair. "There are swarms of these things eating and killing their way across the US. We're missing something."

Plank put an idea forward. "From that video, it might be a seventeen-year cycle and they've all come out at once. It's like what flying ants do, every year."

They went around the table, each adding to the discussion, coming back to the question of toxicity. Google didn't have any suggestions.

"I'll have to take this to Lazarus, as it is. They can get the Science people on it. They're already talking with the CDC in the US. If there's intel about the bugs, they'll get it for us. We can't sit here speculating." She stood. "The most pressing issue is those ships. I want to know why the ones carrying trees aren't coming here. Go over it with a fine-toothed comb. Work up a timeline and go through everything chronologically."

She left them to it and stepped outside. Inside the tent, everything was demanding and immediate. Outside, birds sang, leaves rustled, and Goldrill Beck burbled along. Rather than walk across the field of the encampment to the gateposts through which they'd driven, she walked to a gap that had been cut in the fence, giving access to the bank of the stream, close to the bridge.

She hopped over a stile at the side of the metalwork of Patterdale Bridge. It was a flat structure, with one central pillar of clean-faced stone, supporting the spans of two low arches. The rough, dusty surface of the road ran away from the village in the direction of Hartsop Fell. Fifty yards along, past the fencing that held back the hedge, she arrived at the dual gate of the cottage. One was wide and for vehicles, the other was for pedestrians.

'Not a Public Footpath,' the black and white sign screwed to it couldn't have been clearer or more accurate, considering the massing military presence in the village. She clicked the catch and pushed. The return spring twanged and groaned as she opened the gate.

The path was also gravel, but much finer than on the driveway. Flat slate steps took her to the front door, but she walked around the back of the house. The lounge was glass on three sides, with a cozy fireplace on the innermost wall. It was too early in the day to be lit. The interior was dark, but she could see her father watching her as she walked by.

The other man in the room, Charles Grey, moved to the sliding glass doors to the patio, opening them both when she approached. "Hello, Claire. It's been such a long time since I last saw you."

"Hello, sir." Her professional response was enough.

"I think it was on the last Lazarus exercise, wasn't it?" He stepped back, making space for her to enter. "Is that right, Hunter? Was it then?"

Her father didn't answer or acknowledge her presence. He was scrolling down the screen of a tablet with his index finger.

Grey sat in an armchair, another tablet and papers spread before him on the coffee table. "Frightful business with your chap. Saddened to hear of your loss."

Her father, Artemis, stopped browsing the data, put the screen down and turned to face her. "Do you have something to report?"

"Yes, sir." She was uneasy about telling him anything that wasn't a positive reflection of her capability. "We've been unable to confirm the exact location of the two ships we believe we need to investigate. We are also concerned that we do not understand the immediate threat posed by the insects that are part of the scenario."

He didn't appear concerned that she hadn't given him good news. "That's very unfortunate."

As embarrassing as it might be for him, in front of his colleague, she had to press on. "Sir, we don't understand why the cicadas are so dangerous. We're hoping to get more information from the US. The CDC, perhaps?"

"We've already done that." He wasn't rebuking her, just stating fact. "This is the seventeenth year of the longest reproductive cycle. For some reason, the cicadas have mutated. They are maturing at a staggering rate and are highly toxic. It takes a matter of days before a new swarm emerges."

"That explains the weaponization of the bugs." She said what was obvious, so he'd know she'd understood. "Thank you, sir. We'll factor it in to our planning."

Grey cleared his throat. "There's something else for you to consider, Claire. When you stopped that ship, you'd all been exposed to the airborne pathogen. It's so toxic that even the small amounts on your equipment and clothing could kill, many times over."

She waited for him to continue.

"The chaps in the lab at Latham were able to get some samples, but only from the semi-dirigible boats you abandoned. From their tests, they determined the toxin may be neutralized by salt water." He smiled. "Ordering your men into the sea saved their lives and the lives of those who came to help you."

"Thank you, sir." She'd gotten it right, even if she hadn't known precisely how or why.

"She's always been a smart one, this girl of yours, Hunter." Grey's praise did nothing to alter her father's demeanor.

"Yes. She has." Was that praise? "She's going to need to be, if she's going to find these two ships she knows are out there." If it was, it was accompanied by a verbal slap.

Grey smirked at her. "Grumpy is as grumpy does."

She didn't risk smiling back, in case her father noticed. It was the kind of thing he would see, out of the corner of his eye, when she was a child.

Although Grey was supportive, it didn't alter the timbre of her father's voice. "Do you think you can find these ships before nightfall? Do you even know which ships you're looking for?" The deadline he set suggested there was an urgency to the task. "We've got fires sweeping in all directions from Cheshire. We need to know how rapidly they are moving toward us. If we can't manage the fires, we won't be able to manage the cicadas. Time is of the essence. Be about your task."

She stepped away, slid the doors closed behind her, and trudged back the way she'd come. Her father gave her no quarter as his daughter. Whatever she did, it was always lacking. Her work was never ending. He always told her she had more to do. It wasn't something she needed reminding about.

They were all singing off the same hymn sheet, no matter what he said. They weren't in the Lake District for its natural beauty. They were there because of its natural fortification. Even the Romans built a fort in one of the passes, and they weren't facing an apocalypse level event. Patterdale was an eminently survivable location. The Kirkstone Pass in the south was treacherous in bad weather. To the north, the Ullswater valley was more open, flat and exposed, but very defensible.

Grouse greeted her return with some good news. "The rest of the gang should be here in four hours, boss."

"Two of you can bring them up to speed the moment they get here." She wouldn't be there to do the briefing, so she volunteered Plank and Grouse. "Can someone please give me a Land Ranger map for here?"

Plank opened a crate, flipped his finger along the ridges of purple booklets, then pinched his fingers around the one she'd asked for. He put it flat on the green cotton cloth of their main table and slid it across to her.

"Thanks. I'm taking Mickey for a bit of a hike." She unfolded the concertina of paper inside the protective glossy cover, spreading the 'one inch to one mile' map across the table before her. "We'll drive as high as we can, then we walk to the summit." She placed the pad of her index finger on a concentric layering of contours. "Here. Wansfell Pike." With her other hand, she traced a finger along a road. "We'll take the fork at the Kirkstone Pass Hotel, down to Ambleside."

Of the five, only Nerd was sitting down. "I'm to carry on with the searches, boss?"

"Absolutely. Do your stuff. Keep running through the data." As smart as they were as a team, they couldn't number-crunch like the computers could. "If you get anything actionable, let me know immediately. Let's get geared up and on the move."

"Full gear, boss?" Mickey had stripped his badges as she spoke. His hand was poised over his body armor.

"Full gear. Fully armed." She tugged at her name tag and pulled the rank slider from her tunic. Her own armor was in her kit box, but she retrieved and clipped it onto her body within a minute. "Move out."

It was a nice enough day for a lightweight walk, but the helicopters passing overhead were an obvious sign that it wasn't the sort of day to trek on the hills for fun. The roadblock and sandbags at the high side of the hotel reinforced the idea that the welcome associated with Lakeland had been put 'on hold.'

Mickey slowed the matte black Range Rover to a stop before the horizontal pole of the barrier. Pressing the button on her door, Claire wound her blacked-out window down and beckoned the heavily armed guard from the sentry post. "Make sure you take our registration. Pass it to each watch. We'll be returning in a couple of hours. I want this thing up and open, when we do."

They were not civilians, and they were not regular soldiers. He asked no questions about what she wanted or her right to ask for it. He saluted. "Yes, ma'am." His actions prompted the raising of the bar to their progress.

The A594 would bring them down to the town of Windermere. Although it was also signposted for Ambleside, it wasn't the route they were taking. The more direct route was on a smaller road, called *The Struggle* because of its harsh inclines and tight corners.

"Go right, Mickey." He did as she asked. "After the hairpin right, once the road straightens out, take the left turn onto Stock Ghyll Lane. It's 100 yards on."

Mickey slowed the big SUV, turned hard and sped up again. He would have to work hard to keep the vehicle moving at high speed and in the middle of what was in effect a tarmac track. "They should have called this one *The Struggle*, boss, not the other one."

"It's going to get worse. We're going off-road when we get to the

Stock Ghyll Falls. There's a gate and a footpath, we're going through it and up to the summit." She unclipped her seatbelt. "I'll get the gate."

With the real road behind them, Mickey pressed two buttons on the central console where the selector for the automatic gearbox sat. The entire body of the Range Rover rose several inches. "Ride height's at maximum and the traction control is set to all-terrain. The thing's just a posh quad now." Their tires found good purchase on the soil and grass, as they drove the direct half-mile route to the top of Wansfell Pike. The pile of stacked rocks at the top of the pass, each placed by a passing walker, showed they were at the right place.

Claire got out of the SUV; the height difference was so noticeable there was a definite sensation of stepping down. The panorama also gave her a sense of her utter insignificance, in the raw beauty of the hills and mountains that populated the world around her. To the south, they subsided, gradually declining until the land met the distant sea. As beautiful as that should have been, the view was tainted, darkened and dirtied by a widening ribbon of grey-black smoke. The horizon appeared closer than it was, because of the height at which they stood. More elevation would give her a better idea of the distance.

"Let's put a drone up, Mickey." The unit was designed for covert surveillance, but with an 8k camera and zoom, they would be able to see the fires and accurately estimate the speed at which the flames were consuming Lancashire. Merseyside, Liverpool and the surrounding towns, were almost certainly destroyed.

Her earpiece buzzed. "Team Two, Yogi reporting in. We're here, boss."

Claire could tell it was him. The deep pitch of his double-bass voice was unmistakable. "Good news. Rest and prep." He was her second in command. Yogi, a bear of a man, was her right hand, as Mickey was her left. "All safe?"

"Yep. A regular pick up and drop. Nothing to report." They'd been collecting the remaining Lazarus members. The Cottage would now become the nerve center of decision making and disaster management. Downing Street and Parliament would listen to their advice and execute the plans that they suggested.

The whirring competitive squabble of four small rotor blades filled the air, an annoying characteristic of quadcopter drones. There was a blip in the pitch of the palm-sized airborne camera, as it rose into the sky. When she could no longer see or hear it, she moved to look at the first-person view on the screen of the control system. Rather than have it strapped to his neck, Mickey rested it on the load cover of the trunk.

"That's max operational height." He thumbed a small joystick. The vehicle responded, spinning to look directly south. "That's rough."

She leaned in for a better view. "Oh dear." She closed her eyes, imagining the coastline from above. The Fylde was like a finger that pointed north. It sat proud into the Irish Sea, with Blackpool as a destination for holiday makers. Keeping her mental map, she opened her eyes and came back to the screen. "Zoom in." The tower and amusement park were observable in the daylight. The image was steady and surreal. The landmarks looked like toy models that had been placed before a black curtain, so they would show up better. The curtain was alive, billowing and growing. It darkened the sky to a height three to four times that of Blackpool Tower. It was shaped and held back by wind coming from the sea. If that remained constant, they had four or five days, before the fires would be in southern Cumbria and at the foothills that stretched out before them.

The fires would be devastating, but the poisonous smoke would be worse. The children she had been teaching knew all the gory details of the incidents and deaths. It killed by destroying the body's ability to breathe, choking a person, suffocating them from inside as they struggled for life. Worse still, it disintegrated internal organs and the victim died in convulsions, bleeding from every orifice.

"Boss? You there?" Nerd sounded agitated, enthusiastic. "We've found the ships. Well, we know which ones they are. We know they're in international waters. One's heading for Hull and the other's going to Holyhead on Anglesey."

"Received." She wouldn't get approval to board them until they were in British jurisdiction. She'd been briefed on it, many, many times: Anything else would be considered piracy and would likely start a war. "How long before we can do anything?" He would have calculated that.

"Four days."

She would task her second team with taking the ship bound for Hull. Team One would make ready to take the other. If the ships were like the *Maid of Morning*, they'd have the same crew compliment, if they weren't already dead.

Her mind returned to the mountain top. On screen something bright and tiny pulled at her attention. She put her hand on Mickey's arm and moved her head closer to his chest. Pinpoints of light flickered on the ground. "Pan around." As he followed her instruction, it became clear she was looking at the headlights of vehicles, hundreds of them. A mass exodus, fleeing their homes. The smoke, fires and insects were not the biggest threat to survival. Humans were. Lazarus's limited resources wouldn't support the camp and refugees. Medical supplies would run low. There would be violent clashes, because that's what humans did to survive. "They're all heading this way. We don't have four days—they're going to over-run us in half that time."

CHAPTER THIRTY-NINE

ANAYELI ALFARO. SACRAMENTO, CALIFORNIA

Ash floated from the sky, a dry, gray flurry that caught in Anayeli's eyelashes, frosted Mama's hair, and dusted the dogs' backs and shoulders as they surveyed the parking lot. Where there should have been people, there were only empty, abandoned tents, their flaps snapping in the wind. Anayeli was smoke-sick—nauseous and headachy— and heart-sick. Her sister was gone, out of reach, miles away, flying above the billowing plumes. Jeremy was dead on the hospital roof, the keeper of the exact location of his family's compound, where Carlota was headed. And the most important question—how would they find Carlota?—was unanswerable. At least until Anayeli found her brother.

"What truck is he on?" That was the only question that *did* have an answer, if it wasn't too late. A Jeep, the kind that belonged in TV shows like *M*A*S*H* or movies like *Platoon*, drove out of the evacuation center gates. Sitting in the passenger seat was the ramrod straight back of a man who could only be Colonel Wilson. They were too late. The convoy was leaving. And everyone was either on the trucks or had run through the gates, disappearing into the haze.

"Keep going!" Nurse Kerry shouted in her ear and pointed, not at any of the vehicles that had just exited the evacuation center, but toward the parking garage. "It's one of those!"

Another Jeep with an officer in the passenger seat pulled from the building's exit, followed by a tan-painted troop carrier—the kind Anayeli had only ever seen parked at the National Guard Armory at the fairgrounds.

"You there! Stop!" An armed guard hanging off the back of the troop carrier pointed at them, his words carrying all the authority of an order.

Anayeli used the panic- and anger-fueled surge of adrenaline to push her legs faster. She had to find Ernesto, before the next convoy left the evacuation center. She couldn't afford to be delayed and she couldn't believe she'd trusted Nurse Kerry. The woman had left Ernesto alone with strangers, and his life—all their lives—were still under the military control Anayeli had been trying to escape from. But there was no time for anger. She had to run.

Once she found Ernesto, she'd figure out how to go after Carlota and Bailey Rae. But first: Ernesto. He was close, within reach, somewhere aboard one of the trucks that were inching forward, lining up from the gate into the evacuation center and all the way back into the parking garage.

Anayeli, Mama, and Nurse Kerry ran past another troop transport—this one full of baby-faced soldiers, their expressions all grim lines as they peered out the back at them. The dogs bounded ahead, then ran back, circling, keeping track of their people, the only ones still left.

"*Dónde está mi bebé?*" Mama asked for her baby over and over, an unending mantra that tore at the wall Anayeli had constructed around her heart to keep herself from giving in, from giving up. "Ernesto!"

"We'll find him! He's here." It seemed hopeless, but even if Anayeli didn't know where the hell her brother was, she was not giving up. She grabbed for Nurse Kerry's hand, to pull her along, to keep the only link she had to Ernesto close. As much as she wanted to scream at the woman—*This wasn't the plan! You were supposed to get him on the helicopter, with Carlota*— she could not. Until they found him, she had to rely on Nurse Kerry's help. After that—well. She would reassess everything. Again. Because she kept screwing up. She kept trusting the wrong people. She kept losing her family.

The trucks rolled forward, inch by inch. There was no way to make them stop.

"We have to find him, Kerry. Please! Which truck is it? Which one is he on?" The trucks all looked the same to Anayeli and she'd never be able to tell which was the right one unless she could search them all and there wasn't time for that. She peered into the bed of another troop transport as they ran up to the open back. It might as well have been an exact replica of the last truck she'd looked into. Boys with guns. The military was getting the soldiers out first.

The fire was bearing down on them, danger was closer, and the world had gone quiet. Except for the roar of engines accelerating in low gear as the second convoy snaked through the gates, there was no natural sound of any kind. The air was heavy with expectation, like when a storm was brewing, and only Mama's frantic calling for her baby and the wind could cut through the thick haze. Or, not wind so much as the sucking inhale of flames devouring oxygen, the hot exhale of fire. It was coming. And the convoy was leaving them behind.

"Is he in one those trucks? Are you sure?" Panic edged Anayeli's voice higher as the line of National Guard troop transports followed after the second Jeep. An armored car with a machine gun mounted to it brought up the rear. As it bumped out onto the road, Anayeli fought to keep to her feet, her knees wanting to buckle.

"There's a third convoy for civilians." Nurse Kerry's hand on hers was the only thing that kept Anayeli upright. But as they bolted into the gloom of the parking garage, two more armed guards stepped forward, blocking their way.

"No admittance." The guard's stare made Anayeli think of the dress-uniform photos of soldiers that the newspaper used to run when there had been casualties in Afghanistan: dead, expressionless eyes, a stare that wasn't a thousand-yard stare yet, but would be soon.

Anayeli yanked her hand free of Nurse Kerry's just as the woman spoke.

"You don't understand. I'm a nurse, I've got patients on the convoy." Nurse Kerry pulled at the lanyard around her neck, drew her hospital ID out from under her scrub-top. The guard stared at the ID, then studied the nurse's face for what felt like too long. Finally he waved her on.

But when Anayeli moved to follow, he stopped her with a hand almost to her chest. "What company you with?"

Anayeli had forgotten she was still wearing her borrowed National Guard uniform. She had no idea how to answer. She scrambled to think of something. She couldn't use Colonel Wilson's name. Something like the truth was what she settled on. "My commanding officer... Kassis. She's gone. On the helicopter. I don't know...I was supposed to help this woman." She gestured toward Mama, who had gone silent, watchful.

"There might be room back there. And they can use more help, getting the last evacuees loaded." The soldier pointed a thumb over his shoulder.

Anayeli grabbed Mama's hand and pulled her away from the guards, barking "Come with me" so it sounded like she was ordering Mama around. They had to get moving before the guards changed their minds or asked more questions Anayeli didn't know how to answer.

They hurried to where Nurse Kerry waited for them and Anayeli could have cried, first with relief and then at the sight of one more Jeep at the front and the line of transport trucks behind it. At the very end, barely visible in the dark of the parking garage, there were still soldiers out on the concrete, helping evacuees aboard the last trucks. There was a gurney.

"Is that him?" Anayeli pointed as two soldiers hefted the gurney into the truck. "Is that Ernesto?"

Nurse Kerry's breath caught. Then she pointed to a second gurney, farther back in the line. "There!"

Mama took off in a dead run. Anayeli barged after Mama, the dogs at her heels.

"Ernesto!" Mama's voice cut above all the noise. A voice answered—too faint for Anayeli to recognize, let alone make out the words. But Cricket let out a low woof and kept barking with increasing excitement as they all ran for the very last truck on the convoy.

Mama reached the truck first, just as the feet of whoever was on the gurney disappeared into the truck. Mama whirled to Anayeli. "It's him, Anayeli! *Oh mi bebé*! He's here!"

Anayeli couldn't have stayed fully upright if she'd tried. She dropped her hands to her knees and bent over, her chest heaving. Tears stung her eyes. "*Gracias a Dios*! *Oh gracias*."

"You've got to get on." Nurse Kerry patted her back and pulled at her arm. "Come on!"

As Nurse Kerry clambered aboard, the guard who was helping load the evacuees let his hand go to her buttocks, boosting her up. As he turned, he smirked at the guard on the other side of the bumper, in that joke-y, superior way of a man who'd taken liberties and wanted it acknowledged. It was the creep who'd been at the purples' gate, not dead like she'd expected, and his mask no longer bloodied. The realization hit Anayeli the instant her hands touched the metal edge of the bed to heft herself in. She stopped dead, pulling her cap low so maybe he wouldn't recognize her. But Cricket had read her first intention and leapt from the ground up toward the open back of the truck.

"No." The creep's arm shot out and knocked Cricket aside. The dog hit what passed for a bumper hard and he scrabbled for purchase against the metal, but his claws couldn't hold as the soldier grabbed him by the scruff and hauled him down. Cricket let out a yelp as he landed hard on the ground. "No dogs."

Cruelty. That's what Anayeli was afraid of. That's the instinct that had made her stop. She didn't trust this guard, and she didn't trust the military. Not after what she'd seen. She wanted to get away from anything government-run, not embed herself even further. She had no idea where this convoy was headed, she knew they weren't safe on a truck with that creep, and she didn't know whether they were headed for some place worse, where they'd be subjected to more testing. But they couldn't leave Ernesto—

The creep didn't even spare Anayeli a glance as he forced her aside. "If you're not getting on, get out of the way." He hadn't recognized her. So that was something.

Anayeli stepped back, bumping into Mama.

"What are you doing? Get in!" Mama pushed at her shoulders, shoving her closer to the truck.

She couldn't believe they'd switched roles and Mama was urging her to go with the military after she'd been so reluctant to enter the evacuation center. But they didn't have to be on the military trucks. There were abandoned cars in the parking garage.

Anayeli switched to Spanish. "We'll get a car Mama. We can follow behind." She turned to the creep, switched back to English. "Where are we headed?"

The man didn't look her way. "You think they tell me anything they won't tell you?" He helped another woman—the thin girl from the purple zone—into the truck, one hand taking the girl's, the other going to her butt again, just like he'd done with Nurse Kerry. "Look, either you get on now or you don't."

Anayeli drew Mama aside and lowered her voice so no one would hear. "We can't get on there! I have a plan." They could take a car from the garage, follow the convoy so long as it seemed safe, leave whenever they needed to. They could use the car to get to Montana, to find Carlota. It would be better than being on the convoy.

Mama's eyes dropped to the dogs at Anayeli's feet, then shot back up at Anayeli. "Is this because of your *perros estúpidos*?" Her brows were creased into angry furrows. "You'd leave your brother because of some dogs?" Mama snatched Anayeli's hand, fury in the quickness of her every motion.

If Mama got onto the truck, if Ernesto was aboard the convoy, Anayeli had no choice.

"Mama, please! We need our own transportation. We can take Ernesto, and drive ourselves to Montana, to where Carlota—" The tears that had been stinging her eyes since they saw Ernesto being loaded finally spilled over. It was all so hopeless.

Mama's voice had never been so harsh, not ever in Anayeli's entire life. "Get on this convoy now, *hija*, so help me—" She yanked her hard, scraping Anayeli against the corrugated metal of the bumper.

Every choice was terrible. She hated the only choice she could make.

She clambered after Mama, knees banging on the edge of the truck bed, refusing to look back. She couldn't bear it, seeing Cricket and Roxy's brown eyes go from expectant to confused. The yelping and then the barking was enough to tell her the creep had knocked Cricket down again, that again she had failed.

She hadn't saved everyone.

She'd saved almost no one.

Her sister was alone with Bailey Rae on a helicopter full of strangers. Jeremy was dead. Luz was in the river. Sid was lying in an anonymous hallway. Papa was ash in a burned out field, perhaps the same ash blowing on the wind, sticking to her tears.

She couldn't stop the sobs that ripped from her throat, even as Ernesto reached for Mama, his whole face brighter than she'd seen it in days.

She yanked her hand from Mama's as the two soldiers from the back of the truck clambered on. The creep rapped his knuckles on the frame of the truck.

"Let me off!" She nearly fell as the truck lurched forward and she staggered backward, toward the opening. "I've got to get down."

From behind her a cry went up. It was Mama. There were other voices too—Kerry and Ernesto, whatever they were saying barely penetrating the roaring her ears. It was the churning water in the river, the roaring of the flames in the teff field telling her she'd failed and failed and failed. She wanted out, but the creep and the other soldier, a sturdy, well-fed, well-muscled young man with sandy-blonde hair blocked her path. He was the one who put his hands to her shoulders.

"You can't get off." He shook his head. He had kind eyes. "You really don't want to stay behind. You'd be going AWOL."

"Please! The dogs!" Cricket and Roxy were barking barking barking, and over his shoulder she could make them out, the two of them running hard after the truck as it sped up. "Why can't I bring them? Please!" Some part of her knew she was being stupid, that she was jeopardizing whatever cover she had as a soldier, but the dogs had never left her. They had never let her down. They were loyal.

Ernesto had Mama. Carlota had Bailey Rae. But Anayeli had nothing, belonged to no one. Just like Cricket and Roxy. They were *hers*.

The creep's expression went somehow ugly and hungry and gleeful all at once. He swung his weapon from his back and into his hands, turning toward the opening of the truck. "I can put them out of their misery."

"No!" The way the creep smirked at her scream let her know that's exactly what he'd wanted—to toy with her. To have power over her. And he did. It was a good thing the other guy still had hold of her shoulders because she would have flung herself at the creep.

"You're an asshole, MacIntyre." She could have hugged him for that kindness, for calling out another white man's power trip, except Cricket's barks went silent.

For a split second Anayeli thought he'd gone under the wheels, but then a black-and-white blur rocketed through the truck's opening. He knocked MacIntyre off-balance, so that Anayeli saw Roxy the same instant she made her leap.

The little black dog didn't make it. She only managed to get her front paws up on the edge of the tailgate. But before Anayeli could do a thing to help her, even as she saw Roxy's paws slipping, her nails digging into nothing, the soldier's hand left her shoulder and darted out. He grabbed Roxy by the scruff of her neck and hauled her inside. Safe.

They were all safe, everyone who was hers.

At least for the moment.

READ THE NEXT BOOK IN THE SERIES

Swarm Book 4
Available Here
books.to/ZhUkQ

Printed in Great Britain
by Amazon